Tales short and tall

Michael Tidemann

DEDICATION

To Mother and Father and David and Patricia

CONTENTS

ACKNOWLEDGMENTS

I would like to thank Nicole Buchard for her dedicated work at thewriteplaceatthewritetime.org where many of these stories first appeared.

Alberta

"'And furthermore', said the Belgian, '"I wouldn't help you pull this wagon even if you were a horse like me instead of an ass.'"

"Oh, and what was the name of the ass?" asked John.

Henry hooked his thumbs in his vest and gazed straight ahead. "Wilson."

The whole car burst into laughter, including Mable, who held her new baby on her lap. Asleep until their laughter, Alberta started with a cough and began to cry, and Mable lifted her to her shoulder and gave her a sharp, light pat to coax her into silence. "Oh honey, shush, shush. Don't make a fuss now..." And she sang,

Hush little baby, don't say a word
Momma's gonna buy you a mockingbird
And if that mockingbird won't sing
Momma's gonna buy you a diamond ring

And just like that, the baby quietly cooed to the lyrics.

"Oh my goodness, what a good baby," said Lydia, John's wife, an elegant brunette. It took only a glance to see she and John were of the same station as Henry and Mable – comfortable middle class, successful merchants or landed gentry who were able to afford such things as a coach car from Hazleton to Bismarck where they were all attending Governor Hanna's daughter's wedding – engraved invitation no less. And Mable wouldn't have dreamt of leaving Alberta with their servant girl just because the daft thing thought the baby had the croup and a bit of a fever. Such an idiot, that servant girl. Just barely out of girlhood herself – seventeen, for mercy's sake. She wondered what Henry had in his head when he had hired her. As her mind scavenged for explanations, her eyes narrowed, searing a path toward Henry sitting there now, thumbs in his vest, standing out like a plump tom turkey. Errant images arose – Henry – the servant girl – Henry and the servant girl. No, how ridiculous. She was a foreigner, Irish brogue as thick as prairie sod – so thick a plow couldn't bust through it. Each time she thought of the girl, there were more and more reasons to merit her disapproval, like a garden infested with weeds she couldn't tear out fast enough before more sprouted up to take their place.

"And what's her name again?" asked Lydia, dark, beautiful, elegant.

Mable instantly composed herself. She knew what was expected of a woman of her position; her dark thoughts could be snapped shut at a moment's notice in a box to which only she had the key. It was a practiced art. With a demure glance toward her greatest tangible accomplishment, she turned aside the child's wispy, golden locks, so much like her own. "Alberta."

"Alberta," repeated Lydia. "As in Canada."

"As in Canada," confirmed Mable with a prim sort of pride.

***

The *clackity clack, clackity clack, clackity clack* of the train on the track lulled her half-asleep – sleep perturbed by images of *her*.

"Erin!" she'd called to her just that morning.

"Yes, Mrs. Olson," said the girl, scurrying to her presence, cheeks blanched white so her freckles and fire-red hair blazed as her green eyes lifted like sea turtles swept up in the tide.

"Is this your *novel*?" she asked, disdain in the last word.

"Yes'm." Erin's eyes fell upon the book, then lifted like heavy stones.

"May I ask where you got it?"

"Me grandmum, Mrs. Olson. She give it to me as I boarded at Belfast."

Mable turned the book over in her hand disdainfully. "And you've actually been *reading* it, I suppose?"

Erin cowered. "Yes'm."

"Well I've been reading it too. It's tawdry and common. Is that what you hope to be? Tawdry and common?"

"No'm."

"Then dispose of it." Mable handed her the book with a sneer. "You should be reading the great books – Shakespeare and Pope, Addison and Steele. Certainly not his common Irishman Joyce."

"Yes'm," said Erin, eyes so heavy she couldn't lift them from the floor.

"And Erin? Erin! Look at me."

"Yes'm?" she said, in tears.

"Get rid of that necklace too. It's gaudy and garish."

"But ma'am, that's a gift from me grandmum too." She touched it as though it were the center of her heart.

"Well at least have the common decency to hide it – or to not wear it in my presence at least."

"Yes'm."

"And Erin?"

"Yes'm?"

"Dispose of that book. I'll not have such filth in a Christian home."

"Yes'm."

She never saw the book again – though she knew the girl would never have thrown it away as she'd ordered. That was all right though, she supposed. At least the girl was afraid of her. And that was all that mattered.

Clackity clack, clackity clack, clackity clack.

Henry she'd met at a church social at New Leipzig. Oh, he was such a handsome one, that Henry, riding up in a spotless black carriage and matching black geldings. He hung up the reins and stepped off the carriage like a prince, a person used to being admired. Even at twenty, his hair had started to whiten, like the snowy crest of a young king. Mable learned from the girls' gossip that he already had his own meat market in Hazleton with four men working under him – German butchers, no less. And weren't they the best? Henry would bring in a steer or hog and they would slit its throat, saving the blood, then they would slaughter the animal. He chose only the finest steers and from those he would select the choicest cuts and pack them in ice and sawdust and ship them to the governor and other gentlemen in state government in Bismarck. The best cuts from the hogs went there too, and the rest the Germans made into hot, spicy sausage that bit back when you sank your teeth into it. *That Henry, he makes the best sausage this side of Heidelberg,* everyone said. *That Henry, he's the richest butcher this side of Dresden,* they said too, especially the girls.

Was it any wonder then that as Henry looked past the covey of corseted femininity and settled his sky-blue eyes on her that she fell in love? And he with her?

Clackity clack, clackity clack, clackity clack.

Alberta fussed and as she didn't wish to betray any feelings of intolerance in polite company, Mable took her leave of the others and went to their coach, shunning the snores of those in the berths she passed. Night slid past through the coach window now, twinkling stars growing from the endless prairie. She found solace in the quiet, peace in the solitude. Alberta, finally silent in her arms, regained the familiar appeal of a doll made of porcelain, a thing to be admired. Mabel lay down beside her and coiled her body possessively around the fair child in motherly sleep.

Clackity clack, clackity clack, clackity clack.

She wished she could have interviewed the servant girl first but Henry insisted it was hard to find anyone. *But a foreigner?* she had insisted. *We were foreigners two generations ago*, he reminded her. It was the only argument they'd ever had, and it was a bad one. When Henry rolled up the dusty drive at Potato Butte later that day, the Irish girl's hair flying in the wind like the horse's mane, laughter like water over boulders as they dodged prairie dog mounds, Mable fumed. So *this* was the person who was going to look after her only child? Cook and clean, chop and haul in wood and coal and haul out the ashes? She hadn't even stepped off the carriage when Sigfred, their hired man, hurried to extend his hand to help her down. Then, incredibly, Henry sent him to milk the cows so he could help her down himself.

The girl came down from the carriage and into Henry's arms as naturally as life itself, laughing, green eyes lighting him up like a lighthouse on an errant ship at sea. The first thing Mable did was make her bring in coal, not giving her time to change into her work clothes so her spotless white dress she had bought just to meet her new mistress was forever ruined with coal dust.

She knew the girl dallied with Sigfred. She just knew it the way she would offer to go help him with the milking and come back into the farmhouse, lust written in her lilting voice, sated lust in her eyes. Then, as she served their supper, Sigfred's eyes would rove her body like a map of places he'd already traveled.

Clackity clack, clackity clack, clackity clack.

And Henry. What suspicions were there too. They'd hosted a house party on New Year's Eve and all the neighbors were there – for four miles in every direction at least – packing their home so some had to stand in the foyer and gab as the Victrola played in the parlor as the couples danced. Alberta was but two months old then, so

Mable was still tired from carrying her. Thus, she didn't mind when Henry danced just the first two dances with her before she sat down to rest. But did he have to dance *every* dance with the servant girl after that? Well that's what he did, squiring her around the parlor, strutting like a proud peacock beside her as though *she* were his wife.

She swore could see it in the eyes of her guests as well. They would look at Henry and the servant girl then back at her then back at them. After a time they no longer looked at her at all, letting the scene of Henry and Erin draw their gaze like an audience before a stage. To her horror, they even went up to her and asked who she was and began calling her by her first name. Erin this and Erin that. *What do you think of this, Erin. Do you have a beau? No? Well you should meet our son. He's an attorney in Bismarck. Argued a case before the state supreme court even. Do you think you'd like to meet him? Good. He'll be here next weekend. We'll introduce him.*

With no education, no family or connections, her only apparent asset her vulgar auburn-tressed, emerald-eyed appearance, Erin, in one evening, flew up flights of the social staircase it had taken Mable's family a number of generations and ruthless sacrifices to climb. Everyone in the house that New Year's Eve night loved her, worshipped her. And oh, how Mable hated her.

Clackity clack, clackity clack, clackity clack.

And *that's* why Mabel decided to take her baby on this wedding trip. Despite the servant girl's protestations that Alberta had a croup and a bit of a fever. After all, it was June and the weather was perfect – neither particularly cold nor hot by day with few, if any, mosquitoes. It was ideal weather to introduce an eight-month-old baby of society, to parade her amongst the right social circles, to see and be seen in the city – though Bismarck was hardly a city. But it was the capital and that was something, wasn't it?

Erin had cried when they left. She'd already grown attached to Alberta, rocking her in the chair beside the fireplace, telling her superstitious peasant folklore about fairies and children, putting protective charms and religious idols around the child . . . cooing to her like a silly loon, lifting the blanket from her face, playing peek-a-boo so the baby laughed. Mable could never make her laugh and she was her mother. So why should she allow a mere servant girl to do that? Or, to determine whether her daughter would go on this trip? Following Erin's insistence that Alberta was unwell for travel and the girl's assertion about a dream that "put the heart crossways in me about it," she jerked the baby away from Erin's arms. Both Erin and Alberta cried, and Mable had all she could do not to laugh.

They had boarded at Hazelton at sunset on the longest day of the year, the sun burning the western buttes to glowing coals. As night descended, washing the landscape in shades of violet and mauve, Erin stood there in tears beside Sigfred, holding up her hand to Alberta who waved back, laughing, then cried as her mother boarded with her onto the train.

"I'm so worried about the baby," Erin said to Sigfred, her emerald eyes as forlorn as a monk's island amid the wind-tossed Irish sea.

"I'm sure she'll be fine," said Sigfred, his hand on her shoulder as much as propriety and convention would allow. "Don't you think?"

Erin shook her head then all of her started to shake as tears rolled down her cheek.

***

The porter carried their steamer trunk to their coach and they went to the dining car where they ordered oysters, quail with wild rice, and a magnum of Lafitte-Rothschild.

"Do you really think we should, Henry?" she asked, looking at the massive, expensive bottle.

"Of course. After all, don't I have something to celebrate – a big farm, a successful business, and the most beautiful wife and child between the Red River and the Rockies?"

Mabel smiled as she watched through the window as Sigfred helped the servant girl into the carriage – she refused to even think of her by her first name. *Servant girl.* That's all she was and that was all she would ever be. In the three days they would be gone she secretly hoped Sigfred would get the girl in trouble and she would be able to later say, *See what happens when I leave you two together alone for a weekend? Henry should have known better than to hire an Irish girl.*

Clackity clack, clackity clack, clackity clack.

She looked at the stars now, so bright they shone like white diamonds on velvet. Alberta quiet beside her, she got up and went to the seat in front of the window and sat and gazed at the huge, orange full moon breaking over the prairie so she could pick out every landmark on the horizon. Potato Butte, far to the southeast, nestling their farm in its slope, and Little Heart Butte, pointed like a finger on the otherwise flat prairie. She rested her chin on her hand, wondering about the life she had earned. She had done well, hadn't she? After all, she had married a successful man – wealthy, in many people's eyes. They had the farm and the big, new house and the meat market in Hazelton. And Henry was the admiration of every girl who saw him. So she should be satisfied, shouldn't she? Wasn't wealth, having a handsome husband and child, being both envied and admired the true measure of success? Wasn't this what every woman wanted to achieve? And Alberta was her certificate of proof of all this—Henry's posterity and therefore, her validation, and power over him. No servant girl would ever take what she'd legitimately attained. She wasn't just a wife to be displaced; she'd done what every married woman is told to do--made herself a mother.

Such were her thoughts as she went to Alberta and kissed her cool forehead and covered her up so she wouldn't catch chill; Mable preferred to sleep in cool night air and left the window ajar for herself. "Such a good baby, so quiet. My darling doll." She smiled at the child that reflected her beauty as well as her triumph in marriage and realized it was the proudest moment of her life. Pleased, she left to go to the club car and enjoy herself with the others.

Smoke and jokes and laughter met her, Henry and John fairly rollicking as Lydia cast a smile at her. Mable sat beside Henry and touched his shoulder as a firm reminder, reining him in.

"So how are your stocks doing, Henry?" John said, casting a knowing eye at him.

Henry smiled and sipped his brandy. "I think they might be going all right."

"Let's see now – Standard Oil, Bethlehem Steel, Ford Motor . . . what else do you have now."

"Oh . . . " Henry pondered with false modesty. "I thought I'd pick up a few more automobile stocks, you know – Chevrolet, Packard, Studebaker . . . "

"But Henry. Do you think they'll ever replace the horse?"

Henry leaned forward with knowing intensity. "Mark my word here today. In forty years the horse will have no more value than a pet dog. If will be merely a pleasure animal. Oh, he may have some utility on a ranch, cutting cattle and riding fence and that sort of thing. But draft horses will be no more."

"Oh Henry," John scoffed dismissingly. "And with what do you envision will replace horses in this fantasy world."

Henry sat back with his cigar and blew smoke rings as though each framed a picture of the future. "I see great, mammoth machines picking and harvesting wheat and corn. Someday I even envision one machine doing it all – picking and shelling so all it has to do is dump it into a wagon that will take it to market."

"Oh, oh . . . " John laughed uproariously, holding his hand over Henry's glass. "No more brandy for him. He's had all he can handle."

"Not only that. I see farm equipment manufacturers becoming huge concerns. McCormick-Deering and the others. So I'm going to invest everything in them. And I see huge barges coming up the Mississippi, laden with corn and wheat and sugar beets taken by the thousands of ton to places like London and Paris. And I see war on the horizon." Henry's eyes glimmered through cigar smoke like a seer. "Europe maybe." He faced John and nodded soberly, despite the brandy. "So just yesterday I bought ten thousand shares in the Hormel company that's just started to package beef and pork in tins. An army can't march on an empty stomach, you know."

"Oh Henry, Henry." John mused. "I hope you don't lose it all in these misbegotten ventures."

"Not at all," said Henry meditatively. "Not at all." He peered straight ahead at the future through a window visible only to him – and him alone.

Having discovered little amusement, she found herself weary and in search of a reason to be excused. "I'll go check on Alberta," said Mable.

"You go dear," said Henry, nestling a kiss against her cheek.

***

Their talk continued as the train rolled on, Bismarck now breaking upon the horizon, glowing gas and electric lights dotting the prairie. Beyond was the Missouri River then Mandan and then the great prairie began – wheat fields and ranches stretching all the way to the great, blue, ice-spiked Rockies.

Henry mused at the infinitude of it all. If he could see great cities breaking out upon the prairie, he could also see a downside. Easterners – foreigners, even, as Mable called them – right now were breaking prairie sod they had no business breaking up out west of the Missouri. Honyockers, they called them. Tenderfeet. Greenhorns. Men who could sit a horse no more than a man could walk on the moon – oh, that would happen someday too, but certainly not tomorrow. But breaking up prairie sod was a mistake he could never broach. While rains were certainly good now, they were merely cyclical. Someday those miles upon miles of gumbo out toward the Badlands would dry up and be picked up by the wind and carried all the way to New York and into the Atlantic. Ranching, that's what the western prairies were meant for. The best thing they could have done was leave the buffalo on them and let the Indians have it all.

A white image entered the car, Mable in her nightgown, wonder and horror on her face.

"Mable, for God's sake. What are you doing here in your night dress. This is a public car, don't you know that?"

"Henry," she whispered, all she could manage in the vast gulf between them. "Our Alberta is gone."

"What the thunder," he cried, spilling his brandy as he stood. "She must be somewhere."

"She's nowhere, Henry," said Mabel, lost, forlorn, and alone. "Nowhere to be found."

> *Come away, O, human child!*
> *To the woods and waters wild*
> *With a fairy hand in hand,*
> *For the world's more full of weeping than*
> *you can understand...*

"The Stolen Child" by W. B. Yeats

Amber Alert

Phil was having his best biscuits and gravy ever at a truck stop just off I-65 when the news flash came over the big screen TV. A young girl, blond, blue-eyed, fifteen, had been abducted by a man not long out of state prison. Witnesses had seen the girl lean over to talk to the driver who jumped from the black SUV and grabbed her at gunpoint and screeched off. The quiet Illinois town, streets lined with towering ash and oak, had been violated.

"Headed south on I-65 toward Indianapolis . . . " the newscaster said.

"I'd love to get my hands on that son-of-a-bitch." Ben, another driver Phil had run with for years, studied the license plate on the screen, burning it into his memory.

Phil nodded and finished his coffee and held his hand over his cup when the waitress came over with the pot to top him of. He was running hard to make his Charlotte drop the next morning then he had a backhaul out of Virginia Beach headed for Chicago. He'd run flatbed for years but had turned to running reefer for the last couple years now. It was a little extra work, fueling and checking on the refrigeration unit, but the pay was better and it was a little easier to find backhauls. He'd had enough of deadheading back home – either that or waiting days for a backhaul that might come – or not.

Phil wiped his mouth with his napkin and dropped it on his plate then left a fiver for the waitress. "Well, I spose I'd best be headed for Charlotte."

"865 to 465?"

"Yeah. I don't think I got my Pete tuned enough for the Brickyard."

Ben roughed up a laugh. "Me either. 'N fact, I think the Cat's due for a major."

Phil shook his head in sympathy. "That'll set ya back."

"This is true." Ben swamped down his coffee, eyed Phil's sawbuck tip, and did the same. "I'm headed for Louisville myself so's why don't I run with ya."

"Glad for the company." Phil tugged at his Peterbilt cap and they left.

The July sun had already cooked the inside of his cab by ten. Phil started up his Pete and grabbed his lead pipe from under his seat and did a quick inspection, thumping tires, checking the gladhand and fifth wheel pin, the usual small things that could prevent big problems later, then climbed back into his cab and waved at Ben and they headed out.

It was a beautiful morning as they turned south on I-65, the sky clear except for fluffy white clouds scudding up from the lake-blue sky to the east.

"Looks like it's gonna be a nice day," Ben said over the CB.

"Smog'll take care a that."

Ben's raw laugh tore up the airwaves. "That's you. Always the optimist."

Mid-morning traffic had slackened a bit when they hit the beltway after morning rush. They turned onto 865 then 465 and rounded Indy City on the east and picked up 65 South again, Phil leading with Ben on his back door. At the Franklin exit a black SUV darted in front of him, so Phil had to slam on his brakes.

"Crap, whatcha tryin' to do? Marry my grill?"

"Damn four-wheeler," Phil answered. "He run right in front a me."

"Shoulda known."

Phil studied the plate. A young girl sat in the passenger seat as a much-older man, white, shaven head, middle-aged, drove. "It's him."

"Who's him."

"The kidnapper."

A half-dozen "where's" broke over the CB as other drivers chimed in.

"Mile marker 85, southbound 65."

"Let's get some drivers over here and box the son-of-a-bitch in," Ben said.

Phil hammered down and drifted into the far left lane, black smoke trailing from his stacks. He let his trailer creep ten feet past the SUV then cut in front of him. Ben closed up just behind the SUV and a red Mack pulled alongside the SUV's left and a green Volvo on its right.

"All right, boys," said Phil. "Let's hit our flashers 'n flip out jakes and shut this bastard down."

***

The girl huddled in the SUV, shaking, as the driver held a gun at her stomach. She'd been walking home from morning softball practice, laughing, chatting with her friends, when the man pulled up to her and asked for directions.

"No, you turn left three blocks from here," she said, pointing at the pink stoplight glow through the early morning mist. She didn't even notice as the man slipped silently from the car, wrapped his hand around her mouth, and stuck the gun into her ribs and threw her into his car.

"Make a move, wave at anyone, cry out, and I'll shoot you."

All the girl could think of was the gun against her stomach and how she would never see her school or friends or parents ever again.

For two-hundred miles she had been shaking, sweating, crying, praying – praying to a God she had seldom prayed to since being confirmed and putting God and Jesus behind her as though they were figurines she had collected and set on a shelf and dusted off only when she needed them. And now she wanted God and Jesus more than ever. Where were they and where were God's Angels and when would they save her. She only hoped the man would be quick when he did whatever he was going to do and the pain wouldn't last long.

When the truck pulled in front of them and slammed on its brakes and another truck came up on their back bumper, another fear hit her – that they would be crushed to death by the big trucks and she wouldn't have to endure the horror of torture and rape. Two more trucks pulled alongside, lights flashed, and darkness and a deafening roar sounded like the base of Victoria Falls.

***

Tighter than a Blue Angels formation, they boxed in the black SUV and crawled to a stop, hundreds of cars honking behind. Phil grabbed his .44 magnum Smith and Wesson from the sleeper berth and climbed down. Ben already had his 9mm out and the other drivers came with handguns, pipes, lug wrenches, and even a shotgun and assault rifle or two.

Phil stuck his .44 in the driver's mouth. "Hand me the gun handle first in three seconds and I promise not to blow your head off." The white-faced driver, face pitted, handed Phil his gun and climbed out, shaking with all the guns trained on him. "Someone call 911," said Phil.

***

A score of state troopers, sheriff's deputies, and city police were there minutes later, red and blue lights flashing, traffic blocked for miles behind them. They had driven north up the southbound lane and taken ditches to get there.

An Indiana state trooper tilted his hat appreciatively as Phil handed over the kidnapper. Four more officers helped slam his face into the pavement and they cuffed him and read him his rights. Finally realizing her ordeal was over, the girl popped from the car and jumped into Phil's arms and he held her weeping body.

"I'm glad you boys all got permits for those things," the state trooper said. "I haven't seen so much hardware since Fallujah."

The girl clung to Phil like a bug to a palm trunk in a hurricane, and after she and he had given the police their statements he stayed with her until her parents arrived, frantic, clinging to her as she had to Phil.

***

"Gonna be late for your Charlotte drop."

"You're gonna be late for Louisville too."

"Well I guess that's just tough shit now, ain't it."

Phil laughed. "They ain't ever gonna believe it."

"Nope," said Ben. "We'll have to make up some story they can swallow."

Blizard of '88

"No. The pitch is not steep enough. You must do it over."

Olaf Jensen looked down from his scaffold perch bemusedly. The person who had just addressed him was the new wet-behind-the-ears schoolteacher, but a child herself. Out here in Dakota Territory, a teacher needed only to have finished eighth grade then gone on to a year of normal school to take on her own covey of country school students. And Sonja Hannahsdottir had done just that – qualifying her as a teacher at the ripe old age of fifteen – just two years older than his own daughter Elizabeth. "Oh? And what pitch would you like."

Sonja's arms formed the angle of a country church steeple.

"*A twelve-twelve?*"

"No. A sixteen-twelve."

"*A sixteen-twelve?* Do you have any idea how much wood that will take?"

Sonja stood stubbornly, blond, blue-eyed, unyielding. "If I am to teach here, that is the only way."

"*If* you're going to teach here," Olaf snorted. He glanced to Elizabeth who was handing him another two-by-four. As president of the board of Stateline School No. 2 he was Miss Hannahsdottir's boss – as well as landlord.

17

And *she* was giving *him* – a master carpenter – orders on how to build? He had never heard of such a thing. "What makes you think we'll ever have that much snow."

"The animals."

"Animals?"

"Their coats are still heavy and the dirt around their burrows is deep – and it is only June. The old Viking stories we were told in Iceland say that is a sign of a bad winter."

"Dirt around their burrows?" Olaf scoffed and looked down at his daughter Elizabeth who offered up a shrug. "You'd better do what she says, father. She's the only teacher you could find."

***

By mid-August, a brand new country school, thirty-by-forty, with church steeple pitch had risen on the stark, Dakota prairie. The men on the school board had chosen a particularly pretty spot, a high knoll reaching high above the Bix Sioux River Valley, looking toward Minnesota just across the river. Statehood was fast approaching, and within a couple years Dakota Territory would be North and South Dakota and the South Dakota eastern border would follow the Big Sioux River in the south then jut east, carving out a few extra miles into Minnesota. Then the South Dakota border would veer west again, lapping Big Stone Lake then leaping the north-south Continental Divide to Lake Traverse to the Bois de Sioux that would eventually join the great Red River of the North.

To Elizabeth Jensen, things like borders and rivers and territories and states were not as important as her life, here and now, on the unending sunflower-decked prairie as she watched Sonja Hannahsdottir hang fresh laundry on the clothesline. That had been Elizabeth's job until Miss Hannahsdottir had started boarding with them this summer. Her father had considered Miss Hannahsdottir's boarding as part of her pay. *I have to do something, though. Or else I'll not feel part of the family,* Miss Hannahsdottir had insisted, no doubt prodded by some

18

Icelandic work ethic instilled by her parents. So Elizabeth's mother Emily had chosen a few select chores for Miss Hannahsdottir – nothing too strenuous. Things like laundry and canning and feeding the chickens. That meant fewer chores for Elizabeth – which she didn't mind a bit. So now all she had to worry about was helping her mother with cooking and cleaning while her younger brothers Benjamin and Steven helped her father with field work and caring for the livestock.

As Sonja stood there, hanging laundry, the steady wind limning her legs and stomach like a stream over a boulder, Elizabeth could only think of how beautiful she was – long, blond hair cascading in the wind, rosy-cheeked, blue eyes dancing prairie violets. Elizabeth's skin was far more dusky, hair raven-black, eyes brown garnets. Her parents, neighbors, even a few boys had told her how pretty she was. But she envied Miss Hannahsdottir's nearly white-blond hair, blue eyes, filly legs. She was only two years older, but to Elizabeth she seemed so, so much older and more mature.

Though laundry was Miss Hannahsdottir's job – and Elizabeth doubted she really needed help – Elizabeth left her bedroom window and stepped into the hallway and trotted down the narrow stairs and out the front door to where Miss Hannahsdottir was stretching a sheet across the clothesline, the fabric flapping like a mainsail at sea. "Here, let me help you with that, Miss Hannahsdottir." Elizabeth thrust a handful of clothespins in her mouth and helped stretch the sheet out on the line.

Miss Hannahsdottir crinkled a smile at her, lips cherried from the wind, skin naturally blushed. "Thank you. And you may call me Sonja when we are not in school." She bit her lower lip so it cherried even more.

Elizabeth stepped closer, grabbing the same sheet Sonja had in her hands as though they were about to tussle over it. They laughed, and Elizabeth stepped closer, toe-to-toe with Sonja whose face was inches away. "Your hair. It's so pretty. Can I touch it?"

Sonja smiled curiously as though she found Elizabeth a bit odd. "What a strange request. Yes, you may, if you would like."

Elizabeth reached for Sonja's hair and felt it sift through her hand like flax. She loved how it flowed in her hand as she stroked it, Sonja's eyes closing dreamily. Heart racing, Elizabeth inched closer and studied Sonja's face as she stood with her eyes closed. Elizabeth searched Sonja's face and body for some flaw, some imperfection, but there was none. She was absolutely perfect. Unable to help herself, Elizabeth leaned forward and kissed Sonja on the lips. Sonja's eyes opened and Elizabeth expected a scolding – or worse. But Sonja only clasped Elizabeth's wrist to her shoulder and laughed. "What was that for."

"I only wanted to kiss you. To make sure you were real. I'm sorry. I'm so embarr . . . " She covered her eyes and ran back toward the house, in tears.

"It's all right," Sonja called after her softly. "It's all right," she said again to herself.

***

Elizabeth didn't call Miss Hannahsdottir Sonja for a long time after that – even at home. Miss Hannahsdottir she was to her as a teacher and Miss Hannahsdottir she would remain.

Miss Hannahsdottir called on Elizabeth often in class that fall since she was the only eighth-grader. Seventeen other students filled the classroom, ranging from ages six to Elizabeth at thirteen. Their other teacher, Miss Berdahl, who had been forced to resign after she married Mr. Gregg, had been something of a nag, standing students in the corner when they didn't have the right answer and even rapping a ruler across the older boys' knuckles when they tried to dip a girl's pigtails in their ink wells. But Miss Hannahsdottir was nothing like that. Every student – first grade on up – sat at the edge of the seat, eager to hear Miss Hannahsdottir's questions and be first to give the answer.

If there were a hesitant student in the classroom, it

was Elizabeth. She still blushed with shame whenever she saw Miss Hannahsdottir, and whenever her teacher asked a question, she offered a startled look as though caught doing something naughty.

Summer had crisped to fall, and outside the school windows the slowly browning prairie grass danced in the steady wind like God's hand stroking the fur of some great animal. The other kids were outside playing, their muffled shouts just loud enough for Elizabeth to hear. The boys played a stick and ring game while the girls played tag.

Miss Hannahsdottir gently closed the book she had been reading and laid it on her desk. She had been watching Elizabeth more than reading, pasque-blue eyes meditative. She stood and came around her desk and walked straight toward Elizabeth.

Elizabeth looked up, heart racing.

"Elizabeth, there is something I have been meaning to tell you." Miss Hannahdottir's hand rested on her arm and her warmth soaked clear to her bones.

"Yes, Miss Hannahsdottir?"

Her teacher smiled and with her other hand stroked Elizabeth's hair, touching it lightly then her shoulder. She kept stroking, her hand warm against her back and neck and shoulder. "I feel there is something unspoken between us."

Elizabeth closed her eyes as Miss Hannahsdottir stroked her back, pressing herself against her hand, hoping and praying she would never stop. "Oh, Miss Hannahsdottir." Tears trickled down Elizabeth's cheeks.

The stroking continued, long, gentle strokes going from Elizabeth's hair to her neck to her back and shoulder. "Sometimes all we need is to be touched, don't you think?"

"Oh yes, Miss Hannahsdottir," Elizabeth said, eyes shut so tight she thought they would break.

At home, Miss Hannahsdottir was Sonja after that. Elizabeth couldn't understand why, but whenever she was close to Sonja her stomach would heat up and she felt so wonderful she seemed to be in heaven. And whenever Sonja drifted into the same room, blue eyes lit like beacons, Elizabeth knew Sonja felt the same.

One night a terrible wind came – the last fall thunderstorm. Lightning slashed the sly, shattering the ancient oak in front of the house clear to its base. Elizabeth jumped from beneath the covers and ran to Sonja's room and crawled under the quilt and clung to her narrow waist. "I'm so scared."

The bedsprings creaked as Sonja turned, repeated lightning flashes outlining her smile as she put her arm around Elizabeth and pressed against her, lips inches away. "That is all right," she whispered. Sonja held Elizabeth as she sang an old Icelandic folk song, the melody timed to her stroking her back, as Elizabeth drifted off to sleep.

***

One January morning gray clouds brooded the Dakota horizon. Hovering like a great wall, at first they carried topsoil, hundreds of tons sifting and churning, boiling, a sea of dust, choking everything in its path. And then the clouds turned white as the snow came.

Like many Dakota farmers, Olaf Jensen had learned to read the signs of the seasons. He knew a storm had been brewing. But when and how much was another matter. He had left it to Miss Hannahsdottir if she were going to have school that morning, with a strong hint that she had better if she wanted to keep her job.

So there they were – sequestered in the tiny, one-room school, a full four cords filling the cloak room. Miss Hannahsdottir had seen to that, saying it was going to be hard winter, that a terrible storm was about to come. So she had made every student carry in wood for a whole week, making a math problem out of it. Let's see how much you can add, she said to the first- and second-graders. The third-graders she taught how to multiply chunks of wood and the fourth-graders how to divide them. And the rest? Well she had them determine volume.

A cord is four by four by eight. And how many cubic feet is that? A hundred and twenty-eight? Very good! Now let's see if we can't fit three more cords inside.

And they did. Plus jars of food Miss Hannahsdottir had asked her students to bring all that fall. So why are you needing all this food? the parents asked her. Oh, just in case we get snowed in, Miss Hannahsdottir laughed. Not that we will ever need it. So, all that fall, every Monday, each student brought a pint or quart jar of canned beets or carrots to potatoes or sauerkraut or meat as Miss Hannahsdottir called upon the ancient Norse gods Thor and Odin to prophesy the coming storm.

It descended as a fist, a blow, hundred-mile-an-hour winds and feet of snow day after day. Across Kansas, Nebraska, and the Dakotas, snow-laden school houses collapsed and teachers and children and students froze to death. Cattle froze standing, carcasses upright until spring.

But in one eastern South Dakota school house, the roof held. Snow piled on a foot, two, three, then sloughed off as kerosene lights cast ambered glows onto the snow sifted by wolf-howling winds. Whenever the children despaired into wails, Miss Hannahsdottir made a game of it. See how high the snow's getting? Would you like to go out and play in it? No? Well then let's study geography. And never did students learn more about parallels and meridians and continents and oceans than they did in that little Dakota country school in the Blizzard of '88.

***

Because he raised dairy and not beef, Olaf Jensen's cattle were safely sheltered in the barn. He had strung baling wire all the way from the house to the barn to feed the cattle and hogs and chickens, and every time he returned from milking or feeding the livestock he collapsed in his rocking chair and sobbed, wondering what was happening to his children.

"Don't worry, dear. We have two good, strong, smart girls watching out for the rest of the children," Emily comforted him. By then, Sonja was like their own daughter.

"Oh I hope so." Olaf seized both of Emily's hands in his. "I certainly hope so."

***

As day darkened into night, Sonja and Elizabeth had the children lie on their coats around the banked-up woodstove as they sang them to sleep – first Sonja singing an ancient Icelandic folk song then Elizabeth singing in Norwegian. They sang until little ponies nickered throughout the room.

Elizabeth went over to sleep beside her brothers when she felt a hand around her arm. Miss Hannahsdottir looked steadily at her, a slow smile creasing her lips. "Would you like to sleep beside me?"

Elizabeth's stomach stirred and her mouth went dry. The wind rattled the windows and the woodstove and pipe glowed orange, a dull roar of air feeding the banked-up oak. She let Miss Hannahsdottir lead her behind her desk where they laid down their coats. Miss Hannahsdottir's face was barely lit by the yellowed glow through the woodstove isinglass as she gently clasped Elizabeth's arms then knelt down and patted the coats beside her. Elizabeth sat and looked wondrously at her teacher, her friend. Miss Hannahsdottir stroked her cheek and smiled and lay down and watched Elizabeth. Elizabeth lay down beside her, their faces nearly touching, as Miss Hannahsdottir pulled one of their coats over them. "Don't worry. We'll be warm here," Miss Hannahsdottir said in the fading firelight.

Elizabeth edged toward Miss Hannahsdottir so close they exchanged breaths. "Do you really think so?"

"Yes."

Elizabeth was frozen, aching to hold Miss Hannahsdottir but unable to move closer.

Miss Hannahsdottir's arm went around Elizabeth's back and her lips nuzzled her forehead. "Is this all right?"

Elizabeth sighed heavily. "Yes." She pressed

herself against Miss Hannahsdottir and they drew warmth from each other through the cold, malignant night.

***

When Elizabeth graduated from eighth grade that year, she told her parents she wanted to be a teacher. You'll have to go to normal school, Olaf told her, so Elizabeth enrolled at Madison Normal School while Miss Hannahsdottir continued to teach and live with the Jensens. When Elizabeth graduated, both she and Miss Hannahsdottir took teaching jobs on the Shoshone-Arapahoe Reservation in Riverton, Wyoming. Olaf and Emily's loss was doubled, because by that time Sonja had become a second daughter.

Olaf kept waiting for Elizabeth to write and say she was getting married. You'll have to give up teaching, you know, Olaf was ready to tell her.

But Elizabeth never did marry. Nor did Sonja. They traveled together around the West and the world, teaching and going on to university. They grew from pretty girls into beautiful, elegant women. And still they never married – something no one could understand. Nor could anyone understand why they took in the dozens of misfits and castoff children – the forgotten and abandoned – under their tutelage. Those same orphans, who grew up to become successful doctors and lawyers, bankers and accountants, along with their myriad progeny, thronged the grave of Sonja Hannahsdottir, master's in architecture from Kansas State, who passed away December 1968. They returned three months later to honor the memory of Elizabeth Jensen, master's in letters from the University of Minnesota.

Old maids, what a pity, people said as they visited their graves alongside each other. Together in death as they had been in life.

Buttons

I was eight when my sister Rae gave me the bunny – a white fur ball with pink nose that wrinkled when he looked at me. Right away I wrinkled my nose back at him, nose to nose, touching my nose to his. I thought he would be afraid but he wasn't, and we played like that all that first Easter morning when my sister gave him to me – my touching my nose to his, him scampering around his box, then coming up to let me touch my nose to his again.

"Humph." Dad cinched his thumbs in his coverall straps. "So why'd ya have to get him a rabbit."

My sister's joy at seeing me play with the bunny quelled. "I thought he'd like a pet."

"He already has a dog," Dad said dismissingly. And I did – a shepherd-border collie and who-knows-what-else cross, typical of farm dogs back them.

"But isn't the bunny cute?" my sister insisted.

"Cute. Humph." Dad stared at the rabbit as though it were a rodent he'd just as well trap and eat.

When I asked if I could take him out of the box and play with him on the floor, Dad turned away and said he had to go out to milk cows. Then I asked Mom who said okay, so I reached into the box and pulled out the squiggly bundle of fur and lay back on the living room floor and let him run across my chest then onto the carpet where he summarily shit six rabbit pellets that looked

26

exactly like the sugared cereal I'd had that morning – only they were brown.

"Oh Toby – Look at what your rabbit did," Mom complained. "Now you'll have to clean up after him."

So I did. I was so much in love with my rabbit I was even happy to pick up his rabbit poop. And when no one was around, I'd secretly play with it, flicking the rabbit turds round like billiard balls. I even made a rabbit turd billiard table, with pockets and everything. I cut the side from a cereal box and taped it up and cut six round holes in it and under them taped six thimbles I'd snuck from Mom's sewing kit. When my brother Allen first saw me playing rabbit turd pool, he said I was crazy. But when he saw how easily the rabbit turds rolled then fell into the pockets he wanted to play too. "We need a white cue ball and a black eight ball though," Allen said. I tried feeding the rabbit – whom I finally named Buttons because of his pink nose that looked just like a pink button on my best shirt – chalk and licorice to make cue balls and eight balls. He shit out plenty of cue balls and eight balls all right, but nearly died. After that I stuck to regular rabbit food like warm milk with lettuce and carrots.

I did a good job feeding Buttons – so good in fact that he soon got fatter than a toad. He quickly outgrew his box so my brother built him a cage in shop class, complete with a wooden latch held on by a window screen fastener and everything. Buttons grew bigger and bigger and bigger and plumper and plumper and plumper until he had a hard time turning around in the cage. To exercise Buttons, I would pull him from his cage and lie with him on the living room floor and laugh as he skipped and hopped and deposited rabbit turds all over the living room carpet. I always tried to clean them up, but once in a while when Mom was vacuuming a tried rabbit turd would tinkle happily up the metal tube of her Hoover. "Damned rabbit," Mom would say.

***

October came. Kennedy had been in office for less than

two years and that month faced down Cuba and the Soviet Union and we had daily air raid drills at school. The hippies hadn't come yet though the beatniks were paving the way for them. I had a really horrible third-grade teacher who would try to flunk everyone in the class then ride off with an outlaw biker after she was fired mid-year. And my brother Allen was talking about college. He was a good student – getting A's and B's with an occasional C in courses like chemistry but overall his grades were better than average. And he wanted to go to business school. He was always coming up with ideas for businesses and trying them out on me.

"How about a chicken-raising factory." Allen was lying in bed, seeing his future as clearly as though it were right there in front of him. "You could process the chickens right there. They'd come in as chicks and out as drumsticks."

"How would you feed them."

"Oh, you'd grow your food right there. And you could use their shit as fertilizer."

"Where would you get the chicks."

"You'd hatch them right there."

"How about eggs. Would you sell those?"

"Oh sure. Some chickens would lay eggs and you could gather those and others you'd put in a hatchery and hatch into more chickens."

"How many chickens would you have."

"Thousands." Allen looked off at his future wealth. "Millions."

"Who would take care of all those chickens."

"Oh, you could just bring in poor people from Mexico and Africa. They're not used to making any money anyway. They'd be glad to work for hardly anything."

We didn't realize it them, but my brother at that moment was envisioning the very model of vertical integration that would break the back of family farming twenty years hence. Family farms such as ours – corn, soybeans, oats, hay, dairy, hogs, chicken, and a big garden with canning every summer – would be replaced by production agriculture, huge fields of hundreds of acres taking up whole sections of land. For now, though, we lived on our 120 acres – really an average-sized farm back then – which could have been a model of sustainability had our father really had his heart into farming.

Farm prices were a problem though. Every morning Allen and I would sneak over to the hot air register above the oil burner in the living room and listen to our parents' conversation. It usually went something like this:

"Farmers are dumping milk in Minnesota," Dad would say.

"Dumping milk?" Mom would answer, voice aghast.

"They're under contract, and when the dairies cut what they pay, farmers are getting less than the cost of production."

"Well why can't they just sell their milk to the public?"

"They can't. They're under contract. 'Sides, the dairies control the USDA that makes the rules so it's near impossible for farms to sell straight to the public."

"Oh. So what are we going to do?"

"Keep milkin' an' sellin' it for less than it costs to produce it, I guess."

At first it seemed merely abstract. Cost of production was something people on Wall Street worried about, not farmers. Then one night when we were watching the news it was right there on TV. Farmers were dumping milk right at the end of their driveways as the milk trucks rolled up, hundreds of dollars spilling onto the ground as the truck drivers shook their heads then drove away.

One morning just before school I wanted to grab some of my money from the ceramic cookie jar on the kitchen counter. I reached in but there was nothing. I knew I had put two or three dollars in there – money I'd earned from doing extra errands for Mom or the neighbors. Now there was nothing. "Hey Mom, what happened to my money."

My mother looked up at me, eyes barren and vacant, her half-bowl of cereal still untouched. "We . . . needed it to buy flour."

As I thought then of my money missing from the cookie jar – a dime or even a nickel I'd hoped to have to buy a treat at the store – and Mom's vacant stare, then tears – and now the school bus rolling up, brake lights pink in the wintry morning fog, poverty turned real. It was no longer newscasters talking about the cost of production or radical Minnesota farmers forming unions and dumping milk. It was about a nine-year-old boy who couldn't buy a treat because the family needed his money to put food on the table.

Our meals got smaller. We were down to a half-bowl of cereal in the morning and at night we each had half a potato, half a slice of bread, maybe a tablespoon of peas or carrots, and if we were lucky, maybe a small piece of meat. We ate mush – lots of mush – something my father had survived on during the Depression and something we survived on now. Mush was a watery gruel you flavored with butter and cinnamon and sugar. At first my brother thought it was a treat. Then we ran out of cinnamon then sugar then butter. So all we ate was mush.

I still managed to feed Buttons though. I begged and pleaded with Mom to keep buying lettuce and carrots for him. And she gave in, no doubt softened by the unrelenting cries of a nine-year-old son whose main purpose in life was to feed his rabbit that grew fatter and fatter and fatter and huger and huger and huger while a hungry family stared at a smaller meal every night.

***

It was just about a year after my sister Rae – now married and living in Minneapolis – had given Buttons to me that a big wind came up one night. Roaring, screeching, it rattled the windows in that old farmhouse like the chattering teeth of a dying man. My brother and I knew we were safe, though, because our great-grandfather had built that house – a man who would carry his wooden toolbox every day to the job site where he would build a house for ninety dollars – maybe a half-day's pay for a journeyman carpenter today.

The wind had died down by morning. The days were getting longer, and Easter was coming up – a full year since Rae had given Buttons to me. That made me more excited than ever to go out and feed him.

When I went to the refrigerator and poured milk into a sauce pan to heat on the stove, Mom looked at me. "What are you doing, Toby."

"I'm warming milk up for Buttons." I wondered why she had even asked since I had been doing the same thing for a year.

"Oh." Her gaze drifted out toward the rickety front porch, faded wooden posts barely holding the moss-shingled roof. I dug through the refrigerator crisper drawer for wilted lettuce leaves and carrots – Mom insisted I take those rather than the good ones to feed Buttons – and started out the door.

"Oh Toby . . . " Mom began, then stopped as I stopped at the front screen door.

"Yeah?"

"Never mind." She looked away. "Never mind."

When I went to Buttons' hutch the door was open and he was gone. The clasp had been turned. Then I looked at my dog Rex sitting on the lawn with what appeared to be three small animal organs lined up neatly in a row between his paws. I knew at that moment that the wind had blown Buttons' cage door open during the night and Rex had gotten to him. I burst into tears. But tears wouldn't describe it. It was more like a torrent, gushing from my eyes. "Mom," I cried, running back inside the house. "Rex ate Buttons."

Mom looked at me, concerned yet relieved. "Oh Toby, I'm so sorry."

***

Since it was Good Friday and since we didn't have school that day I cut a piece of weathered wood from a falling-down shed and found a can of old barn paint and painted a sign, DOG FOR SALE, and nailed it on the telephone pole at the end of the driveway. No one stopped to buy Rex, of course. There were too many farm dogs in the country already, roving packs of them killing our neighbor's sheep. To make matters worse, my brother painted a sign, PIG FOR SALE, and since he was taller he hung it above mine on the same telephone pole. I secretly felt he was making fun of me, but I also knew admitting that would be showing signs of weakness, so I didn't say anything.

That night we had meat for the first time in ages. Mom proudly set the platter on the table and we all sat there hungrily with forks and knives in hand as Mom announced, "Chicken for supper tonight."

I looked at the platter as Dad passed it to me. It didn't look like any chicken I'd ever seen. The meat was lighter and the piece I took looked more like a baby's haunch than a drumstick. It didn't taste like chicken either, but with a sweeter, wilder taste.

"This isn't chicken," Allen said with a smirk. "It's rabbit."

The scream came from deep inside me, all on its own. I couldn't have stopped it had I tried. Primordial, it was a scream of atavistic horror. The rabbit I had been eating I spat out all over the table and Dad slapped me, hard, cutting my lip and bloodying my nose. As my blood dripped all over Mom's good tablecloth, Dad slapped me again and again so I bled even more.

"Shut up, you little shit," Dad said, slapping me and slapping me as I kept screaming and bleeding and screaming. Then he turned to my brother. "You! Why did you have to tell him it was rabbit!" Dad jerked Allen from his chair and threw him up against the wall, shattering the frame and glass in a picture of our ancestral home in Norway. For a long moment Allen just stood there. He was nearly Dad's height and could have fought back. But he was only sixteen. And had he fought back he would have been kicked out of the house. So he just stood there as Dad pummeled him with his fists, cracking his lips, bloodying his nose, blackening his eyes. Allen just stood there and took it as Mom and I sat there and hoped Allen would fight back, but he didn't, crying that his own father would do something like this to him more than from the pain of the beating.

"Maynard," Mom said, going to him, grabbing his coverall straps. "You're hurting him, Maynard. Stop."

Dad reached back and cuffed Mom who just stood there, not believing he had really hit her, that he had done the one thing she had said she would never tolerate from him. He stared back not believing either that he had hit her.

Mom ran to the phone on the wall to call our neighbor, Jim, for help. When Jim walked inside the house with his daughter Luann and saw blood all over everyone and on Dad's fists he went straight up to Dad and looked down at him from four inches above and said, "I'm a peaceful, God-fearing man, but I could beat you to death for this."

That finally settled Dad down. Jim could have torn him to pieces right there and then, and Dad knew it. As my brother went out to his dead 1950 two-door Olds to cry his heart out while Luanne went along to hold his hand, Jim put the fear of God – and himself – into Dad.

***

Mom went to file for divorce the next Tuesday. The lawyer was so mad when she told him what had happened that he didn't ask for a retainer and even said he would handle her case pro bono, that it was the worst case of domestic abuse he had ever seen. Mom only stopped the divorce proceedings when she couldn't find Dad one night and went outside and found him north of the hog house with a knife in both hands, ready to kill himself. He didn't put the knife down until she promised not to leave him.

On the way to the lawyer's office Mom had dropped

Allen off at the recruiting office and he signed up for the Navy Reserve and went to the Great Lakes Naval Training Center later that summer for boot camp. He later joined the regular Navy and went to South Vietnam where he received daily doses of Agent Orange and forty-some years later had heart problems, a stroke, and developed leukemia – all of which the VA doctors said were a hundred-percent service-related. Allen died at sixty-eight, a good fifteen or twenty years sooner than he would have had he gone to business school instead. While Allen was in South Vietnam, Dad sold his Olds – now a classic – for scrap.

I never forgave my father. And how could I. After he died from a heart attack years later and Allen flew home for the funeral, Mom asked him to kiss our father's cheek as he lay there in the casket at the visitation the night before the funeral.

"I can't," Allen said, eyes brimming.

When Mom looked at me I shook my head.

"He was a good father," Mom said. But I couldn't see her as she was then. All I could see was her standing there, lip bleeding, back on Good Friday 1963.

"No he wasn't," I said, speaking for Allen as well as myself. "He wasn't a good father at all."

***

Dad had a farm sale not long after Easter 1963, one step ahead of the Federal Land Bank that was threatening to sell him out. He sold all our livestock and farm equipment except for a few chickens and his 1952 John Deere Model B and a three-bottom plow, rake, sickle, and corn planter. He was still going to farm, he vowed, even if it was just crops and not animals.

Dad took a job as a night watchman but fell asleep on the job the first night and was fired. After that he tried to find work but couldn't and finally decided to start laying carpet. I knew he must have been doing pretty well when one night he came home and threw a huge envelope of money on my chest while I was watching The Beverly

Hillbillies and wondering why people laughed because that's pretty much how we lived.

"While you've been layin' on your ass there, boy, I been workin'. That's where that money come from."

I picked up the envelope and looked inside. It was mainly ones. My chest still hurt.

"Six hundred dollars," Dad said scornfully. "How much did you earn today."

I couldn't figure out how a nine-year-old boy could have been expected to answer such a question back then. Even today, at sixty-two, I don't see how I should have been expected to answer him.

Later that spring of 1963 Mom asked me to take the .22 out and shoot the rabbits eating her flowers. There were dozens of them, scurrying through the tulip patch like they owned it. I showed them, though. At first, I saw them as Buttons' brothers and sisters, but the more of them I shot the more I saw them as just rabbits. The thing that bothered me most was that if at nine I could shoot rabbits, why couldn't Dad have done the same instead of making us eat Buttons.

As I grew older, I shot more game – pheasant, deer. And it didn't bother me a bit – not nearly as much as when our family was torn apart over a damn rabbit.

Chancellorsville

After the battle, after the smoke had cleared, after the screams had ended and before the groans and cries began, he picked himself up and walked to the ridge. To the left, blue uniforms lay scattered in lumps, heaps, the officers carefully lifted like religious icons, the enlisted piled like cordwood for burial in mass graves. To the right, Confederate church women picked up all the dead, aided by old men and young boys as they laid each body – officer and enlisted – on each wagon as though all were sacred, all were gods, all had descended from the sky to carry out the Lord's work.

A singing began – from which side he couldn't tell – but it was a singing nevertheless that could have begun from either side – Yankee or Reb. It was a singing that carried over the ridge – the ridge of differences, of philosophies, of ideas, of politics – but not of faiths. It was a singing that was picked up by the other side – part New England Presbyterian, part Southern Baptist, part Negro spiritual. The singing grew louder and louder and louder so it seemed as though even the dead bodies sang.

The singing was in their blood even – White blood, Black blood, maybe even a little Indian blood if you looked long and hard enough – blood that trickled in rivulets from the Northern side, from the Southern side, until it formed puddles, overflowing puddles that became brooks then streams then rivers, Northern blood to the Rappahannock, Southern to the Rapidan, now holy rivers flowing violet and golden and mauve depending on which side you stood – facing the sun or your back to it – rivers that carried their blood with their song, the blood singing it, the blood praising it. The song was the blood and the blood was the song as the two rivers passed the ridge then joined – Northern blood and Southern blood now no longer Northern nor Southern and Yankee blood and Rebel blood no longer Yankee nor Reb but one blood, one beautiful, shining, singing blood that gathered its own energy – coursing, gaining speed, joining other bloody rivers, neither Northern nor Southern, 'til they reached the Chesapeake then the great, sad, gray Atlantic on one, glorious song.

Dad

It had been a bad job. Let me rephrase: It had been the suckiest, rottenest, lousiest job of my life. Managing editor of field communications for the largest fraternal benefits society in the world. Dennis Knaus's pissant – what's the difference. My boss had been a royal pain, all the way from his ass to his elbow. I had just needed out.

"Mom? Is Dad there?" I was actually glad Dad hadn't answered – even though my whole purpose in going to see them was to hit him up for a grand – sort of a grubstake to set me up before I started my next job.

"Is it important? He has trouble getting up to answer the phone, even with his walker."

"Walker???!!!" The last time I'd seen Dad he'd been using a cane. And that was just four months ago. "I didn't know Dad was using a walker."

"Well . . . you know . . . " I could see her looking at him as her voice turned to a whisper. It didn't matter what sort of shape Dad was in, though. He would always be the ruler of the house. The monarch. The kind. The Grand Pubah. No one dared cross him. No one. Then I thought of that huge house with one phone. No, it wasn't important. I'd just quit what they'd thought was the best job I'd ever had and I only had enough money for gas to get to their house. Then it was another four-hundred miles to my next apartment and job in Belle Fourche, South Dakota. Ever seen the movie *The Cowboys*? Belle Fourche was where John Wayne was taking his little cowpokes. And for all I knew, it hadn't changed since The Duke's day. "No Mom, it's not important."

I watched the needle plummet to empty as I crossed Wisconsin, and when I hit Winona I had just enough money to fill up again. I was on fumes when I rolled into Dell Rapids. As I pulled up to the house I finally took a deep breath. Yeah. Dad was good for a grand. That would get me on my feet again.

Mom was there to greet me at the front door. I could never get over how she was able to make herself look so pretty. Every strand, every hair, was always in place as though she had just come from the beauty parlor. She gave me a hug cut short by the worry in her wandering hazel eyes.

"Where's Dad."

Her eyes flicked behind her as though she were afraid to reveal some secret. "Your father isn't feeling very well."

"Aw, it's probably just the flu or something. We had that going around Appleton. It's some really hasty sh . . . "

"Mike!" The house shuddered at the anger, the pain, the demand in his voice.

Mom's eyes froze as the steady thud of the walker came from Dad's chair to just behind her. She stepped aside like a reluctant referee allowing two mortal combatants to engage.

I entered the living room as his gray face labored up from his chest and his eyes peered murkily. A vague hint of a smile creased his lips, but just as soon it was gone. His eyes lifted leadenly, their Norse blueness piercing. "You sure's hell tooka long time to get here. Whadya do? Get a flat???!!!"

"Well, no, actually . . . "

"More'n likely ya stopped off to get a coupla beers. Couple? Shit! Ah bet it was six er eight. Maybe ten. Whadya do after that? Find some whore to roll?"

"Walt!" Mom scolded.

"Shut up!" He thudded his walker on the floor like an exclamation mark. "Can't ya see I'm talkin' to The Prodigal Son?"

"Walt, please."

"Shut up!" he repeated, then mollified that his anger had sufficiently ruined any chance of a warm homecoming, he turned away and thudded his walker back to his chair. "Well come in, come in. Don't stand there an' let all the cold air get inside."

It was April and beautiful, the waving sun casting a violet glow to the east that flowed into a warm orange in the west. I shut the door anyway.

"What's fer supper???!!!" he demanded.

Dishes clattered in the kitchen as Mom hurried against his anger. "Oh. I don't know. How about meatloaf? You like that, don't you?"

"Your meat loaf tastes like crap. Can't ya do any better 'n that?"

Chinking Pyrex in the refrigerator spoke Mom's harried thoughts. "Well, there's some spaghetti left. And I guess there are a few pieces of chicken."

"More like chickensh . . . "

"Please, Walt."

"Crap. That's all she ever feeds me is crap. Crap this. Crap that. Oh, wouldn't you like a little bit of this crap sauce on top of your crap food? She asks. Crap. Crap. Crap. Crap. It's all crap."

I had always known Dad would never be a New York Times food critic, but even I was a little dismayed at his railing at Mom's cooking. "Maybe we could order some takeout?" I offered.

"I'll make a casserole," said Mom, clanking dishes in the cupboard.

His eyes peered into mine in a staredown as his smile warped his thoughts and he nodded. "I ain't seen ya' for a long time."

"Four months, Dad. Christmas. Remember?"

"I remember Christmas," he snapped. "How's the job."

I'd worn one of those fish ties with the scales right where you tied the knot when my boss had been conducting a staff meeting. Every time he turned to the projection screen, I let my jacket slip open and stroked the tail like I was cleaning a walleye and everyone laughed. Dennis had thought everyone was laughing at him, until he spun around toward me when he was talking about first-quarter production figures and saw the tie. Mom had promised she would figure out a better story for Dad.

"I didn't tell him." Mom shrugged up her excuse. "I thought you'd be able to explain better."

"Thanks a *lot*, Mom." I faced Dad like a firing squad. "I quit."

"Quit!" He turned to Mom, wondering if he'd heard right. "Quit? The best-payin' job ya had in your life and ya quit?"

"Money isn't everything in a job, Dad."

"Money isn't everything," he snorted. "Money isn't everything." His grim, dead-on gaze pinned me. "So what the hell is everything."

"Well . . . you know . . . there's enjoying your work. Enjoying your co-workers and your boss."

"Enjoy? What the hell's there to enjoy about a job. I never enjoyed work a day in my life."

Now *that* was a revelation. "If you don't enjoy your work, Dad, then what else is there."

"Oh," he snorted, finally getting his color back. "I worked the ground dawn to dusk for fifty years, sweatin' in hundred-degree heat and drivin' rain. I sat through hail and watched a tornado cross the east forty but had to keep plowin'. I built people's houses and listened to 'em gripe, then hold back payin' me 'cause they wasn't happy. The richer the bastards was, the less they wanted to pay me. An' I did it to feed you kids. You think I enjoyed that? Workin' all day, comin' home to hear a buncha squallin', whinin' brats 'n wife? Ya know how many times I wanted to hit the road, head out with nothin' but the clothes on my back 'n a pocketa change? Ya think I shoulda quit 'cause I got tired of it?" His gaze hardened as he leaned forward and curled his fingers at me as though stroking the underside of a cat – a very large, stupid, fat cat. "How much money ya got in yer pockets."

"Walter!" Mom scolded, taking my side finally.

"I don't have any money."

"Hah, that's what I thought." He settled back into his chair and switched on the remote. "Let's see how that Seattle game is goin'."

We watched Seattle kick Denver's ass – it wasn't even close. When it came time to turn in I went to him again and this time gave him a hug and a kiss – about the third or fourth time that he'd ever let me do that. "'Night, Dad."

"'Night." His eyes held mine even as I climbed the stairs.

He looked like shit the next morning. As soon as he hobbled on his walker to the bathroom I asked Mom. "How long's he been like this?"

"Since you left in January." She worried her cup in her hands.

"*Mom.*"

The toilet flushed and she cast her voice through the bathroom door. "Are you okay in there, Walt?"

"I just took a shit that woulda made Paul Bunyan proud. That okay 'nough fer ya?"

Mom just rolled her eyes into a smile.

We talked then for a while about how maybe Dad's setback was temporary. Working like a draft horse his entire life – who wouldn't get worn down a little. And then of course there was the flu and being pent up all winter. Just as soon as the weather turned a little nicer he'd be able to set aside that walker and he'd be out there for a stroll, beating the crap out of all the dogs in the neighborhood with his cane.

I knew that was all a lie though when he emerged from the bathroom, face the color of the mouth of the Mississippi after a cloudburst. "I don't feel good."

"Maybe you should take your pills. Have you taken your pills this morning?"

"To hell with pills. They don't do a damn thing fer me anyway." Then, for just a moment, the most forlorn, helpless look I had ever seen crossed his face. "Maybe I just need to sit down."

"I think that would be a good idea, Walt," Mom agreed.

I followed him into the living room. I knew what was coming – a continuation of my ass-chewing from last night. Well, let him chew. This time my ass was ready for it.

"So, you quit yer job." His tired, blue eyes peered up at me as he gripped his walker with both hands, even though he was in his chair. I could just see it in his mind that he imagined those hands around my neck.

"Yeah."

"Humph!" He looked out the front window as April greened up the South Dakota of his youth, middle, and old age, as though he were trying to seize them all back, feel them again all at once. "Just like you quit yer marriage to Sandy."

"Yeah, Dad. Just like I quite my marriage to Sandy." I knew what was coming then – how my brother Dave and his wife Patti had just one child – a daughter – and I was the last chance to continue the family line.

"I don't feel good."

That was the second time in his life he'd said that. The first was ten minutes before. "Mother, I don't feel good." The pleading in his voice was so uncharacteristic of him.

"Would you like me to call the doctor?"

"No!" he screamed.

I knew then was the moment I should have called the ambulance myself.

Even as I thought it, freeze frames flashed.

43

His arms moved, in slow motion.

His whole body jerked peristaltically, like a worm on a hook.

His face blackened as he swallowed his tongue and the slow, steady suck of his last breath on Earth seeped into his lungs.

Mom was so rattled, she couldn't even dial 911. Her fingers fluttered over the dial pad like she couldn't even see the numbers, so I had to fight her for the phone and punch the numbers in myself. "Ambulance . . . 103 East Third . . . heart attack?" was all I could remember saying.

The attendants were there in eight minutes. Quick and professional yet warm and kind, they worked on him and worked on him as I stood outside myself and watched. Could this really be happening? It was all like a movie rolling before my eyes – a movie with a script by someone else. And this script was not going to have a happy ending.

Forty minutes they worked on him, the defibrillator paddles shocking him, splaying his arms and legs out like a fish flopping on the shore. Finally, at the end of those forty minutes, they had a pulse and a breath that sounded as though it were coming through a stir straw.

They hastily pushed aside Mom's ceramic figurines – a smiling dog, a little boy fishing, a black smiling cat that we later found had suffered a chip in its tail – and wheeled Dad out, Mom wringing her hands, begging to ride in the ambulance. Certainly, ma'am, they reassured her. We all knew though it was just a matter of time until he was gone.

***

I knew I should have left right away, gone there to help Mom through the terror and anxiety, worry and grief, that was sure to follow.

But I couldn't help but notice Dad's checkbook on the floor.

Green it was – like money. That made a lot of sense, I guessed. Green with an old-man scent to it as I picked it up and sniffed it. I opened it up and saw that he had

$14,029.32 in his account.

I thought about it and thought about it and thought about it again but I knew I couldn't think about it too long because Mom would be there, crying, holding his hand as long at the doctors and nurses would allow it.

It wasn't too hard writing his signature – he'd pressed hard enough when he'd written his last check so all I had to do was trace it. It was the rest of it that was the hard part. I started to write a one then thought about five minutes before I made it a ten. Ten. Thousand. Dollars.

Maury Olson looked a little funny at me when I presented the check at the cashier's window. It took him a little while for him to recognize me, but he recognized me right away when he saw my name on the check.

"Oh, Mike!" he said, shaking my hand. I was thirty-six and the last time he'd seen me was when I'd brought in my brown plastic Dakota Savings Bank piggybank to open my first savings account.

His eyes paled a moment when he looked at the amount. "I'm . . . uh . . . going to need to get an authorization for this amount."

My throat dried up and my knees felt ready to buckle – crap. I knew it. I should have settled for a grand.

When Nate, the bank president, saw the check, he wasn't ready to just rubberstamp it either. "I should probably call your dad about this."

I didn't say anything, knowing that the worst thing I could have possibly said to Nate was *don't you trust me?* I was nineteen when I'd popped his daughter Cindy's cherry – Geeze, you shoulda seen the blood she'd left there on the back seat. Dad complained for months that his car smelled like dead fish – especially after it had sat through that Fourth of July weekend with all the windows rolled up. But she'd given the kid up for adoption so I never had to pay child support. Man, was that a relief.

I shrugged. "You can if you want."

Nate's eyes pierced right through mine to my brain and out the back of my skull like a Lee Harvey Oswald bullet. "Cash it!" he said, then muttering as he walked away, "And let's hope we never see his sorry ass in here again."

***

When I got to the hospital, Dad was already dead. Apparently, he'd lost control of all his bodily functions so he'd crapped all over the sheets and a real evil smell roiled from the room where he'd died to the hallway where Mom stood in tears, my sister Pat futilely trying to comfort her.

"He was such a good man. Such . . . a . . . good . . . man," Mom choked.

I could hear the glorious obituary she'd written for him already, extolling his many virtues, forgetting that he'd been a mean, cynical, old man who'd treated her like crap from the day after he'd knocked her up and they'd had to get married – the moment he'd turned into a mean, cynical young man.

When it came time to picking out a casket, Mom wanted the best, of course. She chose one made of oak with sheathes of grain carved into it – oak because Dad had been a master carpenter and grain because he'd been a farmer. How fitting.

The problem came when Mom had to pay fit it – and the rest of the arrangements.

"I'm sorry, but he only had $4,029.32 in his account," Maury told her.

"But I know he had more in his account. He'd always said, "When it comes time to put me in the ground, I've got plenty of money for the undertaker.""

Maury looked past Mom to me with total disbelief. "Maybe we can . . . cash one of his CDs? He has ten of those . . . at ten thousand each."

"He'd set those side for our grandchildren's college education . . . our ten grandchildren . . . " Mom pondered. "Well," she said, turning to me, her eyes saying I was the trusted son, the son who had stayed to help her through this, the son who had even delayed going to his new job just to see her through her sorrow. The son who had stolen $10,000 from his father and her and one of her grandchildren. "I guess I don't really have any other choice." And with the whisk of a pen there went my niece's college education.

***

I didn't have to start my new job until Monday and it was only Thursday when I got to Belle Fourche. When I saw the stacks of cardboard boxes the movers had left on my one-bedroom apartment, I realized how small it was. The one in Menasha had two bedrooms and a panoramic view of Lake Winnebago. I even had a boat slip on the lake. Here, as I looked out across an expanse of concrete to the ass end of the post office, I felt as though life had totally failed me – or I had totally failed life.

Since it was still April and the nights cool, there were only a couple Harleys at the Iron Horse – the rest of the parking lot filled with cowboy Cadillacs of various vintages. My Alfa did not fit in at all.

I felt better though as I sat down at the bar and ordered up my old standby – a Jack Daniel's on the rocks with a Coors Light chaser. The Jack went down sweet and bitey – the Coors mellowing it out just enough so I didn't get shit-faced right away.

A very interesting blonde took the stool beside me. Blonde hair in pigtails, her blue eyes peered into mine with the obvious question *how much money does he have*? Her tits were huge and appeared to be hard enough for NBA regulation play. "And how are you tonight?" she asked in a heavy German accent.

Interesting. *Very* interesting. "Can I buy you a drink?"

"Oh certainly. I would like a Jagermeister," she said to the bartender, a frumpy, slightly overweight dishwater blonde who didn't hold a candle to her – the difference was more like a blowtorch. "My name is Heidi," said the German girl.

Hi Heidi ho I wanted to say but didn't. I shook her

hand – totally insufficient under the circumstances – but she clarified her intentions when she pressed it inside the crotch of her skintight jeans. "I think maybe you are a very good-looking man."

Within an hour, I had her Jagermeistered up pretty good. The Jack and the Coors had knocked me for a loop too, so knocked up that when she asked me to dance I said sure even though I'd flunked out of Arthur Murray in middle school.

It was a good thing no one else was out there on the dance floor because after a couple minutes she pulled off her T-shirt. She just hung there – like the heads of a pair of panting black labs, just waiting to be petted.

"All right," the barmaid said, strutting toward us like Field Marshall Goering. "You're 86'd."

"Well, hey. Can't she just put her shirt back on?" I turned to Heidi. "Can't you just put your shirt back on?"

"Not her, you," the barmaid said, pointing me toward the door.

"Me???!!! I wasn't the one with my shirt off."

The barmaid looked at me with a dark, no-shit-dumbass sort of expression. "Do you really think if you did you'd have anything anyone would be interested in?" She pointed to the door, one last time. "Out!"

Two bikers, massive, gathered on both sides of me. I learned later their names were Grizz and Snake. "Ah thinks maybe you's oughta do what the lady says," Grizz politely suggested.

Heidi, her shirt still off, came up to me and stuck her tongue inside my mouth and massaged my ass. If she'd done that to Dad right after his heart attack, he'd still be with us today. "You wait outside. As soon as I can, I come outside and we go somewhere and foke."

"Okay," I chippered, as sober as the Jack Daniel's would allow. As I passed by the growing, angry crowd of bikers toward the door, I could have sworn I heard Heidi speaking to Grizz in a sweet Southern accent.

***

48

I waited outside, as hard as Mt. Rushmore. After about five minutes, Grizz and Snake came out and demanded that I leave, so I did. I learned later that Heidi worked at the bar and her real name was Annabelle Marie and she had come up with the Atlanta Devil's Disciples for the summer.

When I came to the next morning, Dad's checkbook was missing. I searched the back left pocket of my jeans – where I always kept it – but it was gone. Then I thought of Heidi's – or Annabelle's – tongue in my mouth as she felt my ass. – a $4,029.32 tonguing and ass feel.

Things are going better now though. I have a girlfriend. She's a nice girl – nothing like the others. We get together a couple times a week and watch TV or go out for dinner and a movie. Mostly we stay at my place, though – where it's safe and quiet.

Heidi – or Annabelle – is sitting out a minimum of two years on a five-year forgery rap. Mom wanted her to get the chair, and it took the better part of a day for the state's attorney to explain to her that they didn't have the chair anymore – just lethal injection – and Heidi's – or Annabelle's – sentence wouldn't have warranted that anyway.

Grizz and Snake just can't wait for Heidi – or Annabelle – to get out. I can't figure out which one she's tighter with – I think maybe the three of them have come up with some very interesting things to do together though.

And me? I stay as far away from the Iron Horse as I can. Hopefully, Grizz and Snake have pretty much forgotten about me by now. All they probably think about is Heidi – or Annabelle.

I think about Dad now – a lot. His irascible ways. His demeanor. His temper. He wasn't a bad man. Not really. He was just crabby as hell. For as long as I can remember.

I sure hope I never get that way.

Dear Virgil
Pella, Iowa
April 1861

"So how much wood does he need split." Virgil Earp and his father Nicholas were sitting at the kitchen table sharing a cup of morning coffee, the sun just breaking over the rolling Iowa prairie to the east.

"Looks to be a couple cords – maybe three." Nicholas stroked his beard and sharpened his keen Irish eye at his son, now nearly his height at just sixteen. "I figures it'll maybe take you the rest of the day."

Virgil nodded and folded his hands on the table as he considered his father's proposition. "So how much is Mr. Rysdam paying me."

Nicholas leaned back in his chair and cast an appraising eye at his son. "Nothing. I just offered you to help. It's only the neighborly thing to do."

"Yes sir." Nicholas nodded. Though he was sixteen and already a strapping lad, he well remembered his father's razor strop from a few years before. "Can Wyatt help?"

"Him I got diggin' garden. 'Sides, he's a might small

to be splittin' all that much wood."

"Well, all right."

"It'll not be that bad. I understand Mrs. Rysdam is quite the baker. She'll make sure to feed you right. 'Sides that, they got a daughter nearly your age."

"Oh?" Virgil's eyebrows curlicued his sudden interest.

"Ellen, I think her name is. Sixteen and pretty as those tulips poppin' up in the Rysdams' front yard."

"I'll hurry right over there then."

"You do that, Son," said Nicholas, clapping his son on the shoulder. "And be sure to eat an extra helpin' of that good Dutch cookin' for me."

***

Virgil saw no daughter – only a huge pile of stumps in the Rysdam's back yard where Mr. Rysdam had led him. The house had the fanciful raised front of an Amsterdam row house, only it was here in the middle of the Iowa prairie. Tulips – yellow, red, orange – poked from the rich, black soil, a testament to the Rysdam's neatness and hard work.

"Earp," said Mr. Rysdam, hand on his hips. "That don't sound Dutch to me."

"No sir. We're Irish."

"Irish!" roared Rysdam, as though Virgil had uttered a curse. Then he broke into a disparaging chuckle. "So how did an Irishman such as your father to manage to find himself in a colony of Hollanders."

"He bought a farm outside of town," Nicholas explained, then nodding back at their imposing three-chimnied, two-story brick home added, "and then the house here."

"I see." Rysdam nodded thoughtfully, not to be daunted by another man's wealth. "Well, I guess the world needs Irishmen too."

"Yes sir."

"Still. If you ain't Dutch, you ain't much."

Virgil chuckled but when Mr. Rysdam didn't, he sobered. "I'll get right to this here wood, sir."

"Yes you do that. Give it your Irish best. My wife she'll serve you dinner 'bout noon."

"Thank you, sir."

As Mr. Rysdam left, Virgil hefted the eight-pound maul, thinking of how he would rather drive it through Rysdam's skull. But no, there was no time for thinking that way, so he rolled the biggest chunk he could find from the pile for a splitting stump then grabbed a mid-sized chunk to set atop it. Fingering the maul edge to test its sharpness, he eyed a slight crack in the oak stump, raised the maul, and brought it down soundly, cleaving the chunk in two. He picked up the split chunk from the ground and raised his maul and split it again.

By a little before noon, he had quarter split and stacked a full cord along the Rysdam's back fence, maybe a third of the wood in the pile. Most was oak, along with a little walnut and cottonwood and hickory. He was just working up a good sweat when a sweet female voice called out, "Oh Virgil?"

He turned in mid-swing and there she was – eyes the same blue as Delft china, blond pigtails trailing over her back. Her haltered dress, intended to hide her figure, didn't do a very good job of it as she stood there, fresh, rosy cheeks and perky-bosomed, already a woman despite her tender sixteen years.

"Ellen?" Virgil answered, slowly setting down his maul.

"Yes." She clasped her hands in front of her and

laughed. "How did you know my name."

"My father told me," Virgil confessed. "Nicholas Earp."

"Oh, Mr. Earp." Ellen laughed, cheeks reddened the same hue as the tulips behind her. "Well, Virgil. Would you like some dinner?"

"I'd *love* some dinner," he answered, then followed her eagerly inside.

The Rysdam kitchen was the picture of tidiness and neatness – yellows and blues and white cascading together in a kaleidoscope of bright and gaudy colors only the Dutch would dare mix together. Mrs. Rysdam turned from the kitchen stove, just as rosy-cheeked as her daughter and far plumper. "You like the Dutch pastries, yes?" Mrs. Rysdam set a plate of the most delicious-looking pastries Virgil had ever seen – so delicious that for a brief moment he had forgotten Ellen. "We have a roast beef and potatoes with carrots and turnips too."

Mr. Rysdam sat in a chair at the end of the trestle table while Virgil sat on a bench across from Ellen as Mrs. Rysdam set heaping, steaming bowls on the table then seated herself at the other end of the table. Virgil reached for a pastry but his hand hadn't even reached the plate before Mr. Rysdam grunted. "First we pray."

"Oh," said Virgil, shame-faced that he hadn't minded his manners.

Mr. Rysdam picked up a well-worn Bible from the table and read. "And I saw another mighty angel come down from heaven, clothed with a cloud: and a rainbow was upon his head, and his face was as it were the sun, and his feet as pillars of fire." Mr. Rysdam read on and on and on. He read so long that steam no longer rose from the food and Virgil wondered if it would be cold before Mr.

Rysdam finished. The answer came when Mr. Rysdam stopped reading and closed his Bible and cast an imperious eye at Virgil. "So what faith are you."

As far as Virgil knew, they didn't have any faith. The only times he had seen the inside of a church were when he had been baptized then later confirmed. Other than that, he figured the only times would be when he married or died. "Christian," he said, figuring that was pretty safe.

"I *know* you're Christian. *Everybody's* Christian, but for the heathen Jews of course. But there are Godly Christians and those who are not Godly. So which are you."

"Godly?" Virgil said, making it sound like a question.

Mr. Rysdam gripped the arms of his chair, losing patience. "And which *sect* does your family belong to."

Virgil knew that the Dutch were all members of the Reformed Church while in Earps, like many of their Scotch-Irish brethren, were Catholic. As he glanced across the table at Ellen, the lie crept from his lips before he could pull it back. "Reformed."

"Oh? And which church."

"I, uh, guess we haven't had a chance to find a church just yet."

"I see. Well if you're a member of the Reformed Church, then you'll have to come to ours."

"Yes sir," Virgil muttered.

The food was better than it looked – far better. Virgil ate as many pastries as his stomach could hold, and when they were done he had all he could do to walk to the woodpile and start swinging the maul again.

"At least he works," Mrs. Rysdam said to Ellen whom he called back inside the house, no doubt to make her safe from an errant, drunken, Catholic Irishman.

Virgil finally finished splitting and stacking three full cords by nightfall, then looking forlornly at the Rysdam's house, picked up his maul and headed home, starlight and a full moon guiding him to his house.

"So how was the woodcutting?" Nicholas asked, just sitting down to supper. Virgil's older brothers were there too – Newton and James – along with his younger brother Wyatt and sister Martha and mother Virginia.

"Oh, all right." Virgil rubbed the calluses just starting to form on his palms from a full day of wood splitting.

"And how was the Rysdam's daughter?" Newton asked, a wicked smile curling clear to his eyes.

"Oh, all right," said Virgil.

"Well I'm glad everything's all right," said Nicholas, passing the platter of corned beef and cabbage without bothering with a prayer first as had the Rysdams.

"Are we still Catholic, Father?" Virgil asked.

Nicholas looked off thoughtfully. "I suppose we are."

"Would it be okay if I joined the Reformed Church?"

Nicholas looked as his son as though he had gone a little crazy. "I don't see that it would hurt anything – as long as you keep working hard." He bit into his corned beef. "So what brought on this joining the Reformed Church."

"I'll bet it has something to do with that Dutch girl," said James.

Nicholas switched his gaze from James to Virgil. "Well did it?"

Virgil looked off in the general direction of the

Rysdams' home. "Maybe."

That night, after tossing and turning for several hours, thinking only of Ellen, Virgil heard a light tapping. He cracked open his eyes and looked out at Ellen Rysdam pressing her face against his window. He pulled himself out of bed and opened the door to the balcony where she stood – quiet, anxious, furtive. "Ellen," he whispered, not wanting to wake the rest of the family. "What are you doing here."

Even in the pale moonlight, her eyes were blue. Bluer than blue, they were part of the night sky itself. She wore only a filmy nightgown and bedroom slippers as though she had just crept out of bed herself. "I had to see you, Virgil." Her breath was humid, her eyes twinkling wondrously up into his. "I had to knock on all your brothers' windows until I found yours."

"We'd both be in trouble if my parents knew you were here." That didn't stop him though from taking her shoulders in his hands, feeling their soft warmth in the moonlight, then the warmth of her body as he edged closer.

"I don't care," she said wondrously. She didn't care either as he leaned over to kiss her, his lips drawing her life from her then returning it, back and forth, until it seemed they could kiss no more. "Oh Virgil," she said, resting her head on his chest. "I want you so much. What will we do."

***

They met upstairs on the porch every night after that, and when he realized his brothers' silence was due to prying eyes, he and Ellen met under a bur oak on a hilltop meadow. As words turned to kisses then more one night, her blue eyes worried her fear. "We can't go any further,

Virgil."

His hand drew reluctantly away from her breast. "Why not."

"We're not married," she said, her eyes reflecting a million stars.

"But we can't get married. We're only sixteen."

"Maybe we could go to the courthouse in Knoxville where no one knows us."

"Okay."

The next morning, Virgil Earp and Ellen Rysdam, both sixteen, told their parents they were going to visit friends. That afternoon, Walter Earp and Ellen Donahoo, both conveniently eighteen, were married in the Marion County Courthouse in Knoxville.

If that bur oak had had eyes, oh what a tale it could have told – of a young couple holding and clasping each other from dusk to dawn, of whispered *I love yous* drifting out into the eternal night to the stars and beyond. They still lived with their parents by day but every night, beneath the bur oak, they were Mr. and Mrs. Earp – in every way.

"I think I'm pregnant," Ellen told Virgil an early October night. It was still warm, the moon haloing their figures beneath the bur oak.

"Are you sure?"

"I'm sure." Her eyes brimmed, happy and afraid. "Oh Virgil, what will we do."

Virgil had no answer for her, and when Nellie Jane came into the world the summer of 1862 and Ellen finally revealed the father, Mr. Rysdam began a slow but steady walk, shotgun loaded with double-ought buck, toward the Earp house. Figuring he had a better chance against the rebs than Mr. Rysdam, Virgil fled that night to Monmouth, Illinois where he joined the 83rd Regiment of Illinois

Volunteers.

***

"I'm sorry, Ellen," Mr. Rysdam told his sobbing daughter. "You should be proud though that he died for the Union cause."

"My baby no longer has a father."

"We'll move west, to Kansas. We can start a new life there. You and Nellie Jane too."

And so, as Virgil Earp fought in major engagements, including one against Confederate General Nathan Bedford Forrest near Fort Donelson in 1863, the Rysdams moved to Kansas then later Oregon then Washington Territory. When Virgil finally mustered out at Nashville June 24, 1865, he returned to Pella to learn Ellen and Nellie Jean had left with the Rysdams, leaving no word of where they had gone. Unknown to Virgil, Mr. Rysdam had declared an end to their marriage.

***

Years later, Nellie Jane was reading a dime novel about the Gunfight at OK Corrall between Morgan, Wyatt, and United States Deputy Marshal Virgil Earp and Doc Holiday and the Clanton gang. Virgil had come away with a leg wound, only to later be drygulched by five shotgun blasts in an arm and above the groin. The next brother to fall was Morgan, murdered as he stood beside his brother Wyatt at Hatch's billiard parlor. Wyatt took revenge for his brothers.

"Mother?" Nellie Jane said, standing at her mother's front door, dime novel in hand.

"Yes."

"Was father's first name Virgil?"

"Yes."

"He's still alive."

58

Ellen sat down to write the first letter to her husband after thirty-seven years. *Dear Virgil . . .*

***

It was Virgil's third wife Allie who urged him to go to Portland to visit the wife and child he hadn't seen since they were seventeen. When Virgil later passed during a pneumonia epidemic in Goldfield, Nevada, October 19, 1905, Allie agreed with Nellie Jane's request to have his remains shipped to her family's burial plot at Riverview Cemetery in Portland where he now rests beside his first wife and daughter. Allie, who died many years later in Los Angeles November 11, 1947, was buried with her sister-in-law Adelia Earp Edwards.

Driving School

When Jessica's father Bob had asked her to do the driving tests when their clients 'graduated', she balked. "Why me?" That seemed to be a question she'd been asking a lot lately.

"I can't." He eyed a highway patrolman in the rearview mirror. They were doing exactly seventy. Just fast enough for the cop to sit on their tail. And who knew. Maybe by now he'd radioed in a NICS check.

"Maybe you could slow down and let him pass," Jessica suggested.

"Okay." By now her father was sweating torpedoes – actual torpedoes – firing from his forehead at some unknown target. He dropped their speed to 68 – then 66. The police cruiser slid by slowly, the officer looking at Bob as though he'd already caught him in the act – and who knows – maybe he had.

"I really wish you hadn't gotten that DUI."

"I know, Jess. I know."

"Maybe you should let me drive." She'd been drawing the surrounding countryside in her sketchbook. Farms. Cows. Clouds. All dreamily floating together into a mosaic where she'd much rather be.

"Hey, that's a great idea." He hit the turn signal and turned off at the first exit for Sioux Falls. "Hey, maybe we could try this town. The sign says 160,000."

"Maybe." As she set her sketchbook aside, she wondered about art school. Then that was as faraway of a dream as anything.

Bob was in the driving school business, and ironically, had lost his own license after his second DUI – pleaded down to first. Six months suspension, the judge ordered, slamming down the gavel. Fortunately, having a daughter kept him out of jail. Jessica suspected the judge didn't want to mess with all the DHS paperwork if she went into temporary foster care while Bob sat it out in the calaboose.

They would pick cities of between 50,000 and 250,000 – big enough to not be noticed but not so big the FBI would catch on to him. The school always started at 6 p.m. sharp Thursdays and went until 10, the same times Friday night, with driving exams Saturday morning. Jessica would take their photos and Bob would crank out fake driver's licenses complete with bar codes and voila – the graduates were on the road. Until their first driving infraction, of course. And then they'd be charged with driving with a forged license. That was why Bob changed the name of the school every town they came to – Universal School of Driving, Columbia Driving School, International Driving Academy – Jessica really liked the sound of that one. Bob would take out ads in the local newspaper a week ahead of time:

DUI? License suspended or revoked? International Driving Academy can help. Just call 555-5555 to save a seat today.

And the calls would pour in. Really? You can help even me get my license back? Absolutely, Bob told them. That's fantastic. My lawyer said I'd be lucky to get it back in five years after I ran over that pedestrian. It wasn't my fault though. He was at least as drunk as I was.

They pulled up at a convenience store, the needle at a quarter. Jessica looked at her father with a *don't tell me we're out of money* look and he shrugged. "I guess this is as good a town as any."

"I guess so." The queasy feeling started in her stomach and ran all the way to her toes and head.

As Bob stepped out, the door molding clattered on the concrete. "Gonna have to fix that."

Jessica nodded, mainly to herself. As Bob went inside to borrow the phone book and look up phone numbers for the local newspapers and shoppers, the HP cruiser stealthed through the parking lot, the driver observing where people were from, checking for outdated plates. As he parked perfectly between the painted lines – exactly 18 inches clearance on each side of his car – he stepped out and donned his wraparound shades and ran a hand through his lawnmower buzzed flattop and headed straight toward the car.

Jessica came up with excuses – knowing that if her dad got into the car and the officer asked for his license and ran a check they were toast. She glared at Bob who smiled back from inside the store, a smile turning to abject horror as he saw the officer.

The officer bent over and picked up the door molding, studied it curiously, and looked at the rusted rivet holes where it had fallen from the car. "Is this yours?"

"No," said Jessica, following Bob's advice to always lie to a police officer whenever possible. Plausible denial, Jess. Plausible denial, he always told her.

"Hmmm . . . " The officer studied the molding, then the bare door, and the molding again. "You know, I've investigated a lot of accidents, and I'd swear this was a door molding for a 1988 Pontiac Bonneville." He nodded at the side of the car. "Just like the one you're sitting in."

"Really?"

The officer looked at the side of the car, kneeled, and fit the molding against the door and with a slight bop of his fist sealed it to the side. He stood slowly, Jessica's guilty-as-hell look reflected in his glasses. "Well, I guess you have a new door molding."

"Yeah, guess so. Thanks."

The officer chuckled and went inside the store. Bob

ducked around him and scrambled outside to the passenger door. "Let's go. You drive."

Jessica turned and rolled her eyes to herself as she slid over and started the car. She cringed as Bob sat on her sketchbook.

"What did he want."

"What did who want."

"The cop. What'd he say to you."

"He asked why a girl as pretty as me was driving a piece of crap like this."

"No. He didn't." Her dad waited for her to continue, but she said nothing. "He didn't hit on you, did he?"

Jessica looked both ways and pulled out on the street. "Something under $40?"

"Oh, a motel. Yeah, right," her dad said, unable to keep two ideas in his head at once. He stared straight ahead, finally calming down. "He didn't hit on you, did he Jess?"

"Yeah he did." She smiled. "He asked me for my phone number and everything."

"You didn't give it to him. Did you?"

"Of course not." A beat. "And please get off my sketchbook."

***

There must have been a lot of drunk drivers in Sioux Falls because the calls poured in. Really? You can even get me a release for my SR-22? Absolutely, her dad told them. Great, sign me up.

By Wednesday night – a day before classes were to start – seventy people had signed up, ranging from a teen who'd had his license revoked for habitual drag racing to a ninety-two-year-old man who'd lost his driving privileges when he couldn't pass the vision test at seventy-eight. At $600 a crack, they'd make a killing.

Her dad had rented a party room at a local tavern to hold the school in, something that troubled Jessica since the students would have to pass through the bar, and since most were probably alcoholics or at least committed drunkards, they wouldn't be able to make it to class sober.

"And you know the drill by now, right Jess? If we're busted?" Her father looked from the TV he'd been watching all afternoon between calls, a beer balanced on his bare belly.

"Yeah. I grab the cash, the camera, the computer, printer, and laminator and throw them in the trunk and split."

"Good girl." Bob smiled and sipped his beer, returning to his program. "I'm so proud of you." Police sirens wailed on the program he was watching and Jessica glanced out the motel window to make sure they weren't for them.

The first night brought in the usual suspects. If there was a profile of a typical student it would be twenty-nine years old, male, severe alcoholic, with a four-page rap sheet of driving infractions. Many had criminal records – some with felonies. There were others too, like a young mom who couldn't afford insurance and whose license had been suspended but she kept driving and had it revoked. And now she was paying nearly a month's take home as a convenience store clerk to get her license back. Jessica felt pretty bad about that one. And then there was an older man, obviously blind, who asked help in finding a seat at one of the tables. She felt sorry for the vet who came in with his wheelchair, jeans pinned back on his stubs – they'd have to waive the driving portion for him since the Bonneville didn't have hand controls. And then there was a fifteen-year-old boy – no driving infractions. In fact he'd never had a license. Jessica found his retro-fifties flat top dorky.

"The driver's ed class was full. My dad asked if this would help get me an insurance discount."

"Sure. This class will get you a fifty percent discount, at least," Bob assured him.

The boy looked narrowly at Bob. "My dad said it would be only twenty-five."

"Oh, I'm sorry." Bob slapped his forehead. "I forgot

this was South Dakota. We're in all fifty states, you know. Canada too. It's really hard to keep track of all these regulations."

The boy looked at Bob as though he had bull crap written all over his face.

After seven or eight more students brought their beers and drinks in from the bar they were ready to start. Bob ran through a series of slides on the projector showing major traffic accidents – mangled cars, some burnt-out hulks, cars wrapped around semis and trains and telephone poles. Injured people sitting dazed beside cars. Corpses covered with sheets and in body bags.

"And not one of them was a graduate of the International Driving Academy," Bob concluded, switching off the projector and turning on the lights. "By Saturday afternoon, every single one of you will not only have your driving privileges restored. You can also rest assured that what happened to these people won't happen to you."

Jessica quickly counted the people in the room, and dividing it into the number of hours available, figured they'd be lucky to have a ten-minute driving test for each student – even if they went all day Saturday.

The rest of Thursday night was taken up with more blood-and-gore slides and mountains of boring statistics. Most of the students were asleep except for the drinkers who had started a couple impromptu poker tournaments, some switching to shots. They seemed to pay the most attention.

Friday night's class started with a driving attitude survey with questions like "Have you ever taken the right of way illegally" or "How often do you speed".

"Are we gonna get 'dem tests back?" asked a heavily tattoo biker barechested except for an open denim motorcycle club vest.

Jessica glanced up at Bob from the tests she was 'scoring'.

"Unfortunately, no."

"Well why not?" the biker demanded, settling back in his chair, arms crossed.

"Well . . . We just take an average of the answers and tailor the rest of the class accordingly. Need I remind you that International Driving Academy has been in the business since 1946? No one does it better than we do."

The biker grimaced through his scars, shrugged, and satisfied himself with another shot and beer back and ordered another round. The bar was making a killing, with two servers scrambling to take the students' orders.

***

Saturday morning came, and it was time for the road test – and graduation. Knowing that the first or second student would attract the attention of the police and get them busted, Bob had finagled a realty company to rent him the parking lot of a defunct home building supply. Knee-high weeds thrust through chunks of broken concrete and the students steered through a litter of beer and soda cans, trash bags, diapers, tampons and prophylactics. Jessica had spent four hours picking up broken beer and wine bottles – those she could see anyway. She didn't have any idea what might still be lurking in the weeds.

At about three, one of the students drove over a broken whiskey bottle and flattened a tire. As Bob scrambled to put on a spare, Jessica scanned the remaining students. Besides the student in the car, the biker registered as Grizz, there were just three left – Darwin, the boy with the flat top, and Mr. Phillips, the ninety-two-year-old blind man.

"There." Bob dusted off his hands and got up from his knees. "Good as new."

Jessica studied the bald spare as Bob got in with Grizz and they weaved through the lot as Bob told Grizz to pretend they were pylons. Since they'd taken photos the first night – it was impossible to flunk provided you paid in full, of course – Jessica handed Grizz his license once they were back.

"'Sanks." He tucked it in his vest pocket where a

half-pint glinted. "Hey, you're kinda cute. Ya wanna go on a date or anythin'?"

"Probably not today."

"Unh, okay." Grizz got on his panhead and kicked the starter and smiled one more time back over his shoulder before roaring out of the lot.

"Your turn," Bob said to Darwin, the kid with the flat top. He cut his driving test short and three minutes later Jessica was handing him his license just as a highway patrol cruiser was pulling over Grizz.

"Great," Darwin chippered. "I can't wait to show this to my dad." He headed straight for the cruiser.

"Dad?" Bob looked grimly at the cruiser which the trooper now had Grizz up against, legs spread, as he pulled out his cuffs.

"Do I get to drive?" the blind man asked, searching for the car right beside him. Grizz securely ensconced in the back seat, the trooper was walking straight toward them.

"You do this one, Jess. Okay?" Bob's voice trailed off into a whisper. "The money's in the trunk with everything else."

Jessica nodded and after she helped the old man get in the door she took the passenger seat.

"Is it running?" the old man asked, unable to hear the engine. The burnt-out muffler was loud enough to get them a ticket.

"Yeah, let's get out of here."

The old man put the car in drive and they surged ahead. In the rearview mirror Jessica saw the trooper questioning her father while Darwin, the patrolman's clone, stood smiling to the side, admiring his new driver's license.

"How far do you want me to drive?" the old man said, eyes filmy with cataracts, barely missing a light pole in the middle of the parking lot.

Jessica flipped on the turn signal and miraculously guided him into heavy traffic. "Omaha. And don't stop for anything." It wasn't until they reached the city outskirts that she realized she had left her sketchbook in the motel.

Erin McDonnell

Harrison Griggs was lonely – so very lonely. It had been but a year since his wife had passed from cancer – a year of remembered birthdays, anniversaries, holidays – all without Emily. And now Harrison flipped his office calendar to Dec. 13, the date she had died.

"Oh, it's nothing," Emily had said, breezing into the kitchen with an armful of groceries, the terrier chasing the cat out and the cat chasing the terrier in, the only remaining chaos they had as empty nesters.

"Did the doctor know what it was?" Harrison probed.

Emily turned to him, a bit paler than her normal blond pallor. "He's referring me to an oncologist."

"An oncologist," Harrison repeated, trying to absorb the reality.

"She's the best, though. That's what he said."

"Honey?"

"Yes?"

"You don't have to be brave for me. Just be honest."

"Oh Harry, honest is so hard."

He buried her less than a year later, and now a year

after that, he was studying the same date she had died, as though staring at it long enough would make it go away, vanish, whisk back the calendar pages until she was alive and whole and well and laughing in his arms. They had scrimped and worked and saved all their lives for retirement. And now he would face it alone.

Harrison was still a catch, though, even at fifty-eight. He ran, golfed, swam, or hit the gym at least once a day. His tan, lean frame made him appear no older than his mid-forties, and he ran a 5K whenever he had a chance. Most woman – regardless of their age – would see him as a prize. But he wasn't interested. All he could think of was Emily, and how their dreams of strolling together into old age had ended with Emily walking off a cliff and Harrison helpless as he watched her fall.

Out of curiosity, he was cruising a dating Website. Just as the digital clock on his desk slipped from December 13 to December 14, one listing caught his eye, even though there was no picture. *DUBLIN GIRL, forty, seeks older man in search of adventure. Redhead, green eyes, weight fifty kilos, height 180 centimeters, breast 100 centimeters.* Harrison pulled his calculator from his desk drawer, and after doing some quick metric conversions, determined that DUBLIN GIRL most definitely was one hot commodity. So he responded.

Nothing happened. Two weeks passed, then three. He didn't want to bother her, but he didn't want anyone else to snatch her up either. Then so many of those places were scams, rip-offs. But the fact that she hadn't answered right away told him she had to be real. So he sent her another message, further detailing his background. *I'm a political consultant, currently managing a Republican Presidential campaign.* He hit ENTER and five minutes later had a response. *Really? That's fascinating. I've attached my photo. Whatever you do, please, please, don't share it with anyone. How soon can you fly to Dublin so we can meet?*

After he saw her photo, sitting on a primordial granite outcropping beside the ocean, coastal breeze streaming her wavy auburn locks past emerald-green eyes, he went online and booked a flight to Dublin the next day.

***

She was holding a sign, ERIN MCDONNELL, in the concourse of Dublin Airport. As he studied her from a distance, Harrison wasn't sure he liked what he saw – sullen, moody, perhaps even cold. He thought a moment of turning around and catching the next flight back. But he had come this far so he decided to follow through so they could at least meet. If things worked out, fine. If they didn't, that would be fine too – at the very least, he could say he had been to Ireland – which he never had before.

As he mixed in with the milling crowd, spilling from planes to ramps to concourses, he matched his pace with the others. Through the bright lights at the end of the concourse her full 100 centimeters stood proudly, the rest of her like a willow along a riverbank. And then, as he came to stand before her, her eyes meeting his, he realized that here was one of the most beautiful women he had ever seen, wavy auburn locks cascading over her shoulder and those green eyes – impossibly deeply green – twinkling from the smoothest, milkiest skin he had ever seen. "Harrison." She lowered the sign and her defenses now that they were joined, the two of them an island oblivious to the hundreds flowing past, a torrent around a boulder.

"Erin," he said, attaching her name to her face.

71

She smiled, hearing him say her name. "For a while I didn't think you would come. But now you're here. Maybe we should have a drink. Or lunch. Or something." Her brogue was so thick he could climb it like a set of stairs clear up to those beautiful eyes and stay there forever.

"Yes, we should." He took her hand and they strolled, looking into each other's eyes, paying no mind to the others passing twice their pace down the concourse, their million voices a din with only two voices audible. "I've rented a car. Should we go for a drive?"

"I know of this inn. Just thirty kilometers from here."

Harrison smiled, figuring that would give them just enough time to learn about each other.

Driving on the left side of the road was a challenge, but Erin laughed, taking his hand, offering directions through a maze of paved then macadam then graveled roads to a limestone inn set amid fairyland rock outcroppings as though it had been carved from them. "They have rooms, too." Erin winked and squeezed his hand before they even opened the roadster doors.

How could I possibly be so lucky, Harrison asked himself, then squeezed back, sealing their compact for the night.

The stuffed Cornish game hen was fabulous, and the burgundy superb. They took what was left of the wine to their room and had just barely finished it when Erin came laughing into his arms. "Oh Harrison."

"Harry."

"Harry." Her eyes flicked up and down his frame, arms over his shoulders. She dangled a high heel from her toe then dropped her shoe to the floor, the first article of clothing to fall victim to their passion.

They made love all night and much of the next day, taking time only to walk the trail behind the inn to the mountain where they could look out as the sun bled into the far western sea. Abandoned stone crofts, roofs long gone, dotted the mountain below, stone fences marking what had once been individual farms hundreds of years before. An early night wind arose, sifting Erin's hair around her face like flower tendrils. There was something unsaid in her eyes – a sadness fueled by some long-hidden, burning anger. He lifted her chin toward him. "Is something wrong?"

"Wrong? No, nothing's wrong." She looked off at something he couldn't see. "We should get back or we'll have to wend our way down the trail in the dark."

***

They took the first available flight after securing Erin's fiancé visa. Harrison's State Department connections whisked it through faster than Seal Team 6 took out bin Laden, and they soon were ensconced together in Harrison's Georgetown colonial, replete with pool and hundred-year-old rose garden. The house said money, power, and influence, but quietly like the brook coursing through the two and a half acres.

"I haven't even met your family. Will they be coming for the wedding? Maybe I can get their tickets for them. I have all sorts of friends at the airlines, you know." Harrison didn't want it to sound like charity. That's why he mentioned his friends.

"I have no family," Erin said as a matter of fact with no emotion whatsoever.

"No family." Harrison laughed. "Why, everyone has family – uncles, aunts, cousins even."

"I have no family," Erin insisted.

"Well who's going to give you away?"

"I need no man to give me away." Erin's eyes were blank and dead, just like her voice. "I can give myself away."

"All right," said Harrison, not wanting to press the matter further. Then an idea occurred. "How about Billy?"

"Billy?"

"Billy Boufon, the candidate whose campaign I'm running. You've certainly heard of him. He was President, twice impeached, but the party wants him back in office again after the disaster that followed him."

Erin's eyes flickered up a smile and she reached for his arm as they sat on the patio. The orioles were chortling, as though laughing along with Erin at his suggestion. "The Republican frontrunner for President of the United States, and former President, is going to walk me down the aisle?"

"Sure, why not? He's one of my best friends."

"Why not. Why not?" Erin said the second time to herself. "Sure. He can give me away."

Billy was thrilled at the idea.

***

"Give your wife away to you? What a great idea. That'll make me seem more human, more approachable. Human and approachable are good. And you know why human and approachable are good? Human and approachable are good because that's the opposite of how the voters see Washington politicians. What a great way to mold my image. What a great idea. You know something, Harry? You're a genius."

Erin was all right with the idea at first. Then, against everything the Democratic news media and pollsters had predicted, Billy was elected President. As their wedding day approached, and the media got word that the newly elected President of the United States was giving away the bride at his campaign manager's wedding, Erin cooled.

"Why does the media have to be at our wedding?"

"My God, Erin. He's President of the United States. And for the second time."

"But the media . . . "

"I can't break my word with Billy, honey."

She looked at him steadily. "Can you ask them to keep the cameras off me?"

"Why would I want to do that, honey? You're absolutely stunning."

Half of her smiled at him. The other half – the half that seemed so sad on that mountain in the Irish countryside months ago – didn't. "All right," she said, as though giving in to something she would later regret.

***

They held the reception at Harrison and Erin's home after the wedding. The rose garden was in full bloom, birds chirping, a string quartet playing baroque as the guests admired Erin in her wedding gown. Erin had been adamant about no photos of the wedding itself – that would just ruin everything, she said – so press photographers were busy catching photos of Billy shaking hands, Billy toasting, Billy mixing it up with senators and congressmen who had finally publicly endorsed him now that he had been elected President a second time. "What a bunch of great people," said Billy. "Great people. Did I ever tell you how much I love great people? Look at all the great people there are here."

Then, when the four of them were standing together chatting, a media photographer took their photo.

"You!" Erin pointed at the photographer. "Delete

that photo."

The photographer shrugged the shoulders of his khaki vest. "But this is a public event. And we were invited."

"My wedding is a private event. And you have no right to take a picture."

"Sorry." The photog smirked. "Tough."

***

Their plane was well out over the Atlantic before they talked again. Erin was simmering like a cauldron. And Harrison was afraid of her, not physically so much as of her mood.

"Are you all right?" He touched her arm as she sat beside him.

"I'm all right." Erin looked straight ahead. Her sullenness melted as she turned to kiss him.

They landed in Athens mid-afternoon and booked into a hotel on an ocean so clear fish shimmered twenty feet below. The sun reflected from the water onto the whitewashed buildings so everything had the aqua patina of a living watercolor. The tide splashed upon the rocks below as they made love, curtains trailing like windborne faeries in the ocean breeze.

The next day they toured the Parthenon and the Acropolis and, if they listened closely enough, they could hear Socrates or Plato or Aristotle carry on dialogues with their students or Homer recite his odes. The oozo and retsina flowed freely, and at night they made love again, the ocean holding the sunlight through the night as phosphorescent jellyfish swarmed the surface, harbingers of the tide. Harrison hoped it would never end, but sadly, before he knew it, they had to return to Washington then turn around and fly with Billy and his wife to London for a meeting with the king.

***

They arrived at Heathrow, checked in to their hotel, and had dinner and drinks then went to their rooms. Erin begged off on going to Buckingham Palace the next day. *I'm so sick I can hardly sit up*, she told Harrison. When Harrison asked if she needed to go to the hospital she said, *no, it must be the fish I had at dinner last night. It'll pass.*

Billy was even more disappointed than Harrison as they entered Royal Albert Hall for the reception. "She's not coming? Why not?"

"She's sick, Billy."

"Well I'll be." Billy's attention was then drawn to the milling crowds, the television cameras, the ceaseless din of voices. "Well let's go meet the Prime Minister."

The PM was a bit cool at first, based on Billy's previous remarks about Great Britain being a socialist state and ragheads taking the whole country over. Billy clasped the PM's shoulder, far more familiarity than normal British propriety would allow. "Now about this terrorist thing . . . "

Harrison felt his phone buzz and pulled it out and read a message from Erin. *Feeling much better. Would love to attend the event but all the cabs in London are taken. Could you come get me? XOXO Erin.* Harrison tugged Billy's sleeve as he was chatting up the PM. "I just got a text from Erin. She's better and wants me to come pick her up."

"Now?" Billy checked his watch. "The King's speech is in just a little over an hour."

"I think I can make it," Harrison said doubtfully.

"Well you'd better leave right now. You'll be

fighting traffic the whole way."

"I will." Harrison pushed his way back through the crowd, trying to remember the parking ramp level where they had parked. Was it eight or nine? Or maybe ten? He reached into his pocket for the stub. Eleven. "I'm sorry." He forced his way through a crowd of disgruntled guests, some undoubtedly from the House of Lords. "Excuse me," he said, making it sound more like a command than a request.

Outside, he ran to the parking ramp, feeling minutes melt away like an ice sculpture at a July outdoor wedding. This was crazy. Erin should know better than this. She was going to ruin everything.

He finally got to the BMW and started it and chirped the tires through the parking ramp. Damn it, damn it. She was going to make him late. She was going to make him miss the King's speech – maybe even the PM's introduction of Billy.

Luckily, there were plenty of spaces in the hotel parking ramp. He hurried into their room only to find Erin not there – only a note fluttering in the breeze from the open window, anchored by a pen. *Harry – I was lucky to find a cab. Sorry to inconvenience you. I'll love you forever. Erin.*

Harrison picked up her note and studied it. A burning doubt coursed through him, starting at the base of his spine and racing through his body. He checked his watch. Less than a half hour until the King's speech. He'd never make it. Billy would kill him. Worse than that, he might fire him.

As he ran down the hallway, a man in trench coat and suit hailed him. "Mister Harrison Griggs?"

"I don't have time now. I'm late," he said as he

brushed past him.

"Mister Griggs, this is important."

"Not now, Harrison screamed. "I'm late. Don't you understand?"

"Mr. Griggs. This is about your national security."

He ran to the parking ramp, got into his rental, and laid rubber the length of the parking ramp and entered the street, cabs and sedans honking as he cut them off. He'd never make it.

The parking ramp was full when he got back to the hall. He circled through every level three times until a Fiat pulled out and he slid into the space almost before the car pulled away, the driver flipping him off. He cut the engine and ran toward the hall, phone buzzing in his pocket. He ignored it but it kept buzzing so he pulled it out and read Billy's text. *Erin's here. Why's she wearing such a baggy dress? She looks like a pregnant cow. Billy.*

Harrison took the rear entrance, and flashing his credentials, stood in the doorway as the PM finished his remarks. "And now, I present the President of the United States, Billy S. Bufoun."

Billy jumped up and smiled and nodded to a mixture of clapping and cheers and boos. He grabbed the PM's elbow and took the mic. "It's great to be here in London. I feel so great to be here, in fact, that I'd like to apologize for a little thing that happened about 247 years ago." The crowd laughed, twisting up Billy's smile as he knew he was winning them over. Then, unexpectedly, he launched into the middle of his speech. "You know, as I stand here in Royal Albert Hall, I think back on how England has historically dealt with its dissidents. And you know what? I think they did the right thing. I know because I saw the movie *Braveheart*. I'm not kidding. I sat through the whole thing. And you know what? I think William Wallace had it coming. And those Welsh poets who threw themselves off a cliff? Well, I say goodbye, good riddance. They wrote lousy poetry anyway. Take the Dylan Thomas, for example. I can't past the first line of that guy. And you know when England sent all those Irish convicts to Australia a couple hundred years ago? I think that was the right thing too. I mean, they didn't kill them, did they? They just skipped that step and sent them straight to hell." The crowd roared.

Harrison smiled and looked past Billy, scanning the dais for Erin. And there she was, beautiful, auburn locks streaming over her shoulders, green eyes vivacious as she smiled and tugged at a loose string on an incredibly baggy dress he had never seen her wear before. Then, for a millisecond, their eyes met, Erin's in shock but with the most loving smile she had ever offered.

The explosion rocked the hall, throwing Billy in pieces from the podium into the crowd. The concussion threw Harrison back through the doorway against a policeman, the last thing he remembered.

***

"Mr. Griggs? Mr. Griggs? Wake up, Mr. Griggs."

"Not now, he's just coming out of a coma."

"Mister Griggs?"

Harrison opened his eyes. Above stood the man in the trench coat he had seen in the hallway. The man reached inside his suit jacket for his wallet and showed his badge. "Simon Moore, Mr. Griggs, mi6." Simon nodded to another suit beside him. "This is Eric Hardin from your CIA. May we speak with you about your wife, or should we say late wife, Mr. Griggs?"

The men's figures blurred when Moore said late

wife. My God, what had happened? Had Erin been murdered? Had others been murdered too?

He got all his answers when they met at mi6 headquarters four days later. Harrison's head was still bandaged from where shrapnel had pierced his skull. The room was nearly dark except for an eerie glow on a projection screen from soft-blue lights above. Moore and Hardin were seated at both ends of a black table, Harrison at the side. "Try not to mind the screen, Mr. Griggs. By the way, you're not in trouble. Far from it. You're a victim, just like the others." Moore clasped his hands, pad and pen in front of him. "Now Mr. Griggs. Could you please tell us how you met your wife?"

"It was a . . . a dating Website. I was really lonely, you know. I'd lost my wife just a year before. Emily. She was such a wonderful person. She died of can – "

"We're well aware of your first wife, Mr. Griggs," Moore interrupted. "We've checked out your background thoroughly since the suicide bombing."

"Suicide bombing?" Tears coursed down Harrison's cheek. "My wife was killed by a suicide bomber? How could they. How – "

"No, Mr. Griggs. Your wife *was* the suicide bomber. And now, could you give us the name of that Website, please?"

"Of course." After he gave Moore and Hardin the name of the Website and how they had met and married, Moore told him everything.

"Erin McDonnell was not your wife's real name, Mr. Griggs." On the projection screen above, Moore flashed a photo of a young woman, seventeen or eighteen, with flaming red butch haircut and angry, green eyes – undoubtedly Erin's. "Her real name was Sinead Clarke, great-granddaughter of John Clarke, instigator of the 1916 Easter Rebellion." Moore flashed more surveillance photos of Erin – or Sinead. "She was an IRA soldier from a very young age, quickly rising to lieutenant. When the IRA finally signed the peace accord, we believe it was your wife who spirited away their remaining weapons cache." Moore showed more surveillance photos, this time of Sinead wearing camos in a desert setting. "Sinead reached out to ISIL, and they welcomed her to their training camp in Syria." More photos of Sinead in camos, camo face paint, firing an AK-47. "Mr. Griggs," Hardin said when the slide show was finished. "You were blissfully married to one of the most dangerous terrorists in the world."

"But . . . " Harrison thought of Erin's note, still stuck in his wallet, something he hadn't told Moore or Hardin about yet because it was the last thing he had of her. "Why did she call me back to get her at our room – and then leave?"

Moore looked at Hardin as though he were about to admit something he didn't want to, then faced Harrison. "Our only conclusion is that your wife was actually in love with you and wanted you spared, Mr. Griggs."

"In love with me," Harrison whispered to himself.

"A total of 78 people died that day, Mr. Griggs. Hundreds of others were crippled, blinded or maimed."

"Billy?"

"DNA traces were all we could find, Mr. Griggs," Moore said. "They were all over the hall. Apparently the bomb had been aimed directly at him. Mr. Boufon's wife, the PM, the king and princes and many of the House of Lords and House of Commons – all dead. All except for Prince Harry and his wife who will now be king and princess of England." Moore looked askance at Hardin. "Given his remarkable military record in Afghanistan, he will likely make a great king."

"But why?"

"Apparently, Mr. Griggs," Moore said leaning forward, "Your wife wanted to rekindle the war between Northern Ireland and the crown." He settled back into his chair. "And she succeeded quite admirably, if I may say. In fact, she may well have won it on her own."

"Oh Erin," Harrison gasped.

"Sinead," Moore corrected.

Faceoff

We were driving the back road from Belle Fourche to Camp Crook because I wanted a steak. Not just any steak. A big, juicy, fat-dripping Camp Crook steak. The best in the world. And so rare it would beller when you stuck in your fork.

Sandy was driving and I was drinking – quite heavily of course. But when wasn't I drinking quite heavily back then. It was my primary avocation.

I had worked with Sandy at the *Belle Fourche Daily Post* but I'd known her before that – clear back to the *Meade County Times*. We both had worked for newspapers for years so our blood ran black. As much as we complained about our jobs, all we talked about when we were off was work.

But now I was on hiatus from the scrivener's profession – driving a bookmobile, of all things, in Butte and Harding counties in northwestern South Dakota. And Sandy was still doing ad composition and paste-up at the *Daily Post*, a job she was more loyal to than it ever was to her.

"Mikey, you're nuts," Sandy said, her red, bulbous

nose pressed against the windshield as sleet cascaded in chunks.

I shrugged. "It was nice when we started out." And it was. It was the first warm spring day we'd had in 1990.

"Well it sure as hell isn't very nice now," she fumed. Sandy was the only person I've ever known who could get so angry with me –furiously angry – but who would tell me she loved me moments later. It wasn't romantic love, though – far from it. Sandy outweighed me by maybe a hundred pounds. But it was a beefy weight. That was what happened to a girl who was the only child of a rancher father who made her wrangle and brand calves, chop wood, drive tractor, and chuck hay bales. By the time she was a senior in high school and most of the other girls in her class dreamt of being prom queen, Sandy could have made first string on the Belle Fourche Broncs defensive line.

Well, we made it to Camp Crook and the steak was great. Afterward, as she finished her eighth rum and Coke and slammed down her glass, Sandy leaned over the table and looked me square in the eye. "Ya know somethin' Mikey?"

"What?" I asked, stewed to the gills myself.

"If we wasn't such good friends, I'd screw your eyes out right now." Her meaty fist slammed the wood, jingling our glasses." Right on this here table."

"Oh."

***

And that's how I liked to remember her – Sandy, the daughter of a rancher who came from a long line of pioneer stock that had settled the harsh and unforgiving gumbo of Butte County along the snaking Redwater. Her father's ancestry was Dane but their name was spelled

Larson. According to Sandy, their ancestor had objected when the immigration official at Ellis Island had spelled his name Larson instead of Larsen. It will cost you a dollar to change it, the official said. Being the thrifty Dane that he was, he left the name as Larson, and his ancestors were left forever with the ignominy of people believing they were Norwegian.

Sandy was similarly stuck in her ways – Monday night Pizza Hut, Tuesday night beef tips at The Rancher in St. Onge, Wednesday night broasted chicken at the drive-in, Thursday night cocktails and endless hors d'oeuvres at Max's, Friday fish night at the Belle Inn, and Saturday and Sunday nights she liked to go to Deadwood and hit the slots and enjoy the cheap buffets.

As a result, Sandy got larger. And larger. When age sixty-two rolled around she didn't hesitate to sign up for Social Security so she could sit home and play computer games. Sandy's ultimate downfall wasn't the volume of food she ate or the six-pack of soda she drank each day. It was her addiction to the Internet.

***

Even though I'd moved to Iowa, we kept in touch over the years. I quit drinking altogether, cleaned up my act, and married an Irish redhead with four kids and at least that many personalities. We stayed over at Sandy's house our first night on our honeymoon trip to the Oregon Coast.

"Mikey," she said, eyes brimming with joy as she hugged me. "I'm so happy to see you."

I hugged her back as my hundred-pound wife looked on jealously. And why shouldn't she have been jealous. Sandy easily topped three-hundred by then so it was like three women my wife's size were swarming me. "Is she kind to you?" Sandy asked as Rose went into the bathroom, a hopeful doubt in her voice.

I paused then lied. "Yes."

"I'm so happy for you," she lied back.

It wasn't long after that that whenever I tried to call Sandy her phone line would be busy. Her Internet addiction was swallowing her as certainly as she swallowed cheese puffs by the pound.

***

Our marriage went south and a little more than a year after our divorce I went west again to the Coast and stopped over at Sandy's. She was fully into her Internet addiction by then and barely had time to visit. Oh, she greeted me at the door and said how glad she was to see me. Then she sat down at her computer, soda to one side and cheese puffs to the other, and continued her video poker game with someone in Mississippi. "You should try this sometime, Mikey," she offered. "You'd like it," she added, as though inviting a nun to an orgy.

I sat there and tried to carry on a conversation but her main focus was on getting a full house. But hers was an empty house, as far as I was concerned.

I met my promise of bringing her smoked salmon from the Coast on my return trip. I know she enjoyed it, saying so between bites as she played canasta with someone in England, chomping down on the creamed cheese mixed with smoked salmon and spread on crackers, probably the healthiest meal she'd eaten in years.

I visited her again – 2009, 2010, and a shorter trip in 2011 when I only made it as far as the Black Hills. By then, there were skid marks on every chair and cushion in her trailer where she had sat in her nightgown without any underwear.

87

"I haven't been feeling very good, Mikey," she admitted. I'd known she'd been diabetic for several years, but this was a new revelation.

"Oh? What's the matter."

She shrugged. "I just don't feel good."

Two weeks after I left, not feeling good meant an ambulance trip to the hospital. No one could find a nursing home that would take a Title XIX trach patient, so she lingered for nearly a year in the hospital until she asked them to pull out her feeding tube and she starved to death.

***

I'd lost track of her months before, so I only learned about her passing when I was curious about how she was doing and called a mutual friend.

"Didn't you hear?" asked Chris. "Sandy passed away." And then she filled me in on the details.

My dear, dear friend Sandy had died. And I'd abandoned her. I kept remembering our last conversation, and how much work it was to get anything out of her as she took long, gasping breaths between every three words. She'll get better, I told myself. But she never did. She just died.

I was on Facebook one night when a message popped up that my friend Sandy Larson wanted to play Farmville. I was outraged, contacted Facebook administration, and told them I was receiving messages from a deceased person and could they please stop them. They promised me they would, so I put my anger and grief behind me.

The next night I received another message from Sandy. Why don't you like playing Farmville with me, Mikey. Don't you like me anymore?

This time I called Facebook and gave them holy

hell. "What's wrong with you idiots. Don't you know this is like watching someone climb out of the grave? Don't you have any sensitivity for a person's feelings at all?"

Sorry sir, they said. We'll take care of it.

I'd just about forgotten about it when a week later I received an instant message from Sandy. Please, please Mikey. Won't you play Farmville with me?

I messaged right back, telling whoever was torturing me they could shove their Farmville up their ass.

"My ass might be pretty big, Mikey. But there's no way you could shove a farm up it. A silo maybe, but not a whole farm," she responded.

I sat there numb. The only person in this life with a sense of humor as sick and demented as mine was Sandy. And she was dead. "What would you trade me for a hundred gallons of butter so you could shove the silo up your ass," I IM'd her.

"How about ten ewes. After all, I've always known you to be a Montana bisexual."

"What's a Montana bisexual."

"Someone who likes cows and sheep both."

We went back and forth like that all night and well into the next day. Finally, I'd had enough. While the person on the other end certainly *sounded* like Sandy, obviously it couldn't have been her. Sandy was dead, cremated, her ashes scattered on the family homestead.

"Who is this?" I finally demanded.

"Why this is Sandy, Mikey. Are you nuts?"

"But Sandy's dead."

"What?"

"Sandy's dead."

"Very funny. Actually, that's not very funny at all."

I went online and found Sandy's obit from the *Belle*

Fourche Post and e-mailed her the link. "There, you're dead."

"Oh, I guess you're right."

And that was the last I ever heard from her.

***

I regret now having told Sandy, her ghost, her spirit, or whatever you want to call it that she'd died. But she did die. That's what Chris said. That's what the obituary said. That's what all her friends who had attended her funeral said. My friend Sandy was no more.

I still go on Facebook, expecting to hear from her. But there's nothing. Only a ghostly hollow cyber sadness, forever silent. Forever gone.

Jailboat

Eric Miller had always wanted to be a reporter – exposing corruption in government, taking up consumer crusades, fighting for the environment – and when he was offered a spot as staff writer at Le Mons, he took it.

Le Mons was a quiet community nestled in the Loess Hills, a band of rolling, oak-studded hills stretching from southwest Iowa into Minnesota. In fall the hills caught fire with color – gold, orange, red. As winter came, the soft mounds turned into sleeping giants – sleeping polar bears, if you squinted when you looked at them.

On the north side of Le Mons, Lake Delton stretched from where it was dammed to five miles north, a slithering snake kissing the banks of the Loess Hills. Early morning fogs would rise up, hugging the shoreline so fishermen emerged like ghosts, Labradors silhouetted with their owners through the pallid mists, trolling motors sputtering, as they continued into the fog bank and vanished.

Eric was lucky enough to have found a place on Lake Delton, a ramshackle red cabin empty for most of the year except when Buck Mause, a modestly famous television fishing show host, asked to have the cabin the second and third week of every July. That was when Buck would return to his old haunts to fish for walleye and northern and renew old acquaintances and when he was done pack up to produce shows in the Lakes of the Woods or Kootenai River.

Eric figured that was a pretty good arrangement. Le Mons was unbearably hot in the summer – even here along Lake Delton – so he planned on packing up for a two-week vacation where he had a rustic cabin his father had willed to him in Elk City, Oregon – once classified as a ghost town but coming back now that everyone in California wanted to move to the Northwest Coast. The rest of the time his cabin was vacant and waiting.

Eric had started at the Le Mons Centennial right out of college, edging out far older and more qualified candidates who had demanded a living wage. Since Eric pretty much lived on a $2,000-a-month annuity his parents had left him, he only needed to earn enough for frills and incidentals. He had no school loans to repay and the three-year-old BMW his parents had left him was paid for. Still, he found that little compensation for his parents being taken from him by a drunk driver two years before. All Eric had left of them was memories – plus the $2,000 a month, BMW, Oregon mountain cabin, and full inheritance of $4.2 million when he reached thirty.

Until then, he would go to work every day, write stories that would please his editor and the public, and collect his paycheck. Opportunities to write harrowing stories about Mob revenge killings or political scandals were pretty much nil, though. So Eric, on the job for a little over two years, now twenty-four, was prepared to cruise through the next six years when he would receive his full inheritance and be forced to accustom himself to an entirely different lifestyle.

**

Alicia Koons was seventeen, tall, blond, blue-eyed, pretty, and as street smart as an East LA gang banger. When she donned her makeup and put up her hair, she easily looked twenty-two. And she could flick on her sex like a button.

After being arrested for taking part in the armed robbery and carjacking of an elderly couple with her twenty-year-old boyfriend, Alicia at sixteen had been remanded to state custody and sentenced until age eighteen to the Lake Delton Youth Reformatory situated on a picturesque island in the middle of Lake Delton. Alcatraz for kiddies, the locals scoffingly referred to it. And in a sense it was. Security was tight but veiled by a veneer of caring.

To work time off their sentences, Lake Delton's 'guests' were required to volunteer for community activities – picking up litter, face-painting children during community events, dressing up like clowns to run a bean-bag toss during the county fair – those sorts of things. That was when the community saw the good side of Lake Delton guests. Their imposture of innocence.

"I'm fuckin' sick of this clown shit," said Alicia, putting on her red bulb nose for what she hoped was the last time.

"Ain't that the truth." Mindy, her often partner in crime beside her, applied clown makeup to her coal-black skin. On the surface, they were complete opposites. Alicia, tall, white, blond, from an upperclass Santa Monica family. Mindy, short, black, dreadlocks, born of a Detroit crackwhore mother who with all honesty didn't know whose father Mindy was. But when it came to getting in trouble, they worked together like fellow career criminals, highly skilled in their plots and schemes, even finishing each other's thoughts.

"There's gotta be a way off this island." Alicia stood back from the mirror and looked at her nose and makeup job, turning her head side to side.

"Maybe we could make a break for it once we hit the mainland," said Mindy, futilely spotting clown blush on her coal-black skin.

"Nah, too obvious. We gotta figure out somethin' where people won't know we're gone for a good six, eight hours."

They'd talked about this before – how they would put the papier-mache masks they'd made in art class on their pillows, roll up their extra clothes under their blankets in the shape of their sleeping curvy hips, slither down the ivy-encrusted downspouts to the ground. Any possible squealers were already silenced – Alicia and Mindy ran the cottage like head bitches on a cell block. It was getting off the island that was the problem. Swimming a good half-mile to shore was out of the question. And the cottage matron kept the pontoons and canoes locked up in the storage shed with the key on her ring with a hundred others. They had to find a boat – any kind would do.

***

As the newest staff writer, Eric was assigned to cover the annual Community Fair, a fundraiser to benefit the local food pantry. It was on a Friday night, which he didn't mind. All he had to do was take photos, Photoshop the images and write cutlines, and then he could leave on vacation the next day. He figured he could make Montana easily that night and hit the Coast in a couple more days. There was nothing between him and his vacation except time.

He bundled up his camera and reporter's notebook and was at the Civic Center – the site of the Community Fair – ten minutes before everything started. He snapped photos of people setting up, making kettle corn, kids getting an early start at the free throw shoot and ring toss. He was especially drawn to where girls in clown outfits clapped and smiled as kids tossed bean bags at ridiculously easy targets.

As Eric readied his camera to take a photo, one fairly tall clown – nearly his height – came over. Smile bright and shining, she invited him to come behind the bean bag target to get a better shot.

"Hey, this is great. It's just like they're tossing the bag right at me." Eric adjusted for better depth of field and slowed hit shutter speed to the tossers' hands blurred as they threw the bags.

The tall clown stepped a little closer, smiled, and touched his shoulder. "Hi."

Eric faced her and saw even through her makeup she was quite pretty. A smile erupted from his face he hadn't expected. Her clown suit tried to be frumpy but wasn't frumpy enough hide some fairly delicious curves. "Hi."

The clown looked side to side and edged closer with a whisper. "Do you have a girlfriend?"

Eric found the question a little blunt, but since he was fairly good-looking, he didn't find it strange. Girls had approached him in college, twirling fingers through his curly, dark locks even. A few even managed to fall in love with his dark brown eyes. "Not now, I don't."

The girl clown laughed, looked side to side again, and stepped even closer so her warm, fruity breath was upon him. "Do you have a boat?" she asked, suddenly going off topic.

"Naw," said Eric, surprised at her sudden intimacy. He liked the attention though – really liked it. "All I have is a canoe."

"How many people will it hold?" the girl clown asked sweetly, now pressing a firm clown breast against him.

"It's a nineteen-footer. It should hold eight-hundred pounds. So yeah, it should hold four people easily."

"Hmm . . . " The girl clown looked down demurely, then into his eyes. "You know what I've always wanted to do?"

"What," asked Eric, embarrassed at the sudden surge in his pants as the girl clown bumped against him.

"I've always wanted to go for a nice, romantic canoe ride on a full moonlit night – like tonight."

Eric thought it over for a moment. It was a little past six now and he hadn't planned on leaving until ten tomorrow and he was already packed. And he certainly didn't see any harm in taking a pretty girl on a canoe ride. "Yeah, that sounds like fun."

"Meet me at Strawberry Point as soon as it's dark," the girl clown said, the hint of an edge in her voice.

"Strawberry Point. That's on the north end of the island, right?"

"Right." The girl clown winked. "See you then. And don't be late."

***

"So what makes you think he'll even show?"

Alicia had turned in her clown nose and suit and was finally removing the last of her clown makeup. "He will. You should've seen the bulge in his pants."

Mindy guffawed. "Okay . . . So what makes you think he'll want me along."

"Isn't it every man's fantasy to have a little salt 'n pepper on his sausage and hardboiled eggs?"

"Girlfriend, you blows my mind. None of my homies even thinks like you."

"That's why we'll break outa this joint – when no one else ever has."

***

Photos worked up and time card punched, Eric finished packing his Bronco and slid his canoe into the water. It was all he could do to move the nineteen-footer by himself, so it helped that Buck had built the rack over the edge of the dock.

A silvery, moonlit trail led him from the dock toward the island as his paddle sliced through water. He really appreciated that Buck had left the canoe here for him. As he paddled, he wondered about the girl who had come up to him and asked to meet him. Had he even gotten her name? He didn't remember giving his. And why on earth did she approach him dressed in a clown outfit instead of waiting until she was more properly dressed. Maybe it was one of those spontaneous attraction type of things. Oh well. He couldn't see any harm in that.

Pelicans and a couple blue heron scampered from their posts as the approached Strawberry Point. The sun was all but swallowed up by the Loess Hills beyond Lake Delton now, washing the water with glints of scarlet, gold, and mauve. He guessed he was a little early – it wouldn't

96

be totally dark for a half hour yet. So he beached his canoe on the pebbled bank at the very tip of Strawberry Point and waited.

***

Alicia had never taken so much time on a makeup job in her life. Gone was the clown makeup and in its place a gorgeous shadow and blush with coral-pink lipstick. With her hair up, she could have passed for someone's date to the Oscars.

She wiggled her rear experimentally as Mindy stood aghast beside her. Her skintight T-shirt she'd cut into a belly buster just below her breasts and her denim cutoffs were trimmed to just below the pockets.

"Don't yo' stretch, girl, or yo' be flashin' yo' headlights." Mindy shook her head slowly. "Daisy Duke be gettin' *banned* from TV for wearin' those."

Alicia stood back, hands on her hips, unable to take her eyes from the girl smiling back at her in the mirror. She was absolutely gorgeous. "This has to work. That means I have to pull out all the stops."

"Don't you worry. They ain't nuthin' stoppin' you, girl."

As dark descended, they made their way down the cottage hall to the window Alicia had loosened earlier so it wouldn't squeak when they opened it. She slid it open and sliced the screen with her contraband penknife and climbed out first, grabbing the downspout and lowering herself slowly into the gathering dark. When she made it to the ground, she tapped the downspout to signal Mindy to follow.

They slipped past the hedge, between the cottage front window and then, staying low, made their way through an open ditch toward Strawberry Point where Eric stood beside a canoe like an expectant Romeo for his Juliet.

"*Him?*" asked Mindy. "He look like a dufus."

"I think he had money though," said Alicia, jaw set and determined.

"Oh my, he handsome then, I guess."

The moon full upon the water, Eric smiled as Alicia's figure appeared in the pearled light. "Hi," she whispered, coming right up to him and taking his hand and kissing him.

She just about knocked him back on his heels, the way she pressed her face against him and stuck her tongue into his mouth. He found her beautiful, though, especially as he pulled back from her to gaze into her pallid eyes dancing into his in the moonlight. "Hi."

The voice came before a second figure emerged from the dark, whispering, "Hi."

"Hi?" Eric said, confused.

"This is Mindy. She's coming along too. To chaperone?" Alicia wrapped her arms around his back, pressing herself against him. "Not that I don't trust you – I just don't trust myself."

Eric couldn't help but emit a deep groan as Alicia ground against him. She wore practically nothing, and his head spun in circles.

"By the way, I'm Alicia," she finally said, going up on her toes to kiss him again.

He never did remember giving her his name.

***

They made it to shore in about a half hour, Alicia and Mindy both helping him paddle. The girls were amazingly strong, and once they got the hang of stroking together, the canoe sliced through the water like a knife, sending them up against his dock in record time. Eric had wanted a more leisurely paddle, but Alicia and Mindy for some reason seemed to want to make shore right away.

He built a bonfire in the fire pit between his cabin and the lake and the girls cracked open some beers with him and warmed their bare legs before the fire. They seemed a little edgy, unable to relax, while he was totally exhausted from working all day then paddling out to the island. "I should probably take you back pretty soon. I have to get up early and get a good start for the Coast."

Alicia looked significantly to Mindy, then Eric. "Which coast."

"Oregon Coast. I head out tomorrow."

Alicia set down her beer and came over to him and sat in his lap and put her arms around him and kissed him. "Can we go along?"

Her firm rear pinching his lap drew his words from him like a deranged dentist pulling a wisdom tooth. "Sure."

She kissed him again, this time twirling his tongue around his before she looked away. "Can we leave tonight?"

"I, uh . . . " Eric tried to decide, then went stupid as Alicia wiggled her Daisy Dukes in his lap. "Sure."

***

Mindy drove as they took the back seat. Eric was tired, exhausted even, but Alicia was all over him. It was somewhere hear Chamberlain when she tugged off her tank top and slipped out of her Daisy Dukes and was straddling him as Mindy glowered in the rearview mirror.

They were well into Montana when he awoke. The sign for Columbus flashed by and the girls were in the front seat, chatting and smoking and drinking Cokes. His pants and shorts were still wrapped around his ankles.

"Man, does you snore," Mindy giggled into the mirror. Alicia smiled seductively over her shoulder as she took a drag from her cigarette, ember glowing. "We used some of your cash to fill up and buy some smokes and snacks. Hope you don't mind."

Eric buckled his pants, blushing profusely. "Where are we?"

"Somewhere in central Montana." Alicia eyed the speedometer. "You're doin' eighty-five. Better slow down, or the cops'll haul us in."

"Huh?" said Eric.

Mindy held onto the wheel like a New York cabbie. "It's okay, everyone's passin' us."

"Maybe back off to eighty."

"Okay."

By noon they were in Dillon and needed gas. When he went to pay, Eric saw he had just over $1,600 in his wallet – he'd brought two grand – and his Mastercard was missing. He still had his VISA with plenty of room on it, so that wasn't a problem. Maybe he'd left his Mastercard on his bedroom dresser. He still couldn't figure out where all that money went though.

***

By nightfall they were in Bend. It wasn't that far to his cabin in Elk City, but everyone was beat, so they pulled over to a motel.

"Single or double," asked the young desk clerk like a zombie, apparently a college student who was disturbed that a customer would disrupt his studying.

"We can get by with one bed if it's a king," offered Mindy.

Alicia grabbed Eric's arm possessively. "We'll take a double."

Eric nodded. "A double."

"A double . . . " the clerk said, switching his glance among them, " . . . for three people. That'll be $78.50."

"Pay the man," said Mindy. "Ah's tired."

Their room was on the second level and overlooking a courtyard where a group of middle-aged men, most likely conventioneers, wolf-whistled at Alicia's short shorts and Mindy's skin-tight jeans climbing the stairs.

"Assholes," said Alicia.

"I'm going to go talk to them," Eric said angrily.

"Naw, ya'll let me do it," said Mindy thoughtfully.

As they entered the room, Alicia turned up the air and pushed Eric onto the bed. "Do you think she'll be okay with those men down there?"

"She'll be fantastic." Alicia tore off her top. "You wanna be on bottom or top."

***

Eric was worried because it was several hours and Mindy hadn't yet returned to the room. By then Alicia had drained all the worry from him and he was sleeping the sleep of the dead.

"Damn, don't he snore," said Mindy, pulling twenties and fifties from her jeans to count them.

"How much you score?"

"I give 'em a package deal. All four for five hundred."

"Damn, maybe I should go see them for a while."

"I gotta feelin' I took care a them right good. 'Sides," she added, nodding at Eric. "Yo' number-one job is to take care a Mistah Money Bags there." She crossed her arms and nodded affectionately. "He is kinda cute, ain't he? Layin' there wid his little thang in the air."

"It's not *that* little."

"Naw? You oughta see some a the thangs the brothers has." Mindy looked askance at her. "Then maybe you has."

"Little or not, I still like *his* thing."

"Girl, I swears ya'll in *love*."

***

After they stopped at the mall so the girls could replenish their wardrobe, they headed for the Coast the next morning. Since he knew the way and they would be going over some fairly tricky mountain curves, Eric drove as the girls chatted up a hurricane, excited about seeing the ocean – Mindy for the first time – and Alicia missing Santa Barbara but not enough to go down there and get nabbed. Eric never could quite figure that one out.

They went through Sisters – looking a lot like Jackson, Wyoming, now with its log-fronted cafes and shops – then Black Butte, Three Fingered Jack, and Santiam Pass. Then they were into the Coastal Range. Eric took a back gravel road off US 20 and ten minutes later they pulled up to a patch of ten-foot blackberries hugging a small cabin.

"*Dis* is it?" Mindy asked

101

"I like it," said Alicia.

"Blackberries get away from me if I'm away for any amount of time." Eric got out and shut the door and stretched as he breathed in fresh coastal air. It was twenty-two miles to the ocean on the Yaquina River that was two blocks away, seventeen on Highway 20, and maybe ten as the eagle flew. A little work on the cabin, and he figured he and the girls could head for the beach.

Mindy approached the dense wall of blackberries. "Now just how does we get through all 'dis."

Eric took a machete from the trunk. "We hack our way in."

Mindy looked around as though for help saving her from an ax murderer, but eased as Eric slashed away at the blackberry plants, soon clearing a path to the front door and inviting the girls in.

The cabin was small but cozy, with a fireplace in one end and a window overlooking the mountains to the south. As ardent environmentalists, his parents had wanted a zero-footprint structure, and this was as close as they could get. Solar panels on one side of the roof made the fireplace merely ambiance and the peat digestion system in the bathroom took care of nearly all waste. The cabin rested on six concrete pilings and below were a sturdy sea canoe and an ATV for exploring the trails and hunting.

The girls brought in their clothes as Eric went through the storage cabinet under the cabin for his rod and reel and tackle box. "I think I'll try catching some steelies for dinner if you want to take the canoe out on the Yaquina."

Mindy eyed Alicia. "Canoe?"

"It's just like the other one except for the outrigger, tiller, and sail. If you know what you're doing and can get past the surf, you could probably go all the way to Mexico."

"Mexico . . . " Mindy pondered.

"Here, I'll help you get it into the water." He

glanced at Alicia's bare legs, totally exposed in her Daisy Dukes. "You might want to wear something a little more substantial than those. You'll be carrying it through the blackberry brambles to the river."

Alicia's eyes misted over. "Okay."

"Is there something wrong?"

"No, nothing's wrong."

Eric went out to hack a second path between the blackberries and the river, then the girls helped him carry the canoe toward the Yaquina. Mindy watched leaves float upstream. "I thought 'dis river went to de ocean."

"It does. It's high tide now, but it should reverse itself."

"Den it would take us to the ocean?"

"Absolutely." Eric helped the girls put the canoe into the water and went back for his fishing gear. As he stood there, looking like a dork in his fishing vest and fly hat, Alicia went up to him and threw her arms around him. "I'll miss you," she sobbed into his shoulder.

"Huh?"

Mindy eyed the sun skittering over the cedars to the west. "We'd best be getting' goin'."

"I'll see if I can't get three steelies – one for each of us," Eric said brightly, heading for the pier. His first cast landed in a deep hole where he knew something would be lurking. A minute later, his line snapped tight and he fought in a twelve-inch steelhead. A scuffling through the rushes drew his attention to the west where he thought he saw Alicia and Mindy both carrying large garbage bags to the canoe before setting out. He found that rather curious, but didn't think much of it.

Toward nightfall, he'd landed two more steelies – one smaller and one larger. As he approached the cabin, he saw the canoe still gone. He cleaned the steelies, washed them off, and put them in the refrigerator. The girls still weren't back, and it was dark.

He went down to the Yaquina and looked both ways and called out, first Alicia's name then Mindy's. As night descended, he returned to the cabin.

His wallet still sat on the kitchen counter where he'd left it before he headed out fishing, but at a slightly different angle. He opened it and counted out his money and saw $1,200, about $300 more than when he'd last checked. And his Mastercard was in there along with a single-word note. *Sorry*.

He searched the room and saw only Alicia's Daily Dukes ploomped on the floor, still holding the shape of *her*.

Jeff

It isn't very often you meet someone who changes your life. But four people? And all in the same night? Well that's just how it happened.

I don't remember exactly how I ended up at the White Rabbit that night. I think I went there with Sarge. So there we were – Sarge, Jeff, Barry, Larry, and me – five compadres deep into their cups as smoke roiled like notes to the music so loud you couldn't hear yourself think much less talk.

It was about then that my future wife Jean crossed the barroom floor, firm, high breasts leading her like a new recruit into formation with the drunken masses.

"I'm going to go down there and ask that girl if she wants to come have a beer with us."

Sarge eyed the girl, eyed me, then eyed the girl again – really *eyed* her. Adjusting the shades he'd perpetually worn ever since a phosphorous explosion nearly blinded him near Danang, he shook his head slowly. "You don't have a chance."

"Oh no?" I finished my beer and studied the girl. "Watch this."

Sarge – Ladykiller Sarge was his full name – laughed. "I'll order you another beer for you to drown your sorrows in when you get back."

I was just hammered enough to maintain my

confidence and still make it down the stairs without falling on my can. The Rabbit was your typical bar for the seventies. The reek of spilled beer, smoke, and the tang of vomit and stale urine all mixed together into one holy smell that offered limitless possibilities. Even a guy like me could get laid in this place.

The girl stood there in a white coat, left hand in her pocket, holding a tap in her right as she studied the crowd as though everyone was a car and she was a deer staring at their headlights.

I snuck up on her side so she couldn't turn away as any self-respecting girl would have done if approached by a geek like me. "Hi."

We chit-chatted about nothing in general. She talked like a sociologist, about how much of a meat market the place was and how everybody was getting drunk so they could get laid.

I had everything I could do to keep my eyes from wandering below her shoulders. "I guess that sort of describes me, huh?"

Her blue eyes sifted through the smoke into mine and she tugged at a light brown strand and touched it to her lips. "No, you're different."

Man, did I have her fooled. "Weird different or interesting different."

She stood there deciding *way* too long. She never did answer – ever

"Do you want to go upstairs and sit with me and my friends?"

Figuring that was as safe as anything, she nodded. "Okay." She must have been incredibly bored.

Sarge had a couple chairs set up for both of us when we got there, seeing me as some kind of lab experiment. After we'd known each other for a few decades he would later tell me that whenever he told me I couldn't do something I would always go ahead and do it just to prove him wrong. And he was exactly right.

So picture this – Sarge, dark, incredibly handsome,

the sort of guy women make themselves fools over; Larry, boisterous, destined for a life as a Republican political consultant, US House candidate, and later homelessness; Barry, tall, urban, a future political consultant like Larry, only quite successful; Jeff, his brilliance hidden by a protective feigned pall of vacuity, not daring to venture beyond 116 Broadway from 1973 until he died there thirty-two years later; and me, a novice at everything, particularly the ways of love.

With four other guys at the same table – though Sarge was the only one I was worried about – I didn't dare go to the bathroom even though I had to go something awful. So I sat there – and sat there – and sat there – until last call when the lights came on and everyone had the chance to see the person they'd been trying to hustle all night – their level of intoxication determined by whether they went home with them.

Jean was stunning, so I decided to hang on to her. Why she decided to go with me, I'm not sure. I think maybe she actually had her eyes on Sarge. So we all piled into the 1965 blue-and-white Ford station wagon my father had broken down and loaned me for college and made our way down to The Bottoms. The Last House on the Left was still popular then, and that's where Barry, Jeff, and Larry lived – the last house on the left on Broadway Avenue, barren of paint, floor still rumpled from the Great 1881 Flood.

We were greeted by a seven-foot cardboard polar bear in the kitchen, heisted from an Eskimo ice cream sandwich display. Past the kitchen and into the living room, we were treated to a stuffed mongoose on the bookcase, a poster of Geronimo with a rifle, and a concert poster for Country Joe and the Fish that I still have.

"Would anyone like to some any dope?" asked Barry, already rolling a fat doobie.

Now before anyone makes any ethical objection to the situation, remember this – it was February 1974 – okay?

The joint passed once around the room, and then I offered to give everyone power hits – mainly so I could give one to Jean. Now for those few who don't know, a power hit is when one person places the lit end of a joint – that's a marijuana cigarette – into his mouth and blows a steady smoke stream into the other person's mouth, forcing said smoke directly into recipient's brain, making said recipient of the smoke incredibly stupid in a very short time.

And I was the master of all power hitters.

Each time I came to Jean, I would move in a little closer, finally clasping her by the arms so she couldn't get away. I'm sure I creeped her out, but she never let on. Three joints later, we were all oozing in our chairs, Jean sitting on my lap because there was nowhere else to sit, Jeff eyeing me, smiling mystically, wondering vicariously where I was going next with her.

So by now you probably think this story is about how I married Jean and we had 2.2 kids and lived happily ever after. Well, it's not. It's about Jeff.

I finally got to go to the bathroom that night, a three-minute throaty roar into the commode that didn't flush and wouldn't again until Jeff had the plumber come in April 1977 – well over three years later. By then, Jean and I had been married several months, Barry and Larry had both moved out, and Jeff lived alone in the house where nature took over, sending creeping Jenny up the rough, unpainted sides and over the roof, the weed-choked yard gathering the city fathers' attention until Jeff mowed it, and when he ran out of money for gas and the mower sat idle in a sheen of rust, swinging a machete like a point man on recon patrol until he tired and refreshed himself with a beer.

I didn't know it at the time, but Jean was the love of my life – a love that lasted just a little over ten years until I succumbed to an infatuation with Lynn – an infatuation that never materialized. That was when I started to call Jeff regularly to commiserate. That was the word he used for it, and it was so profoundly appropriate. I was miserable because my wife was gone and he was miserable because he'd never been laid. And so we found comfort in our mutual misery.

Jeff and I grew closer together than ever when I moved back to Vermillion in April 1992. I'd failed to talk Mary Beth into staying in Rock Rapids where I had an apartment in a party house, so I took an editor's position in Vermillion where I worked a hundred hours a week and drank the other sixty-eight. And most of those sixty-eight hours I spent with Jeff.

One night we just sat there, the Grateful Dead sewing our thoughts together so we didn't even have to speak. We'd just smoked some incredible weed Jeff had grown in his backyard – one of his 'children', as he called it. As I sat there, staring at his gaunt face accented by a goatee, I had no idea that thirteen years later we'd be spreading his ashes on those same children.

***

It's all a haze now as to how it happened. It might have been at a party – in fact it probably was a party since all we did was party then. But one day this girl Lisa came to town. Now Lisa was the sort of girl who belonged to *everybody* – if you know what I mean. Lisa was one of those 'floater' type of girls – floating from one guy to another like a butterfly from flower to flower. And believe me, Lisa lit on a whole lot of flowers.

A couple of those flowers just happened to be me and Jeff. Unfortunately, it was at the same time – and it was the biggest strain Jeff and I would ever have in our friendship.

It was the weekend Jerry and Sandy were getting married. I'd met Jerry through Jeff actually, and Sandy through one of our writer's group meetings. One of our other members had told Sandy about this cool guy Jerry who was a writer and she sat there the whole meeting eyeing me – it was pretty weird, actually. Only when she left did someone tell her who Jerry was – not me – and

Sandy switched her glance between the two of us, trying to decide, and deciding she probably wasn't interested in either of us, left.

I suggested to Jerry that we flip a coin to decide who got Sandy – she was pretty good looking, actually. Jerry won.

So when they got married, we were all already pretty close. Lisa suggested I stay at her house since Jerry and Sandy's place was full with them putting up both their families for the wedding. In retrospect, it would have been better for me if I'd put up a tent in Jerry's yard.

I hate to admit it, but Lisa was pretty damn good in bed. She was a dancer and had a dancer's moves, even horizontally. We were at each other all night as Jeff sat in the next room drinking wine, smoking a joint, listening to Procul Harem. I don't know why, but Lisa had asked him to stay all night – sleep on the couch if he wanted – but all he did was sit there and sulk while we squeaked the springs.

I thought Jeff would hate my guts when I finally rolled out the next morning, but he didn't. Lisa was curled up on his lap as they watched something stupid on TV. Lisa was already drinking and it looked as though Jeff had never stopped.

I could say that Jerry and Sandy's wedding Saturday night went without a hitch, but they were hitched, right there in the Lutheran Church with a lot of guests. When Lisa, Jeff, and I hitched a ride after the wedding with Susan and Cathy – the most contented couple I've ever known – Lisa held hands with both of us in the back seat. Now *this* is going to be interesting, I thought.

But it wasn't. We somehow ventured over to Jerry and Sandy's house where Lisa was charged with babysitting their mixed brood – two kids each for Jerry and Sandy. There was later quite a row over what happened, and time has blurred the situation by now, but as I recall, Lisa let Heidi, one of Jerry's teenage daughters, leave the house at 11:30 – a half hour past her curfew. And when Jerry called at seven the next morning and Heidi still wasn't home, all hell broke loose.

**

There's a cardinal rule that when you're in love – or lust – with someone, and that person does something stupid, your own stupidity can be measured by the amount of love or lust for that person. Well, Lisa did a lot of stupid things – especially when she was drunk – which was most of the time. And I had it so bad for her that I defended and often participated in her antics. A brief list follows:

Lisa applied for a job as a desk clerk at a motel. When she was driving drunk the next day, she turned to me to talk and rear-ended the motel manager, a stern, straight-laced woman who got out of her car to survey the damage, smelled Lisa's breath, and let her go – not getting the job in exchange for not calling the cops. A pretty good trade, I'd say.

I found Lisa kissing another guy in her house one morning. "It's just your imagination. You're so jealous you're reading more into it than there really is." I accepted her explanation and sat there, watching the TV with Jeff, as Lisa continued to kiss the other guy.

Probably the worst thing was when Lisa and I were in bed one night, clenching each other like a pair of minks, when we heard what sounded like a tree hitting the house. When Lisa went to check it out she found Jeff sprawled on the floor in the next bedroom. We found later he'd had a stroke – no doubt from the stress of listening to us grappling with each other as he pined for her.

I could go on and on, but the point is that as my relationship with Lisa intensified, my friendship with Jeff paled. When things were over between Lisa and me, Jeff and I were friends again – though never quite to the degree we once had been.

The last time I ever remember seeing Jeff was at a New Year's party at Nancy's house on Prospect. I was forty-five then and had brought along Anitra, a nineteen-year-old student, for window dressing. "She's *really* young," Steve whispered to me, half admiration, half scolding. I smiled at the admiration half of it and stood there watching Anitra stare at the moon and stars fracture the sky in an unseasonably warm South Dakota winter night, both knowing that nothing would ever happen between us – our ages were too much of a barrier – but we would hang out for a few more dates. I gave her social access and she gave me youth and that's probably all we ever wanted from each other anyway.

As the night wound down, Anitra and I sat on the couch beside Jeff. "Why don't you come down and see me?"

"I will. I'll do that, Jeff," I said, but never did.

That was 1998. I chased another sweet young thing – Nikki – for a couple years after that, unsuccessfully, I might add. And then I married a woman with four kids and didn't hear a word about Jeff until October 2005.

***

"Mikey, this is Jerry. I knew Jerry's voice well enough to realize that when he identified himself it had to be bad news.

"Yeah?"

"I have some real bad news, Mike

"Yeah?"

"Jeff died last night."

What? The same Jeff that I could always count on for a party? The same Jeff I could always commiserate with? The same Jeff who swallowed bait, line, and sinker the story Jerry and I fabricated about helping three beautiful girls put down a convertible top in a downpour and who were so grateful they took us to a motel and two of them made mad love to us as a third – a Cindy Crawford look-a-like – pounded on the motel room door for one of us to let her in? "What happened?"

"Nothing. He died in his sleep."

I learned later that a group of Christian businessmen had pitched together to fix up Jeff's house months before he died. And so after struggling hand to mouth all those years, he lived the last months of his life in relative comfort.

Since both his mother's and father's ashes had been scattered at the base of War Eagle Monument in Sioux City, I guess it was only natural that Jeff would be cremated too – plus it was a lot cheaper.

"It feels like a baby," said Peter through a tearful smile, cradling twenty pounds of Jeff in a plastic bag in his hands. It had been years since Jeff had been in church – probably since his confirmation. So I took it upon myself to conduct the service. A Little *Dust in the Wind* by Kansas, William Cullen Bryant's *Thanatopsis*, and a couple Bible passages later, we reminisced about Jeff.

That was when we all really learned who he was – or had been.

"This man," said a Native man in tears. "This man, he picked me up from the street and carried me down to his house right here and fed me. I'd be dead now if it wasn't for him."

A young girl – *very* young – brunette and pretty and maybe all of twenty, went up to Peter and touched the bag of Jeff's ashes and cried. "I'll miss you, Jeff."

We all raised a brow at each other, thinking that perhaps Jeff had *not* died a virgin.

The accolades, the honors continued until a fuller picture of Jeff emerged. A kind man, a heart as big as the world, who had been a Buddha to us all.

People left, first those who were nodding acquaintances with Jeff. Then it was those who had known him for a couple years or so who slammed the car doors and pulled away, car lights cutting through the descending inky night. The rest of us remained, milling about, smoking cigarettes, cracking open another forty, lighting a joint or two. Peter thought it only natural that Jeff be spread among his children, so that's what we did, each of us taking a handful of Jeff and spreading him through the pot plants that lifted their fat, greasy buds up into that warm, full night as though saying, "Thank you, Dad."

Life Isn't Fair

Once upon a time there were two sisters – a First Sister and a Second Sister.

They were twins, the two sisters. The reason the first sister was named First Sister rather than given a name like Debbie or Susan was because she was the first sister born – exactly five minutes and eight seconds before Second Sister.

Since she was the older sister, First Sister always demanded she be given everything first. *After all*, First Sister reasoned in her First-Sister self-awareness, *doesn't age come before beauty? No, wait a minute. I'm more beautiful too so I deserve all the privileges that entails as well.*

Second Sister always shared her dolls and toys with First Sister who kept them as long as she wanted. When their mother, who was not a First Mother or Second Mother but simply a mother, told First Sister to return Second Sister's dolls and toys, First Sister made sure she twisted off the arms and heads and legs and buried them in the sandbox in the back yard so all Second Sister got back were doll bodies. Second Sister was still happy to play with them, though.

Oh, look at you, First Sister said to Second Sister, *playing with broken dolls. Mine aren't broken. Na na na na na na*, First Sister sang as Second Sister smiled secretively to herself, knowing one day things would change for First Sister.

When they turned older, they discovered boys. First Sister dated the boys with the fastest cars, the best clothes, and the best family names while Second Sister dated the boys she really liked – and who really liked her.

Then the day came that First Sister was to be married. First Sister had a $50,000 wedding with five-hundred guests and a wedding cake so tall the bride and groom atop the cake were decapitated when the cake was wheeled into the hotel dining room. And then they went on a South American cruise where First Sister wore a bikini so revealing it had all the eighty-year-old men ogling her while First Sister's husband justifiably wondered how faithful First Sister would be. They returned from their honeymoon miserable and hating each other.

When their parents told Second Sister she couldn't marry the man of her dreams because he wasn't rich like First Sister's husband, Second Sister and her boyfriend eloped. Their honeymoon cruise was a week in a canoe with a case of beer and all the fish they could catch. The fell asleep in each other's arms every night, their love for each other growing stronger every day.

First Sister tried having a career right after marriage. She wanted to be everyone's boss right away. She even wanted to be her boss's boss. When her boss decided he didn't want his employee being his boss, he fired her.

Second Sister loved her job from the first day. She helped everyone else without trying to claim credit and whenever people suggested how she could do her job better, she accepted their advice willingly and made sure other people received the credit they deserved. Her boss was so impressed that within a few years she was named chief financial officer and head of operations.

Unemployed, hating her husband, hating her life, First Sister decided to have a baby whom she hated too. When the baby cried and cried and cried, demanding her mother's attention, First Sister tried leaving her baby in a car with the windows rolled up on a hot August day. She tried leaving her baby in a car with the windows rolled up several hot August days, in fact. Then First Sister was arrested and charged and convicted of child endangerment and sentenced to a year in prison while her daughter was made a ward of the state and placed in foster care.

Second Sister learned she was pregnant while she was still working. By then, her husband had become a successful financial advisor and could work from home. So after she had her baby, they moved to a new home in Alaska.

First Sister was addicted to heroin, meth, and crack by the time she was released from prison. Her husband had filed for divorce, citing irreconcilable differences and child neglect. He soon met another, younger woman and they were married while First Sister moved to New Mexico where she found a broken-down adobe filled with rattlesnakes and scorpions and her own self-loathing.

Second Sister and her husband and their child thrived in Alaska where his wealth multiplied and the sun low in the horizon stopped aging her when she was twenty-eight. She and her husband were so much in love they had more and more children who were all strong and beautiful and destined for wealth and greatness.

First Sister's skin baked in the New Mexico sun, and with a steady diet of alcohol and drugs, by age forty she looked as though she were ninety-two.

At Second Sister's request, they decided to meet. *After all*, said Second Sister, *shouldn't we compare notes and see how life has treated us?*

When First Sister saw Second Sister, her heart fell from her chest. Second Sister, who still looked twenty-eight, had several gorgeous children and her husband looked like a Greek god. All First Sister had was an ex-husband, a child in his custody, and bills piled so high she couldn't find the top of her kitchen table.

"Look at you," First Sister said to Second Sister. "You have an incredibly handsome husband, beautiful children, and you've hardly aged since I last saw you. Life just isn't fair."

"No," said Second Sister, wrapping her arms around her husband and children in a huge embrace. "It isn't, is it?"

Lost in the Clouds

Joann had lived her entire life in the Driftless Region – a slice of southwest Wisconsin rumpled with mounds and escarpments donned with oak and birch giving way to limestone outcroppings, misty sentinels commanding the landscape. She loved it here – loved the way she and her younger brothers could wander amid lakes and streams like wild Indians in the summer, damming creeks with rocks to trap shiners and perch, finding turtles they carried home proudly until one day they brought home a snapper – oh, did she get in trouble for that – being the eldest. Wallace, her minister father, had tanned her hide for that. Pulled down her pants and reddened her twelve-year-old butt first with his hand and then his belt. And wasn't she a little old for that? Anyway, when he was done she stood before him. *Before* him, naked from stomach to ankles where her jeans crumpled like the petals of a flower and they stood looking at each other. She into his eyes, daring him not to look down. That was when she first understood she had this *power* – a power over men, her father even.

And that was the last spanking he ever gave her. From then on, his scolds had spanks in them, harmless looks that made her laugh to herself – but never at him, of course.

As young womanhood budded her tomboy body,

boys started looking at her differently. She did too, studying the roundness of her pink-petaled breasts. The curve of her hips, the mounding of her down *there.*

The last time she skinny dipped with her brothers was when she was fourteen. They'd wandered a ways from the parsonage on the north side of Ettrick just east of the towering church where her father thundered the word of God from the pulpit each Sunday. They were at a creek where they'd been many times before. This time, it was her idea to dam up the creek, and they piled rocks through the morning and well into the afternoon until they were sweating – drenched to the waist from creek water and above by sweat. She decided then that she wanted to take her clothes off and splash around in the water – and did – first whipping off her T-shirt then her cutoffs so now there was just this *her* standing there, laughing, splashing, inviting her brothers to do the same. It was only natural that she should be this way – they'd done it dozens of times before. This time, though, she looked different. Much different. When she saw how her brothers looked at her all she could do was laugh.

"Come on, sissies," she said, laughing, splashing, smiling her eyes at them mockingly. To her, this felt as natural as anytime they had done it before. And wouldn't it have been more unnatural to stand there with clothes on?

Slowly, her red-faced brothers acquiesced, and soon they were all laughing, splashing. They didn't realize it then, but this would be the last time of such innocence. The last time they would see each other this way.

Joann had blossomed into the sort of beauty that men and women both found striking. Is it right that a *pastor's* daughter should be so beautiful? they asked themselves. But she was – long, blond hair cascading like wheat over her graceful shoulders, sky blue eyes mysterious, deep, penetrating.

Boys asked her out on dates, and once she turned sixteen, her father allowed it. Be home by eleven, he commanded, knowing full well that the last show in Blair was over by 10:30 so that would allow for no more than a few kisses and fumbling grabs before his daughter was safely returned to the front doorstep – eleven and no later, he commanded.

She didn't like any of the boys she dated. First there was Gary, a junior and a running back on the football team who bullied the smaller, younger boys. And then there was Ronnie – a senior and on the football team too, with the trunk of his new 1969 Mustang stuffed with marijuana. On their first date he asked if she wanted to smoke some – which she did. Laughing at first, she wondered why anyone would want to do such a thing, and when she felt what it did to her head, all she could do was lean back and laugh as he unbuttoned her blouse then unhooked her bra and nibbled at her breasts like squirrel. And that was as far as she would let him go.

When her father announced to the family at the end of her sophomore year that they were spending the *summer* – an entire *summer* – in a place called Riverton, Wyoming, they all felt as though their world had been ripped apart. He had wanted to do mission work for years, he explained, and this was a way he could do it without their leaving the country. After all, didn't the Shoshone and Arapaho on the Wind River Indian Reservation deserve to know Jesus too? And the Lutheran pastor there was looking forward to coming back to the Midwest for a summer and was eager to fill in for him. Wouldn't that be just perfect for everyone?

Joann sulked along the banks of the Black River just east of Galesville, her new refuge away from her family – especially her brothers who had become annoying. She loved to sit there on an oak branch over the deep, dark, slow-moving water and stick in her toes. The water was so deep that when she let herself slip off the branch the river swallowed her up until she hit the muddy bottom then kicked herself up, breaking through the coffeed water and gasping for breath. Then she would sit on the branch until she was nearly dry and do it all over again.

Gary and Ronnie were in the past. What remained were shy, quiet boys stealing furtive glances at her in study hall, hands jingling the change in their pockets as she stretched her long, golden legs out their whole length, liking the way they looked at her. But they were nothing close to what she wanted. Neither were Gary and Ronnie. Not even Principal Jorgenson, who sat at the study hall monitor's desk, leaning back in his chair as she rested her arches on the desk ahead of her so he could study her. No, not even him, she smiled to herself behind her book as his eyes burned holes through her clothes.

The Vista Cruiser was packed and ready to go, even the luggage carrier above. And so her mother and father, three brothers and she, were off down the road, away from Wisconsin and into Minnesota, not nearly so hilly but splashed with lakes and fields and red-barned farmsteads. And then it was South Dakota, green at first then browning at the Missouri that yawned before them, a gash in the earth cleaving her from her previous life. Are there kids there we can play with? asked Paul, her youngest brother. Her father sat there, staring straight ahead, hands locked on the wheel. Yes, he said, not mentioning they were all Shoshone and Arapaho.

They had wanted to stop at Mt. Rushmore and Custer State Park – can't we stop to pet the donkeys, Dad? her brothers cried – but they pushed on to where Wyoming opened to a great, open plain. Thunder Basin National Grassland. Nothing but grass, flecked with antelope her brothers counted until she told them to shut up. From there the road plunged south then jerked north again. Can we stop for a bathroom? her brothers wailed. There's no gas station, her father protested, finally stopping so they could all pile out. I peed on a rattlesnake, said Paul. It was just a bull snake, said her middle brother Blaine. How do you know. Maybe he lost his rattle. If it'd been a rattlesnake, you'd already be swelled up you-know-where right now. *Shut up!* their father roared.

Joann laughed, but when she had to pee herself, she

asked her father to stop again, this time just across from Hell's Half Acre. That was pretty funny, she thought, peering over the top of a sagebrush she was squatting behind, rolling a hot coil into the dust until a dry rustle sounded. Why *that* rattlesnake let *her* pee on him without striking her, she could never guess.

Riverton was dry and dusty with well under 10,000 people. What are we doing here? Joann asked after they were settled into the parsonage – a ranch overlooking the cloud-drenched Wind River Range commanded by Mt. Baldy and Wolverine Peak. Nothing to do? her father answered. You have some of the most magnificent scenery in the world right here before your eyes and all you can say is what are we doing here? There's nothing to do, she protested. After you look at the mountains, then what. Her father's glare smoldered, knowing full well that, for her at least, she was right.

***

June burned into July then August and a dry, hot wind that poured from the Wild River Range like a furnace, burning the land to shades of brown. Wisconsin had been rich green, and the only color here was the sky where an occasional cloud scudded across, always reneging its promise of rain.

It was the next-to-the-last service for her father that Sunday. We have a new family coming to church this morning, her father said. Are they white? she asked, not wanting to sound rude, but she did. Her father's glare drenched her hopefulness. Our native people deserve to know Christ too, was all he could say.

On the drive to the church her father was sullen, hostile even. Joann sensed even he was tiring of the dry Wyoming vastness, the treeless, open nakedness of it all. Even he seemed ready to return to Wisconsin. In Wyoming, God seemed to have completely forgotten his coloring box.

As they pulled up to the church, a rider galloped on a horse toward them, sending a high dust plume behind.

Her father stood and watched him approach. That must be the Cloud's son Jerry, he observed.

Cloud? Joann scoffed to herself. More Indians. She should have guessed.

The rider pulled up his horse, dust sifting onto their car as she got out and coughed. As the dust cleared, the young man scanned her family, focusing on her. He rode bareback, boots scuffed and jeans worn shiny. His Western-style shirt stuck to his muscled frame with a veneer of sweat as his brown eyes washed over her, a soft, cool rain quenching the Wyoming dust, his long, black hair tied behind in a traditional braid. He was gorgeous.

"Joann, this is Jerry," her father said.

Jerry looked at her, managing a smile as he held out a calloused palm. "Hi."

"Hi." She let Jerry's muscled hand swallow hers, hating her father for wanting to return to Wisconsin.

Marie

It was the first fight we'd had in quite a while. And it was a good one.

"I don't see why we can't go out to the Coast. We have two weeks 'til you start your new job." Jean's arms were crossed as she looked from the other side of the patio table past me to something – or someone – better.

"But Dad isn't doing very well. He had that stroke, you know. I hear him failing more and more every time we talk."

"Your dad's fine. Besides, it's barely a day's drive back there. You could go see him any three-day weekend."

"But we never do."

Jean's glare cut through me as she flipped her hair over her shoulder. It was times like this – when she was incredibly angry – that the French-Cherokee, the really beautiful part of her, burned through her stubborn Scotch-Irish.

I tried the guilt approach. "We can always go to the Coast next year. I'm just not sure Dad will still be around then."

Jean's cheekbones hollowed as her jaw slipped a notch. She leveled her gaze at me and shifted in her chair and through the glass patio table top I saw her dangle her shoe from her toe, deliberating. "So . . . we go see your dad for two weeks, you come back to start your new job as radio station manager, and a year from now we spend two weeks on the Coast."

"Deal."

"Deal."

***

We loaded up the car and headed out early the next morning, stopping at Wall Drug for Breakfast then Al's Oasis to fill up and have a nickel cup of coffee, getting to my parents' house four that afternoon. Mom was already at the curb, wringing her hands she was so glad to see us, Dad struggling up the sidewalk, thumping his cane as he pinched up a smile for Jean – not me. My brother and his wife had had a girl and decided one child was enough so Dad had been counting on me to carry on the family name. When Jean and I married while still in college, we had decided to wait until graduation. Then we thought we would wait until we paid off our college loans. After that, it was until we had bought a house and later after we had set aside enough money for Jean to take time off to have a baby. Then after we had been married for eight years and decided to take a long-delayed honeymoon on the Oregon Coast, we ran into an abandoned bait shop on the beach at Pacific City. It was an incredible deal – lot complete with building – admittedly ramshackle – for $10,000. We went straight to the realtor's and bought it, knowing in the back on our minds it was our way of delaying a family indefinitely.

When we told the folks about it, Dad's eyes shifted from me to Jean and back to me, trying to decide if we agreed. Surmising we did, he grunted and started talking about how our family had come from Norway to plant new roots and I was only second-generation and he could already see those roots about to wither and die. He even managed to shed a tear which sent Jean directly into the kitchen to help Mom with dinner.

"So when *are* you two going to start a family."

"I don't know, Dad. We're young yet."

125

"You're thirty-one." Dad's gaze leveled at me. "And Jean's what?"

"Twenty-eight."

"By the time your mother was thirty-one, she'd had all four of you kids."

I thought of my brother and two sisters and then myself – the designated sire of the next heir-apparent to the family name. "Like I say, Dad, we're still young."

Dad grunted and grabbed his newspaper from the magazine rack, signaling an end to our conversation.

Dad was pretty much silent all the way through dinner. He finished his meal by buttering a slice of bread and soaking it in high-fructose corn syrup, something he'd done ever since he was a kid. Artery-clogging resin dripping down his chin, he glared at me like a mortal enemy.

"I see your class is having a reunion," Mom said, breaking stony silence as she folded her newspaper and set it on the table.

"Oh? When's that."

"Three tomorrow afternoon," Jean said.

"How'd you know that?"

Jean's jaw shifted as she decided which of a multitude of things she wanted to say. "It was the invitation you got in the mail then glanced at and threw away. That's why I didn't think you were serious about coming here."

I felt a quarrel brewing but decided to let Jean win this one. "Would you like to go, honey?" I asked, maybe a little bit too much like the high-fructose corn syrup Dad had just swallowed.

"I hear Marie's back. She'll probably be there." Dad wiped a stubborn drop of corn syrup from his chin after having dropped the biggest possible bomb he could.

Jean looked more than a little curiously at me. "Who's Marie?"

Mom's eyes flickered from Jean to me to Dad. "She's, uh, well she's . . . "

"His girlfriend," Dad blurted.

"*Former* girlfriend, Maynard," Mom corrected.

Dad's smile crept across the table like a stalking puma. "Pretty, too."

"Oh?" Jean crossed her legs and arms and faced me. "So why haven't I heard of her."

"I hear she just got a divorce, too. And no kids yet. Just like you two." A shit-eating smile creased Dad's face.

"Our thirteen-year reunion," I mulled. Not ten. Not twenty. Thirteen.

***

I was glad it was so informal. The reunion was at city park, amid towering cottonwoods and oaks. Recent heavy rains cascaded the river over the dam built over a hundred years ago to power the town's flour mill, the only remaining vestiges a wall of red quartzite where the river eddied, harboring monster walleye for an occasional lucky fisherman. Because the water was so high, the mosquitoes were terrible, hitting everyone like dive bombers so they ran to their cars, emerging minutes later reeking of DEET as though they'd bathed in Agent Orange.

To my relief, Marie wasn't there. Some of my classmates had seen her, shopping for groceries, going to the drugstore. But no one had really talked to her. Then that was Marie, I guess. Incredibly beautiful but with a sadness deep inside. I had my theories about it. One was that she was so beautiful she was unapproachable. Her beauty set a ten-foot barrier around her that most guys couldn't cross because they were afraid of getting rejected. A lot of girls didn't get close to her either – probably afraid of being upstaged.

When we were sophomores, some of the more daring senior guys asked her out. As far as I knew, she went out with everyone who asked her. But few dared. I suspect most of the guys were afraid to ask her out because she was so damn beautiful. So Marie and her friend Ann started tooling around Sioux Falls in Ann's Camaro, picking up guys – most pretty unsavory. About

127

our mid-senior year I finally screwed up the courage to ask Marie out, and surprisingly, she accepted. We went to Sheila's Shipwreck Inn at Lake Brandt where we had the walleye with salad and fries then drove over to a farmer's private beach on the west side of the lake where we parked and watched the winter sunset pinken the lake ice as Deep Purple blared from the A.M. in my 1960 Catalina. I'd managed to score a case of White Label beer from a bar in Beaver Creek that would serve anyone old enough to put money on the counter so we were sitting there, Deep Purple throbbing the windows, sneaking an occasional kiss. Then Marie reached into her purse and pulled out two tiny, white pills. Her gorgeous Mona Lisa smile crept up to her eyes this time, not making her nearly so Mona Lisa. "Wanna try some?"

"What's that?" I felt like the biggest dork in the world as I looked from the pills to Marie and her incredibly long, straight, blond hair.

"White microdot." Her smile wrapped around her words so she owned them utterly. This was the most beautiful, the most genuine, the most human I'd ever seen her. A million questions raced through my head, like *What is it? What will it do to me? Will it kill me?* "Sure."

Marie handed me one of the pills and I looked at it. It was so small I could barely see it – maybe a quarter of a baby aspirin. Marie popped hers into her mouth and washed it down with a swig of White Label and I did the same and waited. And waited. And waited. Nothing. I drank my beer the same pace as Marie did so when she finished hers and reached into the cooler in the back seat I took her chin in my hand and looked into those iceberg-blue eyes and kissed her. As I leaned back to look again into her eyes, expecting her to pull away, she just sat there. So I kissed her again, and as I let my hand drift down toward her breast she didn't try to stop me so I let it rest there. Marie pulled away and stroked the back of my head. "Maybe we should put the beer in the trunk."

"Huh?"

"So we can use the back seat."

"Okay." I opened my car door and stepped out to a billion stars and planets glaring at me, peering eyes in the endless universe. I felt like I could reach up and grab them and I tried, reaching then jumping, each time failing.

"*What* are you doing?"

"I'm . . . trying . . . to reach for the stars but can't catch them."

Marie started laughing – not laughing but roaring, and when she finally stopped laughing she said, "Why don't you get the beer out of the back seat, put it in the trunk, climb with me into the back seat, and reach for me instead."

A deeper drive than what the acid could conquer drove me on. I don't know how long it took – seconds probably – it seemed like ten thousand years – no, ten thousand light years, a million light years – for me to get the beer out of the back seat and put it in the trunk then open the back door. Marie was already in the back seat, unbuttoning her top. "C'mon, hurry."

"Huh?"

"Hurry up," she said with charming annoyance. "I wanna be doin' it before that acid really hits."

"Okey dokey." I brushed up a laugh from Marie that she couldn't hold, even as she reached behind to unhook her bra. We spun and turned and twisted with the moon and stars from just past sunset until mauve false dawn reached lavender fingers across the lake ice.

***

"Here's Marie," said Wynn, former captain of our football team and more imposing than ever at six-four and a little over three-hundred. Everyone stopped what they were doing – and I mean everyone – as this blond in white shorts and tank climbed from a little red Alfa. The California sun had kissed her body with an incredible tan. She locked her car, no doubt a habit she'd formed in L.A., and strolled past a dozen well-wishers *straight toward me*. If she had been beautiful before, she was an absolute vision now, impossibly long, blond hair sifting in the slight breeze over her shoulder, Birkenstocks sifting coral toenails through the grass and those eyes, those sky-blue mischievous eyes, focusing on *me, me, only me.*

"Harry," she whispered, standing tiptoe to kiss me, not on the cheek but the lips. I kissed her back, of course. She stepped back and took both my hands in both of hers. "It's so nice to see you, Harry."

Jean tried to clear her throat but it sounded more like a grunt.

"Marie, this is Jean my, uh, my . . . "

"Wife." Jean reached her hand toward Marie but Marie ignored it and hugged Jean, kissing her cheek. "Hi Jean," Marie said, turning to me. "She's *beautiful*, Harry."

I nodded, waiting for one of them to explode – probably Jean. And Marie was right. As Jean's French-Cherokee anger boiled over her cheeks fairly glowed like a coral reef. Marie just stood there, Jean still in her arms, caressing her back as though she were a surrogate me. It was then that I saw something inside Marie had been broken. She was still beautiful – more beautiful than ever – but something deep inside her had shattered that even all the king's horses and all the king's men couldn't put together.

I glanced at Marie's left hand still around Jean's waist and sighed relief.

"Oh, I don't know why I still wear these." Marie pulled her arm from around Jean and fiddled with her rings. "I've been divorced for over a year now, Harry." Then she touched her Rolex on the same wrist, not to check the time but to reassure herself it was still there. It was the same watch I'd given her nearly thirteen years before. Her eyes rested on me as though she were starving and I was a banquet.

The way Jean glared at her I thought she was going to walk away, but she didn't. I think she was afraid to leave Marie and me alone.

"It keeps the guys away. They still look, but at least

they don't bother me."

"I see," said Jean frostily.

"I'm sorry." Marie shook her gorgeous blond mop and buried her face in her hand. "It must sound like I'm bragging. But I'm not. I'm really not." She looked at me, desperation creeping into her voice. "Do they have any beer?"

"Kegs." I motioned to where the old gang had gathered. As unofficial brewmeister, Wynn was filling cup after cup, a full one in his free hand.

"I'm sorry. I need a beer." Marie strolled briskly toward the group gathered around the keg and everyone welcomed her, guys and gals both giving her hugs they would never had dared give her in high school. Marie was safe now, with pretty much everyone married with a kid or three.

"She's absolutely gorgeous," Jean said with not a little resentment. "That must have broken your heart when she dumped you."

"She didn't dump me."

"*You* dumped *her*? Were you nuts? She's ten times more beautiful than any other woman here." Jean was usually so Kevlar hard she could deflect the hardest bullet. But there was something about Marie even she couldn't handle.

Jean went to the car to touch up her makeup then we joined the group. Marie of course was the center of everything, telling how she had gone to L.A. and fallen in love with the beach and mild weather and the bands. There were so many bands. She related stories of the L.A. and Frisco music scenes and talked about Grace Slick as though they had been best friends. The beer in her hand had put that old glow back in her face and she was more animated, gesturing wildly, laughing with everyone as the past and present criss-crossed, everyone surprised to hear how former Romeos were now happily married with three or four kids and class clowns were law partners or surgeons. Two or three people were trying to talk to Marie at once as her gaze shifted past them, past me, and her smile carried silent words to Jean. Marie had been glad to see me. But at that moment I sensed a connection – maybe fusion would have been a better word – between Marie and Jean.

Marie excused herself and came toward us, nodding at the crumbling walls of the old flour mill. "Can we take a walk?" she said at least as much to Jean as to me.

"Sure." The way Jean answered Marie I sensed she was warming to my old flame. She felt a connection with Marie too, something solid and genuine. Jean didn't have very many close female friends. But I knew right then that Marie and Jean felt a bond.

We walked down the red quartzite path toward the mill. The water pouring over the dam was so loud we couldn't have heard each other talk if we had tried. Marie held her beer as she carefully negotiated the path down behind the mill wall where the sound of the falls became a sigh. She sat down on a rock, cradling her beer in her hands, as she looked downriver where water frothed and baffled and eddied until it made its quiet journey toward the Missouri then the Mississippi and finally the Gulf of Mexico.

"I just got out of treatment last week – for the fourth time." Marie looked at the beer in her hand and laughed. "Yeah, I know. Sucks, doesn't it." She sipped her beer and looked downriver. I felt she wanted something much stronger.

"Maybe you shouldn't be drinking that beer," said Jean.

Marie shrugged and finished her beer and set her cup on the rock beside her. The Rolex wasn't on her wrist anymore. I figured she must have slipped it into her pocket for safekeeping. "Too late now."

Jean's glance shifted from me to Marie. "Is there anything we can do, Marie?"

Marie looked at me and Jean in one glance. "You're already doing a lot just by being here listening."

"I think you should quit, *right now*."

Marie looked to Jean and shook her head and started to cry. Then the strangest thing happened. It was as though she crumpled from the inside and fell into herself so far no one could ever find her again.

"That's it." Jean took my beer from me and poured it and hers out on the rocks in front of her. I was about to object when she made her point. "We're quitting right now. With you."

Marie shook her head. "You don't have to."

"Yes we do. For you. We're doing this together." Jean stood up from the rock beside me and went over to Marie and knelt in front of her and took her in her arms and held her until the noise of the party died down and everyone packed up the empty kegs and drove off.

***

"So why *did* you break up with her?" I was negotiating the potholes of Highway 77 in my Bronco on the way back to my folks' place. Jean hadn't tried looking away after she asked, meaning she wanted an answer. Now.

"It was the drugs." I shrugged. *Thonk* went the left front tire as I buried it in a washtub-sized crater.

"Try not to hit the potholes."

"Thanks for the advice."

Jean nodded and looked straight ahead, scouting for more potholes. "So what kind of drugs did Marie do?"

"You name it. Pot . . . acid . . . mescaline . . . coke . . . . I think even a little opium and heroin."

Fall 1971 Marie had gone to the U while I went to a smaller state college. We still saw each other weekends, but something about Marie was starting to change. We'd drive to our favorite parking spot, share some beers and kisses and more. Half the time it was as though Marie were somewhere else – some other place, some other party, maybe even with some other guy. I felt like she was a boat I had always counted on sailing but now she was drifting out to sea.

I'd taken a job cooking at Uncle Ed's Café before

classes even started so I could save up the money to buy Marie an engagement ring for Christmas. It was a really nice ring, not a huge stone by any means, a quarter karat, but big enough to be impressive. I walked past the jewelry store every morning to make sure the ring was still there.

I worked at Uncle Ed's twenty-five hours a week that first semester, clear from late August to mid-September. After my last final I went to the jewelry store and asked to see the ring and the clerk took it from the window and set it on the black velvet mat, talking about cut and clarity and other things I didn't understand or care about. I just wanted to buy it and give it to Marie for Christmas. I could already see her eyes light up as she put it on her finger and leaned toward me for a kiss. Then I thought what it would be like to be married to her. Would she be happy with me? Would the life of a radio newscaster satisfy her? Or would she want more. More thrills? More drugs? More guys?

"How much is the Rolex?"

The jeweler stopped in mid-sentence. "I thought it was the ring you were interested in."

"The watch is nice too."

"It is." The jeweler set the ring aside and took the women's Rolex from the case. "We don't sell very many of these of course. They're quite expensive."

"How much."

The jeweler looked me up and down, judging me for the college student that I was. "Eight hundred."

I had $418 burning a hole in my pocket, just enough for the ring. "Could I pay half down and make payments?"

The jeweler's jaw ground a little as he considered. "That depends. We'd have to do a credit check. And I assume you have a job? So you can make the payments?"

I nodded.

"Well why don't you give me the name and phone number of your employer." He set the Rolex back in the display case as though there was no possible way he'd ever sell it to me then he put the ring back in the window and dusted his hands off, dusted me off. "Why don't you stop by tomorrow and I'll let you know."

I cooked from four to ten that night, sneaking glances at Ed to figure out if the jeweler had called him. After we closed and after he cut the front lights he came over, wiping his hands on a dishtowel, to where I was mopping the kitchen floor. "You're plannin' on workin' here 'til school's out in the spring, aren't ya?"

I looked up from my mop. At that moment I felt like life was a five-way turnabout and I had no idea which turn to take. "Sure."

"Good." Ed looked at the spotless grill, the leftovers neatly labeled and put away in the cooler, the shiny floor. "You do a good job. You're a good worker. That's what I told a guy who called here today about ya."

"Thanks."

Four days later Marie and I were sitting together on her parents' living room carpet under the Christmas tree, Marie expectant, her parents expectant, as I handed her present to her. She tore the ribbon and bow and paper off and popped open the box and looked at me, face frozen. "A *watch*?"

Marie's father leaned over for a glance, hoisted his brows, and studied me with newfound admiration. "That's not any watch, Marie. It's a *Rolex*."

"A watch," said Marie, dangling it before her eyes like a dead rat she'd found in the corner.

We spent the rest of the holidays together, but when I called her the first Thursday night after classes started, the night I usually called to set things up for the weekend, Marie said she was busy. She was busy the next weekend too and the weekend after that. Ed was a little surprised when I asked if I could work weekends since I'd always asked for them off before but he was glad for the extra help. The jeweler was also surprised when I came into his store late February and laid $400 on the counter. He wrote PAID IN FULL on a receipt and handed it to me.

"Anytime you want to buy anything on time, just come on in. Your credit here's solid gold." I thanked him and when I left, I saw the ring still in the window.

***

Jean's eyes were still frozen to the road. "Did you ever do any drugs with her?"

My loins surged when I thought of that time at Lake Brandt. "A little acid, maybe."

"I see." Jean turned on the radio, and not liking what she heard, popped in a cassette.

"Just once."

"You never did acid with me."

I glanced at Jean, this time dropping the right front tire in a rut.

"Pothole."

"Yep."

"So was sex good with her?"

I felt my Adam's apple bulge as I swallowed. "It was okay."

"Liar."

"Huh?" *Bam.* The biggest pothole yet.

"I bet you two screwed from dusk 'til dawn." Jean waited for me to answer. "Well did you? And don't hit any more potholes. I can already feel my teeth falling out of my skull."

"It was pretty intense," I admitted, sweat trickling down my forehead, the air on full blast.

"Thank you for being honest with me," Jean lied.

***

Mom already had dinner – or supper as she and Dad called it – on the table when we got there. Dad already sat at his place at the head of the table, fork and knife in hand, ready to devour whatever Mom set in front of him. Jean went into the bathroom to wash her hands and sulk and I sat at the side of the table, trying to figure out how to get past my memories of Marie and the constant bickering with Jean that I knew could eventually make her a memory too. I loved Jean. I really did. What I didn't love was her insistent prying about my and Marie's past.

Jean returned from the bathroom, eyes a little redder than when she had gone in. "That looks great," she said, Mom's food reviving her.

"We have peas and carrots and roast beef with mashed potatoes and gravy," Mom said proudly, setting the ladle in the gravy. "Well, she said, untying her apron. "Let's eat."

Dad dove straight in, dishing himself two, huge scoops of mashed potatoes then making a bird's nest and overfilling it with gravy dripping over the side of his plate. Then he stabbed a slab or roast beef as big as his hand and laid it alongside. He took about a teaspoon of peas and carrots.

"You should eat more vegetables, Maynard," Mom advised.

"This is enough," Dad grunted. "Damned peas make me fart and carrots give me the shits."

"Oh Maynard."

Jean started laughing so hard tears ran down her face, spilling as though she'd been bottling up anger and joy and sadness all together in one noxious brew. Her laughter spread to me, Mom, and even Dad who had broken the tension between Jean and me with one of his always-inappropriate remarks.

After we topped the meal off with hot apple pie puddled in vanilla ice cream we sat with the folks and watched Lawrence Welk, Myron Floren playing up a storm on the accordion. Dad was always proud that Myron was his cousin, something he never failed to mention every time he watched the show. After Lawrence Welk we watched a very unmemorable Western, Dad's choice, of course, then the folks turned in to bed. Jean and I listened to the news, and when the sports were over, Jean reached for the remote on the coffee table and switched off the television and drew up her knees and rested her head on my shoulder and stroked my chest. "Can we talk?"

Her sudden desire for romance threw me. "Sure.

What do you want to talk about?"

"Us."

"O . . . kay. That's a pretty broad topic. What is it about us you'd like to talk about?"

"Just us. Our future. Our marriage."

"Is our marriage in trouble?"

"I probably shouldn't have had that beer this afternoon."

"So how does your having one beer put our marriage in trouble."

"I think I'm pregnant."

Jean could have dropped an anvil on my head from ten feet up and I wouldn't have been more shocked. Less than a year after she'd moved in with me while we were in college, she got pregnant. We were both terrified of what our parents would think, so she had an abortion. I'll never forget how I sat in the waiting area for them to finish the procedure. All the other girls had gone in and come out maybe an hour later, but Jean had been in there for over two hours when a couple guys in white coats rushed in the front door, one carrying something that looked like a vacuum cleaner, and asked which room they should go to. I figured then that something had gone wrong and they had come to save Jean. When the third hour passed I thought Jean had died and I started planning her funeral. Then, after Jean had been in the OR for three and a half hours, the two men in white coats emerged. "You need to clean that machine more often so it doesn't clog up," one of them admonished the girl at the front desk, and they left.

Jean later told me the machine had broken down in mid-procedure and she had to wait for the technicians to come fix it. I couldn't start to imagine what it must have been like for her, another life half out of her, half in. What she had planned as a simple procedure, *like getting rid of a bug*, had turned into an ordeal from hell. Afterward, Jean emerged from the OR, barely able to walk, and we took a cab to the home of a kindly woman who had taken us for a pair of street urchins and sheltered us for several days as Jean slowly recovered. They'd given Jean some pills to stanch the bleeding but she still bled a lot. That's normal, the receptionist at the abortion clinic said when Jean called. If it gets real bad, call us.

We were halfway back home when Jean checked her purse and said to me, "The pills. I must have left them at that house. What will that woman think?"

***

"Harry. Are you awake?"

"I'm awake."

Jean's apple pie-vanilla ice cream breath whispered, "Are you happy, Harry? Are you mad? Are you afraid?" A pause. "Harry? What are you?"

"Happy," I said, reaching around to cradle all of her in my arms. "I'm happier than I've ever been in my life."

***

The call came a little after three. The hall light framed Mom's silhouette so for a moment she looked younger than I'd ever seen her – no wrinkles, no age spots, just Mom. "Harry?" she whispered, trying to wake me but not Jean who turned over anyway and looked at Mom standing in the doorway like she didn't know her.

"Yeah," I sighed.

"Wynn's on the phone, Harry. He has some bad news, he said. He didn't say what. He wanted to talk to you himself."

"Okay," I muttered and kicked on my slippers and followed Mom downstairs.

The phone receiver was on the table, the cord coiled around it like a python. I picked it up and tried not to sound annoyed but did. "Yeah Wynn."

"Harry." Wynn was choked up, something I'd never heard before. "Marie was in an accident."

"Is she all right?"

"She died, Harry."

"What?"

"I'm on search and rescue, you know. We got a 911

call a little after midnight and headed straight out. Her car made the first two turns just west of town but missed the last. The patrolman said her car flipped at least a dozen times before it landed on its top." A good ten seconds passed. "Harry?"

"Yeah."

"I'm really sorry, Har. I don't know what else to say. I know how you two were back in school. I just thought you should hear it from me and not the TV."

"Thanks, Wynn."

"Oh, one more thing. Did Jean lose a watch at the picnic?"

I had all I could do to muster an answer. "Not that I know of."

"It's a really nice women's Rolex. Somebody's gonna miss it."

"Thanks, Wynn," I said, wanting our conversation over.

"You bet. Take care, buddy."

I knew what had happened. I didn't need to ask Wynn and he knew he didn't have to tell me. Marie had stopped at the tavern by the city park just for a 'quick one' and stayed there half the night then tried to drive home. I should have known. I should have had Jean drive the Bronco and I should have driven Marie's car back to her place.

Jean was half asleep when I got back to our bedroom. She spooned herself against me as I held her and imagined I could already feel our baby's heartbeat. "Who was that?" she whispered in her sleep.

I could tell her the truth and we could wait the usual four days for the funeral or we could head out first thing in the morning after telling Mom and Dad the great news about the baby. "Wynn."

A sigh. "What did he want at this hour?"

"Someone lost a women's watch in the park. He called to see if it was yours."

Jean's right eye poked open at the nightstand clock.

"He called at three in the morning *about a watch*?"

"It was a Rolex." I curled against Jean and nuzzled her back to sleep.

Masterpiece

Kelly made it *sound* like a good gig – Eagles Landing, a tony retirement community for the ultra-rich, nestled on the shores of Lake Onagonda. The people who lived there had money – lots of money. Living in a retirement community for them was merely transitioning from posh, lakefront villas to a posh, skilled nursing facility for the rich.

"How many books should I bring."

"How many do you have."

"A couple boxes – maybe fifty."

"Bring them all."

"Wow. You think there'll be that many customers?"

"Believe me. These people have money. The parking garage is filled with Mercedes and Audis."

"Great."

"Meet me in the assisted living lobby – right out front."

This was the opportunity for which I'd been waiting – to get my book into the hands of community leaders – more like national leaders, in this case. Lake Onagonda was known as one of the premier retirement communities in the country – and this was the reading for which I'd been waiting.

So I loaded up two cases of books – fifty total – into my PT Cruiser and made the half-hour drive through pelting sleet. A crawling feeling up my spine told me this was not going to be a good day. I shrugged it off as beginning-author jitters and made it with twenty minutes to spare.

Instead of Kelly, a somber woman of about forty met me at the front door. She wore a nurse's smock and her blond hair was brushed back severely – maybe painfully would have been a better way to put it. Devoid of makeup, jewelry, perfume, or facial expression, she looked askance at the two boxes of books with which I had lumbered in through the door. "*Oh*," she muttered, knife-edge frost in her voice. "So are *you* the *author*?"

I had never before heard the word author expressed with such imperious disdain. "I guess so."

"Well *are* you or *aren't* you."

Instinct told me to leave – or flee. "Yes, I'm the author," I admitted, wondering whether I truly deserved the appellation in her eyes – or anyone's – at that point.

"And *what* do you have in those *boxes*?"

Wounded rattlesnakes to complement your glowing personality, I wanted to say. "Books?" I offered, feeling as though TSA was just about to nail me with twenty pounds of C-4 strapped to my legs at JFK.

"You'll need only one – to read from."

"O . . . kay." I huffed back through the doors into a sleet storm pelting bullets, wondering if maybe I shouldn't just leave. I felt about as welcome as Dzhokhar Tsarnaev at a pre-Boston Marathon pasta bar. The storm worse than ever, I tucked a single copy of my book inside my coat and returned inside.

I must have taken too long because the woman – MARIAN I saw from her name badge – was tapping the floor with her toe so hard it looked as though she were trying to stomp a cobra to death. Then a cobra's bite probably couldn't have fazed her since she already had plenty of venom flowing through her veins. As we passed through an ultra-elegant lobby with a white grand piano and a fireplace so massive you could have stood up in it, she turned to me with what could have possibly passed for a smile – or extreme gas. "So what's your book about?"

"Oh," I responded, feeling as though I had connected with an actual human being. "The title is Doomsday. It's about how terrorists destroy the Internet and civilization collapses. With the collapse comes the total disintegration of the utilities infrastructure, communications, and law enforcement. People starve and freeze to death by the millions and the only ones to survive are those who live in isolated rural enclaves. The Amish do just fine . . . "

"You have got to be kidding," said Nurse Ratched, standing between me and a massive steel door that said NO ADMITTANCE WITHOUT AUTHORIZED ESCORT.

"No, really. The Amish do just f . . . "

"Do you have any *idea* how our residents will react when you tell them that?"

"I'm sorry. Don't they like the Amish?"

"*No*," she uttered, daggers in her voice. "They'll think it's really happening. Do you have any idea how long it will take us to calm them down?"

"Uh, no."

"Weren't you told that you'll be reading to MCU residents?"

Not knowing nursing home lingo, visions of patients hooked up to tubes and wires ran through my head. "They'll still understand what I'm talking about – won't they?"

"I'm sorry. We simply can't have you terrifying our residents. Isn't there a passage that doesn't deal with death and destruction?"

Since pretty much everything in my novel that didn't deal with death and destruction was a sex scene, I offered, "Yes."

"Good." She nodded and opened the door that at that moment could just as well have had a sign above, ABANDON ALL HOPE, YE WHO ENTER HERE.

On the other side of the door, it was just as nice, but

a lot more clinical. Residents wandered up and down the halls to locked doors, tried them, then walked back to the other side of the hallway where they tried another door, stared at it as if failed to open, and started the process all over again.

Saturday was when a lot of families visited their relatives, so a pretty good mix of people clustered in chairs and sofas, glimmers of recognition flitting in and out of the residents' eyes. Baby Boomers – probably the residents' children – seemed insistent on getting their relatives to recognize them while their grandchildren and great-grandchildren seemed bored to tears. Kelly was nowhere around.

"I don't give a damn what her name is. She isn't supposed to be here."

I turned toward where the voice had come from and saw a man, sartorially comfortable in a wool sport jacket and gripping a cane. The face of the woman he had been addressing, his daughter, I presume, was blanched with tears. Somewhere down the hall, a woman screamed the most horror-ridden, terrified scram I had ever heard. The man screamed back mockingly, adding, "Aw shut up."

Marian led me to the Great Room where I was to have my reading. A grand piano and fireplace identical to those in the lobby were suitable appointments to the room featuring plush chairs and sofas. At the south end of the room a three-story window shaped like the side of a cathedral gave way to a quiet dark lake where the sleet storm had turned to snow, quiet, silent, elegant, each flake like a note as someone started playing the piano – something Chopin.

One man seated in the front row kept getting up as though wanting to go outside and walking straight into a large window as though he couldn't see it. An aide would lead him back to his chair where he would do it all over again. Finally, they led him away.

One woman, also in the front row, farted a bass line to Chopin, pausing as one of her farts turned into something more and an aide led her off, dark stains rohrschaching the back of her white slacks. Another aide removed the chair.

My audience was dwindling.

As the clock ticked down to a couple minutes before ten, I went to the podium they'd set up for me. I set my book on the small table with a chair behind. Apparently, someone besides Nurse Ratched had been thoughtful enough to make my reading comfortable.

The woman playing the piano, a ravishing platinum blond wearing a black cocktail dress and pearls, smiled directly into my eyes as she played. Apparently, she knew her music very well, because no score was visible on the piano as she played from memory Chopin's Etude in E minor, Opus 25, No. 5, lilting, beautiful, haunting, each note perfectly executed. As her ice-blue eyes rested upon me, her lips slightly parted as though singing silently to me – and only me. I could have sworn she was mouthing something about making love until dawn. She was so spectacularly ravishing she could have been any age – and age didn't matter. As one of the aides rested her hand on her shoulder to signal that she was to stop playing so I could begin, she segued perfectly into the refrain, haunting, beautiful, sad, and ended.

Applause shattered the room as the woman stood back from the piano bench. It had been a performance worthy of a President or king at Carnegie Hall or Lincoln Center. I have never heard anything so magnificent before or since.

Taking Nurse Ratched's admonishment into consideration I began my reading with the standard reasons for why I had become a writer – the authors who had inspired me, my writing habits, work published and about to be published. The entire time, the blond who had been playing Chopin so magnificently nodded and laughed in all the right places, making intense love with her eyes – and all for me.

I managed to find a couple passages that weren't

too traumatic – or sexual. Both were about how my hero and villain had both gone into the basement of an old house and found canned goods left by a past resident. Grandma reaching back from the grave to save them, I think was how I had phrased it. The residents and their families seemed to hang on my every word, clapping several times, offering an overwhelming applause when I had finished. They were the best audience I've ever had.

By then I was determined to ask the blond – probably one of the residents' daughters – out for dinner. I didn't have long to wait. She came right up to the podium, ice-blue eyes sparkling, luscious lips opening to speak – thank God audibly, this time. She opened a napkin to me upon which she had apparently dipped her finger into her water glass and written some epic – a story of war and love lost and found – a story that transcended anything penned by Homer or Shakespeare or the Romantics. "What do you think of this?" She stood there, smiling, awaiting my pronouncement, my verdict of what I thought of her creation. "Beautiful. Beautiful," I repeated, meaning her.

A female aide came beside her and touched her elbow, preserving her dignity the best she could. "You must be tired, Linda," the aide said as she looked to me. "I'm sorry."

I couldn't think of what to say as the aide led her away, the napkin falling to the floor, her masterpiece forgotten amid the scuff and scrape of chairs getting put away.

I snatched up her napkin and when I was alone, held it to my nose and sniffed and found her all over again. Her smile, her perfect playing, her great novel. I still have it, tucked safely inside an envelope I take to every reading where I sniff it just before I begin, not knowing what great artist the audience might hold.

Meeting Paul Newman

Ole was worrying a stripped nut off an oil pan when Ed Duncan pulled up on his dirt bike. Engine sputtering, smoke roiling out the pipe like a cigar chain smoker, Ed was pissed. He killed the engine and strutted toward Ole's shop, spewing fumes himself. "I thought you said you'd fixed that cocksucker."

Ole set down his wrench and emerged from his greasy, oil-rag-soaked shop and went to the Yamaha caked with mud and sand from the kickstand to the handlebars and seat. "I thought I did." He turned to Ed. "What's the matter?"

"It ain't got no power 'tall." Ed set his ballcap squarely down on his head, kicking the bike so it nearly toppled. "Acts like the rings is shot."

"Well . . . let me give her a try," said Ole, tired in his voice. He was tired of Ed and all the movie people coming and going for the past month, racing bikes and busting them up then expecting him to perform miracles with them – like raising someone from the grave. He kickstarted the engine and all it did was roll over once, then kill. He tried it again and it did the same. Third time, nothing. "Sounds flooded. Where ya been ridin' this anyway."

"Over there on the dirt track right up Harlan Road," said Ed. "We got us a race goin' in the movie. Tried jumpin' a dune at Depoe Bay yesterday. Damn thing killed just 'fore I was to hit a board goin' up t' other side. Gotta mouth fulla sand."

Ole tried not to laugh as the image of hotshot dirtbike rider Ed filled his mind. As far as he was concerned, Ed had it coming. "I gotta new 600cc engine I could put on it. Just come in a crate yesterday. Lot more power 'n you're used to with that 250. I could swap her out 'n you'd be flyin' over those sand dunes like a seagull."

"Do it," Ed demanded. "Those movie people got all kindsa money."

Over a year ago production crews had been scouting out the area, and they'd settled on Toledo, a slice of the Siletz River up north, and right here in Elk City. Filming had started this spring. Grandpa Hank Fonda himself strutting his stuff, ordering free drinks for everyone at The Timbers in Toledo. Even Paul Newman was along, famous now with his new movie, *Butch Cassidy and The Sundance Kid*. Especially how Newman and Robert Redford got shot up at the end.

"Should have her done tomorrow mornin'," said Ole, kicking up the kickstand and rolling the bike toward his shop.

"That ain't a gonna be soon enough," Ed protested. "They wanna refilm that Depoe Bay scene afore sunset tonight."

"I'll have it done by four, then," Ole agreed. He didn't know why he agreed. Saltwater-drenched sand coated the oil pan and crankcase like sprayed-on texture. Just cleaning that off took a good hour. And then there were the constant interruptions of his friends.

"Hey there, Ole," said Frank, moseying into his shop with a beer and a shit-faced grin. "I see you're workin' on a motorcycle."

"No shit, Sherlock, what was your first clue." Ole didn't even look up. He had the old engine off now and was cleaning everything up, hoping to make the 600 fit.

"Aw, Ole. Is that any way to talk to an old friend?"

"You can call me friend again when you pay me for that transmission I put on your Olds."

"Pay you? It went out last week."

"I put it in four years ago."

"Has it been that long?"

"Yeah, I been countin' the days. Here, help me slide this engine in here."

"Whooee, that's a big one." Frank sidled over and helped Ole lift the engine on a chain and they lowered it slowly. "Transmission gonna fit?"

"I'll make it fit."

Untruer words were never spoken. That was the hard part. About noon their friend Paul Allison ventured in, beer in hand. "Wahtcha doin'? Workin' on a motorcycle?"

"No," Ole answered, perturbed at yet another stupid question. "We're makin' a porno movie – an' Frank's playin' the part a the girl."

"Oh? And who's the unlucky guy?" Paul guffawed.

"Asshole." Ole slithered his gaze to Paul. "Whaddya know 'bout puttin' a 600 engine into a 250 Yamaha."

"'Bout as much as makin' a porno movie," said Paul.

"Thanks a lot."

Three heads trying to figure out the problem turned into four when sixteen-year-old Billy stuck his head into Ole's shop. "Hey. Whatcha doin'? Workin' on a motorcycle?"

"No," answered Paul. "We're makin' a porno movie."

"Really? Where's the girl? Can I watch?"

"Frank's playin' the girl," said Paul.

"Yuck. Hey . . . " Billy looked at everyone holding beers. "Can I have one too?"

"Now you know you're too young for that," said Frank.

"I've drank beer before. Lotsa times."

"Give him a beer," Ole sighed. "Tell you Ma

though, Billy, we'll kill ya."

"Okay," Billy said brightly as Frank handed him a beer, figuring the beer was worth it. Billy took the church key hanging from a string on Ole's workbench to remove the cap and sipped. "I've worked on motorcycles before. Can I help?"

"You can try," said Ole.

They all surrounded the bike to discuss the best way to make everything fit when a blue-eyed, curly blond-haired man stuck his head into Ole's shop. "Say, someone said I could get a beer here. Any chance of that?"

Too busy to be bothered, Ole pointed to the battered, old refrigerator. "Help yourself."

The man opened the refrigerator, found a beer inside, found the church key, and opened it and sipped. "Ohh . . . Tastes good."

"You know anything 'bout mountin' an engine?"

"Maybe." The man took another sip of his beer and came over. "Aw. You have it all wrong there. You're going to have to lower it a good inch to get everything to link up."

"Well can you help?" Ole asked, perturbed about advice with no action.

The man sipped his beer and set it on the workbench then got down on his knees beside them. "Let's see what we can do."

By three they had the engine mounted, gassed up, and Billy took it for a spin, romping over a bump on the way toward the covered bridge and the track. "Careful now, I don't wanna have t' go fixin' it after you wreck it," Ole called after him.

The stranger, also named Paul, sat with them through a couple more beers as they talked about booze, barbeque, and broads. Everyone bragged about the broads part – more like lied – and the handsome stranger just sat there, eyes twinkling, enjoying the companionship.

When Ed came back for his bike, Billy still wasn't

back. "You let *him* have it? It'll come back in pieces."

"No it won't," said Frank. "We promised him another beer if he brought it back okay."

"Brother."

Sure enough, Billy was soon there, beaming brightly. "Boy that's fast. I bet I could jump ten cars with that."

"Better not," Ed growled, switching places on the bike. "Need a ride back to the set, Paul?"

"Paul?" asked their friend Paul.

"No, not you," Ed growled.

The stranger Paul finished his beer and rose. "Sure. I'll take a ride. He climbed on back and held on as Ed wound up the engine and they crossed the bridge, the sweet, smooth sound of massive power echoing all the way to the other end.

"That's funny, meetin' somebody else named Paul," said Paul. "They ain't too many fellas named Paul round here."

"Thank God," said Ole, and to that they all agreed.

Missing

"What's the matter, you idiot? Can't you get anything right?" Rose waved the twelve-pack of toilet paper like an ancient Amazon warrior holding the head of a freshly killed enemy. "I send you in with a grocery list of items. And you come back with this? Don't you know what T.P. means?" She threw the toilet paper in his face and kept driving down the road.

"Hey Mom, can we stop so I can pee?" Jimmy had stopped playing Angry Birds just long enough to ask while Marie, just finishing her first year in college, and Lynn, a disturbingly early budding fifteen-year-old, primped themselves for whatever boys – or grown men – they might be able to pick up on their vacation.

Rose held the wheel steady and peered down the road, firm and determined. "We just stopped an hour ago."

"But Mom . . . "

Rose slammed on the brakes and the side of Harry's head slammed the dash – he'd unbuckled his seatbelt to hand the toilet paper to Lynn in the back seat – then he rubbed the welt Rose had given him with the toilet paper as blood oozed from his nose after hitting the dash.

"Oh, stop faking it, Harry," Rose said, doing her best to ignore him and deride him at the same time. "And stop the pity party. You make me want to vomit."

Harry wiped the blood on his jeans.

"And stop wiping that blood all over those jeans. Do you know how hard it is to get those stains out?"

"If I'm faking it, then why am I bleeding?"

Rose slammed the brakes and Harry's head hit the dash again. He asked Lynn to hand him one of the rolls of toilet paper and used half of it to stanch the bleeding.

Harry didn't recall bleeding this much since an outlaw motorcycle gang had beaten him half to death and he had turned state's evidence and entered the federal Witness Protection Program.

***

Rose handed him another grocery list the next day. They were just coming up on the first town in Missouri and the dead raccoons along the road were already turning into armadillos. "Gee, isn't that fascinating," Harry said, watching what resembled miniature suitcases as they passed. He was sitting in the back seat by himself while Lynn and Jimmy occupied the third seat, fighting over leg space.

"Hey Mom, can I get a tattoo?" Marie asked from the front seat as they merged onto the main drag and drove past tattoo and piercing parlors mixed in with gentlemen's clubs.

"No, it's a good way to get a disease."

Marie gazed longingly at the tattoo parlors as prostitutes and drug addicts emerged from the gentlemen's clubs and entered the same place where Marie wanted to get a tattoo. "No it's not. You get diseases by having unprotected sex. By . . . "

Marie went into such intricate detail about foreplay and bodily fluids that Harry wondered how she had ever had time to study at all during her freshman year.

Once they passed the gentlemen's clubs and tattoo and piercing parlors and entered the regular business district, Rose slammed on the brakes, this time smashing the left side of Harry's face against Marie's headrest.

"What's that noise back there?" Rose asked.

"It was just my face, dear. Or what's left of it."

"No great loss, then," Rose said as she whipped into the strip mall parking lot. "Here's a Walgreen's. Let's see if you can get it right this time."

"Yes, dear."

"And don't use that smart-ass tone of voice with me."

"Yes, dear." As Rose simmered to a furious boil behind the wheel, Harry entered the brightly lit drugstore and went straight to the cigarette counter. "Old Gold kings, please." He paid for the cigarettes separately because he didn't want Rose to see them on the cash register receipt. She always inspected and double-checked everything he did – even the narrative he had written of his previous marriage when she forced him to pay for an annulment so they could get married in the Catholic Church where she piously played the organ and piano every Saturday. Rose had said if she ever found him smoking again she would file for a divorce. Harry wondered how Father Schumer would accept *that* as grounds for annulment since the good priest smoked like a train himself.

After he bought his cigarettes and went into the men's room to shove them down his pants, Harry bought everything on the list – including toothpaste – and returned to the car. Rose looked into the bag as he handed it to her.

"What! Toothpaste? I wanted toilet paper, you idiot!"

"I'm sorry, dear."

"What did I say about using that tone of voice with me?"

"Sorry. I thought it was toothpaste you wanted since you were so upset about my buying toilet paper yesterday."

"That was yesterday," Rose screamed. "This is today. Don't you know what day it is, you fool? Do I need to put you in a rest home? Because of your thoughtlessness and stupidity, I had to give Marie a fifty-dollar bill to buy toothpaste at that convenience store at the campground last night. By the way, where's my change, Marie?" Rose asked, holding out her hand.

Marie looked at her mother, the elf tattoo beside her right eye smiling back.

"I'm sorry, dear. I just thought we already had plenty of toilet paper," said Harry.

"Well, first of all, you can't think. You're totally inept at it. And second of all, you've been wasting all kinds of toilet paper by wiping all that blood off your ugly face."

"Well, maybe if you'd stop slamming on the brakes and smashing my skull I couldn't bleed so much, dear."

"Do you want to argue? Is that what you want? Because if you want, we can argue all day. And where will that put us? That will make us late for our vacation. Is that what you want?" Rose turned to Marie in the seat beside her and then to the kids in the back. "What do you think, kids? Your stepfather wants to do nothing but argue and make us late for our vacation."

"You suck, Harry," said Jimmy.

"Yeah, Harry. You suck," said Marie.

Lynn, the one kid of Rose's Harry could tolerate, smiled and said nothing.

"Well maybe I can take this toothpaste back and exchange it for toilet paper," Harry offered.

"It's too late now. And it's all your fault. Get in the car before you make us even later."

"Yes, dear."

"What did I say?"

"Yes, dear." After Harry handed Rose the bag and went around the van to the back door, waiting for Rose to turn her head around three times and puke green vomit, he realized he *really* needed a cigarette.

***

They were just coming up on Bentonville the next morning when Rose handed him another list. By then Marie had totally commandeered the front seat, waving at passing truckers who honked as they looked down at her overfilled sports bra and legs splayed across the dash, paying particular attention to her Daisy Dukes. "Hey Mom, you spose we'll find any hot guys this trip?"

Rose's warped grimace reflected in the mirror. "I don't *know*."

"There aren't any hot guys down here," Lynn said appraisingly. "They're all fat and ugly and look like they should be starring in *Duck Dynasty*."

"The *black* ones are okay though," Marie amended.

Harry wondered what was going through all three female minds as silence pervaded the van and Jimmy played Crazy Birds.

Rose had almost passed another Walgreen's when she remembered and slammed on her brakes. The impact of his skull against Marie's headrest resulted in a mild concussion, so a thrum filled Harry's head. He stumbled from the van into the Walgreen's and returned and handed his purchase to Rose who screeched the van tires as they left the parking lot.

They were just about to central Arkansas when Rose opened the bag. "Tampons? Tampons! What in the hell did you buy tampons for?"

"I'm sorry, dear. I just thought that, given your mood lately and everything, that when you wrote T.P. this time is must have been your time of month."

Lynn lifted a wise, knowing eyebrow as she whispered, "She's always like this."

"No I'm not."

"Not when she's asleep, she's not." Marie giggled and waved at a honking semi.

The thumping started a little south of Little Rock and continued all the way to the Texas line. Harry had been enjoying the Southern scenery out the other window so it was the other side of his skull that was concussed when Rose slammed the brakes this time.

"Go see what that racket is back there," Rose demanded.

Knowing the command in her loving tone of voice was for him, Harry got out and went around and saw the bolt had come off the spare holder so the wheel was flapping back and forth. He opened the back door and found an extra bolt and wrench in the toolbox, then remembering his cigarettes and matches in his shaving kit, grabbed those too. He twisted the bolt on securely. Then, admiring a job well done, he removed the cellophane and paper from the cigarettes and put one in his mouth and lit it. The nicotine rush went straight to his brain so he could finally think again.

The front passenger door closed and Marie came around and gawked at him. Today's tissue-thin Daisy Dukes were even shorter than yesterday's and she apparently wore no underwear, making her a perfect match for the gentleman's club billboard just behind her. "Mom, Harry's smoking," Marie yelled.

"What?" Rose screamed.

"Harry's smoking, Mom. He has a cigarette in his mouth and everything."

"Get in the van, Marie," Rose ordered.

Marie got in and shut the door and screeching tires sent the van off into the distance.

Harry smoked his cigarette down to the filter then used it to light another. Rose had married him for his money, Harry mused. And despite her vigilant spying on his 401K balance and stocks, even she didn't know the true extent of his holdings. Comsat, Amazon, Microsoft, Berkshire-Hathaway. He'd bought into all of them heavily. Plus he had plenty of investments safely tucked away in Switzerland and the Caymans. And he could hide out indefinitely in a cabin in the Oregon Coastal Range she knew nothing about.

Several cars passed as Harry continued to smoke. After his third cigarette he turned and held out his thumb and the first vehicle approaching, a conventional semi, hit its jake brake and rolled to a stop. Just before he climbed in, Harry spotted a dead armadillo along the road. He removed his Hawaiian shirt and soaked it with armadillo blood then tossed the shirt into the ditch. The driver, week-old stubble covering his jaw and a cigarette dangling from his lip, eyed Harry as he climbed up into the cab. "Break down, didja?"

"Naw, just travelin'," Harry said, climbing into the seat and buckling his belt.

"Travelin', huh?" The driver eyed Harry's ARKANSAS, THE NATURAL STATE T-shirt. "Where to?"

"Central Oregon Coast," Harry chirped like a parakeet finally freed from his cage.

"Why, ain't you in luck." The driver hit his four-ways and eased the truck into gear and pulled back onto the road. "Ah's takin' a loada swingin' beef to Newport then backhaulin' a loada oysters outa South Bend to Chi-Town."

"Newport's perfect," said Harry. "There's a place you can drop me off right on Highway 20."

***

About ten miles down the road, Rose did a U-turn and headed back.

"Aw Mom," Marie said, checking herself in the mirror. "You aren't going back for Harry, are you? He's such a fuddy duddy."

"Yeah, fuddy duddy," said Jimmy over the chaos of Angry Birds.

Lynn said nothing.

"Well you don't expect *me* to pay for this vacation, do you?" No response from the kids, she continued. "He *does* make quite a bit of money," she admitted.

Rose slowed the van to a crawl when they reached the spot where she had left Harry. Traffic whizzed past on the four-lane, swerving and hoking. "Where could he *be*?"

"Hey, there's his shirt, Mom," said Marie.

"Where?"

"Right there."

Rose pulled up alongside Harry's crumpled Hawaiian shirt in the ditch. Marie piled out and returned with it, holding it at arm's length. "Ew, Mom. It's all full of blood."

As traffic whizzed past, Rose wondered what had happened to Harry – and his wallet. "I spose I'd better call the state trooper and tell them his wallet . . . or he's . . . missing."

A half-hour later an Arkansas state trooper was grimly holding Harry's shirt and shaking his head. He'd called in search teams and dogs to comb the area.

"Well, what do you think happened to him?" Rose asked.

"I'm afraid he may have met a bad end, ma'am."

"You don't think – "

The trooper nodded slowly.

That was when Rose really started to panic. Harry, the man who had been so kind, so gentle, so understanding, so free with his money, was gone. She and the kids joined in the search until nightfall then continued the next day. But they found nothing. There was no sign of Harry at all.

"The FBI is joining the search since he may have been kidnapped and taken across the state line." The state police reginal commander nodded at the beginnings of Texas just over the next rise. "The forensics report should be back from the state crime lab in a couple days. That will at least allow us to make a positive ID if we ever unearth his remains."

"Oh my God." Rose crumpled into pieces at the thought of losing Harry. Of no longer having him there to rely on. His smile, his caring touch, his steady paycheck. "I wonder what became of him. What's going to become of us?"

"I'm sorry, ma'am," the regional commander said. "Like I said, I'm afraid he may have met a bad end."

***

"So we going through Nevada?" Harry asked. He was behind the wheel, his nearly forgotten years of truck driving coming back to him.

"We could, I spose," said the driver, tilting his cowboy hat to eye Harry as Tex Ritter crooned on the A.M. "Just pick up I-80 a little ahead here."

"Do they still have those – "

"Yep. Certain counties."

"Will we be going through any of those certain counties?"

A sly smile crept across the truck cab to Harry. "Ah spect so."

Harry beamed. "This is going to be a great trip."

***

"We're calling off the search. I'm sorry, Mrs. Griggs," the FBI agent said.

Rose drew in jagged sobs as the true impact finally hit her. Harry gone. Her husband gone. Her life partner. Gone forever.

"We can only assume Mr. Griggs is dead, Mrs. Griggs. Maybe you'll want to make some sort of final arrangements – minus the body, of course."

"Rose's face blanched at the thought. "I guess I'll have to do that, won't I?"

"Yes, Mrs. Griggs. I guess you will."

And then the state crime lab report came in the next day.

"Armadillo?"

The same FBI agent who had told her the day before to give up all hope, that all was lost, that her husband was likely pushing up daisies or whatever else grows in Arkansas, confirmed the verdict. "Yes. This gives us some slim hope that he's still alive."

"Well why would there be armadillo blood on his shirt?"

"There could be any of a number of reasons, Mrs. Griggs. Maybe he was abducted and the kidnappers wanted to throw us off his trail. Or maybe – "

"Yes? Yes?"

"Maybe Mr. Griggs staged his own murder – to make it look like someone had killed him."

"Why on earth would he do that?"

After meeting with her over the past couple days, the agent tried his best to keep a stone face. "I'm not sure why, Mrs. Griggs," he said, though he knew exactly why.

***

"Boy, that was a great time, wasn't it?" They were just pulled out of Battle Mountain, the Santa Rosas looming to the northwest.

The deep, satisfied look on the driver's face was his only answer.

"When ya think we'll get to Oregon? I can hardly wait to see my friends there."

"Should be in a day," the driver said, covering his face with his cowboy hat and settling into a well-earned snooze.

***

"All I can say is, Mrs. Griggs, return home and wait until the kidnappers contact you."

"Aw, does that mean our vacation's over?" asked Jimmy.

"I'm afraid so." Rose lovingly stroked the top of his buzz cut.

"And I didn't even get to meet any guys," said Marie.

"I'll miss him," said Lynn.

"I'm sorry, folks," the agent said. "We'll keep doing everything from our end we can. We'll notify you the moment we hear anything."

And with that, they packed up and returned to Iowa.

***

"Thanks." Harry climbed down and shut the cab door and waved as the driver headed east on Highway 20, smoke trailing from the stacks. The first thing Harry did was go to the Bank of the West in Toledo where he still had a substantial account. He wrote a check for $50,000 cash under another assumed name – Gary Harrison – then went to breakfast at The Timbers. Then he bought a faded-red 1985 Dodge pickup and drove it straight to Elk City. His twelve-by-twenty log cabin was still standing, a testament to the entire summer he had spent building it.

Billy and Frank were there, along with Paul and J.R. Paul had a big bonfire going at his place next door and they all took a log and caught up on old times.

"What kind of blood?" Billy asked incredulously as he finished his beer.

"Armadillo."

"Don't see too many of them 'round here," said Frank.

"Cougar, maybe," said J.R.

"They's too quick to be road kill though," said Paul.

"Not if I'm drivin', said J.R.

***

"Ashes to ashes, dust to dust," the minister intoned as Harry's Hawaiian shirt was lowered in a small casket into his grave.

"That's so sad. That's all that's left of him," said Rose.

"It's okay, Mom," said Marie. "You'll find another guy."

"But no one like Harry," she wailed. "There's no one else with his money anywhere."

Night Talks With My Brother

The image is frozen in my mind forever like a photo from an ancient Brownie camera. As we say good-bye, my brother flashes a gang sign at me, no doubt an homage to the rebellious black leather jacket I wear well into my forties. The rest of the family offers kisses and hugs. My L.L. Bean-accoutered brother flashes a gang sign. So I do what's natural. I flip him off and climb in my 1950 Studebaker pickup and don't see him again until my second wedding three years later.

***

My brother passed away August 25, 2014, the day before I was to start teaching a new college class. Quite frankly, finances also prevented me from going to his funeral on the East Coast. I was eight years into a newspaper job that hadn't given me a raise for six years, so college teaching was really a way to subsidize my position as a newspaper staff writer. I also felt a certain ambiguity about my brother who had always referred to me as his 'little' brother, even as we both approached retirement. I loved my brother. I always did and I always will. It was only natural though that one would react, internally at least, to a lifetime of imperious put-downs and name calling and shame.

***

When we were young, it was at night when the truth would

come out, in fits and jerks, in his words so honest they fazed me into silence. When we were alone, when no one else could witness it, my brother would babble his guts out to the stars and icy wind seeping through the cracks between the boards of our unsided home stop a hill in a small town in southeastern South Dakota. That was the first time I remember my brother talking that way – open, honest, his words unencumbered with vain witticism.

I was three when I first remember it. My fourth birthday was the next day.

"I can't wait for you to see what I made you for your birthday tomorrow," David said excitedly.

His spirit caught me up as well. "What is it?"

"I can't tell you now. But you'll see."

At my birthday party the next day, I remember our border collie Laddie standing next to me as I opened my Christmas presents outside by the trellis already covered with vines in the tender May warmth. The first one I opened was the sailboat. I started to play with the boat right away, asking if I could take it down to the creek and see how far it could sail.

"You'd better not do that," Dad said. "It will probably just float on down the creek to the river then out to sea."

"So the creek runs to the river?" I looked in wonder at the silver trickle slicing past our yard down the hill to the wetland below. And, yes, I suppose it led from there to the sea.

"All creeks and rivers do," my father said.

"Can I float it just a little way?" I begged. The tears are still in my eyes in the picture I have of me holding my birthday cake as Laddie stood beside me in front of the trellis.

"Oh, I guess so," Dad said, giving in.

"Aren't you going to open my present too?" my brother asked anxiously.

"You'd better open your brother's present, don't you think?" Mother said, putting her hand on my shoulder.

I wanted to put my boat in the water, though, and since I was the youngest and the 'baby' in the family, it was my tears that won out. Only after playing with my boat all that afternoon and my big surprise present, a Radio Flyer wagon in which my brother and his friends would push me at breakneck speed downhill so I would continually crash laughing into the creek bed below, did my brother again ask me to open my present from him, which I did. It was a cross made of popsickle sticks, embedded in plaster of Paris, JESUS written horizontally and SAVES vertically so both words shared the S.

"Do you like it?" my brother asked excitedly.

"I guess so," I said. What else could I say. I was four. And a Jesus Saves cross wasn't a hoot in a holler compared to a wooden sailboat or a Radio Flyer wagon.

After that, I was always the 'little brother'. Maybe even the spoiled little brother. From that point on, my brother was always quick to compare how many pieces of candy I got to how many he received. How many Christmas presents did he get compared to how many I received.

When we moved from our house in town to our ancestral farm in 1958, that distance between us grew. I was but five while my brother was twelve. I was still a child – a mere baby. My brother, though, was expected to work. Drop bales down the hole from door in the hay loft, break them apart, and feed and water and milk the cattle. He had to herd them too, going to get them every night after school from our summer range a half-mile to the east along the Big Sioux River to the barn where he would milk them then herd them back even as the ponderosa windbreak to the west side of our house drank the sun through their nettles. Then he would feed and water the hogs and chickens, and if it were summer, help plow the field and bale. By the time he reached sixteen, my brother had learned to hate farming and our father who beat him bloody one night in the kitchen for no reason. David, who was big enough so he could have defended himself, just stood there and took it as our father shoved his head against a photo of our ancestral home in Norway, breaking the frame. The picture was one of a set of four and I still have the other three. My brother signed up with the Navy Reserve the next day.

***

The next night I most remember talking with my brother was just before he shipped off to Vietnam. The Navy, my brother's ticket out of an abusive, poverty-stricken adolescence, would send him to a Seabee unit in Danang where he would have a daily dosage of hundred-degree heat in the summer and monsoons in the winter and Agent Orange year round so he would die prematurely at 68 after more than two years of heart attacks and strokes and leukemia.

"I'll miss you, Mike," David.

I lay there stunned. Had he really said that? Had my brother really told me he would miss me? "I'll miss you too, Dave." My words drifted off into dark silence.

"You know, I might not come back." A choking sigh punctuated his words.

I looked to the Jesus Saves cross on the dressing table silhouetted in the cold, white, rising full moon. "You'll come back."

"How do you know that?" he asked brokenly.

"I'll pray that you do."

That was enough to settle him into sleep so he could catch his plane the next morning.

***

My brother never did come back to South Dakota. He met a good-looking blond at a bowling alley in Jersey and once he saw her in a bikini at the shore that was it. No more farming. No more memories of poverty. No more South Dakota. His life took one road and mine took another.

Our last night talk was in a motel room in Drummond, Montana, while we were on vacation in 2007. Just before that my brother had encouraged me to

167

proposition a girl he believed was a hooker (she probably was) in a room just down from the two my brother and his wife and I had taken. David was sorely disappointed when I didn't try to "date" her.

He came into my room and laid on my king-size bed and asked me to lie there too so we could talk. It seemed awkward at first, but for my brother it was like the 'good-old days' – those nights when we talked about birthdays and leaving home and which girls were cute and which ones to stay away from. We agreed that I hadn't done a very good job picking a second wife while he had done a good job picking his first.

That night he thanked me for paying back a loan he had made to me and for being his brother. I was surprised and taken aback. It had been years since he had been so honest with me. That was our last real face-to-face talk together.

I stopped by that same motel on my way out to the Northwest Coast this summer, not to stay there but to see if the motel was still there. It was. The same faded paint and railing backdropped by a gray, cloud-shrouded mountain rearing up just behind. I looked at the second-floor balcony rooms where we had stayed. I thought I remembered which were ours, but wasn't sure. It didn't matter though.

The point was that that I had remembered.

One Horse, Franny, and The Drummer
Deadwood, South Dakota
July 1981

One Horse was feelin' his oats – and his Miller Lite – as the No. 10 house band struck up another tune. They weren't a bad band, really. And the fact that they played *Amy*, his favorite song, by Pure Prairie League in just about every set didn't hurt a bit either. As the rhythm guitar played his riff, the voices blended together, harmonizing on the title refrain, "*Amy* . . . "

He'd just sold a good-sized load to the mill – sixteen-foot ponderosas straight as an arrow that commanded a premium price. Sheba, his skidding horse so beloved by him that he had received 'One Horse' as an appellation, had balked at first on pulling such heavy logs, but he had coaxed her, sweet talked her, and finally whipped her to get the logs to the landing. When he was done, though, and after he'd taken the load to the mill and cashed his $300 check, he fixed her a batch of molasses-soaked oats.

And now here he was, watching the band as silhouettes drifted in through the bright summer outside, denizens of Deadwood finding their rightful place at myriad stools and tables purchased by years of usufruct, of elbows bent and shots pitched down and alcohol-fueled fights started and ended until everyone settled into a mantra of the same boozy buzz.

One of the shadows, tall, weaved through the light not a little unlike Jesus coming to earth on a holy beam – or maybe like a Martian on a spaceship. Standing before him, weaving in a small circle, she fell into the stool beside him. Brown-eyed Franny looked at him accusingly, mockingly, maybe revengefully even. "So where were you?"

He just remembered then that he'd promised to pick her up right after he'd cashed his check from the mill. They were supposed to have gone to The Sluice for chicken enchiladas and margaritas. The only real date he'd ever had with her, and he'd blown it. "Aw, I'm sorry, babe." One Horse patted the stool beside him. "It slipped my mind. Why dontcha set down here an' I'll getcha a beer – an' maybe a little shota Jack t' go along?"

Swaying in circles as she decided between staying mad and having a drink, Franny acquiesced to the latter and plopped into the stool. After One Horse ordered them up a round of beers and shots, she downed hers and pushed it back toward Gary the bartender for another then washed it down with half her beer. "'Sanks for the drink." Her eyes lifted like boulders toward him, trying to decide if she were still angry. "I'm still pissed," she admitted. "Get me drunk though, an' I'll forget it."

Since she was a good twenty sheets to the wind already, One Horse wondered how drunk that would be.

A couple of gays came into the bar, city boys with their skintight leather pants and colorful shirts, chatting it up as they sat together – nestled would have been a better way to put it – and ordered something pink with umbrellas and giggled into their glasses.

One Horse downed his fresh shot so fast he hadn't prepared himself for its bite, gagged a second, then washed it down with half a can of beer and thumped his chest.

"God you're gettin' to be a lightweight," said

Franny, disgusted.

"It ain't the booze." He nodded to the gay couple. "It's them."

Franny turned in her stool and waved at the gay boys. "Hi."

The pair looked at her, trying to decide whether were making fun of them, and deciding not, sallied over with their drinks. "I'm Evan," said the slightly taller of the two, dark hair, narrow sideburns, a meticulously managed three-day growth, and a lingering scent of two-hundred-dollar cologne. He could have modeled for any magazine in the country. "This is Pauley."

Pauley, a bit slighter but toned, had gay California surfer boy written all over him. "Hi," Pauley echoed, shaking hands first with Franny then One Horse as he daintily sipped his drink. "You folks must be locals," said Pauley, dangling his pinky. "You look so, so *Western*."

One Horse couldn't decide if Pauley were making fun of him or not, but shook hands with him anyway. Pauley had a surprisingly strong grip, so One Horse reserved his disparaging remarks about the pair's sexuality for later.

"I've lived here twelve years," said Franny, then turning to One Horse, "And him? He was born from the knothole of a tree. That's why all he ever does is sit there like a bump on a log and mope."

Pauley waved his finger. "Mopey, mopey, mopey." He and Evan laughed, chatted it up with Franny, asking about the best restaurants and motels and whether there were any with whirlpools, then returned to their stools.

"That wasn't very nice," said Franny, edging her stool away from him.

"What wasn't very nice."

"The way you acted toward them. You were rude."

One Horse shrugged, lifted his beer and looked in the bar mirror at a man he didn't recognize, and finished his beer and ordered another. "I hate fags."

"Shh. They'll hear you."

171

"I don't care," said One Horse, louder this time. "I hate fags."

Franny glared at him. "I can't believe you."

"Oh? Then believe this." He leaned around her and called down to the pair a few stools away. "I hate fags."

Pauley and Evan looked hurt at him at first, then deciding he was just like countless others they'd met, turned to each other.

Gary clanked One Horse's beer in front of him. "That's the last you're gettin' tonight. You've had enough. One more remark like that and you're 86'd. They're customers too."

One Horse sipped his beer guardedly, biding Gary's admonition.

"So what would you think if I decided to take up with a girl?"

"You? A girl?" One Horse laughed. "Come on."

"Why not?" Franny leaned toward him. "Maybe there's nothing I'd love better than curling up next to a nice, warm female body."

"Hah. You'd never do that in a million years."

The band finished its set, and the lead singer, a rangy Billy Gibbons look-a-like, stepped up to the mic. "Sorry, folks. That's gonna have to be our last set. Our bass player's feelin' poorly an' we just can't continue without a bass line."

The crowd groaned – had the band been bad they would have cheered – and Gary crossed his arms angrily. "See what I get fer two grand a week?"

"Yeah," One Horse agreed, nudging his empty toward Gary. "Kin I have another if I behave myself?"

Gary pondered his request for a moment. "*If* you behave yourself."

Franny plopped out of her stool and went to the band that was just starting to put its gear away. She passed by a second later. "I'm gonna grab my bass."

"Oh here we go now. This is gonna be interestin'."

A beer later Franny was onstage, plugging the

hookup from the amp into her guitar. The band conferenced a little, and above them lifted Franny's voice, "I want somethin' fast, hard, and clean." The band whipped right into *The Devil Came Down to Georgia*, substituting Charlie Daniels' original version of "son-of-a-bitch" instead of "son-of-a-gun", and Owen the fiddler played it hot. The crowd went nuts, flooding the dance floor, jitterbugging like bunches of boxelder bugs butt-loving in a blizzard.

As they sequed into *Orange Blossom Special*, One Horse couldn't help but notice Franny eyeing the drummer, a short little brunette of a gal, maybe four-ten tops. She was so short he hadn't even seen her above her drum kit, but she was banging the pots like she'd been born with them.

Franny was playing it hot too, working her magic on the bass line. By the end of the set the regular bass player would be fired and she and the rest of the band would go on the road for six months. As Franny leaned into her ax, she smiled at the drummer, her total opposite. Franny was easily five-eleven, maybe pushing six foot. But her surging bass line matched the drummer's solo so well the band parted for everyone to see. The drummer shook her head like a maniac, hair blurring as she banged the pots, then Franny took away the solo, throbbing her riffs like a Harley in second gear. They exchanged solos, going back and forth, LA-studio quality sounds that had the dance floor a jumpin' and a jivin'. The rest of the band jumped in to finish the number, and as she did her last lick, Franny bent over and French kissed the drummer, tongue so far inside her mouth her cheek looked like a garter snake swallowin' a bullfrog. The crowd went nuts on that too, and the leader stepped up to the mic. "What kin ah say, folks. We're in love with our music."

As the crowd roared, One Horse groaned, settlin' back in his stool like he'd been shot. As dusk drenched Deadwood Gulch in pearly twilight, it seemed like everyone was pairin' up. Where before there had been tables of guys and gals there were now couples. Franny and the drummer were paired off, it seemed, and then there were the gay boys. And here he was, One Horse, in love with his horse.

"You sure blew that one," said Gary, setting another beer in front of him. "It's on the house. You look like you need it."

"Thanks," he said, feeling the humiliation heaped upon him. Hopefully, when he got back to his cabin on Yellow Creek, Sheba would be in the mood.

One of the Guys

They had just about framed the first house when Bud Spate shot himself in the femoral artery with a nail gun. And wasn't that something – Bud lying there screaming – a sixteen-penny nail shot clean into his leg, lodged somewhere against the bone, blood spraying like the fire hydrants they opened up every August to keep the South Side kids busy and out of trouble. What was really bad was Bud's scream, an unholy wail sounding like two cats with their tails tied together. It was so exciting no one thought right away to call 911.

Once they did, the paramedics were there in minutes, careening over discarded cutoffs and the ubiquitous house wrap. As they deliberated whether to pull the nail out, two-sixty Bud howling like a monkey and curled up like roadkill so it took eight men to straighten him out and strap him to the gurney, they wisely decided to leave it in. The nail was partially blocking the blood flow from his artery, keeping him from bleeding to death.

As the ambulance careened away, tires picking up God-knows-how-many nails, the contractor crossed the muddy job site, shaking his head. Louie took a pack of Camels from his pocket and flicked one into his mouth and took out an ancient Ronson and lit it, the slow burn and wispy smoke tracing his thoughts as he looked at the nicely framed house standing there like an embryo waiting to be born. "Nice job, boys. Nice job." Louis took another drag, cigarette embering his pondering. "Too bad about Bud."

"Yeah, too bad about Bud," said Larry.

"Real bad," said Matt.

"I hope he pulls through okay. Bud's a nice guy," said Paul.

"Well . . . " Louie decided. "Might just as well pack it up. Runnin' a three-man framin' crew is like invitin' a one-arm man to a round of golf. And from the looks of it, Bud's gonna be laid low for a while. Why don't ya pack it in an' head home. I'll call ya back once I hire a fourth crew member."

"That damn Bud," said Larry.

"Screwball."

"Jackass."

The imprecations worsened as Louie finished his cigarette, flicked the butt into a dirt pile, and drove off.

***

No one expected Louie to find Bud's replacement right away so they'd spent the better part of the night at the Corner Pocket playing darts and seeing who could slam down the most boilermakers. So when Louie called them back to work the next morning they slithered back to the job site like something that had crawled out from under a rock. Larry, bald as a Corner Pocket cue ball even at twenty-eight, had to lean against his pickup to keep from falling over. Matt wasn't much better, leaning his lanky frame against Larry's truck, steaming cup of coffee and cigarette jerking him awake. Paul was last to get to the site, but in a far better mood because he was still drunk.

When Louie rolled up to the site in his crew cab with a statuesque blond in the passenger seat, they all came to attention like Parris Island recruits. Louie killed the engine and stepped out and the girl got out from the other side. Her long blond hair was pulled back in a ponytail, iceberg-blue eyes piercing. She was a tall drink of water at all of six feet, so her 44Ds seemed almost normal. As she smiled then turned and bent over to tie her shoelace, more than one member of the crew seriously considered making a wax impression of her ass to mount on an altar and start a new religion.

"This is Carissa Struthers," Louie said, crossing the weed-strewn lot to introduce her.

Larry, Matt, and Paul exchanged glances of doubt.

"Carissa graduated from a construction trades program out in Denver an' she's been workin' jobs 'round the country. Thought she'd move back to Illinois to live with her folks since her dad's been ailin'. She's pretty near journeyman." Even old Louie's eyes were drawn down Carissa's frame past her tool belt. "Maybe I should say journeywoman."

"Whatever you say, boss," said Larry, running his hand over his head as though he still had a full head of hair.

"Sure thing," added five-eleven Matt, who had to look up into Carissa's sky-blue eyes.

"Glad to meetcha." Paul beamed effusively, tripping over a two-by-four and falling flat on his face.

As soon as Louie left, the jokes and innuendos started right away. First was Larry who shook his head and went up behind her. "Aw, now, there ya go, your tool belt all loose like that. You're gonna lose your framin' hammer that way." He sauntered up behind her, and to the surprise of even Matt and Paul who was still dusting himself off from his face plant, put his arms around her and undid her tool belt and cinched it a notch tighter, trying to goose her. If he'd been tall enough, he would have succeeded.

Carissa turned her smile to him, unfazed. "Thanks. I was wondering if that wasn't a little loose." She looked from man to man, then took them in with one sweeping gaze of her twinkling aqua eyes. "Well, should we get to work?"

**

Even sober and not hung over, it would have been hard to keep up with her. She worked like a man – a young, virile man loaded with testosterone. They finished framing the house by early afternoon then moved on to the next unit.

"I'm not so sure about that deck plate," said Carissa, hands on hips as she studied the board like a seasoned contractor. She pulled a level from her belt and bent over and laid it on the board. "Just as I thought. We're gonna have to shim up this sidewall maybe a half inch to make her level." Still bent over, she turned to the crew whose six eyeballs were glued to her rear like flies to flypaper. "Enjoyin' the view, guys?"

Matt, the lady killer of the bunch if there was one, smiled and stoked his beard. "Yeah, but not long enough."

"Don't you worry," Carissa reassured him with a smile. "I'm sure we'll all be doin' our share of bendin' and stoopin' before this job is over."

***

By week's end, under Carissa's leadership, they'd framed every unit in the development so they had to call the roofing contractor early. Louie was so happy with the work they'd done he gave them all a hundred-dollar bonus.

Carissa had taken all their jokes and sexual bantering in stride, often joking back. Do you have a nut that could fit around this? Matt asked her, holding out a foot-long bolt a couple inches wide. I might find one in the toolbox on my truck, she said. Then you might be able to handle me, said Matt. All Carissa did was laugh.

Any other woman would have sued the company for gross sexual harassment – with an emphasis on gross. But Carissa took it all without batting a baby-blue eye, laughing and joking right along with them. As a result, by the time Louie handed them their checks at the end of the week, the whole crew had fallen in love with her.

Larry and Paul both stepped aside to let Matt have first shot at her. Besides, Matt was the only one of them that wasn't married. They were at the Corner Pocket, Carissa racking the balls up then clearing the table, spinning the ball in crazy bank shots most of them had only seen on TV. When she jumped the cue ball over another ball to sink the eight into the pocket, they all knew they were toast.

"How about dinner after this," asked Matt suavely, echoing the thoughts of every guy in the place who had been watching Carissa bend over for each shot.

She smiled down at him, as though considering. "I'd really like to, but some other time. My dad has an appointment at the VA clinic early tomorrow morning and Mom doesn't drive anymore. Thanks anyway."

"Oh, by the way, if you do decide to go out with one of us, maybe this will give you some ideas." Larry stepped between Carissa and Matt and handed her one of the filthiest smut magazines ever printed.

Carissa thumbed through it, noting bodies in improbable positions.

"They's even some pretty hot girl-on-girl action in there." Larry nodded like a fool. Even Matt and Paul turned red-faced at that.

"I see that," said Carissa, thumbing through the magazine with more than a passing interest, pausing on one page, then another, even turning the magazine so the half-sized centerfold spilled nearly to the floor. "*Very* interesting."

Matt, Paul, and even now Larry waited for her to rail at them, to cry out sexual harassment, but she tucked the magazine in the back of her jeans, a place where every man in the bar wanted to be. "Thanks." She smiled broadly and left.

"That was really stupid," Matt said to Larry as the three of them perched on their bar stools, not a lot unlike The Three Stooges.

"Whadya mean?" asked Larry. "She took everything good-naturedly."

"Ya know what she's gonna do with that magazine? First thing Monday mornin' she's gonna shove it right under Louie's nose and tell him to fire every one of our asses or she's gonna sue the company. Then, after we're fired, she'll probably sue anyway."

"She won't do that."

"Oh no? You just wait an' see." Matt finished his beer and slammed the empty on the bar. "First thing in the mornin', I'm gonna go to the union hall an' see what they got posted."

***

Since she'd had only a couple beers and hadn't capped her buzz off yet, Carissa stopped at the liquor store for a twelve-pack and a half-pint of Jack Daniel's. The hundred-dollar bonus and eighty-five bucks she'd won playing pool were burning a hole in her pocket, and she really would have liked to have stayed at the bar, but she needed to get home to check on her dad.

"Hi Pop," she said, streaming through the door and giving him a hug. "How's life treatin' ya."

"Well, you know . . . . " He looked down at his useless leg, an old war injury now finally taking its toll as he entered his last years. "Not worth a crap if ya wanna know the truth."

"Love ya, Pop." She bent over and hugged him again, so hard he squeaked like a squeak toy. As she stowed her twelve-pack in the refrigerator, her mother, not even half her size at barely five-three, worried her coffee cup in her hands. "Did you have a nice week at work honey?"

"Great." Carissa unscrewed her half pint of Jack, took a sip, and wiped her lip. "The guys are a gas."

Her mother's gaze flicked to the whiskey bottle in her daughter's hand then into her eyes. "I wish you wouldn't drink so much, dear."

"Aw Mom, ya know I'm no lightweight. Pop and I will be through this twelve and half-pint quicker 'n ya can say shit or shinola." She held out the bottle. "Wanna short snort, Ma?"

"No thank you, dear. You know me. One drop of alcohol and I just go crazy." She set her coffee cup on the counter and wrung her hands together. "Oh honey, if you

180

only knew how much I wish you could meet some nice, young man and get married and give us some grandchildren."

"Aw Ma, you know that'll never happen." She pulled the magazine from her back pocket and headed for the bathroom with her half-pint. "Ya know I'm not the marryin' kind."

Saga

Reporter Harrison Carter knew his editor had really lost his marbles when he gave him the story assignment. "A morning what?"

"A *moor*-ing stone," David repeated. David was the apotheosis of the small-town newspaper editor – short, fat, balding, ashtray filled with cigarettes. "Some farmer east of Viking Rapids says he has a buncha mooring stones in his pasture. Says the Vikings used 'em."

Harrison was visibly impressed. "The Minnesota Vikings were in Iowa?"

"Nooo," said David, sliding open his desk drawer and twisting the cap off his half-empty whiskey bottle to sweeten his coffee. "The *real* Vikings."

"Vikings. In Iowa." It only took Harrison a half-second to mull the idea over before he relegated the story to the category of the farmer who had written a four-foot shelf of prophecy dictated by God, the cat lady with 177 felines, and the man who had tracks from the Underground Railroad in his basement. "Is this guy nuts or something?"

"Prob'ly," David admitted. "Like most of the rest of our subscribers."

"All . . . right. So where's this guy at."

"First farm on the east side of town. Can't miss it. There's an old falling-down stone barn on the north side of the road."

***

Harrison called the farmer and made an appointment for that afternoon. It was late fall, and the sun was already falling toward the oak-rimmed bluffs to the west when he pulled into Olaf Olafson's yard, scattering a plethora of chickens and goats and pigs. A tall, broad, blond man emerged from the ancient farmhouse that hadn't seen a coat of pain for generations.

"Neinn," Olaf said to the goats trying to climb Harrison's Taurus. A billy got a good foothold and jumped on the hood, his yellow eyes peering satanically through the windshield. "Neinn, I said." Olaf swatted the billy who jumped bleating to the ground, leaving a dozen hoof-shaped dents in the hood. "Sorry 'bout that. He just likes to meet new fo'lk, I guess."

Harrison thought of protesting what was easily $1,200 in damage to his car until he saw Olaf easily stood six-eight and probably topped 375 – without an ounce of fat. "That's okay . . . I guess."

"I need to put them goats out in the hagi, I guess. They just get too rambunctious. Well let me show you what you drove out here for."

Olaf led him to a car-sized granite boulder on the edge of his pasture and pointed to a hole drilled into the rock. "You see? That's proof the Vikings was here."

To Harrison the hole looked something he could have made with his Black and Decker and a half-inch masonry bit. "Uh huh." Harrison looked at Olaf and wondered if he would be able to outrun him if he tried something really crazy. "I, uh, guess I don't exactly understand, sir."

"Vell, you see the Vikings would put their steel mooring pins into the rock to hold their ships. Then they would get off their boat and rape and pillage do all other sorts of viking things." Olaf pronounced boat like boa with a T on the end.

"I see." Harrison pulled out his camera and took a

picture of the hole in the boulder then bit his lip and nodded.

Olaf pointed at five more boulders across a deep valley to the north. "Do you notice anyting similar with dose boulders to this one?"

"They're at the same elevation?"

"Ja'," Olaf boomed so loudly he nearly bowled Harrison over. "Now you have it. The only difference is that a thousand years ago that valley was all water."

A pickup swung into the drive, swirling a tornado cloud of dust, dodging the livestock until it ground to a halt in the pasture. The driver, sporting a shock of red hair and beard, studied Harrison then looked to Olaf. "So you have da company, I see."

"Ja' Sven. This is the newspaper reporter and he's doing a story on my mooring stones."

Sven, who closely resembled an FBI wanted poster for an outlaw biker gang leader, nodded his approval. "They's gno'tt of them. Dat's for sure." He nodded at the two men in the truck cab with him. I brung Ole and Peder. We're goin' fishin' tomorrow and wondered if you would like to go." He nodded to Harrison in afterthought. "You too."

When Harrison saw the size of Ole and Peder, a couple more biker types with sun-bleached hair, he wondered how big of a boat it would take to haul all of them. The four men alone probably topped 1,500 pounds.

"Oh, it's been a long time since I caught a fiskr," said Olaf. "Ja', would you like to go too?" he asked Harrison.

"I, er, think I have something going on."

"Neita, that's too bad," said Olaf. "We usually catch some really big fiskr."

"Really big fiskr," Sven, Ole, and Peder echoed.

"I brung a little aquavit. I thought maybe we could have a couple short snorts and plan our fishin' trip."

"Ja'," Olaf said eagerly. "And maybe we can fill our reporter here in on da mooring stones."

***

Sven stowed six one-liter bottles in Olaf's freezer and set a seventh on the table as Olaf grabbed an armful of jelly jar glass tumblers from the cupboard then poured them all a drink. Harrison looked suspiciously at the twelve-ounce glass filled to the brim then sipped the sweet, smooth, anise-flavored liquor. It went down like milk. "Hey, that's pretty good."

At the same moment Olaf, Sven, Ole, and Peder all boomed out a laugh measuring 8.0 on the Richter scale, swelling the sides of the house. "We make a viking out of you yet," Sven boasted.

Harrison's drink went down so easily that when Sven offered to pour another round, he held up his glass and Sven filled it to the brim.

"So, you like drykkja the aquavit," Olaf observed.

"It's great," said Harrison.

"Ja', you have the viking dreyri in you," said Sven.

"Ja', there is nothing argr about you," said Ole.

"And if you drink a little too much, in the morning you can have a little more. A little haddr of the dog that bit you."

There was only one more question Harrison had. And he'd had enough aquavit to ask it. "This place looks like it's been here a long time," he said to Olaf. "Did your ancestors homestead here?"

"Oh, you could probably say dat," Olaf said, topping off his glass. "It was maybe even before the homesteading days though."

"Maybe before the skraelings even," said Sven.

"Ja', maybe even before the skraelings," Olaf agreed.

The more they drank, the more strange words came to fill their speech, until finally the four monstrous Scandinavians were not speaking English at all but a foreign tongue somewhere between German and the ineffable rantings of skid row drunks.

Deciding it was the latter, Harrison figured he'd had

enough of their tall tales of mooring stones and viking ships and raids. But not before he polished off a fourth glass then turned the bottle and saw 100 proof printed on the side.

As he stood to leave, the room spun wildly and the four men laughed.

Say, give him another bjor-ker so he can find his bearings."

"Ja,' they's gnott more where that came from," Olaf added.

"Ja', they's nothing argr about him."

Harrison nodded and waved his way out the door, nearly stumbling over the billy goat who was breeding a nanny. When he finally made to his Taurus he fell into it and turned the key. "Mooring stones, wikings," he slurred to himself. "Bullcrap." He barely made it out the drive, down the gravel road, then to the highway when a highway patrolman lit up his lights and pulled him over.

***

"Too bad 'bout dat reporter fella," Olaf said the next morning after the four of them finished listening to the police report on the radio.

"Ja'," said Sven. "I thought maybe he could handle his aquavit but I guess not."

"Ja', said Olaf.

"Argr," said Peder. They all agreed.

"Well, I guess it's time we go see how many fiskr we can catch," said Olaf.

The four carried their tumblers of aquavit out to Olaf's stone barn. They set down their glasses and the other three rolled open the massive barn door while Olaf started up his John Deere and backed it inside the barn. The tractor emerged a minute alter, towing a trailer with a thousand-year-old Viking ship.

"Ja'," said Sven, checking the red-and-white striped sail. "*Now* we see who catches the biggest fiskr."

Viking lexicon

186

*Neinn – no.
*Fo'lk – people.
*Hagi – pasture land.
*Ja' – yes.
*Gno'tt – abundance.
*Fiskr – fish.
*Neita – to refuse, deny.
*Aquavit – A Danish anise-flavored liquor of 100 proof. Dating to the viking era, it tastes like candy and goes down like milk.
*Drykkja – drinking.
*Dreyri – blood.
*Argr – cowardly, womanish.
*Haddr – hair.
*Skraelings – Native Americans.
*Bjor-ker – beer goblet.
*Gnott – plenty.

For more on mooring stones:

http://www.stormlakepilottribune.com/story/18324
83.html

Shadows in the Sand

The roar of surf and cry of gulls lay heavy upon the beach. Ebbing tides left teaming life – sand dollars, kelp, hermit crab – gulls sweeping into their midst, finding food so they could soar and cry and drift for eternity.

Shadows flickered in the sand – one a strong, right ankle, strengthened by years of marching and leading Marines in the jungles of South Vietnam and later the deserts of Iraq and mountains of Afghanistan. The other was a prosthetic – metal with wood fitted into a shoe coursing through the sand, the surf, marching through kelp and gulls, marching to the roaring surf as though it were a distant echo of the drums of war.

Gunnery Sgt. Ret. Phil Davis adjusted his faded green USMC ball cap and peered down the beach where the surf cast mist clouds all the way from the beach to the point and towering Cape Lookout, a silhouette shaped like a sleeping bear in the pre-down glinting over the Coast Range like the glimmer of a sea-gleaned pearl. The smell of sea life and ocean was rich and rank, waking his senses to its abundance. And he was here – at least most of him – awake and alive to enjoy it.

Most of his life he'd given to the Corps – the better part of it anyway – and they'd given him his life back again with a disability to comfortably live out the rest of his days – or as comfortable as he could, one mangled foot left moldering somewhere in Afghanistan after an IED had blown him and three other men and their Humvee into the air and insurgents had peppered it with bullets. Cpl. Hodges had managed to cut loose with his .249 SAW and Phil had nearly emptied the last clip of his M4. Only then was he able to cradle Hodges' head in his lap as he bound a tourniquet around his own stump and radioed for air support. By then, all the insurgents were dead, along with Cpl. Hodges and Sgts. Ramirez and Koske. For some reason, he was the only one left alive.

The tang of salt and ocean life along the beach, the golden halo of the sun rising above Cape Lookout, the constant roar of surf, and the incessant cries of gulls reminded him of his former life. There had been a girl then. He'd just gotten out of basic and had a few days leave before heading to Pendleton when he'd met her at Balboa Beach – Joann – tall, blond, blue-eyed, high-cheeked, and Nordic in every aspect. Her voice was like water – not the roaring crash of surf in his ears now but more like a stream – steady, soft, reassuring. The first thing he noticed about her was her leopard print bikini strolling down the beach. But when she turned and smiled it was her eyes that held him, blue eyes matching the deepest waters of the Pacific. The same ocean where he walked now along in Oregon. The same ocean that quite possibly still held a few molecules, a few atoms, of her essence.

They were drawn to each other as would any attractive young man and woman – he taut and fit and she slim and curves in all the right places. They didn't need to say anything to each other – their eyes did all the speaking. And when they did finally speak they talked of making a life together – maybe even a family.

And then the war came – the war for which he and the Marines had trained, and then came her opposition to his role in it. What can I do. I'm a Marine, he said. And the wall was drawn between them. He chose a path of fighting for his country, of saving the South Vietnamese people.

She went to Berkeley and led protests against the very war in which he fought. When he came home, heavily decorated, she didn't recognize him. And he no longer recognized her drug-enhanced gaze, unkempt clothes, and patchouli-drenched lifestyle.

Oh, he still pursued her – caught her a few times even – but she always ran away. Ran away from him in LA. Ran away from him in New Mexico. Ran away from him even in a car that she crashed in a snowy farmer's field mid-afternoon December 13, 1984.

He'd been training recruits at Pendleton when his mother called him about it. I have some bad news, Son. Time passed now like the slap of surf in his ear. They said she had been on drugs.

She was beautiful, lying there in the casket. How could she be dead, as perfect as she was. The funeral director smiled and nodded at what he took as a compliment and folded his hands together as any proper undertaker would before the service began. Afterward, her father, the minister who had conducted the service, handed him a locket Phil had given her thirteen years before. I thought Joann would have liked you to have this.

No, oh God no, he thought. He had wanted her to have it. But all he could do was clench on to it as they shoveled earth on her burial vault at the cemetery that overlooked the farm where he had grown up, a half-mile to the west. A necklace he had worn ever since she had died, still even now, next to his dog tags.

She had been his last love, his only love if he were truly honest with himself. Oh, there had been women. But they were just women – stopgaps to keep him sane as he drove through life like a drunken man in a rain squall.

And so now he was here, walking an Oregon beach empty except for a willowy, dark-haired figure drifting from out of the mist. As she came closer, her loose-fitting dress showed her shape and shadows, hair billowing in a seawind that rose as the sun lifted boldly, melting the mist. Her dark eyes met his – eyes so dark her pupils and irises were the same color. Her slightly curving lips and gently rounded chin suggested a smile about to erupt as her brows lifted as her eyes held his, nose crinkling as she smiled.

"Hi." He stopped to look at her. All of her. Because she was beautiful.

She smiled until she saw his prosthetic then tilted her head in sympathy.

"Pardon me, but I forgot to put my foot on this morning. I seem to have left the original somewhere in Afghanistan."

She crossed her arms against the chilling mist and laughed. She was so beautiful it was ungodly. "I'm Victoria," she said, as though that would help him forget.

And it did. "I'm Phil."

Her full name was Victoria Koronis, and she was from Macedonia and working as a doctor in Portland. He turned from the direction where he had been headed and walked beside her. Together they darted in and out of the surf that chased them as they strolled along the beach, every fifth wave chilling their ankles as the sand sifted under their feet. They walked for miles, interminable miles.

He would never forget Joann. Never.

But it was Victoria within whom he would share the rest of his life.

The Accident

Celeste was frantic when she called. Ray? In an accident? The true horror of it all became clear as she unfolded the details.

Ray had been driving south on 101 when a northbound semi hauling for a major discount chain sideswiped him, sending his Miata over the embankment onto the beach below. Another driver behind him had witnessed it all – how Ray's shattered convertible had shot directly off the road like a projectile, how the semi driver had kept going, how the Miata just *sat* there – waiting for the next high tide to swallow it up and carry him out to sea. Thank God the tide was at its lowest when the accident happened.

I asked the fateful question. "Is he . . . going to live?"

"I don't know." Then Celeste broke. "He's the only man I've ever loved."

***

Ray and I went back years. He'd stumbled up – virtually – up from San Diego to stay with his friends Stig and Ingrid supposedly to dry out. I was living in what was then still a mining town – until rock-bottom gold prices would close the mine seventeen years later. At that time, Oretown was still a mining town, its populace split between miners and non-miners.

As a private practice attorney with a shingle hung out on Upper Main, I dealt mainly with court-appointed DWI and drug-possession cases and an occasional domestic case. Probably my most notable case was when I got a guy off for second-degree murder because of a botched police search.

I met Ray when the court clerk asked me if I'd take his DWI case. I didn't have much of a choice, since my name was next on the court-appointment roster. At first I thought we'd try to plead down to reckless driving, but when I read the police report and saw the patrolman had pulled Ray over for a loose license plate bracket, I thought we actually had a case.

"He can't pull you over for this," I offered, dropping the report on my desk.

Ray looked up meekly from his chair, disheveled surfer cut brushing his eyes. "So you think we can fight it?"

"Absolutely. There was no vehicle malfunction and your driving looks pretty decent. I think we have a helluva case."

Ray jumped up and shook my hand. "Thanks."

"No problem." As I stood to shake hands, I took an immediate liking to the guy.

***

We won the case and turned around and filed a countersuit for false arrest which resulted in a tidy settlement for Ray. I bought a new Beemer with my third and had enough left to take a nice vacation.

If this sounds like everything turned out rosy for Ray, well, it didn't. The day I handed him his settlement check, he asked me out for drinks. I should never have agreed.

"You be the *man*, Harrison." Ray clapped me on the shoulder as we sat lodged like hood ornaments on our barstools at the Number Ten. "You be the man. Can I call you Harry?"

No one had ever called me Harry in my life. It had

always been Harrison Charles Richardson III, since the day I was born – even in grade school. "Sure, I guess so," I acquiesced.

"Harry Richardson, Harry Richardson," Ray pondered, well into his cups with his fourth beer. "Hey," he said as though lightning had just struck him. "Anyone ever call you Harry Dick?"

"I can't say that they have."

"Do you care if I call you that?"

"I would prefer that you not."

"I think I'll call you that anyway. Harry Dick, Harry Dick. It has a real nice ring to it, doesn't it?"

I said nothing and nursed my second scotch as Ray ordered his fifth beer. "I'd be careful," I cautioned. "After what we've been through, the police are probably gunning for you."

"Aw, I don't have nuthin' to worry about. I have Harry Dick for a lawyer. I have a big Harry Dick." As Ray laughed uproariously at his own joke, my face purpled and I soon left.

As I should have expected, I had a call from Ray the next morning. "Can you come bail me out?" Ray asked meekly. There he was, sitting in jail, not a penny in his pocket, and the judge demanded cash bail.

"I'll be right down."

After I bought him breakfast and poured a half-gallon of coffee into him, we went to my office. Ray had refused the breathalyzer, of course, mistake number one. But when he told the cop he had a big Harry Dick who would ream his ass, the officer shot him with a taser, beat him with his stick, and pointed his gun at Ray's head so he screamed, "Okay. I did it. I've been drinking and driving. Please don't shoot me."

At first I didn't believe Ray's story, but when I replayed the video from the squad car camera, I knew it was true. And it all happened before they read him his rights at the station.

"As incredible as this seems . . ." I surmised,

steepling my fingers on my desk to better put Ray into perspective " . . . I think we might have a case."

"Really?" Ray rose from his chair like a phoenix.

"I won't guarantee it, but with what very clearly appears to be your forced confession coming before Miranda, I think we have a very solid case, in fact."

The jury agreed, and in the police brutality countersuit, another jury awarded Ray $1.2 million. That amount I can divulge since it was in all the papers.

"I think the first thing I'd advise you to invest in is a good treatment facility – preferably several states away."

"Okay," Ray readily agreed. And the last thing I'd learned was that he'd headed back to California.

Celeste had called because she found my business card tucked inside Ray's wallet – plus the stories he'd told her of what a great lawyer I was. I'm glad she couldn't see me blush over the phone because that's exactly what I did. As a lawyer, I was no better than average. It was my willingness to take Ray on as a client and his incredible luck that shook the alignment of the stars. As I was soon to find, Celeste would realign them even more.

***

My flight landed at San Diego International ahead of schedule, so of course I didn't expect anyone there. All I could think of the entire trip was how glad I was I'd kept up my California license to practice – it only made sense to get my initial license there since I'd graduated from Berkeley Law. I only hoped see my old friend one last time before his passing.

I scanned the crowd for the sort of girl I thought Ray would marry – scatter-brained, perhaps, bug-eyed, maybe retro-hippy. The only woman I saw was a statuesque beauty – probably five-eight or five-nine. If you'd asked me then what her nationality was I would have never guessed. Her olive skin and jet-black hair said Mediterranean – Greek, perhaps, but the freckles across her nose and her saucy temper said Irish. Then her high cheeks and iceberg-blue eyes said Norse. But a bit of

African-American traced the figure of a Nigerian princess. She was without a doubt the most gorgeous creature I had ever seen.

"Harry?" Her pinched smile led her down the concourse where I took her hand in both of mine. Her perfume was ravishing as her eyes devastated me. I knew then that God had not created such beauty as this upon planet Earth for eons. Her beauty was timeless. "Celeste?" I answered, feeling privileged to be able to say her name.

She stood there, wanting me to clasp her in my arms, to comfort her, and I desperately wanted her to do the same with me. "Ray's said so much about you. I'm glad we could finally meet."

"How is he?"

"Not good . . . " She looked away, his image drawing her from the moment. "Not good at all."

"I'm so sorry, Celeste. I'm so sorry." That was when she broke and embraced me and I so willingly took every inch of her that I could into my arms.

***

When we went directly from the airport to the hospital ICU, I was numbed by what I saw. Ray's face was barely recognizable. It hardly seemed human. As the chief trauma team physician explained it, Ray had sustained massive internal injuries as well. His trachea had been crushed and he breathed through a tube, but fortunately was stable. Both femurs were broken and he had a punctured lung. "I'm so sorry, Ray buddy." As I stroked his forehead reassuringly, I thought a hint of a smile cracked his face – no doubt Ray's spirit fighting through his induced coma.

I went to work on Ray's case right away. I'd booked a room at the Sheraton but Celeste demanded I stay at their house, and when she led me to the guest room with a bank of windows overlooking the tossing Pacific, I was sold.

Celeste's record-keeping was impeccable. She had the police report all laid out, along with witness statements she'd taken herself. Not just one but five drivers had seen what had happened.

I also learned that Ray had done quite well for himself as a jazz bari sax player – that explained the La Jolla beach house – so that made projected loss of earnings stratospheric. That, compounded by the fact that the semi driver had left the scene, made for enormous potential punitive damages. I filed the next week.

As expected, the company played the waiting game, hoping to time the case out. I was a pretty savvy ambulance chaser myself by then, so every time they filed for a delay, I filed an amended complaint, seeking higher punitive damages. We were going for $100 million, and I knew we had a solid case.

Since it was just me taking on a bank of attorneys representing one of the biggest megacorporations in the world, I put my regular practice on hold. I was throwing everything at Ray's case – even my career.

After several months, Celeste and I had talked the case to death. We were tired of the filings and amendments and delays, tired of the entire California legal system itself. And I was tired of ignoring her, of ignoring such exquisite beauty, and she was tired of no longer having a man to hold her at night.

Is it any wonder then that it happened?

We were sharing a bottle of the finest Napa Valley merlot, Celeste on one side of the expansive living room and I thirty feet on the other. The deck door was open, and a strong sea breeze lifted the sheer curtains and our errant thoughts like ghosts.

I was taken aback when Celeste asked if I wanted to smoke a joint. Then I reminded myself that this was California, where pot was the conventional five-o-clock cocktail. "Sure," I readily agreed.

Celeste sat there, fingers fumbling as she tried to roll. Tears streamed down her face and she sniffed. "I can't do this. Ray was the one who usually rolled." She looked up at me and tears dammed up for months broke loose.

I went to her – what person wouldn't – and held her. The tide was at its highest then, and with a strong sea wind the curtains stood straight out. The ocean roared, hiding our thoughts, our glances and questions and doubts. As I leaned back from her I held her glistening black hair to one side, wondering how a woman so beautiful could ever be mortal. Her eyes peered into mine, begging, pleading. Her soft, coral lips tried to form unspeakable words. "Here, let me help," I said and sat on the white leather davenport beside her to roll the joint.

Celeste laughed – a quick, curt laugh filled with nervousness and frustration, tears abating as she leaned forward, hands clasped on her knees as she watched me roll. "You're pretty good at that – do you know that?" Her eyes peered into mine, inches away.

"At what?"

She laughed again and clasped my arm and gazed at the tide, now beating the jetty so fiercely the ocean sprayed forty or fifty feet. "This is wrong."

"Smoking dope?" I asked, putting the joint into my mouth to light it.

"No," she said, not laughing for once as I handed her the joint. The pot was excellent. She took a hit and handed the joint back to me. "My thoughts."

"You have thoughts?" I said, taking a good hit now, the golden buds crackling like a Napa Valley wildfire. "This shit should take care of that," I said, handing her the joint.

Celeste laughed then toked, the ember lighting her azure eyes, her olive skin, her raven-black hair the sea wind wisped and eddied. She shifted and touched her knee against my leg. I thought of moving away but didn't, and she smiled as she handed me the joint. "God, I needed this."

Needed what, I wondered. I toked, burning the joint down to an inch. "There's not much left, is there."

"No there's not." She took the joint from me and

toked then turned to the ashtray, her body fully facing me like a question mark as she faced me. I couldn't resist the chance to openly admire her sheer, white dress, dragonfly wings revealing her everything. I felt her gaze before I could look away. Her eyes were upon me, drawing me toward her, her lips again forming those unspeakable words, *make love to me.*

I touched her hair, caressing it like a waterfall past her ear as her eyes flickered in the dying light, picking up glints of the sun streaking a path through the turbulent ocean, joining us together in its hallowed beam. I leaned over to kiss her and her lips readily agreed, Celeste breathing in my breath as I breathed in hers, our mutual exchange matching the tides and time and eternity.

***

I awoke to the smells of bacon and saltwater the next morning, a sheet between me and the bracing chill. We apparently hadn't made it further than the davenport that night, but it had been large enough for the two of us.

"How did you sleep?" Celeste swept down from the kitchen stairs into the living room, trailing the edge of her nightgown behind, and handed me a cup of coffee. As always, she was devastating.

I sipped the coffee to gather my thoughts. "Like a rock." The coffee knocked any trace of a wine or pot hangover from my head. I looked at my reflection in the coffee where an ogre approaching middle age stared back. "This coffee's fantastic."

She laughed and sat beside me and gripped my arm. "So were you."

As I looked around the room, visions of Ray lingering in the hospital filled my head. He was the reason I was here. If it were not for his trauma, suffering, and near death, I would never have met her. I sipped again and set the cup down on the coffee table. "Pretrial conference is today and the trial starts tomorrow."

Celeste's smile faded as I brought us back to reality and her hand slipped away. "Yes, I guess it does, doesn't it."

The pretrial conference went extremely well. Several weeks before I had filed a discovery motion for the driver's logbook – something the driver had claimed had been 'lost' in the accident – and the judge looked the company attorneys in the eye and told them that without it they were starting with a losing case. When the logbook miraculously appeared later that afternoon, the last entry was more than a day before the accident – and the driver was already far beyond his allowable hours of service.

As I slept in the guest bedroom alone that night, I heard Celeste sobbing in her and Ray's bedroom down the hall. I should have felt guilty about the night before, but instead I felt guilty about not sharing her bed as I knew that was what she wanted. So beautiful, so alone, so sad. As guilt clenched my soul, I vowed to win the case for her and for Ray. That was the least I owed them. So I absolved myself from her body, willing myself to focus on Ray's case and nothing else.

***

The trial took two full weeks during which expert witnesses hired by the company paraded facts and statistics before the bleary-eyed jury whose members all nodded off at least once. My presentation was far more straightforward. I laid out the chain of events on an overhead – a fatigued truck driver had crossed the centerline and knocked Ray's car from the road and left the scene, and then I showed slides of Ray's injuries. By then the jury was swaying our way, but when I put Celeste on the stand, I figured that cinched it. Jaws set, they left for the jury room.

We were still waiting a day and a half later in a coffee shop across the street. Celeste had left her tuna croissant untouched, and I barely forced down half a sub myself. Celeste's question came from so deep inside her I knew there was no bottom to it. "What do you think they'll decide?"

I looked grimly across my coffee cup to her,

wishing I could be more optimistic. "As determined as they seemed going into the jury room, at first I thought they'd come right back and rule in our favor. Now, I'm not sure." I set down my cup. "I'm not sure at all, Celeste."

She smiled and clasped my wrist. "You were a real lion in the courtroom, Harrison. No one could have done better."

"Thanks." I realized then that was the first time she had called me Harrison. Until then it had always been Harry.

My cell rang. The clerk summoned us back to the courtroom. The jury had a verdict.

***

I learned later the reason for the delay. It wasn't the verdict the jury had disagreed upon but the amount of the award. I had done everything I could to convince them they should give a $100-million award. Well, the jury disagreed. They awarded $200 million.

Celeste was ecstatic. Then, as thoughts of Ray quelled her joy, she asked me to go with her to the hospital to tell Ray, that somehow in his comatose state some part of him might understand. He was no longer in induced coma but remained unresponsive. The doctors were stumped by his case. His pupils were no longer dilated and they thought he should possibly have been able to speak, but the extent of brain damage was unknown. The casts had been removed from his legs, so now we could only hope and pray that his brain would heal.

We stepped into his room and shut the door, Ray's ventilator whispering as his oxygen and heart monitor beeped softly. I'd been in hospitals often enough to know his heart rhythms were near normal. Just as I was about to say something to Celeste, she went to Ray and cried as she took his hand. "Oh, Ray honey, I know you probably can't hear me, but if you can somehow, I want you to know the jury decided in our favor. They awarded us $200 million, and I'll see to it that you get around-the-clock care from the best specialists in the world for the rest of your life."

Ray's eyes popped open and he rose up, tossed off the ventilator and monitors, and planted his feet firmly on the floor. "Yeah babe, that's what CNN just said – one of the largest damage settlements in California history." He stood up and sank his fingers into her rear and his tongue into her mouth.

Celeste backed away from him and caught her breath. "I . . . you . . . we . . . " Celeste's gaze switched between Ray and me several times, finally settling on him. "You were *faking* it?"

"The whole time, babe," Ray said, leaning over to slap his thigh. "The whole time."

Celeste stormed out, and all Ray could say was "Where'd she go? Where'd she go?"

I flew back, knowing Celeste would send a cashier's check for my fees when she had the chance. It arrived, along with a note asking me to meet her in Mexico. I took the first flight that day.

As Ray's legal guardian due to his incapacity, Celeste got everything – except for my $66 million fee, of course. Ray got nothing.

***

So here we are in Mexico, the two of us in a whitewashed villa with red-tile roof overlooking the blue expanse of the Pacific. We make love every night – and morning – and afternoon. The servants are very cheap down here, so we have our private barista for the daytime and bartender for after five. Our swimming pool and spa are aqua steppingstones down to our mile of private beach below.

All is bliss here – all is perfect. And yet I feel Ray lurking somewhere, his saxophone sonorous in the Sonoras every sunset. Watching, waiting, plotting his final revenge.

The Bathers

How Benny wound up in Philly was a mystery even to him. But here he was, in Philadelphia Museum of Art French Romantics room, gazing at a life-size painting of a clutch of women in a stream. *THE BATHERS* by Renoir. On the lower right was a young woman with the most impish smile. Fourteen, fifteen, sixteen at the most. The rest of the women looked like a painting. But the girl on the lower right, splashing water on her friend, was fully realized. She emerged from the canvas as a living, breathing girl.

Every day Benny came here. Past the Miros and the Picassos. Duchamp's *Nude Descending a Staircase* he could even live without. But every day he came to see *THE BATHERS*, especially THE BATHER – HER. And when he was done looking at her, digesting her visual reality to his very core, he would leave the museum fully.

He had moved to Philly after being laid off from his job at the tractor factory in Iowa. His plan had been to go to New Jersey to help his dying brother with his towing business. He told Allen he loved him and his brother garbled the same thing back over the phone, and Benny headed out as soon as the human resources office handed him his last check.

***

Jess felt pretty bad about dumping Mr. Heinrichs off at the bus depot in Omaha, but she knew she didn't have any choice. By now the police would be searching all of South Dakota and maybe Iowa too. In Nebraska she'd be safe – for a few hours anyway.

"You want me to *what*?" cried Mr. Heinrichs, standing there in front of the diesel-spewing Greyhound as she handed him his ticket.

"Just ride the bus back to Sioux Falls, okay?"

"But why can't I drive? I drove all the way down here, didn't I?"

Jess was still shaking from the ride. "I can't go back with you. I need the car because I have to go somewhere else."

"Well why can't you go with me?"

"Because the cops are probably after me."

"Oh, well why didn't you just say so. I can drive with my new driver's license when I get back to South Dakota then?"

"As long as the cops don't stop you."

Mr. Heinrichs winked as he stepped on the bus and turned to her one last time. "That was really fun. What was that music we listened to?"

"Lil Wayne?"

"Yeah. Little Wayne. I'll have to listen to more of him. He's sort of catchy."

"Yeah . . . bye." Jess waved as Mr. Heinrichs boarded the bus, not realizing that even God could not reinstate his driving privileges.

***

The trip out did not go well. He was barely out of Iowa when a weird grinding and crunching sounded under his car and he rolled to a stop in front of a repair shop at Prairie du Chien. A little over a thousand dollars later Benny was on the road, scratching. It had taken six days to find and install a transmission, so he had spent the whole time in the cheapest motel he could find.

"Bedbugs," the doctor in Janesville announced.

"Are you sure?"

"I'm sure. I've seen them hundreds of times."

He did as the doctor said, stopping to do all his laundry and take a shower and spend the night in a motel room in Peoria – a room infested with bedbugs.

***

Jessica laughed as the bandit-faced raccoon caught the bread and tore at it with his paws, the sign DO NOT FEED THE ANIMALS nailed to the tree above him. She didn't care, though. Raccoons needed to eat too, didn't they? And what harm would it be to feed one just this once.

Her fun with the raccoon was disrupted when a phalanx of motorcycles roared past her campsite – probably the most isolated in the Missouri state park since she was still hiding from the cops. The leader, a huge man who sat atop the Harley-Davidson like a sumo wrestler on a football, stopped to smile at her through bug-encrusted teeth. "Hi honey, wanna have some fun with my bros an' me?"

Jessica acted as though she hadn't heard and went to the Bonneville where she got Bob's .38 special from the glove box and turned to fire three shots in rapid succession just above the raccoon she had just fed. "Damn raccoons were trying eat my breakfast. That'll show 'em."

The gang leader gawked at her .38 and roared off, the rest of the gang clinging behind.

As she swung the cylinder open to reload, Jess thought about guys in general. All she wanted was a real man – maybe a laid off tractor mechanic down on his luck. Maybe someone whose brother had just died and who was bussing tables, paying his own way.

***

He was really itching when he pulled up to his brother Allen's house in Moorestown. His cell phone had gone dead because it had been a few days since he'd charged it, and he didn't want to stop to plug it in. And so here he was, staring at an empty five-bedroom colonial, featuring a pool in the back and a brook coursing through the highly desirable 2.2-acre lot. There were no deer and turkey abounding right now, though.

His sister-in-law Lynn, niece Taylor and her husband Rod, and their daughter Kristina arrived four hours later to tell him that his brother had just passed. They didn't really come out and tell him right away though. It just sort of eked out, the same way they piled out of Paul's SUV as though frozen, even though it was August and humid as a four-hundred-pound gorilla's armpit.

"Grandpa died," said Kristina, taking out the ear bid just long enough to tell him. "Where were you."

"Well, I broke down in Wisconsin then got sort of . . . sick a little later." He knew he must have seemed to be pleading for forgiveness when he looked at them, trying to decide who was his ally and who was not. "Did he pass . . . peacefully?"

Rod cleared his throat, deferring to whoever dared speak first.

"He was in agony, Ben," Lynn finally said.

He'd better find a motel.

"I have a room ready for you, Ben," said Lynn, turning from him, no longer able to face him. "It was ready a week ago."

Things really didn't warm up after that – especially after the funeral. And when he asked Lynn if she still wanted him to help with the towing business she told him she was planning on selling it to their foreman. "There's no sense in your starting there now. He wouldn't want to keep you on anyway."

That was when Benny knew he was out of a job. And when Lynn found out about his bedbugs, he was out of a home and what was the rest of his family.

***

The drivers started changing once she was east of Illinois. After she passed through a tollgate, a roaring engine from behind soared past, the driver flipping her off.

Bob had always said the Bonneville was a fast car. "Be careful when you're driving it, Jess. If there's a top end to this thing I've never found it. We (he always said

206

we as though her complicity somehow assuaged his guilt) need that extra horsepower though in case the cops come after us." Her father had rambled on about things she didn't understand – dual overhead cams, high-rise something, headers, supercharger . . . she didn't understand a word of it. The next time someone tried to pass her and cut her off, she munched the throttle and tires screamed a smoking, unholy wail that left the other driver, the tool booth, and a good portion of Butler County, Pennsylvania in a burning cloud of smoke.

***

With the last of his money, he rented a gritty coldwater studio in Chinatown. His landlord ran a restaurant on the main level. In the foyer glittering orange fish and crustaceans swam and crawled happily until they were plucked out and boiled or baked to perfection. Benny knew right away it would be difficult dealing with his landlord when he went into the restaurant to hand him the $2,400 for the first and last month's rent plus deposit.

That was when he saw the HELP WANTED sign. "You're looking for help?" he asked the owner.

The owner glared at him, angry for his asking. "So you even know how to read. I always looking for help. Cooks, servers, dishwashers, bus boys. I need them all. Why? You want job?"

"Sure."

"You pay rent first. Then we talk."

***

Jessica pulled over at a rest area in central Pennsylvania to go to the restroom and have a cool drink. Before she headed out again, she opened the trunk and set the spare on the ground and lifted the carpet and flipped through Bob's license plate 'collection'. Oklahoma, Oregon – there they were – Pennsylvania. She unscrewed the Ohio plates from the brackets and threw a couple handfuls of dust on the new plates so they matched the rest of the car and headed out.

***

And that was how Benny became the only Caucasian employee of a staff of twenty – all Asian except for himself. Chinese, Korean, Vietnamese, and Lao voices buzzed about as he started work the next day. Pointing, laughing, elbowing each other, it was a feast of languages and he couldn't sample the hors d'oeuvres.

"No. You no do that right. Carry more like this," said Mr. Chen, the owner, as he carried four tables of dishes in his bussing tub to Benny's one. "Otherwise you waste time I pay you for."

The first time Benny tried it, three plates and a cup tumbled out and broke on the floor. "That cost you day's pay," Chen said.

How Mr. Chen figured wages was a mystery to Benny. Chen paid cash so there was no check stub, and when Benny looked at the $283 for working from eleven to nine, ten hours a day, seven days a week, he couldn't believe it. "So you took out for taxes?"

"Of course I take out for taxes. What you think? I some kinda gangsta?"

Benny already wanted to quit. That changed when Chen gave him a raise.

"Gee, thanks, Mr. Chen," said Benny, counting out the $347 – another $54 for the additional 21 hours. "Uh, how much am I being paid an hour, Mr. Chen?" He knew it wasn't over six bucks an hour after taxes – and that was at straight time.

"What???!!! You no paid by hour. You paid salary. You such a big shot already to question me? Maybe you want to go back to bus boy."

"No, Mr. Chen. The pay is fine."

"Good," said Chen, nodding at the dining area filled with people. "Now hurry up and cook so you can go take their orders and bus tables and do dishes."

***

Hands gripped on the steering wheel as though choking a chicken, Lil Wayne blaring from the CD player, Jess entered Philly on the Schuylkill Expressway, ready to rip the city apart. With her determination, the city didn't have a chance. She was going to be an artist, damn it. It didn't matter if she had to sleep in the alleys along with the winos. No one was going to stop her.

***

Even working eleven hours a day, seven days a week, Benny found he was barely making a living with rent at eight-hundred a month. It helped that he ate all his meals at the restaurant, but he needed to earn more, so he took a part-time job delivering the *City Paper* once a week. Chen bristled when he asked for a day off with no reduction in pay. Surprisingly, Chen gave in, and Benny found himself with Mondays off – a whole day he could spend at the art museum.

"You must like that painting," said a museum guard, impeccably attired in Armani.

"She's beautiful," said Benny, entranced in his own bit of heaven.

"There are other artworks here, you know," said the guard.

"I know that. But just standing here admiring her is all I want to do."

The guard shrugged. "It's up to you. You paid to get in." After that, Benny was visually monitored from the time he entered the museum until he left.

***

She spend her first night at a wildlife refuge just west of Philadelphia International Airport, jets roaring over as she sat under a shelter half Bob had left in the trunk, heating a can of beans on the fire. She'd managed to catch a couple fish in Cobbs Creek, and they went well with the potatoes and onions.

As the fetid blanket of night descended, she decided to go skinny dipping in the creek. The cool water felt wonderful, washing away the grimy miles behind her. As she stepped from the water and dried herself with a towel, she couldn't decide what to do with her hair so she did it in a braid. For some reason she felt like transforming herself into someone who lived in an age long ago.

**

One Saturday night when Benny was just finishing up he came from the kitchen with his bussing tub when he saw her. The girl from the painting was there in the flesh, just a little older.

Benny slowly approached, picking up one table then another. The restaurant was empty except for the girl, pulling back her light brown plait, the most beautiful girl Benny had ever seen – the girl from *THE BATHERS.*

With Chen standing there, tapping his foot, Benny knew he wanted to tell the girl to leave. After all, all she'd ordered was a cup of egg drop soup and tea. It was ten after nine and Chen's naturally dark complexion burned darker every minute she remained. As Benny approached her table, she looked up at him.

"Excuse me, but . . . "

Jess smiled up at him. "Yes?"

"You really remind me of someone."

"Oh, who's that?" said Jess, wrapping her hands covetously around her tea as she sensed they wanted her to leave.

"Someone I knew a while ago. A long time ago." As Chen tired of waiting for Benny to chase her off, Benny stepped closer. "Would you like to go to the art museum?"

Jess looked at him, her smile spreading to her eyes. "Yes. I'd like that a lot."

The Bill Collector

I don't remember exactly what year it was. But it was 1962 or '63 or '64. It could have been even later. But there Mom was, bricks piled up in the yard, a fire going under the copper boiler, washing clothes. Dad couldn't pay the propane bill so what would have been antiques for most people were for us necessities – the copper boiler, the wooden stirring stick, the wooden-handled plunger to churn the clothes in the hot, soapy water to try futilely to remove weeks – maybe even months – of sweated-in dirt on Dad's coveralls. As Mom stood to look at me she laughed, blowing aside a tired, blond wisp. She was still a pretty woman then – blonde, petite, hazel-eyed. She could have married a banker or doctor or lawyer but she was married to my dad – an already-broken farmer who had failed but didn't want to admit it. A man whose sullen silences were broken only by false braggadocio, pathetic in his rantings but something you pretended to believe and accept if you wanted remain a family member. Dad had set up the bricks and laid down the kindling and brought the dented, antique copper boiler down from the summer kitchen upstairs and said, "See, that will work" as Mom glared back, near hatred in her eyes.

A gray trail of dust curled up from a newer blue car coming up the gravel road from past the Peterson place.

The roads were always dusty like this in summer – until the late-August rains. Then would come fall with its first cold snap then gold and red leaves in the ash and oak and sumac along the Big Sioux River. Now, it was early August and hot and dusty and I was wanting a glass of fresh lemonade more than life itself.

The blue car turned up the driveway, seizing Mom's glance as it rolled to a stop, dust still sifting past it because no one had told it to stop, an army of dust motes invading our farm grove.

"It must be the Fuller Brush man. Or . . . no . . . maybe the Watkins man."

As the man got out of his car he pinched up a well-worn smile. He pitched his fedora on the car seat. His blue suit matched his dark-blue car almost perfectly, just as his shiny black shoes matched the tires as he looked around the farmyard seeming lost, as though he had ventured into a place where he wasn't sure he wanted to be. "Mrs. Griggs?" the man said politely, strolling up the sidewalk sprouting a fresh crop of grass and weeds.

"Yes?" Mom covered her hair with her hand, afraid to be seen such a mess by a stranger.

The man's face settled into a smile that didn't quite reach his eyes. "Your husband home, Mrs. Griggs?"

"Why, no. He went to town to buy some fence. Our cattle have been getting out, you know, it's such a trouble . . ."

The man cut Mom short. "Do you know when he'll be back?"

"Why no. Sometimes he comes home right away. Sometimes he doesn't." Actually, Dad never did come home right away. He always stopped at the card parlor, his own haven against poverty, sometimes staying there well into the night while his supper sat on the kitchen table, getting colder and colder.

The man pinched up his frozen smile. "Well maybe I could just speak with you then, ma'am. I'm with the Federal Land Bank. I'm here to speak with your husband about his past-due loan."

"But my husband isn't here."

"I realize that, Mrs. Griggs. But I thought maybe you . . ."

"I said my husband isn't here," Mom said, getting an edge to her voice. She held her washing stick like a club as she glared at the man, as though wanting to beat him to death.

"I realize that, ma'am. I just thought . . . "

"Do you think I can just sit down and write you out a check?" Mom's eyes blazed, and if I didn't know better, I could have sworn they changed color, like a bull's when he's ready to charge. "I'm washing clothes, outside, over a wood fire, because my goddamn lazy good-for-nothing husband can't pay the gas bill. Do you think I can just whip out a checkbook and write you a check?"

"Well, no ma'am, I . . . "

Mom threw the stirring stick into the boiler and crossed her arms and squared off with the man. "If you want this farm, you can have it. In fact, you can take it and shove it up your ass."

"I'm sorry, ma'am." The man retreated. "Maybe I should come back later."

"Make it two or three in the morning. That's when he drags his worthless, good-for-nothing ass home and sleeps just long enough to have coffee and go into town and play cards again."

"I'm sorry, ma'am. I'm sorry." The man got back into his car, and revving the engine a little too loudly when he started it, pinged gravel against the undercarriage as he drove away, the same dust motes following him that he had brought in.

I watched the blue car get swallowed by the distant dust cloud. "Good for you, Mom."

Mom glared at the cloud too. "Son of a bitch."

"Son-of-a-bitch," I repeated.

Mom's gaze narrowed. "I should wash your mouth out with soap."

"But Mom, you just said the same thing."

"You get to be my age, you go through the crap I've gone through, then you earn the right to say son-of-a-bitch. 'Til then, watch your mouth."

"Okay, Mom." I don't think I'd ever seen her that mad before – or since.

"Take the farm," she snorted. "He can take the son-of-a-bitch and shove it up his ass, silo and everything."

The Mentor

Harrison Griggs studied the invitation as he and his wife had afternoon cocktails. He was still deciding if he even wanted to go.

"What's that, honey?" asked Glenna from the other side of the patio table. Her yellow slacks and matching tank did nothing to hide her figure – still vivacious at fifty-eight. It was one of the many things he loved about her, finding her just as intoxicating as she had been when they were in their teens. She noticed the way his glance was taking in the view of her. She decided to use the opportunity in that distraction to probe the matter of the letter with a sly, prying smile.

"Oh nothing." He dropped the envelope on the table along with circulars for drugstores, vitamin supplements, and hearing aid companies. Neither of them needed drugs or vitamins or hearing aids, though. They both ran a 5K every morning and played doubles every Saturday, not to mention golf every Tuesday, Thursday, and Sunday. They were as fit as near-retirees could be, poised to live the sort of retirement of which most people only dreamed.

"Well it has to be something." Glenna's fingers walked across the table toward the envelope. She opened it and smiled. "Well it's your fortieth high-school graduation."

"Forty years," said Harrison, pronouncing each syllable like a death sentence.

"Don't tell me you're already feeling your age." Glenna set down the invitation. "You certainly don't look it."

"Thanks. I guess I should take that as a compliment – even though it's from my wife."

"Oh Harry." Glenna clasped his wrist. "Don't be so dour. I'll bet you make ten times what most of your classmates do."

And he did. Griggs Custom Machining, with over three-hundred employees, commanded a good percentage of the ag and classic car parts replacement parts market. At the persistence of their son Tommy, next year they were going global with plants in Indonesia, China, and Mexico. Harrison had fought taking manufacturing overseas, preferring American labor. Buy American, hire American, had always been his mantra. But when overseas sales grew – they had surpassed domestic – it only made sense to base plants where their orders were.

"Don't you want to go, honey?" Glenna persisted. "Maybe to show them how well you've done – even just a little?" She giggled into her drink and touched the invitation once more. "I can't wait to see their sorry, sad, little faces."

"Nor I." Harrison chuckled, giving in as he knew his wife had already made his mind up for him.

***

School had started badly that first day. He had just stepped off the bus and headed for his first-grade classes – they didn't have kindergarten back then – when his cousin Freddie, then a second-grader, came up to him and pasted him in the mouth and wrestled him to the ground. He may have only been a year older, but a year meant a lot when you were in first grade and not used to fighting. Freddie was getting the better of him when Harrison's father Maynard drove by in his gray Korean War-era Navy

216

surplus truck. "Whatcha doin'? Fightin'?" His father said it as though it were Harrison's fault, even though his cousin had started it and was now pounding his face in. Harrison hoped his father would come pull Freddie off him, scold him, tell him never to do it again. But his dad just sat there in his truck, watching with a smirk, as Freddie rearranged his face and muddied his clothes and called him names he'd never heard.

His teacher – Mrs. Beerdahl – scolded him as he entered the classroom with shoes and clothes caked with mud so the other kids laughed at him. "Who are you and why are you such a mess?"

"I'm Har . . . ry," he said and started to cry. That only made the kids laugh even harder.

"You're also dir . . . ty," his teacher mocked. "Now go to the washroom and clean yourself up and sit down at your desk. Har . . . ri . . . son." The kids roared even louder.

Harry headed for the washroom. Then, deciding he hated his cousin Freddie and his teacher Mrs. Beerdahl and his classmates, he walked right on past the washroom and all the other classrooms. He pushed open the north emergency door, setting off the fire alarm, and kept walking. He walked off the school grounds and across the street and past Mrs. Johnson's barking German shepherd that he petted to quiet down then went down the hill to the creek where he crossed the footbridge and kept walking. Past the tree nursery he walked, then Mr. Knudsen's cattle yard where he climbed the wooden fence and wandered among the huge, 1,400-pound steers to the other fence that he climbed until he came to the river where he saw the old dam that his parents had told him to never, never, ever cross alone, and he crossed it as he had a number of times, feet chilling in the ankle-deep water as the surging river tried to push him over the edge into the churning, frothy water. Several times he thought of turning back, but that would have meant returning to his cousin Freddie and his teacher Mrs. Beerdahl and his classmates so he kept walking, crossing the dam to the other side of the river where his feet squished in his shoes, shooting water out like a squirt gun. He walked through the city park to the field and crawled under the barbed wire fence, ripping his new shirt, and kept walking until he came to a dark, wooded grove where Old Man Bates lived in a log cabin his great-grandfather had built in 1866, now the oldest structure in the county. He knocked on the door.

Old Man Bates cracked open the door and the aroma of kerosene and a woodstove and beer and whiskey and cigarettes roiled outside in one rank, heavenly Old Man Bates aroma. Old Man Bates' quizzical eye hovered like a caterpillar as he studied the young truant before him. "What're you? A salesman?"

"No, Mr. Bates. It's me – Harry Griggs. I had my first day of school today and decided I didn't like it." Several times Harry and his folks had driven past the Bates house, muttering things under their breath about how he was a hermit, always staying to himself. Harry felt that way about himself too, though, going to his room whenever his mother scolded him. He often wanted to be like Mr. Bates. Now was his chance.

Old Man Bates grinned. Of course he'd recognized the Griggs boy—he knew the family, though he didn't associate with them, nor any of the other townsfolk for that matter. Couldn't see the point. They'd already made up their minds and their myths about him. He avoided them and they avoided him. But Harry seemed like a decent enough kid whenever he crossed paths with him on rare supply runs into town or when the youth wandered over to play in the woods nearby. Bates spat a stream of tobacco juice into the Butternut can beside the door like a grasshopper. "Well, boy, ah didn't like school none too well neither. Why doncha come on in an' dry them duds off an' we'll go fishin'."

***

After Harry sat by the crackling woodstove for an hour, Old Man Bates pulled out a couple fishing roads, and sizing Harry up, handed him the shorter one. A lifetime of walking and hunting and fishing had hardened his body like a steel wire, so he was amazingly spry for a man pushing sixty. "Ya ever fish before?"

Harry looked at the complicated fishing rig and shrugged. "Maybe a little. I tried it once. The fish broke my pole though."

"Hmm . . . " Old Man Bates fingered the reel. "No fish'll break this. Catch a whale 'n you'll reel him in, if ya kin hold on to 'em."

Harry eyed the rod and reel as though it were a religious relic. "That would be great, to catch a whale."

Old Man Bates chuckled and led Harry out to his recently harvested vegetable patch where he showed him how to dig for worms, turning the black, silty loan with a spade until night crawlers squirmed like snakes. Harry jumped back as the old man pulled one out and held it in front of his face. "This here crawler is gonna catch us a walleye."

Harry watched as Old Man Bates set the night crawler in the can with several others and a goodly mixture of dirt then they headed down a path through weeds as high as Harry's head to the reedy riverbank where Old Man Bates showed him how to bait his hook and click off the reel drag as he cast. The big night crawler flew squirming through the air and hadn't plopped into the water but a second when something huge tugged at the hook.

"Whip yer rod 'n reel 'em in."

Harry did as Old Man Bates said, and a minute later he had a sixteen-inch walleye flopping on the riverbank.

"Now ah'll show ya how to clean 'em." Old Man Bates whipped out his filet knife and slid it back along the spine then cut behind the head and pulled it off then slit open the crop and cleaned the walleye in a couple minutes then rinsed it off in a bucket of water. "A few turnips 'n carrots 'n taters 'n this here'll be a meal fer a king."

After they caught a few more fish – a couple catfish for Harry and a couple walleye for Old Man Bates – they headed back to the cabin where he showed Harry how to cut the walleye into filets then dip it in egg and roll it in cornmeal. By noon they were dining on some of the most succulent walleye ever prepared by human hand. That afternoon they hunted rabbits and squirrels – the old man showed Harry how to hold his .22 and let Harry shoot a squirrel. Then at a little before three Old Man Bates pulled out his pocket watch as they walked back toward the cabin. "Well, I spose we'd best head ya to back to school so's ya kin catch the bus home."

Harry looked forlornly at the rod and reel and rifle hanging on the wall. "Can I come here to hunt and fish again?"

"Course ya kin. Anytime ya wants."

Harry nodded and followed Old Man Bates out to his old pickup and climbed up into the musty cab as the engine started. He couldn't wait to tell his classmates the things he'd seen and done.

***

The other kids were heading toward the buses when Old Man Bates let Harry off at the school. Harry looked for a bus with a number 2 on it and climbed up the stairs and sat behind the bus driver, Mr. Floren, who turned in his seat and looked at him as though he were a ghost. "Where you been all day. They even got the police lookin' for ya."

Harry shrugged. "Fishin' 'n huntin'."

"Fishin' 'n huntin', huh?" Mr. Floren pulled out his tin of Copenhagen and thumbed a pinch under his lip. "Well take me 'long next time, will ya?"

"Sure. Long as it's okay with Mr. Bates."

"Bates, huh? Well, folks say he's a strange old codger, but he'll learn ya huntin' 'n fishin' if anybody kin."

***

Harry's parents' short-lived relief gave way to a surge of verbal scolding for the worry he'd caused over his reckless rule-breaking and departure from school

220

grounds. They asked countless questions without pausing to let him answer. When he saw them finally tiring from the joint tirade, he told a long and involved tale of how he had dug worms and caught a walleye as high as his knee then shot a squirrel, then . . . They exchanged looks before each grabbing an arm to drag him inside so they could wash his mouth out with soap and spank him for lying on top of his other crimes. He didn't bother to tell them to check the details with Old Man Bates—partly out of pride, partly out of a fear that they would keep him from going there again or give Bates trouble. Silently, he took his punishment as a man in miniature.

***

"And the fish was *how* big?" asked Mrs. Beerdahl, the rest of the class roaring.

"This big." Harry held his hand at his knee. If he had been a foot taller, holding his hand at his knee would have been a little more accurate.

Mrs. Beerdahl's smile dropped as she crossed her arms. "In show and tell we tell the truth, Harrison. We don't lie."

"But it's true. And you should have seen the squirrel I shot."

The class laughed even harder as Mrs. Beerdahl marched Harry to the corner and faced him to the wall. "Now you stand there until you're ready to tell the truth – and not until then."

Harry faced the wall, tears streaming down his cheeks. Throughout his young life, he had never told a lie, not even a fib. But now his teacher taught him that if he wanted to stay out of trouble, he had to lie.

Whenever his parents asked him if he'd gone over to bother Old Man Bates, he lied about that too. But Harry went there whenever he got in trouble in school or with one of the other kids. Mr. Bates was his refuge.

***

One day when he was in seventh grade Harry was walking out the west door of the school when Steven Coster stopped him. Steven was three years older but had been held back twice so he was an eighth-grader. Rippled muscles bulged from Steven's T-shirt and a knowing smirk etched his face. "Pussy."

"Huh?"

"I said you're a pussy." Steven stepped closer, just inches away. He was about three inches taller, breath rank with cigarettes. "I said you're a pussy. Whatcha gonna do 'bout it."

Harry stood there. He knew what was coming. A fist to the face. It would hurt – it would hurt like hell – but there was nothing he could do about it. It came a lot faster than he had expected, faster than the blink of an eye, cracking his lip so his head bounced back against the glass front door, gashing the back of his head so blood trickled down his back.

Steven hit him as he tried to leave earlier through the west door the next day and the day after that. Harry avoided him by going through the east door the following day but the day after that Steven met him there too, jeering in his face as the other kids looked on as Steven pasted him in the face yet again. Harry regretted having ever gone to school. He even regretted being born.

***

If there was one class Harry liked, it was mechanical drawing. He loved the rough wood feel of the drawing board and how the T-square slid along it and how he could use the triangles to make different shapes. He even loved how he could use the French curve to make arcs. He hated the new math, but without realizing it, he was learning the essence of algebra and geometry and trigonometry from the ground up. As he did the arcs and loops the algebra formulas he had so long disdained drifted into the back of his head and came together with the pencil in his hand.

***

Old Man Bates didn't answer when he knocked. Harry followed a high-pitched whine to the shop behind his cabin. Harry stood in the doorway, watching the old man expertly, sparks and metal filings flying, peering through his goggles like a scientist peering through a microscope. As he finished his cut, Bates shut off his saw and lifted his goggles and smiled. "Howdy stranger."

It had been a couple years since Harry had visited the old man, and he felt guilty for that. And yet Old Man Bates seemed content in his ways, hunting, fishing, trapping, and working in his machine shop, sometimes all through the night, the high-pitched whine of saws and drills drifting even across the river where kids went to surreptitiously smoke cigarettes and kiss and feel up girls. "Whatcha makin'?"

The old man smiled, kindly blue eyes drifting through the dust motes of the hazy, late-afternoon light. His eyes said a lot. They said they welcomed his visit and that, while he may have regarded a visit by anyone else as an interruption, Harry was always welcome. "Ah'm makin' a receiver fer mah rifle."

"Receiver?"

"Come hear an' ah'll show ya."

Harry went to the workbench where Bates held up the metal tube. The grooved swirls inside looked like something he had been doing in mechanical drawing class. "Ah'm makin' a .308."

"*Making?*" Harry said, half-believing.

"From the stock up. Here. Ah'll show ya." Bates went to the corner and came back with a rifle with a finely polished stock and gleaming blue barrel. "This here's an ought-six ah made. One-in-ten twist. It'll drop anythin' you aim it at from four-hundert yards. Open sight even."

The rifle was beautiful. It was one of the most beautiful things he had ever seen. Harry thought back to when he had come to visit Bates that first day of school and shot his .22. He wondered if he had made that gun too. He probably had. "Where did you learn to do this?"

Bates smiled up a chuckle. "Was a machinist mate in the Navy. When everyone complained how they wished their rifles was more accurate, I decided to make my own barrels. Then ah went a step further an' started makin' mah own guns."

Harry delicately touched the stock. The depth of the swirled grain seemed to go on forever. "What kind of wood is this? It's beautiful."

"Burled walnut," said Bates, taking the gun back from Harry to run his finger along the pattern of the grain. "This here tree got taken in a lightnin' storm. Since it had a mind to work all them years to make a grain, ah decided to do it the honor of makin' a gun stock outa it." Bates set the rifle butt on the table. "This here gun'll be 'round fer a good five-hundert years – prob'ly shoot fer two or three hundred of that. After that, it'll prob'ly rest on some rich man's wall 'longside paintin's an' such."

Harry knew what the old man said was true. He had never seen anything so beautiful – not even Glenna Olson who had just started school the previous fall. "Can you show me how to do this?"

Bates looked at him steadily, deciding. "How much time ya got?"

"As much time as it takes."

"Then I got time to show ya." Bates kept looking at him, then touched his cheek. "What happened here."

"Oh, nothin'."

"Nothin'." Bates' keen, blue eyes pierced through his fib. "Looks to me like some bastard's been usin' your face fer a punchin' bag."

Harry looked at Bates, unable to pull his eyes away. More than his father, more than his mother, more than his teacher or minister, Bates had a way of piercing to the bottom of his soul, and sometimes it scared him. Maybe that was why he hadn't been around for a couple years. "It's this kid at school."

"Only one?" Bates looked long and hard at him. "Here. Afore we starts machinin', we're gonna learn how to box."

Bates showed him how to hold his hands, how to feint and duck and weave. How to side step and jab then follow with an upper cut that seemed to come out of nowhere. For six hours they practiced, and by the time Harry went home that night, he knew of twenty ways to knock Steven Coster right on his ass.

***

Steven wasn't at school the next day. Harry even went to the east door to wait for him, then the west door. The next day Harry heard that Steven had been suspended from school for three days for smoking. When Harry still stood at the east door of the school waiting for Steven three days later, he learned that Steven had decided to drop out of school. Harry was surprised at how sorry he was that Steven decided not to come back. He'd looked for the opportunity for retribution.

***

"How's this?" Harry handed the barrel to Bates who eyed it keenly, imagining how the bullet would spin through the grooves. As he set it on the workbench, he offered his pronouncement. "It's perfect."

***

Harry started engineering school on an ROTC scholarship. He had taken every math course he could in high school, and in college everything came together for him. He had been dating Glenna Olson ever since his junior year in high school, and when he proposed to her the day after he graduated with his mechanical engineering degree, she accepted. Shortly later, Harry was commissioned as a second lieutenant in the U.S. Army and went on to teach marksmanship at Fort Benning. He was promoted to captain, and led a rifle company in the Gulf War. After receiving the Silver Star and Distinguished Service Cross, he retired as a lieutenant colonel and started Griggs Custom Machining.

He'd written Bates time to time. The replies were short and sparse, but kindly. As life intervened, Harry's end of the correspondence fell away and Bates wasn't the sort to continue it himself.

Harry and Glenna had Tommy in 1992. During that time, Harry tried to bestow the best traits he could on his son. Whenever he searched for those traits, the image of Mr. Bates came into his mind. He was the one who had taught him self-reliance and thrift and courage. It was Mr. Bates, the same Mr. Bates his parents and the town ostracized as a hermit and recluse, that Harry looked up to more than anyone. So he figured that was the sort of person he wanted to be. And that was the sort of person he wanted his son Tommy to be.

***

Forty years had passed since he had driven this road, past the gently sloping hills into the river valley. By some ancient instinct, Harry was drawn to the ancient dirt road meandering along the river.

Glenna raised her sunglasses to her forehead. "Why are we pulling off here?"

Harry shrugged. "Someone I used to know lived here once. I just thought I'd drive by and see if there's anything left of the place."

Glenna shrugged and lowered her sunglasses. "Whatever you need to do, Harry," she said, trying to understand this sudden strange request.

Harry pulled the a8 up in front of the ancient cabin, the roof caved in like the backbone of a dead whale. Waist-high weeds had seized the property, parted by teenage paths leading toward scenes of smoking, drinking, and long, illicit summer nights in the tall grass. Harry got out of the car.

"Harry? Harry, what are you doing?" Glenna got out the other door. "Harry, this is trespassing."

Harry looked around. "Probably. Let's go have a look inside."

"Harry. Oh . . . " Glenna groaned and followed him through buffalo grass, Russian thistle, and milkweeds.

Harry knocked, though he knew no one was home, and opened the door barely on its hinges and stepped inside. Yellowed light beams traced through the rotten roof, criss-crossing through dust motes. The sharp, rank pungency of wood smoke was still there, along with an empty whiskey bottle on the table. Two fishing rods still hung on the wall, the same ones he and Old Man Bates had used fifty-two years ago, for some reason overlooked by vandals and looters who had considered them of no value.

"Har . . . ry. What are we doing here?" Glenna asked impatiently. She shuddered as she studied the old wreck of a cabin and shop. "This place always gave me the creeps – still does."

"Let's go check out back."

"Oh, for cripes sake."

He led the way to the shop where the door was askew. All the machinery was gone, no doubt lost to looters ages ago. The workbench was still there, though, with a receiver and barrel and block of fine, burled walnut. He turned to Glenna, her face blurring through his tears. "Remember when I told you about someone who helped me through my school years. Well, this is where he lived." His eyes were drawn to the receiver and barrel and wood. "I want to buy this place. I don't care how much they want for it, I'm going to buy it."

"Okay, Harry. Okay," she said, knowing that the real significance of this visit to the past wasn't to laud success in the faces of the unimportant majority who didn't understand him, but to pay homage to the one important soul who did.

The Counselor

Benny Johnson awoke to a bright, crusty dawn. Past the jumble of downtown buildings scattered like a baby's blocks, a yellow, sun-fueled, gaseous hue bled into the grungy sky. The constant drone of traffic told him he was still downtown, still locked in the city's greasy grasp, stomach gnawing and growling like a lion's. The putrid tang of fortified wine filled his swollen tongue clear to his throat.

He rolled over, shedding his bed of cardboard and newspapers, as a robin chortled a morning song, mocking his decrepit state, his fall from grace, his very existence. Today, he told himself. *Today* is the day I'll try to stay off the sauce. Maybe find a job. Even if it's loading trucks. Even if it's for just today.

Then the putrid funk of him rose into his nose, the same aroma he had smelled on others as well as himself. The same odor as winos throughout the city and the state and the country and the world.

"Hmm . . . " Benny started moving to get away from the smell. The graffiti-splashed alley glimmered and faded, depending on how long the artwork had been there. And some of it was really artwork, colors blended and fused like a masterpiece at the MET – some even better, if his artistic judgment meant anything.

Something black and hanging from a dumpster

caught his eye. He lifted the lid and pulled out a complete suit, still in a plastic bag with the warning KEEP AWAY FROM YOUNG CHILDREN. He sniffed the suit through the plastic and drew in the fresh dry cleaning smell. A faded sign, FILBERT'S DRYCLEANING EMPLOYEE ENTRANCE told him someone had failed to pick up his dry cleaning for several months – who knows, maybe years? – and a cache of expensive clothes had been tossed into the dumpster and oblivion. A further search turned up another suit, two dress shirts, and a couple ties. Benny continued his scavenger stroll, finding a pair of socks and shoes that pinched his toes. But they would do. He carefully folded his find into his backpack and continued down the alley.

He may have had a wardrobe fit for a trial lawyer, but that same funk chased after him all the way to a large, grassy space where the pish pish of sprinklers made him want to relieve himself. He set down his treasures and stood in the corner of a building and let loose a happy, gurgling stream.

A thought struck him as he turned toward the sprinkler spraying his greasy jeans. He stripped and stepped into the sprinkler's midst and splashed water over himself. Cold, bracing, and soapless, but it would do – for today, at least.

After he put on fresh clothes and checked himself in the mirrored glint of a window backed by a darkened hallway, Benny smelled the greasy aroma of food. He cut a dry path around the sprinkler and came to a large, green dumpster. He hoisted the lid and peered inside. Wilted lettuce, bread crust, and many unknowns greeted him. He reached in for a barely munched hero sandwich and tasted it. Ham, turkey, salami, and cheese. He finished the sandwich and found another completely untouched but for a film of cottage cheese. After he finished that sandwich, he realized he had to take an absolutely monstrous dump.

"Mr. Johnson?"

Benny jerked toward the previously darkened window, now alight and framing the visage of a blonde in her early thirties. "Why didn't you come in the front door, Mr. Johnson? This is the long way to your office."

Benny looked behind, above, and below, checking to see what alternative universe he had entered. "Sorry."

"No bother." The woman's smile was full, vivacious, maybe even flirty. "Let's get you settled into your office before the kids start coming in. It looks like you have a full slate of referrals through the day. And oh, I'm sorry . . . " The woman extended her hand. "I'm Laura Shoenauer, the substitute principal while Mrs. Henricksen is on maternity leave." Laura smiled and blushed as she secreted her opinion to Benny. "She's so lucky."

As Benny fell behind Laura in the darkened hallway, he couldn't help but notice how trim and muscled her calf muscles were – twin wires sending megavolts to some deep part of his brain. The urge to make a nature call faded as another impulse took over.

"Here's your office, Mr. Johnson," said Laura, waving at a metal door with a printed sign MR. RALPH JOHNSON, COUNSELOR in the plastic name holder. "And here's your office key along with the keys to the front and back doors and the men's faculty restroom." Laura's smile turned up into impossibly endless blue eyes. And was that a wink? "I *love* your beard, by the way. It's so . . . so masculine." Then she glanced at his backpack slung over his shoulder. "The kids should relate to your carrying a backpack too – instead of a stuffy, old briefcase." She glanced over her shoulder at him as she strolled away, heels clicking her thoughts in Morse Code.

Ralph. So that was his new name. His first thought was to run to Laura – or Laura Schoenauer – and tell her this was some mistake, that he wasn't Ralph Johnson but Benny Johnson, a wino for the past twenty years who had been lucky enough to score a new set of clothes, a free shower, sub sandwiches from the school dumpster, and to be greeted at the back door of a school by an absolutely stunning, blonde, blue-eyed, substitute high-school principal.

But wait. He could fake it for a day, couldn't he? Go along with his imposture until the *real* Mr. Johnson came along? And what would he do then? Run? Hide? He'd been running and hiding all his life – so he could go along with the charade. For a day, at least.

***

He'd been running hiding ever since Jean had died. He and Jean had married young. He was twenty-one and she was nineteen when she walked into his study with a pink piece of paper. He'd been burning barrels of midnight oil studying for his abnormal psych exam. Jean stood there, a warped smile on her lips, a cross between joy and fear and terror in her eyes. "I guess I'll just have to get rid of it, huh?"

They'd talked about this very thing before on at least a philosophical level. If she ever got pregnant, she would get an abortion. After all, Jean reasoned. It's just a bug, isn't it? Something you pulled out of you and stepped on and squashed? And it isn't that much of a procedure anyway, is it? Just go into the clinic and voila – an hour later you're out on the street, free again.

And so that's what they did. They took the five-hour bus ride to the nearest available abortion clinic where Jean sat through an hour-long video directed, produced, and starring actors sympathetic to the right-to-life state Republicans who had made the film mandatory before abortions would be permitted. Jean's mind had been made up before the video. But when she saw the young couple – and they were exactly her and Benny's age, weren't they? – when she saw that young couple decide to keep their baby and at the end waltz through a field of sunflowers, baby in the girl's arms as the credits rolled across the screen, Jean started to change her mind. *Are you sure you want to terminate this pregnancy after seeing that film?* the man asked. And of course he had to be a man. A middle-aged man with kind, brown, puppy-dog eyes asking the biggest rhetorical question she had ever faced. *Sure,* she answered, not sure at all but not wanting

231

to disrupt the career of her boyfriend who sat in the waiting room, wringing his hands as he wondered how many hours he would have to pump gas at the local service station or flip burgers in a restaurant to keep their noses above the drowning swells of poverty. *You're sure?* The man asked again. The girl to her left broke into tears. *I can't do this*, she cried, and ran from the room, the lights just now coming on as the final credits rolled. *I'm sure.* And she was – at that moment. Then the girl to her right broke. *It's a baby*, she pleaded. *How could you.* And she fled the room after the other girl. That left her and the man and no one else. A man paid – no doubt handsomely – by the very organization that had jammed the law through that said she had to sit through the film and listen to his harangue before she underwent the knife or vacuum cleaner or whatever it was. *I'm sure*, she yelled, half-standing as she said it, ready to hit him in the face if he dared ask again.

"All right," the man said, an abortion-prevention counselor who was likely no counselor at all but some whacko religious hack who undoubtedly prowled the local shopping malls on his days off, searching for girls just like her to impregnate then talk out of having abortions. Talk about the ultimate ethnic cleansing. "All right," he said again, sadness filling his buck-brown eyes as his allotted ninety minutes were up and she was free to undergo the procedure.

All she could think of as she undressed and put on the hospital gown and let them lay her on the operating table, ankles bound in the stirrups as the anesthesiologist finally made her not care what happened, was how she wanted to keep her baby. How she longed for her and Benny to walk through those same sunflower fields, babe in her arms. And what would she name him? Or her? she wondered as the life was sucked out of her. Would he – or she – be smart? Attractive? Kind? Caring? By the time she wondered how proud she would feel when her child had graduated from college and been married and had children, its life had been totally sucked out of her.

***

But then Jean had never told Benny that story – not all at once anyway. It came out in dribbles, like a hole in a leaking bag of sadness that led to her huge void of nothing. Gone were her smiles, giddiness, and laughter. Instead all he saw from her was a constant, deep sadness that never left her eyes, and when he wasn't around, hours of tears, the only trace the redness of her eyes.

Pressured by her Methodist Bible-thumping parents to no longer live in sin, they married. It was a cheap, brief ceremony without the frills of an upper-middle-class wedding, their honeymoon a night in a cheap motel where they kissed each other good night then fell asleep without making love.

Benny finished his master's then his PhD in psychology as Jean kept getting sadder and sadder. Had she opened up to him, had she bared her soul, he could have helped her. After all, he was the expert, wasn't he? But she didn't.

She declined to accompany him on his first job interview – therapist at a prestigious clinic. And wasn't that something? So he flew to Pasadena and flew through his interview and was hired. When he told her he had the job her only response was, "That's nice. Now you should make it through life okay. Goodbye." The goodbye had been prolonged, the *bye* lilting then fading like her whole life in one syllable.

On his return flight, Benny wondered at her response as the circles of dryland irrigation faded into the checkerboard of row crop farming from 30,000 feet above, the twinkling blue and yellow lights of farms and towns and cities peopling the earth. Why wasn't she happier? Why wasn't she more excited? Why didn't she, already nearly an accomplished artist herself, want to jump at the chance to pack her canvas and brushes and oils and hurry out to the Golden State where she could paint boats and seagulls and tossing aqua waves whenever she wanted?

The first thing he did after the plane landed was pull out his bulky cell phone and call her. The phone rang ten times then the answering machine picked up. *Hello, this is the Johnsons. We're not home right now, so please leave a message.* And then the beep – ten of them. Then he tried her cell. *Hi, this is Jean. You know what to do.* Six more beeps.

"Well I'll be damned." He tried his folks who lived an hour away, but they weren't home either. So he tried his best friend.

"Hey Jer? This is Benny. I'm here at the airport and Jean isn't picking up. Can you come get me?"

"Sure, bud. Hey, you get the job?"

"Sure did. Eighty grand to start."

"Crap. You'll be rollin' in the dough. Hey. Let me throw on a jacket and I'll be right there."

Benny studied the milling concourse crowds, people coming and going, all strangers so they let their true feelings show – fear, anger, grief. His only feelings were excitement and joy.

Jer met him at the luggage claim a half hour later. "Eighty grand! Isn't that something?"

Benny could hardly believe it himself as they drove toward his and Jean's apartment. Their black cat Jinx was in the hallway when they got there, meowing up a storm. "Jinxy." Benny picked up the cat and held her in his arms, wishing she were Jean.

He turned the key in the lock as Jer carried in his bag. "Geez, I gotta take a whiz. Mind if I use your can?"

"No problem." Benny scanned the room. "Jean?" Only a hollow, vacant echo answered.

"Oh my God!"

"Jer?"

Jer slammed the bathroom door, face white. "Don't go in there."

Benny heard all except Jer's first word. Jer stood in the way to keep him from entering the bathroom, but Benny fought past him.

In the pink tub of water Jean lay naked, brown hair spooled in a halo around her head. A long, red slit traced each of her writs, her blue eyes staring stark and wondrous at the next world she had entered.

Benny never did go to Pasadena. He didn't even call. After Jean's funeral he went straight to the closest bar and paid $4 a shot for JDs on the rocks until they 86ed him and then he bought a fifth at the liquor store next door. He didn't stop drinking for twenty years.

***

"I'm thinking of killing myself."

A slight, frightened boy the other kids undoubtedly teased mercilessly peered at him from across the desk. Besides being undersized, even for a high-school sophomore, Carl's acne pustules raged like a hundred volcanoes ready to explode.

"Why do you say that?"

Carl looked at the blank wall as though he wanted to crawl through it. "The other kids. They . . . "

Carl didn't have to continue. Benny already knew his story. Carl had been a straight-A student all the way through grade school and junior high. And this year, his first year of high school, his grades had plummeted. Benny leaned slightly over his desk, just enough to show his interest yet giving Carl his space. "Carl?"

Carl turned to him, a frightened-rabbit look in his eyes.

"You're going through a real pile of crap right now, aren't you?"

Carl's lips muttered up his answer. "Yes."

"The other kids give you grief every time you turn around, don't they."

"Yes."

"And you feel like you're the only person in the world who's treated the way you are. Don't you."

"Yes," Carl peeped.

"Well you're not. Thousands of kids – millions – feel exactly the same way you do. And they have the same

235

feelings you do right now, Carl."

"They do?"

"Absolutely. You're not alone, Carl. There are others who feel just the same way you do."

Carl's eyes flitted side to side. "So where are they?"

"They're all around you. They're hiding in the corners, sitting along at lunch tables, feeling the same way you do."

Carl looked at him as though he had plunged through his eyes and into the pit of his soul.

"Make friends with them, Carl. Tell *them* how you feel. And when they tell you how they feel, *listen*."

Carl's tears came, a flood. "I can do that, can't I?"

"Yes you can, Carl. You have the power in you to change your life and the lives of others."

"Do you really think so?"

"I know so." Benny stood and came around his desk. "Stand up."

Carl slowly rose from his chair, shaking.

Benny threw his arms around Carl in a big bear hug. "I care, Carl. I care," he whispered, imaging for the briefest moment that it was Jean he was holding in his arms.

***

The cool kiss of dawn pried open his eyes. Judging from the light, he figured it was just before 5.

Benny chuckled to himself as he thought of the kids he'd seen the day before – eight of them. The teacher referrals said they were low performers, behavior problems, lacking motivation. But he just saw them as kids – all the same except for the barriers adults had placed in their paths to keep them from succeeding.

Benny also realized yesterday was the first full day he had gone without a drink since Jean had taken her life twenty years before.

He bolted up and looked around. He had pitched his shelter half in a state park, far enough away from the campground to remain undetected. Last night he had gone to bed figuring his foray into the school would be but for a day. But he knew the kids needed him. And because they needed him, he needed them. He figured he could walk to the school in less than an hour.

He bathed in a crackling cold stream then put on the same suit – different shirt – and rolled up his camp with his backpack and laid it in an animal burrow in a side hill. He guessed the badger or cougar or bear or whatever it was would just have to find a new home.

He made it to the school a half-hour early, time enough to gloss his appointments. Twelve today with an afternoon faculty in-service.

A light rap drew his eyes to his door where the hall light framed Laura Schoenauer's smile. "Good morning, Mr. Johnson."

Benny returned her smile. He liked this woman. He liked her a lot. And it wasn't just because she was so incredibly attractive. She cared about kids, just as he did. Then he guessed that was why they were both there. Benny stood and motioned for Laura to sit in the chair on the other side of his desk. "Have a seat, if you have a minute."

"I have three or four even," Laura said eagerly as she took the chair, her smile perking through. "I saw Carl Tillman in the hallway yesterday."

"Oh?" Benny wondered where her conversation was leading.

"He was smiling."

"Yeah?"

Laura tilted her head at him. "What on earth did you *say* to him? I've *never* seen Carl smile."

Benny shrugged. "I just gave him some words of encouragement."

"Well whatever those words were, they worked. I guess he even asked the cross-country coach about joining the team. Carl has *never* shown an interest in sports before."

Benny hoisted an eyebrow, surprised himself. "I

guess that's pretty good, huh?"

"That's fantastic. Oh, by the way . . . " Laura handed him a spiral-bound book she'd carried in. "We'll be going over standards and benchmarks at this afternoon's in-service. I thought you might like a little light reading before the meeting."

Benny hefted the half-pound document as Laura handed it to him. It was a good inch thick.

"And your first appointment today is a real case."

Benny cast an appraising glance at her. He hated when people were quick to judge others. Especially kids. "Oh?"

Laura stabbed her finger at the list on Benny's desk. "Jose Martinez. The biggest bully in the school. I wish we could just get rid of him."

Benny looked at Jose's name then back at Laura as he tried to determine what was going on. "I'll see what I can do."

"Well, good luck. You'll need it." Laura rose from her chair, lingering at the doorway as her fingers caressed the frame as she looked over her shoulder. "Would it be okay if I called you Ralph when we're alone?"

"Ralph?"

Laura cupped her hand around her laugh, echoing it to herself. "Your first name, silly."

"Oh sure, Ms. Schoenauer."

"Please call me Laura."

"Okay . . . Laura."

She winked and curled her fingers at him in a goodbye wave. "Bye . . . "

Laura Schoenauer's heels clicking down the hallway drew his errant thoughts away from Jose Martinez and standards and benchmarks and every other thought that had been in his head before she had entered his office that morning. Was it his imagination, or was she flirting with him?"

Jose Martinez was there ten minutes later, the chain on his wallet long enough to strangle an opposing gang member. The tattoo on his neck said hardcore. Jose came in and kicked the chair out from Benny's desk and plopped into it and crossed his arms defiantly. "So what kinda shit we talkin' about?"

Benny could already see why Laura found Jose a problem. He would have too if it hadn't been for his last twenty years on the street. His academic studies would have done nothing to prepare him for Jose. "I don't know. What do *you* want to talk about?"

"What *I* wanna talk about?"

"Yeah."

Jose's smile curled up inside itself. "How 'bout booze an' weed an' pussy?"

"I guess that's as good a place to start as any."

Twenty minutes later, Jose was hanging on Benny's every word. When Benny quit talking, Jose's eyes lifted gravely. "No shit? Your old lady was dead when you come home an' you lived on the streets twenty years?"

Benny nodded slowly. Jose was the only person who had ever heard his whole story. Then Jose was probably the only person in the building who could have understood it.

"Man . . . " Jose sat on the edge of his chair, hands clasped, shaking his head. "Ah's sorry, man. Ah's real sorry."

"If someone like me can pull himself up by his bootstraps, don't you think you can too, Jose?"

Benny's question perked up Jose's ears like a racehorse hearing the bell.

"What is it you want to do with your life, Jose?"

Jose stared at him, the walls between them crumbling beneath shared tragedies. "Well, ah thinks it'd be real dope to be a lawyer."

"Well, that will require some study now, won't it? Courses like English and government."

"Man, I hates them courses."

"You want to understand the system and how to change it, don't you?"

239

"Yeah."

"Well then that's what you need to do."

"Ah don' know. That sound real hard."

"Life's hard, Jose. I know that. You know that. Trouble is, none of those mother fuckers out there in the hallway know that."

"Jose's smile brimmed. "Did you just say *mother fuckers*, Mr. Johnson?"

"Damn straight." Benny stood up from his desk and came around and knuckle-bumped Jose. "So you know where the shit is now, man."

Something glimmered in Jose's eyes. Something he'd never understood before but did now.

Benny put his hand on Jose's shoulder. "Come talk to me whenever you want. About anything you want. Even girls."

"Okay, man. Okay." Jose nodded to himself. "Ah'll do that."

***

Benny could tell right away no one else wanted to be at the in-service – even Laura. After Laura introduced him as the new school counselor and everyone shared introductions, the faculty engaged in side conversations, locked arms already showing they were closed to hearing any new ideas or following new mandates. After Laura discussed a PowerPoint on standards and benchmarks, Gil Haus, the history teacher, shook his head slowly.

"Yes Mr. Haus?"

"If our students are doing so great in English, then why can't they write a decent essay question?"

Sharon Leitz, the English instructor, looked aghast at Haus. "Gee, why don't they know a damn thing about the Civil War when we discuss *Red Badge of Courage*?" And then the riot began.

Laura had everything to shout them down. "Listen! Could everyone listen! Could we please have a little *order* in here?" She turned to Benny who had been holding up his hand for a good minute. "Yes, Mr. Johnson?" she asked, tone lightening.

Benny hoisted his pants cuffs from the tops of his shoes and stood. "How about if we taught basic competency skills across the curriculum – history teachers could assess a writing component, writing teachers cold assess a history component, that sort of thing."

Gil Haus was living. "I'm a history teacher, not an English teacher. It's not part of my job."

Benny shrugged. "Well what *is* our job? It's teaching kids, isn't it? Encouraging and guiding and molding them? And how is our arguing accomplishing that."

Stunned silence.

"We're so preoccupied by our own personal standards and benchmarks that we're failing to see the whole picture. I'd suggest shared rubrics across the curriculum. Ten percent of assessment, say, could be based on rubrics from other disciplines. That way, stellar student achievement would be require students to demonstrate not just a grasp of basic concepts but a direct application to their daily lives."

"So does that mean I have to teach public speaking?" asked Daryl Rusche, the CAD instructor.

"Do engineers have to give presentations? Do they have to speak to groups in response to RFPs?" Benny challenged.

"Well . . . yes," Rusche acknowledged.

"Then would you agree that quite often it's not the best engineering firm that gets the professional services contract but the one that gives the best presentation?"

Rusche's eyes paled over. The silence in the room was deafening.

Laura cleared her throat to break the silence. She stepped from the overhead projector to the center of the room and looked down, searching for words. "I think Mr. Johnson has presented some very important points." Her gaze shifted to him with newfound awe. "Some very penetrating and fascinating points, in fact. I think what we need is a retreat to develop some shared rubrics we can all agree upon."

Light assenting murmurs sifted through the room.

Laura nodded at him. "Thank you, Mr. Johnson."

After the in-service, Benny went to his office and logged on to his computer and downloaded and completed an application to renew his professional license.

***

A week later, a half-dozen students were at his door when he got to work. The first in line was Jose Martinez – with books in his hand.

Between bells Benny saw Carl Tillman talking to a girl by his locker. She was a little mousy and seemed shy with enormous glasses, but give her an updated pair of glasses or remove them altogether and give her a fresh hairstyle and some makeup and she would have been downright cute. Benny knew that would all happen if Carl talked to her long enough. He clasped Carl's shoulder as he passed. "You go, tiger."

Carl beamed a smile over his shoulder. His acne seemed to be clearing. "Good morning, Mr. Johnson."

Benny chuckled to himself as he passed down the hallway. He suspected Carl might have an enormous impact on the girl's transformation – and she on his.

"Oh, Mr. Johnson." Laura bounded down the hall, almost in a run – something she didn't normally dare do because she always scolded the students for it. She stood before him breathless, eyes shining, skin glowing. "I was wondering, Mr. Johnson, Ralph," she whispered under her breath. "Would you be interested in heading up our across-the-curriculum committee?"

"Sure," he agreed, without knowing exactly what all that would entail. Then it was his idea, wasn't it? "So when's the first meeting?"

"Wednesday afternoon after our usual early dismissal."

"All right." He stood there and looked into Laura's

glacial blue eyes and realized how incredibly beautiful she was. Not a blemish. Not a hair out of place. She was absolutely perfect. "I, uh, I'd really like that."

A light *hmmm* emerged from deep inside Laura's throat, a *hmmm* she couldn't control. "I was wondering, Mr. Johnson . . . " Her eyes darted side to side as students wove around them.

"Yes, Ms. Schoenauer?"

"I was wondering if we could have dinner tomorrow night. At my place." She looked off at the students, their lockers, at nothing as though her hand were caught in a cookie jar. Then her head snapped up toward him. "To go over the rubrics, of course."

Her reason for their meeting was so facile, so obvious, he had to hold back a chuckle. "Certainly, Ms. Schoenauer," he said, saying her name as though it were rare jewel. "Just name the time and place."

***

Laura Schoenauer's apartment was upscale but not posh – exactly the sort of apartment where Benny expected an up-and-coming substitute principal would live. Benny figured even he could swing an apartment there on his $36,000 salary.

He buzzed the intercom and she answered seconds later. "Is that you, Ralph?" He had to think a moment as the lie caught in his throat. "Uh, yeah." The buzzer rang and he entered the door and took the elevator to the eleventh floor and found her apartment by the aroma of her cooking – *Do you like hot curry?* she had asked. He loved it. For the past twenty years, it had been his favorite meal he had dug from the restaurant dumpsters along Lake Street.

Laura met him at the door, hair down and slung over her left shoulder like a perfect, glistening waterfall. He wanted to bury his face in it just to inhale it. To inhale all of her. "You're early," she said, making an excuse for the apron she removed to reveal a casual aqua top that matched her eyes and skinny jeans. "Grab a seat in the living room. I have a snack tray set up."

Benny smiled at her, a smile that faded when he saw the meat and cheese tray with a bottle of wine and two glasses beside it. The glasses were close but not quite touching. A signal of how close she wanted them to sit?

"I hope you like my curry recipe. I had all I could do to talk it out of this quaint little chef in Singapore when I was there on a Fulbright a couple years ago. Have you ever been to Singapore?" Laura asked, her words and face peeking at him from around the kitchen doorway.

Benny stood there, afraid to even get close to the wine.

Laura angled her gaze at him. "Is something wrong, Ralph?"

He wanted to grab the wine bottle and drain it without a pause. He closed his eyes slowly, wishing Laura and her apartment and the kids and the job he had stolen would all go away and he could be on the street again. "I, uh, I don't drink." He opened his eyes. "Alcohol, I mean." A sheen of sweat broke across his forehead and a slight shaking started somewhere deep inside his gut and went all the way to his hands and feet.

"I'm sorry." Laura looked to the wine bottle then him. "Are you okay?"

"Yeah, sure." He couldn't look back at the wine. Or the meat and cheese tray. Or Laura. "I . . . uh . . . " He wanted to finish his sentence with *think this is a mistake* but couldn't.

"Yes?" Laura stood inches away, her aqua top almost brushing against him, her darting eyes searching his.

"I . . . uh . . . think maybe I should go."

Laura's eyes shimmered in the kitchen light fighting to invade the darkened living room where a single candle glowed to the sound of soft jazz.

"I'm not who you think I am, Laura."

"Well none of us are," she said, a sudden edge to her voice. "We all have barriers. We're all afraid to show our true feelings, Ralph. Why – "

"I'm not Ralph."

Her eyes froze in their sockets. "What?"

"I'm not Ralph Johnson."

Laura coughed up a laugh. "Well who *are* you then?"

"My name is Benjamin Johnson. I've been a skid row wino for the past twenty years. I found a couple suits in an alley in a drycleaner's dumpster. I took a freezing cold shower in the school sprinkler system and put on my suit and had just finished a couple hero sandwiches from the dumpster behind the school when you first called me Mr. Johnson. And oh . . . you can call me Benny, not Ralph."

Laura's gaped as her face paled and she stood away from him. "Get . . . the hell out of my apartment before I call the police."

"I'm sorry."

"And don't you *dare* set foot on school property or I *will* have you arrested."

"I'm sorry. I'm so, so sorry," he said as he closed the door behind him.

***

He retrieved his backpack from the cave and returned to the city – the place where he knew how best to survive. He asked about the HELP WANTED sign in a greasy spoon diner window and was flipping burgers and pouring coffee ten minutes later.

After a full month of sobriety, he had his first paycheck in his hand in twenty years. He found a room with shared kitchenette and bath three blocks from the diner and settled into his new life.

***

"So his name wasn't even Ralph Johnson." Dr. Stoeckman gazed across his desk at her, measuring the full impact of what she had said.

"No. It was Benny. Or Ben. Or Benjamin or whatever." Laura's ramrod-straight back was so rigid it didn't touch the back of her chair.

A light knock and his office door opened. "Dr. Stoeckman?" His administrative assistant entered and held up a manilla envelope. "I hate to bother you, Dr. Stoeckman. This came for Mr. Johnson from the state Department of Human Services. Would you like me to open it?"

A light flashed in Dr. Stoeckman's eyes. "Sure."

"Thank you," said his assistant, closing the door.

"Opening the U.S. mail? Isn't that a little *illegal*?" Laura asked.

"How about impersonating a school counselor. Isn't *that* illegal?"

A knock again and the door opened. "Dr. Stoeckman? I think you should see this," she said, handing him the opened envelope.

Dr. Stoeckman sighed and leveled his gaze at Laura as he slid a sheet from the envelope and peered down at it. "Well, what have we here? A professional license issued by the state Department of Human Services to a Benjamin Johnson, PhD."

"*PdD*?"

"Apparently he was masking as a mental health professional too. This," Dr. Stoeckman said, waving the document in his hand, "is going to put Mr. *Benjamin* Johnson exactly where he belongs – behind bars." He studied the document. "Part of this whole mess is probably my fault. I should have come here to meet him when he first started. Then I would have realized he wasn't the man I had hired. I was so tied up in meetings with the state school lobbyist though. I just wonder whatever happened to Ralph Johnson," Dr. Stoeckman said, looking out his window.

***

Laura felt as though a truck had run over her when she got home that night. Had it been less than twenty-four hours since Ralph – or Benny – Johnson had been in her apartment? A fake, a fraud, maybe even a serial killer for all she knew? The open wine bottle still sat on the living room coffee table, the two glasses still there, nearly touching. The dried-up meat and cheese already curled up. She shivered as she thought how close she had come to giving herself to him – offering herself up as a sacrifice.

She tossed the meat and cheese in the garbage and poured the wine down the sink, hating Benjamin Johnson with all her soul. The phone interrupted her thoughts and she tossed the bottle in the recycling along with the thought that she never wanted to ever see Benjamin Johnson again.

"Ms. Schoenauer, Dick Stoeckman. I'm glad I caught you."

"It's not like I have a social life anyway," she said, slamming the recycling container lid shut.

An extended silence. "I just got off the phone with the state social services director."

"Oh?" She glanced at the curry still in the glass-covered casserole dish on top of the stove. She bet that if she left it there long enough, she wouldn't be able to tell the rice from maggots. Now wouldn't Benny Johnson enjoy *that* on his dumpster diving forays? "Do they have Benjamin Johnson in custody yet?"

"*Dr.* Johnson."

"What?"

"Apparently he has a PhD in psychology from Berkeley."

"Are you *kidding*?"

"DHS never kids. They verified it."

Laura twisted the phone cord through his fingers. "Why did he take a school *counselor* position? With a *PhD*?"

"I have no idea. All I do know is we were getting one hell of a deal at $36,000 a year."

"So why the story about his being on the street for twenty years?"

"That's quite possibly true. Apparently he first obtained his professional license in 1997 and it lapsed

247

when he failed to renew it."

"My God." She looked at the recycling container, the meat and cheese in the trash, the curry on the stove, her head swimming. Why didn't he tell me?"

"Did you give him the opportunity?"

"No."

"Well there you have it."

A dry, hot wind ran through her body as though she didn't exist. "So what are you doing to do?"

"I've had a constant stream of students coming to my office all day. They're demanding to know what happened to Ralph Johnson." A pause as he mulled his answer. "I'm going to find Benjamin Johnson, PhD, *from Berkeley*, and offer him a position as school counselor at Lakeland High School."

Her heart fell to the pit of her stomach then bounced back to the base of her throat. "Do you think you can find him?"

"I'm sure the police can."

"I'm sorry." She scrunched the phone cord between her fingers. "I should have given him the chance to explain himself."

"Your reaction, given what you knew at the time, was quite appropriate, Ms. Schoenauer. I'm sure Mr. *Benjamin* Johnson even found it appropriate. "Goodbye."

"Bye . . . " she said, voice trailing. She hung up the phone and thought of Benjamin Johnson – or Benny. Her mind drifted back to the night before. Twenty years on the street. Twenty years. What terrible thing had happened to him for that to happen? And where was he now?

She got her pepper spray from the kitchen drawer and put on her coat and headed out for the most dangerous part of the city.

***

"You missed a spot there."

Harry looked over the mop handle. "You never was this picky before when we was together on the street."

"I have a job now. And so do you. And we'd better

do our jobs if we want to keep them."

Harry grumbled and finished mopping the floor and rolled the mop bucket into the back room to empty it.

Benny topped off everyone's coffee at the counter then took an order from a young couple in a corner booth. They were apparently in love, the way they held hands against the cold seeping through the plate glass windows. On the other side of the window snow drifted slowly like notes written to the jazz station Benny had playing on the radio. No one had noticed when he switched it from the oldies channel so he decided to leave it.

The bell above the door tinkled and a woman came in. Snowflakes dusted her black wool coat as she pulled off her stocking cap and shook her blonde hair and took another empty booth beside the window.

Benny grabbed a menu, glass of water, coffee pot, and cup and went to her. He set the cup on the table and filled it.

"Thank you," she said.

"I didn't even need to ask. You had *I need coffee* written all over your face. By the way, I'd recommend the grilled cheese and chili."

"Oh my God, it's you."

Benny finally looked at the woman. Laura. He tried to swallow but couldn't.

"We've *scoured* this city for months searching for you. Where have you been? What have you been *doing*?"

The coffee pot in his hand suddenly felt as though it weighed a ton. "I've upgraded my living accommodations, you might say. And I've been working, catching up with the news of the world, not drinking . . . that sort of thing."

"Dr. Stoeckman wants you back."

"He does?"

Her eyes peered up fervently at him. "So do the kids. So do I."

Benny set the coffee pot down on the table and sat across from her. The snow was heavy now, silver-dollar flakes gliding past the window. All unique, pressing them together into a much-smaller world. He reached across the table for her hand. "I'd really recommend the grilled cheese and chili."

***

"Dr. Conrad, the patient is reviving."

Dr. Nelson Conrad rushed to the patient's side, the nurse checking the patient's vitals. "Nearly four months in a coma. Remarkable. You are one lucky man, Mr. Johnson. We never thought you would survive that car accident."

Ralph Johnson opened his eyes and tried to determine his surroundings and wondered where he would be tomorrow.

The Dare

The whole house was crazy over Sofia's quinceanera. Their mother Carlotta had hired a band – traditional mariachi no less – and all of Maria's brothers and sisters were decorating their house with bunting and Mexican flags. Little Isidro was even in on it, filling the piñata he had made himself with candies and toys and those whistles that when you blow on them sound just like the police sirens in Juarez where they visited their relatives every other year – or third – or whenever they could afford it. The reason they were in such a rush was that Sofia's quinceanera – a party for Mexican girls who were formally ready for courtship at age fifteen – was five Saturday afternoon.

Maria pinched a smile as she listened to the others, so excited that every tio and tia and primo and prima would be there. Some were even coming from Mexico. Even her father Juan would be there, provided the police released him. Maybe, just maybe, he would be out of the carcel in time to see her graduate from DARE on Thursday.

Maria held out little hope for that. She was but ten, a fifth-grader, merely a child, eclipsed by Sofia's event and her own disappointment in her father who had been arrested for drunk driving the weekend before. It wasn't the driving drunk that was so bad but her father's inability

251

to follow the instructions of the policia. According to their report, when they had asked him to recite the alphabet he had stumbled over the letters like little Isidro had over his blocks when he was a baby, giving him the scar still blazed across his forehead as he now filled the piñata that looked more like a rhinoceros than a horse. And when they asked Juan to walk in a straight line, he tripped over his own foot he'd hurt at the packing plant the day before. When they tested his blood it was exactly .08 – just enough to send him to the carcel.

It wasn't his drunk driving arrest that got him fired so much as that her mother couldn't raise money for bail. Monday, Tuesday, Wednesday their mother counted off the days. And today, Wednesday, his supervisor called to say he no longer had a job.

And that was the pall cast over both Maria's DARE graduation tomorrow night and Sofia's quinceanera Saturday. All the food, all the frijoles and carne asada and tamales and enchiladas for Sofia's great day her mother had already made. And could they take food they'd already made back to pay their father's bail? Maria wondered. She had to only once look into Sofia's brimming tears to realize that was out of the question. And besides, whoever heard of a tienda de comestibles taking back food once it was sold.

And so they went ahead as planned, Sofia with her quinceanera and Maria with her DARE graduation. One a great, blazing Mexican sun and the other a far and distant dwindling star. Both overshadowed by their family's shame.

***

Her mother had just put dinner on the table when the front door opened and in walked her father, looking sheepish and a little worse for the wear, with her tio Manuel following closely behind. They all knew the story without having to ask. Tio Manuel had come up with her father's bail, just as he had helped him out of scrapes so many times before. Had her father called him right away instead

252

of hiding behind his machismo, he would have still had his job.

As the rest of the family stood aghast, seeing her father almost as an intruder, Maria ran up to him and threw her arms around him and sobbed into his belly that still smelled like the carcel. "I missed you, Papa," she cried, feeling his hand in her hair as he looked at the rest of his familia.

Her mother turned back to the stove where she had been making supper. "I see you're back," she said, not looking at him.

He stroked Maria's hair, drawing strength from her dark locks. "Manuel said maybe he could help get me my job back."

"Thank you, Manuel," her mother said looking at her tio but not her father.

Manuel nodded from where he still stood beside the door, feet shuffling his thoughts. "You shouldn't be so hard on your husband," he said, trying not to take sides.

Her mother clanked the lid on the pot of frijoles, hung up her apron on the wall, and turned to her uncle. "Hard on my husband? How can I even begin to be hard enough on a man who spends every night in the bodega and who comes home smelling of beer and whiskey. How can I be hard enough when he finally falls asleep when he should be getting up for work. How can I be hard enough on a man who thinks more of his compadres than his own wife and children."

Tio Manuel could only stand there and hold out his hands. "Maybe if you weren't so hard on him he wouldn't do those things."

With no place else for her anger to go, her mother's face reddened. "Are you staying for supper?"

"No." Tio Manuel waved her off. "I have to do." He faced his brother and gripped him in what was a warning as much as reassurance. "You'll be okay now, okay?"

"I'll be okay," her father said sheepishly.

As Tio Manuel left, Maria was able to focus her

father's attention on her. "Will you be coming to my DARE graduation tomorrow night, father?"

"Of course, daughter, yes."

***

Maria heard her parents argue in the bedroom above through the night, her mother speaking of divorce. She had hinted at it before, maybe cajoled and threatened, but this was the first time she had laid it down so hard and firm. *You have no chances, Juan. You've used your last one.*

Maria lay there for what seemed like forever and finally drifted off to sleep broken by fragments of dreams so vivid they sometimes woke her. The most vivid was of her father stuck in quicksand. She went to help him, but didn't want to fall into the quicksand herself. So she knelt before him for what seemed like forever as he thrashed violently, quicksand finally swallowing him up and entering his nostrils so he drowned.

Maria awoke sobbing. Sofia was shaking her. "Wake up, you're having a bad dream."

Maria looked up at her big sister, looking like an angel in the dim light streaming through the windows and her filmy pink gown. "I was dreaming of our father."

Sofia bent down and hugged her. "Don't you worry now." She was warm against her. "He can't hurt you now. He won't sleep with you like he did me. If he even thinks of it, I will kill him."

***

Sofia's revelation about their father and herself hung with Maria through the morning. A father sleep with his own daughter? How horrible. As much as she loved her sister, she now hated her father even more.

She sat at breakfast with all the other children and her father around the table, their mother and Sofia scurrying to feed everyone. Before they began to eat, their mother had them all join hands in prayer. "Padre, please heal this house and all the evil that has come into it. Help us trust each other again. And most of all, Padre, help Juan get his job back again."

A knocking came at the screen door just as they were finishing breakfast. Her father rose to meet Jose at the door – his often partner in crime whom their mother had branded as no better than a common criminal. If her father had been arrested for drunk driving once, Jose had been arrested three or four times. And each time he begged and pleaded with the judge, saying he needed to drive to keep his job and feed his wife and children. For some unknown reason, the judge granted his request, even though there were rumors that Jose was selling marijuana. And now Jose was driving her father to work.

When her father went to kiss her mother goodbye she just stood there, wiping her hands on a towel after doing dishes as though wiping her hands clean of him. "And you will be home on time by five so we can go to Maria's DARE graduation?"

As her father looked from her mother to Maria, he had the same look in his eyes as in her dream – lost, forlorn, abandoned. "Of course I'll be there."

Maria didn't believe him. Even after all the nights he had come home drunk, even after he had been arrested, she had loved him and believed in him. But after what Sofia had told her, she didn't love or believe in him at all. "I don't think you'll be there."

Her father looked to her mother, expecting some discipline, maybe a matriarchal slap across his daughter's face. But her mother only stood there, still wiping her hands and her husband from her life.

"I'll be there," her father promised, now in tears.

Maria looked to Sofia, knowing her father would certainly be at her quinceanera – probably for more reasons than one. But would he show up at her DARE graduation? "I dare you to show up," Maria said, again challenging her father. "If you love me at all, you will."

"I'll show up," he said, bowing to her like a child to a parent. "I'll be at your graduation, Maria. I promise."

***

For six weeks, DARE graduation was all anyone could talk

255

about in the school, a hundred-year-old, ivy-encrusted brick building that could have been taken for a college. Still known as a packing town, Millville attracted all ethnicities – Hispanic, Laotian, Hmong, Sudanese – so whites were now a minority, at least in Maria's class.

Following their after-school program the students gathered in Roosevelt Auditorium, named not for the second but the first President Roosevelt. Students chattered like a thousand squirrels, bouncing a dull roar all around the ancient chandeliers and the stage curtains, scrambling their teachers to keep order. Finally, Officer Donnelly, the DARE officer they had all come to love, stood on the stage with his German shepherd Rex. After the futile efforts of their teachers to get the kids to shush, Rex barked once, quieting the kids with wonder.

"Thank you, kids, and thank you, Rex, for bringing everyone to order." Officer Donnelly laughed and petted Rex and the kids laughed too, Rex wagging his tail appreciatively. "Today is the day we've all been waiting for. Today is the day you graduate from DARE."

The kids roared, a sound that set off Rex barking, which only made the kids roar louder and Rex bark even louder yet. As she plugged her ears against the roar, Maria scanned the crowd for her family. Everyone else's was here – or at least it seemed like it. There Anna's parents were, along with her brother and sister. And Pedro and Camilla's families too. Everyone's family was here – everyone's. Except hers.

She started to cry as Office Donnelly talked about their accomplishments, about how *great* everyone had done, and how proud he and Rex were that everyone had taken the DARE pledge to stay away from drugs and alcohol. "Just say no, just say no," the kids chanted, and then Maria saw her parents come in. Yes, there they were! Her mother and Sofia and Isidro and the others, and yes, even her father trailing behind. All the seats were full, so they had to go all the way to the front, just below the stage where Rex was barking, suddenly pulling at his choke collar. Officer Donnelly jerked Rex's collar so the shepherd sat, but he stood again right away, barking at her family. "Rex!" Officer Donnelly commanded, jerking Rex's chain so the dog whined and barely lifted his tail.

Mrs. Anderson, her homeroom teacher, played a slide show of the kids in their DARE activities – making signs, giving speeches, writing essays. And then it was time to award the winning essays. First it was Danny Orillo – she should have known, the showoff. The student winning from the next class was Suzy Olson – what a little snot – she hated her. Then Gloria Norman – she was a snot too. Darlene Caruthers – yuck. Maria Ortiz . . .

The students on both sides of her elbowed her. "Go up and get your award, Maria," said Miguel Padilla.

"What? Me?"

"Go up, go up," they urged.

So there she was, Maria Ortiz, rubber legs so soft she could barely stand, shaking as she climbed the stairs. Only when she reached the stage did it all sink in to her. She was one of five essay winners, five out of over a hundred students.

As she reached the stage and went to join the others, they looked differently at her than they had before. In their eyes, they accepted her as one of them.

Next was the fun part, the part all the kids had been waiting for. Officer Donnelly had hidden a hollow ball filled with marijuana somewhere on the stage and Rex was going to help him find it. Officer Donnelly explained that Rex would sniff around, looking here and there, high and low, then sit beside the spot where the marijuana was.

So there they were, Officer Donnelly and Rex, Officer Donnelly calling out, "Where's the dope, Rex? Where's the dope?" Rex sniffing, tail low, sniffing at a table, the lectern, the stage curtain. "Where's the dope, Rex?" Rex went to the edge of the edge of the stage, wagging his tail, getting a great laugh from the kids, then, despite all Officer's Donnelly's attempts to restrain him, he leaped from the stage. "Rex!" Officer Donnelly called out.

Rex sat beside Maria's father, tail wagging, and all Juan Ortiz could do was pet Rex and say, "Nice doggie, nice doggie."

***

God answered Maria's prayers that Officer Donnelly wouldn't arrest her father – he called in a couple other officers for that – and they politely escorted him from the auditorium to the outside hallway where they searched him and found the marijuana and took him downtown for booking.

Sofia had her quinceanera, though it was far more subdued than she would have wished. Without their father around, it just wasn't the same.

The years sent Sofia into marriage then family and then Maria too. Paul was tall, blond, blue-eyed, Anglo, and Lutheran – as far from her family heritage as she could get. They fell in love beside the fountain inside the quad where she had been writing a poem about her father who was hooked up to a dialysis machine and had only a few months left. In the poem she tried to sort out her feelings for him, the ambiguity of loving him yet hating him for what he had done to Sofia, the shame he had brought upon the family with two arrests in one week. And then the shame of her parents' divorce after Maria had told her about her father and Sofia – the first divorce anyone ever remembered in their family.

"Hi," said Paul, sitting beside her. She wore white shorts and a huggy top that set off her best features and she had fortunately spent more than the usual amount of time on her makeup that morning as the man of her dreams came into her life. "Hi," she said, thinking it would go no further.

Oh, but it did. Paul saw to that. He asked if she would like to finish her poem over a pizza and beer at the craft brewery and pub at the edge of campus and she said she would. And there they sat, he gazing into her garnet-brown eyes and she into his that were as blue as the sky.

After her mother had passed away and she and the

other kids were going through her things, she found Sofia's diary – no doubt forgotten in her mother's house when she had married. No one objected when she asked to have it, and it sat in a drawer for over a year before she had the courage to break the lock and open it and release a torrent of memories. The smell of Sofia was even there, a hint of fruity perfume that brought her sister back to life again. Sofia had written of her first period, first date, first kiss, her quinceanera, and how she had lied to her sister about her father sleeping with her.

She reached up on her bookshelf and found the poem bookmarking Romantic Poets. As she sat looking at the struggling lines, her daughter Sofia, named in memory of her sister who had died in a car accident, asked if she could borrow her car keys to go see her boyfriend. "Be careful," she cautioned, as always, and Sofia shook her head and kissed her on the check as she left.

A cool rush of wind came through the window as Maria closed her sister's diary. She wondered if things would have been different if Sofia had never said those things about her father. The lines that had at one time seemed so heartfelt and honest now rang with falseness and bitterness.

She sat for a time then looked once again at the poem and took a pen from the drawer, and thinking of her father with a smile, decided to finish it.

The Final Season

The soft contours of Sarah matched the far-reaching hills. The lift of her thigh sloped gradually, like the start of the Coastal Range as it eased up from Yaquina Bay, reaching to her hip, so like Marys Peak – soft, gentle, yet unyielding. Then the slope of her stomach, Yaquina Valley, rising to the plateau of her ribcage and the softly unfolding foothills and finally her smile.

"What are you going to do today?" Sarah asked, her mild curiosity tinged with her longing for him.

He stroked her mountains and her valleys, hoping to make her landscape his again, before he headed out that morning. "I was thinking of taking some of those yearling steers to market. Then maybe stop in town and have coffee with the boys and buy you something nice."

Sarah scrunched up her strawberry-blonde smile, the part of her he loved the best. Even considering her mountains and valleys. Then her gaze shifted toward the west. "What about Harry? Were you going to visit him before he leaves?"

Harry was a writer friend who had drifted into the Yaquina Valley from Iowa and set down summer roots. They were deep roots though – as deep as the blackberry canes drifting all along the banks of the Yaquina and Siletz. "I spect I will. He don't come out here but once every couple years. And then maybe a couple weeks at a time at most."

Sarah turned and wrapped her arm around his stomach and studied the hole in the roof as though it still mattered that he fix it. "Why'd he build that cabin if that's all the longer he's here?"

"I don't know. He's a writer. I guess they can get by being all sorts of crazy."

Sarah turned to him. "Like a logger or a fisherman or a cattle rancher?"

"Something like that." He kissed her and studied how the green of her eyes drifted from her saucy Irish face. "I'd better go bring them steers in."

***

After he hauled his steers to market at Lebanon he cashed the check and bought Sarah a nice necklace and a bottle of wine for that night. Then he dropped off his cattle trailer at the ranch and drove up the snaking Yaquina Valley to Elk City. Not very big for a city, he mused as he passed by vacation cabins and campers interspersed among the handful of permanent residents. They were his friends, though, friends for as long as he could remember, and like all friends, they had their ups and downs. He only saw Harry often enough to be friends though. He guessed that was why he was so happy to see him when he did come these few weeks every couple years.

Harry's cabin was a bit outlandish. A glassy gondola-shaped thing about the size of a school bus with no privacy at all. Sarah had said she liked the cabin – it was a little larger than the one she and Billy lived in – but she didn't like the idea of all those windows. *I want you to build me one exactly like it*, she had said. *Except for all those damn windows. You don't want all the neighbors to see me stark naked, do you?*

He thought of a pretty funny answer for her but it would only have given him a cold shoulder – or worse. *The only neighbors are cougar and bear*, he had answered. *And if I built you a cabin exactly like his, it would be full of windows.* That last remark set her to simmering like week-old elk stew.

Harry was up when Billy got there – no surprise since he usually woke to the first false dawn to hit the valley. He was just finishing breakfast and dunking his dishes in hot soapy water. "Howdy," Harry said, settling back in his canvas chair and setting another cup on the small table between the other empty chair where he nodded for Billy to sit.

Billy sipped the chicory-laced coffee and nodded appreciatively. "Tastes like N'awlins."

"Nothing tastes as good as N'awlins." Harry sipped his coffee and tipped his head back into some memory stew only he could savor.

"So . . . " Billy proposed, setting down his coffee. "When we gonna head up Murderers Creek way and get that big elk's been hauntin' them canyons longer 'n a coon's age?"

Harry finished his coffee and topped off their cups and returned the pot to the camp stove. "I don't know. You figure my ought-six would bring him down?"

"Hell, my .270 would. Hit 'em in the right spot."

"Left flank, just behind the shoulder. Right?"

"You remembered." They laughed and drank coffee and talked hunting and fishing and women to death until it was time for Billy to leave. "One-eighty grain now, and not a grain less," Billy advised.

"Ought-six is cleaned and oiled and ready to go."

***

Sarah liked her necklace really well. After a dinner of grilled salmon and salad and potatoes, Billy pulled out his guitar and noodled a few tunes as a full blood moon rose over Yaquina Valley. Sarah sighed and rested her head against his shoulder as Billy matched the notes to the rolling Yaquina's baseline and the frogs and crickets came out with rhythm and percussion. Not a bad night, Billy figured. Not a bad night at all.

He was at Harry's place the next morning just as the sun was hoisting itself over the ridge. He and Sarah had

had a few words over his wanting to take Harry elk hunting at Murderers Creek.

"What? You have to drive a good day, maybe a day and a half, just to hunt elk?"

"I have a special depredation license," Billy answered, feeling a bit rankled.

"Well why didn't you just get a regular license?"

"Chances are, I'd never win a draw."

"Oh, all right. Go on your elk hunt and I'll just drive up the Coast to see Tina in Astoria."

Tina was the one person in Sarah's family he couldn't stand – and Sarah pretty much felt the same way. A visit to Sarah meant she was filled to the brim with him. "Suit yourself. I hope you have a *lovely* time."

"Ass." She pushed him so hard he fell out of his chair and came up laughing from the ground, despite the handful of blackberry nettles in his hand.

Harry wasn't up yet though. He lay there looking out the window as though he could see something so far away it would take the Pine Mountain Observatory at Bend to find it.

"What's this? Not up yet? Somebody else be getting' that ol' elk we don't hustle over there."

Harry rolled his feet to the cabin floor and clacked his dry tongue to the roof of his mouth. He reached for a cup of water on the table beside his bed. "I don't know. I've been feeling poorly lately." Harry lifted his eyes at him as though he really meant it.

"Poorly as in hangover poorly or as in gettin' old poorly."

Harry looked at the bottle of Jack on the table, the whiskey down to the neck. "Maybe a little of both. There was a time when I would never have gone to bed with nearly a full bottle of whiskey on the table."

"Well you didn't have *me* around last night," Billy chuckled then sobered. "You *don't* feel real well, do you? 'N fact, you look like shit."

"Thank you for confirming my high opinion of

myself."

"You're welcome. Say . . . " Billy mulled his next move. "Why don't we go to The Timbers in Toledo. I hear Jessica's workin'. You know, that cute brunette whose jeans you can never stop talkin' about?"

"Really?" said Harry, perking up.

"Yeah. I'll tell you what. Why don't we go have breakfast then go to the beach an' laugh at the tourists? Maybe we could slip into the Bay Haven for a sip or two afore we call it a day."

"Suits me."

They made a day of it – an expansive breakfast, served personally by Jessica – the seemingly endless beach flecked with the cries of gulls and a sky so blue it hurt to look at it – then the Bay Haven, dark as a tomb with its wood floor and red vinyl stools until their eyes got used to it and they stepped outside into the blinding white light of the Bayfront. It was still early, so they capped the day off with a chowder bread bowl at Mo's they washed down with a couple beers and headed back to Elk City but not before they grabbed a twelve-pack for the trip back.

It was just getting dark when they got to Harry's so Harry started a fire and they settled down with shots and beers. "What a wasted day," said Harry.

"Wasted?" Billy scooted up on the edge of his chair. "Why, we had a big breakfast served by a waitress you can't keep your eyes off of then we went to the beach an' rated girls from one to ten – with maybe a few minuses an' elevens or twelves thrown in. Then we drank 'til we couldn't walk so we had to drive but not afore we ate an' drank some more. An' now we're settin' here drinkin' more yet. An' now we're gonna smoke a little weed," Billy said as he pulled a joint from his shirt pocket and lit it.

"Oh boy," said Harry, taking the joint and toking so deeply the ember glowed his features and Billy saw how Harry looked as though the day had drained the last drop of blood from his face. That was the first time Billy had to admit maybe Harry didn't look that good at all. But they decided for sure they were going to Murderers Creek the next day.

Sarah was upset of course when he finally made it home after two, smelling like a brewery and a distillery and a wildfire racing through a field of pot. "Hunting my ass!" she said as she rolled over and punched her pillow as though it were his face. "You disgust me."

"Sorry, babe."

"Don't you babe me, you horse's ass."

Billy lay beside her, thinking of horses and asses but not horses' asses. "Are you mad, babe?"

"What do *you* think?"

A sudden thought came to him. "So why aren't you at Tina's?"

"The only person who disgusts me nearly as much as you is her."

That was when he realized romance was not in the picture that night.

***

He was up long before dawn. Still drunk, he drank himself sober with coffee until the valley started to lighten then he repacked his cooler with salami and cheese and beer – mainly beer – and headed for Harry's. This time he wasn't taking no for an answer. They were going to Murderers Creek and they were going to get that big elk if Harry were ready to go or not.

Smoking ashes still lay in Harry's fire pit from the night before and the drained whiskey bottle sat on the table, a dead general with the dozen dead soldiers of their empty beer cans scattered below. Billy was disappointed to see through the window Harry was still in bed.

"Come on, lazybones. Time's a wastin'. I hear that bull elk callin' our names." Billy nudged Harry's arm that fell limply to his side. His eyes were closed to some eternal dream, his freshly oiled ought-six standing in the corner with two boxes of rounds on the shelf beside it. "Oh crap, Har. Oh crap."

***

265

After the sheriff's deputy went through Harry's personal effects, Billy offered to call his niece back in the Midwest tell her the bad news. *No, I don't think he suffered*, Billy told her. *I don't think he suffered at all. It was just like he went to sleep.*

The ambulance came to pick up Harry's body so the mortician could prepare him for the flight back home for burial. Billy and Sarah stood there and looked at his cabin, now vacant except for his bed, dresser, and writing table.

"He had everything he needed. Right here. Didn't he," Billy said, Sarah's face blurring through his sheen of tears.

"He did." Sarah took his arm and looked into his eyes as the ambulance pulled away. "I only wish you two could have gone to Murderers Creek."

"I do too, babe. I do too."

***

As she lay beside him that night, Sarah wondered what Billy would do now that his friend was gone. Granted, they had seen each other but a few weeks every year or so. But they had been good friends, with Billy falling back into his boyhood she so detested yet adored.

As he lay there, his sadness melting into the solace of sleep, she traced her finger along the rising mountain of his thigh to the peak of his hip then down to his waist, still narrow for a man his age. His chest – a mountain unto itself – rose and fell slowly as the blessedness of sleep finally overcame him.

She spooned herself against his warm, naked back and legs and wrapped her arm around his waist and clutched him tightly. "I love you, Billy," she said as his light nicker answered. Then she wrapped the contours of her landscape against his.

The Golden Years

I was a college junior and already calling myself a writer when I took a room in the Johnsons' house on Clark and Plum. Their house was across the street from a sorority – which offered some interesting sights – and just east of the college tennis courts. The rent was $40 a month – a steal for even forty years ago. I saw moving in with the Johnsons as a new start. I'd just come off a couple bad breakups – one a girl I'd been seeing for four years and another who nearly destroyed me.

Mr. Johnson had to be the most hen-pecked man I'd ever seen. He would drive his 1967 Oldsmobile home every night from his watch and clock repair shop, park squarely in the garage as he had for the past forty years, and walk into a wall of flying invectives.

"Henry, why are you home so late."

"I'm sorry, dear. Isn't it exactly 5:15? The usual time I arrive home?"

"Oh, I guess it is. Well, why couldn't you have gotten home sooner. I could have used the buttermilk for this recipe. I'll bet you forgot it."

"Here it is, dear."

"Oh. Well, I suppose you forgot the vanilla then."

"It's right here dear. Right along with the buttermilk."

"You don't have to get so smart with me."

"I'm not trying to be smart, dear. I was just telling you that I'd brought the vanilla."

"Well change out of those awful frumpy clothes and go check on the furnace. I think we need a new filter."

"Yes, dear."

I and Will and Lee, the other guys who rented from the Johnsons, would gather at the top of the staircase that was a megaphone for the Johnsons' conversations. Afterward we would explicate their exchanges. Will, a psychology PhD candidate, had determined with absolute certainly that Mabel Johnson was manic depressive while Lee, a PhD candidate in biochemistry, thought she had a severe chemical imbalance possibly exacerbated by intense radon poisoning. I suggested the problem was merely biological – that Mr. Johnson needed to grow a set of balls.

Since the rent was cheap, I stayed on longer than I had expected – all the way through undergraduate and graduate school until I acquired the house through unforeseen events I'll talk about later. It was that first fall I began to see signs of Mr. Johnson's demise.

He started to forget things. Obvious things. I found that a bit odd since he was just sixty, but he began to forget the buttermilk and vanilla – unforgiveable, in Mrs. Johnson's mind. The night he came home without his Oldsmobile and asked Mabel if she knew where it was, she exploded.

"You idiot. What's the matter with you? Are you losing your marbles? I'm going to put you in a nursing home if you're going to be that stupid."

Apparently Mrs. Johnson later checked into the *cost* of a nursing home, because she no longer insisted Mr. Johnson go into one. But her tirades continued.

One early November day when the leaves had crisped to gold and scarlet and mauve all along Clark Street, a sure sign of fall and football and girls bundling up and burying their treasures until spring, Mr. Johnson failed to leave for work. My first class didn't start until ten, and I listened from the top of the stairs as Mrs. Johnson screamed at him.

"Henry, what's the matter with you? Why are you just sitting there? Are you listening to me? Henry!" Then I heard her voice calling my name from the bottom of the stairs. "Harrison?"

I just about jumped out of my shorts, thinking she knew I'd been spying on them. I waited a couple seconds then crept downstairs. "Yes, Mrs. Johnson?"

She stood there in mid-fume, as though confused about what to do next. I looked past her to Henry – seated in his chair, staring blankly out the window.

"Is Mr. Johnson okay?"

"I don't know." Mrs. Johnson worried her arms together into an impossible knot. "He doesn't respond to anything I say. All he does is sit there and stare."

I approached Mr. Johnson, quite frankly a little afraid. He looked fine – blue eyes clear, healthy glowing skin. Actually, he looked pretty damn good for sixty. The only problem was he just sat there, staring straight ahead.

"What do you think's the matter, Harrison?"

Behind Mr. Johnson, I motioned for Mrs. Johnson to follow me through the dining room to the kitchen where I quietly closed the door. "I'm sorry to have to tell you this, Mrs. Johnson, but I think he has Alzheimer's."

Mrs. Johnson looked up at me like a small bird caught in a trap. "Alzheimer's? That's impossible. He's just sixty. He was doing just fine the other day."

"Yeah, but crazy as it seems, I think that's the problem."

"Oh my God."

I wasn't sure just then how much money the Johnsons had. I figured they were comfortable, but I didn't think they were by any means rich. They had the income from Mr. Johnson's shop and three or four student tenants – and I figured that was about it. I knew if he went into the nursing home Mrs. Johnson would have to sell the house and the money wouldn't pay for Mr. Johnson's care before he passed on. For the first time, I felt sorry for her.

I skipped my first class and helped Mrs. Johnson walk her husband to their car and went along with them to the clinic. I stayed with her in the waiting room until the doctor came out and confirmed her worst fears.

The young, prematurely balding doctor rested his hand on her shoulder as he told her. "I'm sorry, Mrs. Johnson. All tests indicate your husband has Alzheimer's." He handed her a handful of brochures – nursing homes, in-home care options. None of them sounded very good – or cheap.

With no possibility of any response from her husband to her rants, Mrs. Johnson's tone toward him mellowed – maybe even softened – now that she had to feed and bathe him and help him to the bathroom. I saw a vastly changed Mrs. Johnson. What had before been an evil, malevolent shrew was now a sweet, tender woman who saw to her husband's every need. Incredible as it seemed, she became a saint.

***

I think just about every guy in the college tried to get into Anika Sorensen's Introduction to Philosophy class. Anika was a twenty-six-year-old grad assistant, Swedish, blue-eyed with blond pigtails, and built like a proverbial brick outhouse. She was a 44D at bare minimum, but lithely proportionate at five-ten.

I needed a humanities class, so at spring registration I asked a jock next to me if he had any suggestions.

"Have you heard about Miss Sorensen's philosophy class?" Easily six-four and three-hundred – most likely a defensive lineman judging from the bruises on his ankles – I could have sworn he panted like a dog.

"No, I haven't. Why don't you fill me in about it." What he told me had very little to do with philosophy and far more with anatomy – so I registered.

The normally boisterous jocks were as silent as Tibetan monks as they filtered into Miss Sorensen's class.

Since it was 1975 and Ms. hadn't quite taken hold in the Midwest, that's what everyone called her. And no one was ever late – ever.

Miss Sorensen wore fashionable short heels – in high heels she would have topped six feet – cradling a pair of the sweetest feet and ankles you'd ever seen and legs rising like the pillars of Hercules for three feet to a miniskirt – always a miniskirt – then a skintight sweater hand-knitted by her Swedish grandmother. "Und who can tell me vat morality is," she pondered.

"It sure isn't what I'm thinking right now," jested a jock in the back. Everyone sniggered.

Miss Sorensen must have had great hearing, because she went straight back to the guilty party and leaned over his desk so Grandma's sweater bulged nearly against his face. "Oh? Und vat are you zinking right now." The class' snicker faded to silence.

"I, uh, well . . . " The jock was tongue-tied along with the rest of him.

"I zee. Vell, ve vill start at de beginning. Ethics is how ve study morality." Every male head in the class, mine included, followed Miss Sorensen from her taut calves and thighs to a vision of heaven itself, our eyes dissecting her like a chicken in a meat market. Yeah, it was sexist. Yeah, it was chauvinist. But to *not* look at her would have violated the laws of nature – and philosophy. I think there was one girl in the class – a cute redhead that would normally have gotten more than a casual glance – but she wasn't even close to Miss Sorensen's league. All she could do was sit there and shake her head.

When class was over, the guys all filtered out and wandered around as though they'd all had electric shock treatments or lobotomies. If Miss Sorensen's goal was to reframe our thinking, she had certainly succeeded – but maybe not in the way she had intended.

My other classes were a creative writing seminar, earth science, the American transcendentalists, and the American novel – a fairly light semester, but I wanted to focus on my writing – and Miss Sorensen.

***

It was a hard winter for Mrs. Johnson. Any extra time I had I spent helping her – scraping snow off the sidewalk and blowing drifts from the driveway. Before, Mr. Johnson had done everything so she was pretty helpless. I offered to take the Olds into the service station to have it winterized, and she gladly agreed. I did quite a bit of work for her. If she'd had the money to pay me, I know she would have. Just before the end of the spring semester I found a job as a camp counselor – something I'd always wanted to do. They were even going to let me teach poetry and guitar. Before I left, I offered to plant a vegetable garden for Mrs. Johnson, and she was pretty happy about that. I tilled up a nice, sunny ten-by-twenty patch and planted lettuce, beans, carrots, potatoes – just about all the vegetables she would need through the summer. She promised me she would let me have my room back in the fall then we hugged and both cried when I left. She had turned into a real sweet lady.

***

Camp was a blast from the first day when I met Jean – an art student from Laramie. She was there for the same reason I was – to make a few bucks over the summer, build a resume, and maybe meet somebody.

Jean was no Anika Sorensen, but she was pretty damn close. Five-seven, raven locks falling to the middle of her back, dark-brown eyes, olive skin, and a laugh that curled its fingers around you and held you in its clasp – that was Jean. She was maybe one-fifteen and gave the Levi Strauss company a whole new image.

We shared ideas too – I guess that was where Miss Sorensen's class came in handy. After seven every night was free time, and we would sit on a granite ridge and watch the sunset burn through the mist-troughed Black Hills all the way to the Bighorns a couple hundred miles away. I took her hand the second time I met her there and I kissed her the third and by the fourth time we went there we were in love. She wasn't real happy with Laramie – too many cowboys, she said – and I told her about the BFA and MFA programs at the U and she decided to transfer. I knew what that meant, of course. I'd have to find a different place. There was no possible way Mrs. Johnson – or Mr. Johnson when he still had all his faculties – would let an unmarried couple live together in their home.

"Mrs. Johnson?"

It took several seconds for her to answer the phone. "Yes?" Her voice sounded tired and weak.

"This is Harrison, Mrs. Johnson. How's your summer been."

" . . . Well, you know. It's an awful lot of work taking care of Henry. So I didn't get out much, you know."

"How's the garden doing."

"Well . . . you know . . . I haven't really had time to get out there much to weed, you know. What with Henry and all."

She sounded like she was a hundred years old. My heart plunged at what I had to tell her next. "I'm real grateful that you promised me the room again this fall, Mrs. Johnson. It's a great deal. But I'm afraid I'm going to have to find something else. I'm sure you can find another renter pretty easily."

"Why on earth aren't you taking it?" I swore there were tears in her voice.

"Well, I met this girl here at summer camp, Mrs. Johnson. She's transferring to the art program at the U. We'd like to rent a place together." I was awful careful not to say *live* together. That would have been far more than Mrs. Johnson could have handled.

"Well . . . Is she a nice girl?"

"She's fantastic, Mrs. Johnson." I waited for her to give her blessings and let me move on with my life.

"Well, the other two graduated and moved out. Would you be interested in their rooms too?"

I wondered then if she was starting to suffer from

Alzheimer's too. "I'm sorry, Mrs. Johnson. This girl, Jean, is moving in with me and . . . "

"I could let you have all three rooms for a hundred. That would give you a study and maybe a little art studio for her."

"Mrs. Johnson. We're not married. We'd just be living together. In your home." There. I'd said it.

"Well, you said she was a nice girl."

"The best, Mrs. Johnson."

"I trust your judgment then. Will I still be seeing you this fall?"

"Yes . . . Yes, Mrs. Johnson." I almost choked.

"And does a hundred sound okay?"

"That's way too cheap, Mrs. Johnson. Beside, you could probably use the mo . . . "

"You've been a big help, Harrison. If you can pay me a hundred dollars a month you and your girl can have the upstairs."

It was an absolute steal. Even back then it was easily worth two-hundred. "Thank you, Mrs. Johnson. Thank you."

I knew I should have talked to Jean first, but when I told her how nice Mrs. Johnson was – meaning the *new* Mrs. Johnson – she wanted to move in just so she could help with Mr. Johnson and keep up the house too.

***

I couldn't believe what I saw when we pulled up to the house. The grass was over a foot high and large branches from a summer storm cluttered the yard. The worst was the garden, now a patch of four-foot weeds. Jean huddled close and clasped my arm. "Are you sure this is the right place? It looks abandoned."

I double-checked the address. Yep, 820 East Clark. "This is the place, all right."

"It looks spooky."

"Well, let's go say hi to Mrs. Johnson and pay the rent."

We went to the front door and I rang the bell. It

was totally silent. I knocked, and a hollow echo sounded as I turned to Jean. "Something's wrong."

As I opened the door, a rank smell roiled from the back of the house – a mixture of garbage and cooking smells and moldy dishes. We entered, and a fly buzzed me like a Japanese zero. "Mrs. Johnson?"

The floor creaked, and I turned to a bare, sparse figure weighing maybe ninety pounds. Mrs. Johnson's hair was severely tied back from a blanched face and eyes that had the thousand-yard stare of someone who had seen war. She crept toward us with a cane, the first time I'd ever seen her use one.

"Mrs. Johnson?"

She tried to bite up a smile. "Harrison, it's so, so good to see you." When she looked around me to Jean, she finally managed a smile. "And this must be your girl."

When Jean went to shake hands with her, I swear it was just like Mrs. Johnson received a blood transfusion. Their connection was instant. "This is Jean, Mrs. Johnson. We'll both be living here."

Mrs. Johnson's smile filled her face as she turned to me. "Such a lovely girl. You're such a lucky fellow, Harrison."

"I sure am," I admitted. "How's Mr. Johnson?" I asked, hating to ask if he were dead – which I presumed.

"Oh, he's in the living room. The TV's on – just to keep him company, you know."

I took Jean's hand. "I want you to meet Mr. Johnson." We went through the pantry then the dining room where I heard a chuckle. I looked around to see where it had come from. "Mr. Johnson?" I asked as we entered the living room.

The iron-gray head froze in the lounge chair. Jean and I went around to the front and there Mr. Johnson sat, staring straight ahead, as a sit-com played on the television. "Is someone else here?" I asked Mrs. Johnson as she entered the living room.

"No . . . " she croaked – I swear it was more of a

croak than a voice. "It's just the two of us."

"Huh." I looked a little closer at Mr. Johnson. His face was ruddy and his arms looked like a prizefighter's. Compared to Mrs. Johnson, he looked half her age. "How are you doing, Mr. Johnson?"

Nothing. Absolutely nothing. Just a blank stare at vast, empty space.

I turned to Mrs. Johnson. "I'll tell you what, Mrs. Johnson. Why don't you let me hit that yard with the mower and pick things up a little bit. Then Jean and I can see what we can find in the garden."

Mrs. Johnson lifted her nose like an ancient bird's beak and peered through tired, fading eyes. "That would be nice."

I paid the rent – she looked at the money as though it was the first she'd seen in months – and we took our luggage and my guitar and Jean's art supplies upstairs. We'd just gotten up there when Jean turned to me. "She's so sweet. But she looks terrible."

"I know." I honestly wondered how much time she had left.

As soon as we'd brought everything upstairs I went to the garage where Mr. Johnson's Olds sat, cobwebs glistening in the late-afternoon light as I opened the garage door. Cobwebs even drifted from the antenna to the ceiling. I brushed my way past them and found the mower and a nearly full can of gas and filled the tank. I knew it would be pretty tough going so I raised the wheels as high as they would go and started the mower and pushed it through the grass. It kept clogging up and killing, but I finally made it around the yard, piling up branches as I mowed.

In the weed patch that was once a garden we found some lettuce, onions, carrots, and even a zucchini or two. Jean made dinner while I finished weeding the garden, first finding a vegetable then weeding around it until I found another. It was an absolute mess. When I was done I had what somewhat resembled a garden with a couple pickup loads of weeds.

Jean offered to feed Mr. Johnson – who responded pretty well to her – and Mrs. Johnson ate like a starving lumberjack. Jean had made a salad and zucchini with chicken and herbs and Mrs. Johnson cleaned her plate and asked for more.

We managed our schedules so we could help with Mr. Johnson. He needed help with everything – going to the bathroom even. I hated to ask Jean to do that but she offered. After she'd helped him to the bathroom one night she tugged at my sleeve to follow her into the den. Her eyes looked as though they'd seen a ghost.

"After he finished, I bent him over to wipe him and when he sat up, there was this, this . . . "

"A what."

She looked at Mr. Johnson, sitting quietly as laughter came from the TV in the next room, then at me. "His boner was absolutely huge."

I held back a laugh. "Bigger than mine, even?"

Jean's eyes gazed into mine. "Yes. Way bigger."

"It must be some biological thing. Maybe the blood from his brain all flowed to his . . . well, you know."

"He was absolutely *huge*," said Jean, eyes wide with wonder.

***

Mrs. Johnson was the first to go to the hospital. Jean had gone downstairs one night to get a glass of milk and I heard her cry out. When I ran downstairs Mrs. Johnson was lying right there, staring off like she was already dead. I called the ambulance.

The doctor said it was a stroke. I have to admit I felt a huge responsibility right then. Here I was, just a renter, and one of my landlords had Alzheimer's and the other was in the hospital. I sat with Mrs. Johnson and held her hand for a while until the nurse said it would probably be better if Jean and I went home so Mrs. Johnson could get some rest.

When I got back Jean was reading to Mr. Johnson

from a book of Jack London stories she'd found in their library. She said she thought he liked them. When I said that was impossible because he had Alzheimer's, she insisted that she thought she detected some response, that she felt his eyes on her as she read.

We helped Mr. Johnson to bed then went upstairs. As much as I wanted Jean right then, I had all I could do to kiss her good night before I drifted off. She continued to toss and turn, and I asked her what was the matter.

"I keep thinking about that story about the man they left alone with the wolves all around him and then I keep thinking of Mr. Johnson and mixing them up in my head. Maybe I just need to finish the story to find out what happened."

"I can tell you how it ends."

"Don't spoil it. I'm going to go get that book and come back and finish the story." She tossed off the covers and headed into the hallway completely naked – that's how we slept.

"Aren't you going to put something on?"

"Who's going to see me? Mr. Johnson?" I caught a glimpse of her hip as she laughed and continued down the hallway and felt myself stir. Maybe I wouldn't go to sleep right away after all. I waited for her to come back. And waited. And waited. Annoyed, I got up and put on my bathrobe and went downstairs.

She wasn't in the living room so I poked my head into the Johnsons' bedroom where Jean was bent over looking on the night table beside the bed for the book. This time I *really* felt myself stir because I could see *all* of her. As she walked around the table, still looking for the book, in the glow of the nightlight I saw Mr. Johnson follow her with his head, the bedcovers lifting over his lower body. As Jean spread her legs and bent over to pick the book up from the floor, the covers lifted even higher and Mr. Johnson sat right up in bed to look at her. "Oh, I found it." Jean picked the book up from the floor and I met her in the living room. "Oh, you came down." She smiled. "Were you lonely for me?"

"Very lonely." As I wrapped my arms around her to kiss her I wanted to open my bathrobe and close it again with her inside.

"Ooh, is Mr. Happy waking up?" asked Jean, pressing against me.

"He's been awake for a while."

"Ooh, let's see if we can't do something about that," she said, taking my hand and leading me upstairs.

***

Mrs. Johnson never did return home. I found her daughter's phone in her address book and called her first thing the next morning after her stroke. I was all set to apologize for not calling her the night before, but all she seemed concerned about was her father.

"How's Dad?"

"Well, physically he seems fine." I certainly didn't want to go into detail about what I'd seen when Jean was in her parents' bedroom. "But his Alzheimer's seems pretty severe."

"I'll tell you what. I can't get away right now, but the term at the high school where I'm teaching ends the twenty-fifth. Do you think you could possibly stay with Dad until then? I'd like to see him for myself before I decide on what to do with him."

"He needs to go to a nursing home."

"You're probably right. Will that work though – if I'm there the twenty-eighth?"

It will have to, I thought. "Sure, that's fine."

Other than having to care for Mr. Johnson, it wasn't such a bad deal for us, actually. Our classes were over on the tenth and it would give us a couple weeks to unwind before we returned to our jobs at the camp June 1. It would also be a year since Jean and I had met, and we couldn't wait to see everyone's faces when they saw the couple we'd become over the past year. We'd have to sleep apart for a few weeks – that was a real bummer – but we still had our secret meeting spot and I had some pretty imaginative ways of how we could make use of it.

When Marie came – that was the Johnsons' daughter – she was all business. The first thing she did was balk when she heard how much rent we'd been paying.

"A hundred a month? That's ridiculous. That apartment would probably be two-fifty in Topeka."

"But we've been caring for Mr. Johnson, though," said Jean. And that takes . . . "

"I don't care what it takes," Marie snapped, sitting there severely in her business skirt and blouse. "As far as I'm concerned, the two of you have been robbing them. It can't be that tough to feed an old man and put him to bed. I'll probably just stay here through the summer and do it myself."

I knew right then that Marie didn't have a clue about the rest of it. Helping him to the bathroom, the bathing, the wandering around in the middle of the night – three times the police had brought him back to the house after they had found him jogging around the block in his pajamas – and no telling how long he'd been doing that. I also knew we would have to find a different place in the fall. Marie was definitely her mother's daughter – the Mrs. Johnson I'd first met when her husband still had all his faculties. Jean started to cry so I put my arm around her. I think she had grown to love the Johnsons even more than I had. "Well, we'll probably find a different place then." I gave her the camp phone number. "Could you please let us know if there's a turn for the worse for either of them? We've gotten really attached."

"I suppose," Marie snapped, tossing the paper I'd given her into her purse.

***

It was absolute hell being away from Jean every night. Even if we'd been married, camp rules were that each of us had to stay in a cabin with the campers. So at two each morning, when their nickering little snores made it impossible to sleep, we would grab our sleeping bags and meet at our spot and make love in the cool mountain grass. We started sleeping there together for part of the night, so things got better. It wasn't the same as sharing a bed at the Johnsons', but it was okay.

The camp was closing for the summer and we had just packed up and gotten our last paycheck when the call came. "She's dead," Marie said.

"Oh my God." Jean would be heartbroken. I had no idea how I would tell her. "Could you tell me when the funeral is? We really want to be there. She was just like a grandma to us."

"It's two tomorrow afternoon."

We would have to push pretty hard to get there by then, but I guess that was better than grieving for several days. "How's Mr. Johnson?" I asked. The only answer was a dial tone.

Jean took it even harder than I thought she would. She wailed – actually wailed – then sobbed for half an hour as I held her. "I never knew either of my grandmas. Mrs. Johnson was the only grandma I ever had." Then she broke into tears again and I held her until the camp had nearly cleared out and the caretaker patiently waited for us to leave so he could lock up for the summer.

I cried a lot too. What I couldn't figure out though was why the Johnsons' daughter had hung up on me when I asked about her father.

We'd both taken the news about Mrs. Johnson pretty hard, so instead of driving all night we got a room in Wall. Jean was still whimpering over Mrs. Johnson, but as soon as we both realized it was the first time we'd been together in a real bed for nearly three months, she let me kiss her tears away. After we made love then later lay there watching a fat August moon dance across the sky through our balcony room window, we were able to talk about Mrs. Johnson and even laugh a little bit about some of the things she'd said and done. Jean said not ever being able to talk to Mrs. Johnson again made her want to see Mr. Johnson again even more – even if it was just to hold his hand and read one last story to him – if his daughter would let her.

***

Wall Drug still had two eggs with toast and coffee for a quarter then, so that's what we had for breakfast. I took a picture of Jean sitting on the lap of one of the concrete cowboys – she giggled the whole time. Then we topped off our gas tank and grabbed another cup of coffee and hit the road. If you've ever driven across western South Dakota between the Black Hills and the Missouri River, you know how desolate it can be. Well, our thoughts were pretty desolate too.

We made Vermillion by one – just enough time to stop and see Mr. Johnson before the funeral. I was grateful for that because it would give Jean time to see him again and work out her grief with him.

As we drove down the elm-lined street, Jean and I reached for each other's hands, not knowing what we would find at the house. What sort of reception would Marie have for us? Was Mr. Johnson even still alive? If he were, would Marie even let us see him? Let alone Jean read him one last story?

When we got there, we found the house exactly the same as it had been when we came here a year before – knee-high grass, litter in the lawn, a screen window banging loose in the wind. The one change was in the detached two-car garage. Beside Mr. Johnson's 1967 Oldsmobile was a new, cherry red BMW roadster.

Jean turned to me, her mouth hanging open aghast. "Do you suppose someone else lives here now?"

"Let's go see."

We went to the front door and rang the bell. There was no answer so I knocked. Still no answer, I cracked open the door and called out. "Marie?"

"I'll be right with you."

Jean turned to me as though she'd just heard a

282

ghost. The voice was just like Mr. Johnson's.

A minute later, Mr. Johnson came to the door, carrying a cardboard box. He wore crisp, white shorts and a red polo and a light sweat glistened across his forehead, but otherwise he looked as healthy as a Triple Crown winner. "Harrison, old boy, great to see you," he said, reaching out a bone-crunching handshake.

"Mr. Johnson . . . I . . . you . . . we . . . "

"Remarkable recovery, Harrison, remarkable recovery." He winked as he took in Jean – *all* of her.

"Your daughter Marie. Is she . . . "

"Oh let's talk about something pleasant now, shall we? Oh, forgive me. Come in, come in."

Mr. Johnson seated us at the kitchen table and opened the refrigerator and cracked open beers for Jean and me and himself. "So how was your summer?"

Jean and I couldn't help but exchange glances with each other, both of us convinced that the man seated with us at the table was either an imposter or a ghost.

Mr. Johnson smiled – maybe leered would be a better word – at Jean then focused on me. "Oh, I have something for you." He jumped up and went to the kitchen counter and returned with a large manila envelope.

"What's this, Mr. Johnson."

"Open it up and see." He smiled as he downed his beer then went to the refrigerator for refills.

I pulled out two documents – one the deed to the house and the other the title to the Oldsmobile. "Mr. Johnson, I can't accept these."

"Oh, you earned it, Harrison. And especially you, Jean," he added, winking at her.

He said Jean's name as though he'd known her from the time they'd first met – when Mr. Johnson was in a catatonic state. "Where will *you* live, Mr. Johnson?"

"Oh, I was thinking of getting a place on the water – Myrtle Beach, Padre Island, maybe Malibu. Well, Harrison, I guess we'd better drink up. We have a funeral to go to."

I rolled the deed into a tube in my hand. "This doesn't feel right at all, Mr. Johnson. Are you sure?"

"As sure as I am that as soon as this funeral's over I'll be doing a hundred forty on my way out of town." He eyed Jean one more time then winked at me. "Pretty cute girlfriend you've got there, Harrison. Hope you burn up a couple sheets for me tonight." He took one last swallow of his beer and looked off with dreamy determination. "Wouldn't mind something like that for myself. Well . . . " He crumpled his beer cans in his fist and tossed them in the trash. "I'll see you at the funeral." The screen door slammed behind him. Moments later, a cranking engine sounded, a wailing engine, screeching tires.

When I thought back to when I first met the Johnsons and Mr. Johnson's illness and Mrs. Johnson's demise, I had an epiphany. Like a vampire sucking the blood from his victim and continuing to live through eternity, Mr. Johnson had not only gotten even with his wife – he'd done so royally.

Jean looked at me, as lost as I'd ever seen her. "That night, when I came downstairs to get that book from Mr. Johnson's bedroom so I could finish the story?"

"Yeah?"

"I wonder what all he saw."

The Homecoming

The dawn call of the whip-poor-will woke her. She turned in the thick tick mattress in half sleep and reached for Philip and grabbed a bolster. She had been dreaming of him again. They were sitting on the banks of the Yaquina in faraway Oregon – as distant as the moon.

As she cracked her eyes open fully, dust motes danced on the yellow beam streaming through the east window like the souls of the fallen. Billy Ellis, the neighbor to the north, had fallen at Manassas, a Yankee mini ball to the heart. Then it was Harrison Griggs, her neighbor to the east, his life cut off by a Yankee officer's sword at Seven Pines. Toby Miller, the neighbor to the south, had been wounded in Pickett's Charge and fought the surgeon who wanted to cut off his leg until it was too late. He died in the wagonload of wounded before they were long into Virginia. Carl Moses to the west had died at Cold Harbor. Cholera, the doctor said. Those who knew better said he had flat plain died from shitting green corn like thousands of others.

It was Philip, though, she wondered most about now this morning, that Yankee boy who had held her hand long before there were Yankees and Rebs, long before a North and a South, as the cold, rushing water slid past, carrying his I love you's out to sea. He had told her so often she wondered if the ocean had heard it too, if it had fallen in love with him as much as had she.

That had all changed when he signed on with Sheridan and rode with him all the way from Oregon to Booneville then Perryville. After that, she had lost track. That was just as well. She had married Charles, who had proven his bravery and loyalty to the South many times. That was all in vain, though, for Vicksburg had fallen nearly two years before, right after the Yankees beat their men back at Gettysburg. She had waited for months for Charles and her father to return from the war after she had heard General Lee had surrendered at Appomattox.

She had resigned herself that she would be married to Charles for the rest of her life. Perhaps she could even learn to love him.

She rose and went to the smoke-smudged foyer mirror she had salvaged after the Yankees had torched the big house where she had been born and married Charles and where the Yankees had killed Abraham as he tried to hold them back, sweat beads glistening down his angry black face, bulging white eyes showing his fear at the same time. The Yankees, who said they were waging war to free the slaves, shot him right there at the door. But Abraham had given her just enough time to flee out the back door and into the pecan grove where she watched them loot the house then set fire to it, an eerie glow far into the night. After the Yankees had left the next morning, she went to the smoking ruins and sifted through the ashes until she found Abraham's charred body, eyelids burnt off, death gaze staring back at himself in the mirror.

The face staring back at her in that same mirror now asked her why. Why had the South seceded. Why did the South fire on Fort Sumter. Why had the North declared war. And why did they say it was over slavery when they had killed a slave as fine and true and brave as Abraham, whom her father had trusted to let her sit on his knee as he told her stories of talking animals and sang to her until she drifted off to sleep against his coveralls tinged with the smells of ham and hickory from the smokehouse. Her face stared back, no longer young but drawn and a bit haggard, turned dark olive by the Alabama sun. Carry your parasol whenever you go out, elst you'll wind up looking like a quadroon, her father had always cautioned her. After he had spent his own money to raise a regiment of volunteers, she had stowed the parasol in the foyer closet where it was now among the ashes. Now wherever she looked she only saw ashes. The ashes of the house. The ashes of the Confederacy. The ashes of the dead.

It hadn't rained for months, and that hot, dry afternoon a red dust plum rose in the far yonder of Birmingham Trace. Slender as a dust devil at first, it puffed to as wide and high as a tornado until it birthed a team of horses and wagon and a raw, ragged voice urging the team on. As the voice grew louder, Carissa saw it was her father. She shut the slave quarters door against the growing Alabama heat and went to meet him.

Wallace O'Malley turned the team up the dusty drive, stirring up more of the red Alabama clay, halting the team beside the naked chimneys and marble columns, ghostly in the wavy sea of ashes around them. His gaze fruitlessly roved the ashes for signs of life. He turned to her as she ran toward him.

"Father." Her joy quelled as she saw what had become of him. Hard lines etched his face like rivers through delta, sweat-drenched dust caking his eyes burnt to pissholes in the insufferable heat. His look said he had not just given in but given up. He banged his dusty red hat against his knee, turning the color butternut. A moan sounded behind him and a pile of crumpled quilts rolled in the wagon box.

"Father. Is that Charles? Is he all right?"

Her father stared at her. "Charles is dead," he said flatly, as if it were something he had said a thousand times before, making it no longer important. His road-weary eyes focused on her with bottomless sadness. "I brought Philip back."

"Philip?" She raced to the wagon box where Philip

lay, shivering beneath the pile of quilts. His powder-blue eyes flickered in his sunburnt face. She reached for his hand beneath the quilt and only as he squeezed back did she remember her husband. "Is Charles dead?" She tried to catch her breath with her hand but her grief poured out, choking her.

"Five Forks," was all her father could say. "We got overrun by Sheridan. There was nothing else I could do." He looked off, seeing it all over again.

"And you brought Philip back?"

"There's no more blue or gray anymore, Carissa. It's all gray."

The truth sinking in, she let go of Philip's hand just long enough to fall into her father's arms. His wearied body charged with her embrace. "I did as much for Philip as I could – which wasn't much. Least I saved him long enough so you can say your good-byes."

***

As weeks passed, Philip mended and her father told her the truth. When Charles had heard that Sheridan was advancing, he looked for Philip's regiment. As her father watched in wonder as Philip led the charge, a Union bullet crashed into her father's shoulder, sending him to the ground. Philip saw he had fallen, dismounted, and dragged him behind a stone wall to protect him from Union fire. As he reached up to clasp Philip's hand, Philip grimaced as a bayonet pierced his side, Charles holding the rifle. The last thing her father remembered was raising his .36 Navy cap and ball to his son-in-law.

As the shock of losing Charles faded, her thoughts turned to Philip. She realized then that she had never stopped thinking of him. Even when she and Charles were married, the image was in her mind of Philip standing there before the altar with her, Philip saying his vows to her, Philip placing the ring on her finger. Her body had married Charles but her mind and soul had married Philip.

One day Philip was finally able to sit up and talk and

she brought him his dinner – nothing fancy – cornbread and beans with ham hocks and the bravest smile she could muster. She fed him, spoon by spoon, mopping up the beans with the cornbread and teasingly touching it to his mouth then pulling it away so he grabbed her hand.

His eyes searched hers like a dying man in a desert seeing a mirage. "I'm sorry."

"For what."

"Charles. The war."

"The war's over, Philip." She looked down at her hand in his and squeezed back as hard as she thought he could stand it. "Welcome home."

The Hunt

"Four years ago today." The ancient grandfather clock ticked sonorously over Emily's fading words. Now it was Norman's turn to pick up the same conversation they had had three years already on this date – how their daughter Marie had died in an unexpected accident on an icy South Dakota road. Her subcompact had flown through a stop sign and flipped sixteen times. A passing farmer found the car and her in a frozen field, the last moments of life draining out of her as she whispered, "Daddy . . . no." That's what the farmer told the deputy who was there even before the ambulance – both too late.

"I wonder what Marie meant by that . . . Daddy . . . no." Emily's glassy eyes glassed Norman. "Her last words were to you. How she must have loved you."

Norman turned his coffee cup in his hand. "I don't think she suffered . . . for very long, anyway," was the only solace he could offer.

"She was thirty-one." Emily took a breath so deep it seemed a miracle she could even hold it then let it out slowly as though it were the last breath she would ever take. "Thank God we have three other children."

Oh yes. Michael, Miranda, and Matthew. Norman had almost forgotten about them. And how could he. They were wonderful, remarkable young people. Yet the loss of Marie was a huge crater in his heart – a hole he would never fill. She had most definitely been his favorite – even though a parent isn't supposed to have a favorite. But she was.

"Oh, I forgot to mention. Pastor Yackle called yesterday

and asked if you could fill in for him this Sunday."

"That's pretty short notice."

"This is only Tuesday. So it's five days from now. You've done it on shorter notice. Besides, he said he already has his sermon written. The rest you've done hundreds of times before."

Hundreds of times. From when he had preached his first sermon as a student pastor in Wisconsin, all the way until he gave his last sermon in a quaint rural church in South Dakota forty years later.

"So do you think you'll do it for him?"

"I'd rather not."

"Why? You always have before."

"I'd rather not."

"You'd better call him then. I think he was expecting you to. After all, you've been willing to every time he's asked before."

"Could you call him for me?"

Emily's jaw shifted just a little at his request. "I *suppose*."

Norman's gaze shifted toward the west picture window of their A-frame. Huge snowflakes sifted slowly, enemy paratroopers invading his heart. Four years. Four years today. "Any idea what we'll have for dinner tonight?"

Emily studied him as though he were an intricate puzzle she had been trying to solve for years. "I was thinking of going to town and getting a pot roast. There isn't much else in the refrigerator."

"What about the freezer."

"You helped me clean that out last week, remember? We threw most of it out."

"The roads might be getting pretty bad right now. The county plow doesn't come by until late afternoon, you know."

"I know . . . " Emily peered out at the same snowflakes Norman was gazing at. "I spose I could heat up some soup."

"I heard a rooster in the grove when I was out shoveling the walk this morning."

"Pheasant would be nice. I could make some wild rice and peas. There's a little of that cheesecake left too."

"Sounds delicious. Well, I'll grab my 20-gauge and see if I can't hunt us up some dinner."

***

Norman and Emily lived on forty acres of western Wisconsin forest sliced by Brule Creek, a meandering stream passing out of the St. Croix hills to the west and slipping past another range of hills on the south side of their property. With a road to the north, national forest surrounded them on three sides, giving them all the privacy they could want.

Not long after Marie had died, they bought the land and started sketching out plans for their dream home, something they'd been planning for twenty years. Things never seemed to work out, though. Since a minister was always subject to being on call – and often the vicissitudes of a fickle parish – they had never lived in one place long enough to find the acreage they wanted. Then, just after Norman retired, they started looking for a place to build in earnest. That was about the time Marie was killed in the accident – drugs or alcohol and probably both were likely involved, the deputy sheriff said.

They had had trouble with Marie ever since she started high school – skipping classes, smoking, drinking. And then it was the marijuana and staying out all night with boys. When Emily found a pill bottle with over forty hits of LSD in it, they laid down the law. Stop the smoking and drinking and drugs or move out.

So Marie moved out.

I just can't understand it, said Emily. She was always such a good girl. And then when she was eleven or twelve . . .

I know, said Norman. I know . . .

***

Now he was walking up a deer trail along Brule Creek, the same sort of crystalline powder that made perfect skiing – cross-country or downhill. It was so fluffy that he didn't even feel the cold as he trudged through it. A geigle sent a rooster up not ten feet in front of him, fluttering in an arc then soaring, a perfect target. Norman just then remembered the gun in his hands. He'd had a good eight or ten seconds to take the shot, and now it was too late. What was wrong with him. The rooster was now somewhere along Brule Creek, maybe a couple hundred yards away. He chambered in a shell and continued up the trail.

***

It was about his third parish the first time it happened. Emily was at choir practice and he was left with making supper and giving the children their baths and scooting them off to bed.

292

Marie was taking an awful long time so he opened the bathroom door and there she stood in the bathtub, shampooing her hair, pink rear to him. Norman stood aghast as he stared at his eight-year-old daughter and thought how perfect she was – long, lean legs flowing to her dimpled derriere.

***

The rooster lifted, even slower than last time, stiffened by the hardening cold. The wind was picking up and the snow was getting heavier, turning from fluff to icy pellets that felt like bullets. He lifted his shotgun and followed the rooster as it reached the top of the arc of his flight, then soared to the other side of the Brule.

***

He did his fatherly duties, giving the kids their baths every Thursday night. By the time Marie turned ten she would call to him through the bathroom door and he went willingly, following her sweet voice slipping from girlhood on one side of the door to young womanhood on the other. Within a year, things had moved much further.

Marie's attitude toward her mother started to change. Whenever her mother asked her to do something, Marie would either forget or totally ignore her until Emily would walk up to her and scream in her face and Marie would run to her father and pile in his lap as he sat in his favorite recliner, watching a football game or some documentary. "Daddy, don't let her make me do it," Marie would say, nuzzling her lips up against his neck as though *they* were married couple and Emily just some old hag. And every time Norman would take Marie's side, even to the point where Emily would grab her car keys and storm off for hours while Marie sat in her father's lap until she drifted off to sleep and he carried her to bed.

One Thursday night just before Marie's fourteenth birthday – about the time she started noticing boys – Norman tried the bathroom door and it was locked. "Marie? Do you want me to come in?" he asked once the other kids were out of earshot.

"No," she said firmly.

Marie was a real handful after that. She started dating boys – none the sort of which either Norman or Emily approved. She started smoking cigarettes and drinking and doing drugs. And then her parents gave her their ultimatum, a bluff she

293

easily called. She barely made it through one year of college then drifted off to California and oblivion.

A shell of her former self, when she turned 31 she returned to South Dakota. She was in and out of treatment three times in rapid succession before the accident. The sheriff's deputy said Marie had blown through the stop sign going at least eighty – maybe a hundred. Her car had flipped sixteen times – no skid marks. The driver's door had popped open and Marie was thrown from her car that landed on her – probably the second flip – and ended up in a tree line a hundred and ninety feet away, a dent the size and shape of Marie's skull on the right front corner of the roof. When Norman asked if she had died right away the coroner said it was more likely she had lain there quite some time before she froze to death since the blood coating her body had formed a brittle, bright red sheen by the time she was found.

***

Early in his ministry, while he was still in Wisconsin, Emil Jensen came to him, beside himself.

"The farm has been in my family for five generations. And now I'm about to lose it."

Norman patted Emil's shoulder. "It can't be that bad, can it? There must be some way you can make the payment."

Emil wrung his seed cap in his hands. "I have no money. No crop. And my annual payment was due last week." When Emily told Norman how much the payment was, all Norman could do was shake his head.

"Well you have a lot of skills as a farmer. You should be able to find work in town."

"You don't understand. To a farmer, his land is his life. Take his land away, and he might just as well be dead. I've been driving around with my shotgun in my trunk for several weeks now. Maybe I'd better just go ahead and do it."

"And burn in Hell forever?" Norman thundered. "Don't you know suicide is the unforgivable sin? What would your family think? Do you want to leave them with that burden?"

Emil's tears ran in creeks down his sun-weathered face. "I don't know what else to do."

"The farm is merely something material and will eventually no longer exist. Your soul is eternal. Do you want to spend eternity in Hell?"

Emil's jaw shuddered in sobs. "No."

"Save your soul and let the farm go. Find a good job in town and buy a nice house and take care of your family." Norman smiled. "And start coming to church every Sunday."

"All right." Emil grimaced through his tears. "So what do I do with my shotgun."

"Give it to me for safekeeping. I'll put it under lock and key and you needn't worry about it."

"Okay. Okay," Emil repeated, looking off through the rectory window as though he could see his farm that would soon no longer be his.

So Emil gave him the shotgun. After a while, when Emil had found a job as a welder and bought a comfortable home in town, Norman asked Emil if he wanted his shotgun back. Emil said no, it would only remind him of his grief. The shotgun was a small payment for Norman's saving his life.

What a terrible *accident*, Emily had said to Norman after he said the last words over his daughter's graveside service.

***

Yes, *accident*, Norman told himself and continued to tell himself up until even now as the rooster fluttered before him, a perfect shot, rising to the apex of flight, then hanging there, still, then drifting slowly to reed-flanked Brule Creek fifty yards away.

***

Emily was searching for spices when the shotgun popped not far away. She smiled and grabbed the flour. Oh, wouldn't that pheasant taste wonderful tonight.

The Pileated Woodpecker

Pileated woodpecker: A spectacular, crow-sized woodpecker with a conspicuous red crest. Resident of woodlands from Nova Scotia, New Brunswick, and Manitoba south to Florida and Gulf of Mexico. (A Field Guide to the Birds. Roger Tory Peterson.)

AK-47: The AK-47 is a selective-fire (semiautomatic and automatic), gas-operated 7.62X39mm assault rifle, developed in the Soviet Union by Mikhail Kalashnikov. There are places around the world where AK-type weapons can be purchased on the Black Market for as little as $6, or traded for a chicken or a sack of grain. (Wikipedia.)

Under certain circumstances, many claim the sound of the pileated woodpecker pecking at trees and the AK-47 are exactly the same.

Thwock thwock thwock thwock thwock. The Taliban had them pinned down, their only cover their rolled-over Humvee and a few scattered boulders. Two of their four-man patrol were dead, with no radio contact in the rock-strewn, icy pass.

"Where's their fire coming from, Sergeant?" his corporal yelled above his M249.

"I don't know." Enemy fire echoed off both sides of the pass so it could have come from either side, bullets ringing like hail on their vehicle, now useless but as shelter.

"Are we going to get out of this, Sergeant?"

"I don't know."

***

"I don't know . . . I don't know . . . " Lynn was shaking him, leaning over him in bed in her filmy blue nightgown. "Charlie. You've been having nightmares again. Wake up, Charlie."

He ripped open his eyes and grabbed the side of the bed to make sure he was here and not Kabul or some other God-forsaken place in Afghanistan.

Lynn was frantic as she leaned over to hold him. "It's okay, honey. It's okay. I'm here."

As he felt her warm, soft body against his chest, he knew he was more than okay. And after a few minutes with her, he would be magnificent.

***

Like a lot of other young men his age, Charlie Harris had volunteered soon after the Sept. 11, 2001 terrorist attacks. He'd been a star athlete in high school and was offered football scholarships from three Division I universities, but when the attacks came at the start of his senior year of high school, his view of college and football and girls and parties changed. It all seemed meaningless, like some stupid, silly game. And when he walked into the United States Marine Corps recruiting office, he found two sergeants more than happy to confirm his beliefs.

"So you want to serve your country," the First Sergeant said.

"Yes sir," Charlie said, ramrod-straight in the chair on the other side of the desk.

"You can drop the sir in boot camp. There you call them drill instructors."

"Yes, Sergeant."

"See?" the First Sergeant said to his Staff Sergeant. "He's smart. He's learning already."

***

While some claimed boot camp would be the hardest part,

Charlie found it the easiest. Then it was on to MOS training and deployment to Iraq. Charlie's fire team fought from Fallujah to the Kurdish villages in the north, and when Iraq was secure – for a time, at least – it was on to Afghanistan.

It was between deployments when he met Lynn, a stunning, blue-eyed, blond ornithology graduate student from the University of Michigan. She was on spring break from college and he was on leave when they met at St. Petersburg. She walked past him eight or ten times before he noticed her, and when he finally did, he couldn't take his eyes from her – nor she him. Their first date was electric – they both felt a shock when their hands touched. And when their bodies collided that first night it was like a meteor striking the earth – a hot, white meteor that burned everything around it.

"Be careful," she said as he boarded the KC-130 that would eventually land in Kabul.

"I always am. Besides, I have my buddies to cover me." A long kiss and hug later, he was off, the huge transport soon a spec in the sky, then nothing.

It was right after he and his corporal survived the Taliban attack in the pass that he called her and asked her to marry him. He'd planned a career in the Marines, but the thought of losing Lynn was more than he could bear. Their only arguments were over what if something should happen to him. But Charlie had remained invincible – right up until the attack in the pass. When he and his corporal were the only two out of their four-man team to survive, he realized keeping Lynn meant leaving the Marines.

***

"What are you reading?"

Lynn smiled and lifted her glasses to the top of her forehead and showed him the cover. "It's a book I found in the giveaway bin at the public library. *A Field Guide to the Birds*. It has some great information here about the pileated woodpecker."

"Pileated woodpecker?"

"Here. Listen to this." Lynn lowered her glasses to read. "The Northern Pileated woodpecker ranges from Manitoba, New Brunswick, and Nova Scotia south to Minnesota, Iowa, Indiana, and Pennsylvania. Isn't that fascinating?" She looked up just in time to see him looking down her nightgown. "You weren't listening to a word I said."

"Oh, I was listening all right."

"No you weren't. You were staring at my breasts the whole time."

"Let's just say that I'm feeling a little like a pileated woodpecker myself." He studied her eyes for a second. "How would you like a nice, big woody."

She bonked him over the head with her book. "You're awful."

"Ha ha ha ha ha," he said just before he ravished her.

***

Thwock thwock thwock thwock thwock. He cracked open his eyes to see Lynn looking through the binoculars he had brought back from Afghanistan into the woods beside their house. "Look at him. He just keeps pecking away, like he wants to entertain us."

"Who's he?"

"A pileated woodpecker, silly."

He finally made the connection that the woodpecker had been cause of his returning nightmares. "Why does a woodpecker peck anyway."

"To get at the insects living in the dead tree branches," Lynn explained, looking through the binoculars as she leaned toward the window.

"Isn't there any way to get him to stop."

"Why would you want to do that." Lynn set the binoculars on the nightstand. "It's such a neat sound."

"I hate it."

"Why on earth do you hate it."

"It reminds me of something else."

"What else."

"Oh . . . just something else."
***

He tried earplugs, but they fell out. And even when they didn't, the persistent thwock thwock thwock sounded like an AK with a suppressor. His nightmares turned more vivid, always ending with their being pinned down in the pass, the radio out, Taliban fire coming from every direction. And every time he would wake to the sound of the same damned woodpecker.

Finally, he'd had enough. He left right after breakfast one morning and came back late that afternoon with a present for her – a life-size oak carving of a pileated woodpecker.

"It's beautiful," said Lynn, leaning over his chair to kiss him. "Where did you find it."

"Oh, there's this old 'Nam vet on disability living back in the woods who carves them – that's about all he does."

"I hope it didn't cost too much."

"Naw, it was pretty cheap, actually."

"Well thank you." She leaned over to kiss him again. "I think it will look great on the mantle, don't you?"

"Yeah." Charlie smiled. "I think it will look great there."

"Well, I'd better put this up and hurry over to the college. "I'm giving my last final this afternoon and I don't want to be late. Can I take the Jeep?"

"Uh, why would you want to take that."

"The HR's been overheating."

"Well . . . okay. Can I get something out first?"

"Sure. We'll I'd better go."
***

Charlie slept better that night than he had in years. When he woke, it was to chirping birds and the sun streaming on the bed beside him. He heard Lynn on the deck just outside their bedroom, so he threw on a robe and went outside.

She was sitting on the deck bench, frantically

scanning tree to tree. "I can't find him."

"Find who?" he asked, settling beside her.

"The woodpecker. I didn't hear him this morning, and when I came out, I couldn't see him. What do you think happened to him."

"Search me." Charlie stretched and yawned and took in the morning sunlight.

Lynn set down the binoculars and studied him. "What did you have to get out of the car yesterday."

"Oh, I'll show you." He went to their bedroom closet and returned with a 20- gauge pump and laid it in Lynn's hands.

"Did you buy this yesterday?"

"Yep."

"I thought after Iraq then Afghanistan you'd be tired of guns."

"Oh, it doesn't hurt to have a gun or two in the house. I still like to hunt, you know."

Lynn twisted her eyes narrowly at him. "What is it you like to hunt."

"Deer, mainly. Maybe a little pheasant and waterfowl in the fall."

She turned the cold blue barrel in her hand. "Not woodpeckers."

He laughed long and hard and loud. But he never did answer her.

The Pink House

I had just come home from football practice when Dad asked me to go help him lay carpet. I was fifteen and in pretty good shape – small, but strong. I guess when Dad asked me to go along to help I should have seen it as a compliment, but I was tired – dead dog bone tired. That was why I curled up against the window in his old panel truck as we cruised down Highway 77 to Sioux Falls, gas fumes just as ripe as Dad's smoking Camel and his body that had gone for two weeks without a bath. Along with the funeral home-smelling formaldehyde-treated carpet padding, tile samples, and asbestos-fibered tile cement, it all blended into one strange, rank, lovely aroma – the aroma of Dad's Chevy Apache 10 panel truck that I'll never forget.

"You look pretty tuckered out there, boy," Dad said, a hint of concern in his voice. "That football practice there gettin' to be too much for ya?"

"I don' know," I muttered, my head lobbing against the window.

"If it is, I kin sure use ya layin' carpet 'n stead."

"That's good to know," I said, not meaning it to sound as sarcastic as it did.

Dad laughed – probably because he was always sarcastic too. "Ya know, boy. Ya follow me 'round a while an' learn this carpet trade – 'long with some farmin' – an' ya might amount to somethin' yet."

I smiled as I thought of our 120 acres of corn, soybeans, and hay – we no longer had animals. They were gone after the big farm sale back in '63. We had a forty with a commanding view of the Big Sioux River Valley to the east, another forty on the Big Sioux west bank – the place I had always gone to play with the neighbor kids. And then the forty of bottomland on the Big Sioux east bank. It wasn't a big farm by any stretch, but it was big enough for a young boy to get lost on and later to sneak around on with cigarettes, beer, and girls.

And then there was Dad's business – which hadn't turned out so bad. He had been laying carpet, linoleum, and tile for a few years now, and word had spread that he was pretty good. The wholesaler in Sioux Falls even recommended him – in fact he was at the top of their list. Someone would come into Paint and Glass and look over carpet samples and as soon as they decided the salesman would say, "Oh you want Maynard Griggs to lay it. He's the best." I guess in a city of 50,000 that was a pretty good recommendation.

Yeah, I guess I could see a worse future. Vietnam was raging right then and students were demonstrating at Berkeley and Cornell. They'd just had some big demonstrations in Chicago with lots of arrests. Dad hated anything having to do with hippies, even the mere mention of them, and when my sister had given me a paisley hat for my birthday and Mom had given me a paisley zippered suitcase to match and then I picked up a strong of love beads, that was more than Dad could take. He scornfully spoke of hippies and drugs and 'jungle music' and asked if I had tried drugs yet. I shook my head and he grunted, satisfied that I was enough of a dork to not fit in with the drug crowd.

The carpet tied down on top of Dad's panel was heavy, and we had all we could do to roll it off the top of the truck to the dolly and ease it toward the front door. Dad had put a lot of thought into loading and unloading, so it was pretty amazing what he was able to do by himself or just me to help. We pulled that six-hundred-pound carpet toward the front door, Dad proud to be installing it in a doctor's new home in southeast Sioux Falls. He had nailed down the tack strips and laid the padding the day before, so all we had to do was measure and cut and stretch and lay the carpet. And then he could turn in his bill.

The work went pretty fast. Dad did the cutting – he always did the cutting. I didn't want to be blamed for messing that up. Then we both took a hammer and wide-bladed chisel and drove the carpet into the crack between the flooring and wall. Then Dad would take his stretcher out of the box along with his kick stretcher and we could stretch that carpet tight and tack it into the opposite wall.

It was just a little after noon when we had finished and Dad had laid his bill on the kitchen counter. Usually he didn't even leave a bill. He thought that was rude, I guess. He would just wait until people asked how much the bill was before he would give it to them. When he died, he had thousands on his books – much of it no doubt from people who had never received a bill.

We stopped for lunch at the Frisco Inn in downtown Sioux Falls, a favorite of both mine and Dad's. "Order anything you want," said Dad, now a big shot as he already felt that $1,200 in his pocket from the carpet job.

"Really?"

Dad coughed up his horse laugh followed by a cigarette hack and I didn't want to push it any further so I ordered a bowl of chili with a hamburger and Coke. George, the white-haired owner, served up the best chili and hamburger this side of New York. The chili was all meat with no beans and a thin layer of grease floating on the top along with oyster crackers. The burger was basically the same loose meat and both were redolent of chili powder and cumin and I suspect a little curry. Even today, I can still taste that wonderful chili and burger in the back of my mouth, the cumin heavenly wafting itself through my senses.

As we sat down to eat, George would always come over and pull up a chair and talk politics. His Greek accent was still as thick as fishing boats on the Aegean, and he would rant and rave about hippies and drugs and rock 'n roll and the terrible things the world was coming to. "How 'bout you?" George would say, pointing right at me and I finished my chili. Dad had already finished his meal and was sitting there with a cup of coffee and a Camel and a rare smile. "You do drugs?" George asked the question like a semi rolling over a cat.

"No," I said, already feeling guilty for what I thought I might do years later in college.

"Of course not," said George. "You a good young man. You work with your father here, right."

"Right."

George clapped my shoulder. "You have a good boy here. More boys should work with their fathers. That's how you really lean a trade – generation to generation. That's where the quality comes from, learning it by the watching then the doing. Not by going to college and being everyone's boss and not knowing what their jobs are."

At that moment, I felt my college prospects dwindle significantly.

"Well, I have more customers," said George as the front door opened.

After we finished, Dad and I drove over to the doctor's house. A black Mercedes sat in the concrete driveway and a man about forty stepped out and smiled at us. He had blond hair and sunglasses and wore dress casual slacks and a polo shirt with an alligator on the pocket. People actually wore those back then. I guess if you had an alligator on your shirt it was a subtle way of saying you had a lot of money. The man smiled two rows of the brightest teeth I'd ever seen and stuck out his hand. "Mr. Griggs. You must be the one who did this fine carpet job. Why don't you come inside and I'll write you a check."

Dad seemed to want to look behind himself when the doctor called him mister. Probably the only people who called him mister were highway patrolmen. He followed the doctor who went inside and pulled out his checkbook and leaned on the kitchen counter and wrote the check and handed it to Dad who stared at it. "This isn't right. You made it out for $1,300."

"That's right," the doctor said, flashing a smile. "For a job well done."

"But I can't take this." I wanted to kick dad right then and tell him to take the money and run.

"Well why not? You did a great job. I fired the first two installers before I was lucky enough to find you. You deserve it. You're the best."

I was pretty damn proud of Dad just then. Here there was a doctor – a noted surgeon, even – heaping praises on my dad. And that didn't happen very often – if ever.

"Well thank you." Dad tucked the check into his wallet.

"I'm telling everyone in the development here what a great job you did too."

"I'd appreciate that."

As we went outside, the doctor – whom I later learned was Doctor Beck – twisted a wry glance at an older pink house next door. One car was leaving just as another was turning in the half-circle drive. A woman – maybe I should say a girl – not much older than myself opened the door. She wore skin-tight white shorts and a gray sorority sweatshirt and blond pigtails tumbling past her shoulders. Behind her, barely lit by the early afternoon sun, was a brunette with equally long hair, wrapped over her front shoulder. Both girls appeared to be college age, maybe a bit older.

Dr. Beck shook his head. "You know, this would be a great neighborhood if it weren't for them." I wanted to ask Dr. Beck why.

"Oh?" Dad's voice and eyebrows rose with sudden

interest.

"They moved into that house about six months ago – about the time I started construction. Men come and go day and night. None of them stays for more than an hour. And that can mean only one thing."

"Well," Dad pondered. "I guess it takes all kinds."

All I could think of was how much the girls charged.

"Well," said Dad, casting a quick glance back over his shoulder. "I guess we'd better be on our way."

***

When I got up the next morning, Dad was already up which wasn't unusual since he was an early riser. His mood had suddenly changed. He was whistling – chortling would have been more like it – and even more surprising, he had taken a bath and was wearing a pair of dress slacks and a polo shirt with an alligator on the picket just like the doctor's. I guess Mom must have given it to him for Christmas and he hadn't had the guts to wear it yet. He'd even colored his hair – not a very good job, I might add – a stubborn black streak was still on his forehead so it looked bruised from a bar fight. Mom had been in Worthington, Minnesota, all week helping my aunt who had just had an operation and who needed help with cooking and cleaning around their farmhouse. Since it was Saturday I didn't have football practice.

"So, boy," Dad said, looking me up and down. "Wanna go to Sioux Falls?"

"Sure." What the heck, it was really boring around the farm on Saturday anyway. I still couldn't figure out why Dad was so dressed up – I mean really dressed up for him. The only other times he dressed up were those rare occasions when we went to church for a baptism, wedding, or funeral. People had to either be born, get married, or die to get Dad to dress up.

Dad chuckled. "Well, you'd better grab a bowl of cereal or something afore we head out."

I ate and Dad got Mom's '67 Delta 88 out of the garage. The car was only a year old and was Mom's pride and joy. Dad only drove it when Mom said he could. She was that possessive of it. This time, though, she wasn't around for Dad to have to even ask.

I felt a sense of adventure as we drifted down the gravel roads toward Highway 77 where the car carrump carrumped over the poorly sealed joints. Back then, before highway contractors knew what they were doing, every highway had its sound – and Highway 77 was carrump carrump.

The closer we got to Sioux Falls, the more nervous Dad got, as though deciding something. We were just rounding the curve by the Pioneer Monument past Al's Place and the Alibi Club on the way toward the penitentiary when Dad turned to me. "So you're fifteen now, huh?"

"Yeah," I said, thinking it a strange question for him to ask.

"Humph. Little young yet."

For what, I wanted to ask, but didn't.

About twenty minutes later we rolled up in front of the doctor's house. The Mercedes wasn't there and the lawn contractor was spraying water over the freshly laid sod. Dad looked over at me, as though still deciding something. "I gotta check the seam on that carpet – make sure nothin's showin'. All right?"

"Sure." I sat there and watched as Dad went to the front door and knocked then went in. A little while later he came out the back of the house, glanced once in my direction, then walked over to the pink house.

I sat there for well over an hour – two hours would have been more like it – before Dad got back to the Olds and opened the door and got in. The look of supreme satisfaction on his face faded. I knew right then where that extra hundred dollars had gone. I also knew that Dad knew that I knew. "You keep quiet 'bout this, boy."

"Okay," I muttered. I was silent all the way home. It wasn't that Dad had gone to the house and cheated on Mom that bothered me so much because going to see a prostitute back then wasn't really cheating, was it? It was more like a ritual, something men did at least once in their lives, whether they were married or not.

What really bothered me was that the girls were nearly my age and Dad hadn't considered me man enough to go along. That was what really hurt.

The Settlement

It didn't bode well for Dave Jefferson's marriage when he moved back to his hometown in the Oregon Coastal Range. They'd already had problems – Gloria social climbing like an orangutan up a tree. Dave preferred to stay on the ground where it was safe.

So when Dave said he was thinking of coming back home and his dad gave him first option to buy the bar that had stood like Mount Gibraltar on Upper Main in Toledo since the late 1880s, Dave took him up on it. After all, it was a great excuse to get away from Gloria.

So there he was, holding down the bar at McBaron's, something of a baron himself in his own domain, eighty-sixing people whether they deserved it or not, guys and girls alike. Depending on how cute a girl was, she'd get a second, third, or fourth chance even. And if she were beautiful, the chances continued forever.

The divorce complaint came as no surprise to him. As the deputy handed him the registered letter, Dave turned it in his hand, studying the address.

"So Gloria finally went and did it," the deputy said, having him sign.

"Guess so." Dave sighed and looked out the window at the pearled, rimming light spilling onto the ancient wood floor.

"You have my sympathy. I went through a nasty

divorce myself." The deputy stood there, nodding. "Or in your case should I offer congratulations."

"Congratulations. Definitely congratulations," said Dave. "When you get off duty, come back for a cold one on me and I'll tell you the whole story."

"I'll do that," said the deputy. "Can't wait to hear it."

***

It hadn't started out that badly. They had met just north of Florence, Dave busting up sand dunes with his modified Volkswagen in the Mini Baha, the crowd cheering him on. He had entered as the favorite, so it was no surprise when he crossed the finish line to accept the hallowed trophy, a cup with a dune buggy rearing into the air with his name later etched on the brass plaque below. Presenting the trophy was a luscious blond, well-built, in a bikini and high heels. When she went to kiss him on the cheek as she presented him his trophy, Dave impulsively turned and kissed her fully on the lips. It was the only impulsive thing he had ever done with a woman in his life.

Apparently the Mini Baha queen was impulsive too, because she turned squarely toward him and sucked his brains out. They spent the next day and a half burning the sheets in a Gold Beach motel, the surf timing their lovemaking like a metronome.

That weekend should have been his first clue that Gloria went for the stars – the guys who shone above everyone else. Little did she know that he was more like a comet – one flash then falling to earth.

Their marriage even started out badly. They drove his Suburban all the way to Fairbanks, Dave talking the whole time about how he'd love to bag this animal with this caliber of rifle. How big of a gun it would take to drop a grizzly, and how much time and how many shots a guy could get off before the grizzly ate him. Gloria's response was a yawn, and she slept all the way from Fairbanks to Denali.

That wasn't the worst of it though. Once they hit

Victoria on their return, Gloria whipped out her credit cards like a poker hand. And when they weren't enough, she sexily coaxed Dave out of his. Is it okay if I get this, honey? Is it okay if I get that? she asked. You're so sweet. We're going to have a wonderful marriage.

That was the biggest lie she had ever told him – and she told a lot. Seven years into their marriage, Dave had to sell his mountain cabin west of Sisters just to pay off their credit card debt. And when Gloria wanted to start charging again and he told her no, she played back a recording of his snoring and told him if he didn't start sleeping in another room she'd divorce him. So when McBaron's came up for sale in Toledo a couple hundred miles north, he jumped on it.

***

When he opened the divorce complaint and the endless list of what Gloria wanted, he was leveled. She wanted everything – the house, the beach cabin, the Lexus, the Range Rover. She even wanted half of his 401K he'd put money into for the last twenty years – starting long before he'd met her. When he called her attorney and asked if she'd forgotten to ask for his balls too, the lawyer hesitated, then admitted she'd mentioned it in passing.

The only things Gloria didn't ask for were what she couldn't get – the family tavern he was buying on contract – or didn't want – his 1978 Ford F350, a mammoth beast that ate gas like a Saudi oil sheik's fleet of Ferraris. He'd be paying on the bar for the next fifteen years, and then he'd be ready for retirement. And his pickup was likely to conk out any day now.

He contested nothing. He saw it as an expensive lesson that the next time he looked for a wife he shouldn't decide with a part of his anatomy other than his brain. When Gloria finally *did* try to go for the bar, urging him to finance it at the bank so there would be some paper she could go for, he hung up the phone.

"Good move," said Craig Orris, the police chief. "I've been through a divorce too, and they wanna take your nuts an' everything."

Then Dave told Craig what Gloria's lawyer had said.

"See what I mean?" answered Craig, sliding his glass on the bar toward Dave. "Gimme another pounder. Duane's on duty tonight so I should be fine drivin' home."

***

When Dave saw the check he'd received from his portion of the sale of the joint assets, his head hit the ceiling fan. Gloria had sold his .223 Ruger, .257 Roberts, .270 Winchester, .338 Browning, and two .45 Colt 1911s for a dollar – to his brother-in-law. The check was for his half, fifty cents. Everything else in the house or on the property she had claimed for herself.

"Whatcha gonna do about it?" asked Cole Barnes, the county sheriff.

"I'm going to drive down there, and then I don't know what I'm going to do. But I'm doing something."

"I would too," said Cole, finishing his Windsor-Seven. "I been through a divorce too." He leaned over the bar toward Dave, sequestering their conversation. "Anybody ever asks me about it, I'll say I never heard a word." He held up his hand and leaned back with a wink.

***

All Dave could think of on the drive down to Cave Junction that Friday was the release on the joint deed he'd signed. Until he handed it to Gloria and she had it recorded Monday, the house was his, wasn't it? And if it was his house, he could do whatever he wanted with it, couldn't he?

Such were his thoughts as he pulled up at a convenience store in Grants Pass. Country western was all he could get on the ancient AM radio, so Tex Ritter strummed and yodeled as Dave pulled over to call Gloria and say he'd be there in a couple hours. She'd demanded advance notice before he came – no doubt to avoid being caught en flagrante delicato with her latest boy toy.

"What's that awful screeching? Did you run over a cat or something? Please put it out of its misery."

Dave took a sudden liking then to Tex Ritter and turned up the volume. "I'm sorry, honey. What was that?"

"Oh, it's the radio. Can't you turn it down?"

He turned it up instead. "I'm sorry, I can't hear you. The radio's too loud. Could you speak up, dear?" Her squawking rivaled Tex Ritter's, even surpassing it, and Dave laughed so hard he almost peed his pants. Having had enough fun, he decided to end the conversation. "I'll see you in a couple hours, dear."

"You can go to hell."

Dave continued to laugh all the way down I-5, visions of Gloria squawking like a chicken percolating through his plans for the future. It wasn't all that terrible, really. That new bartender, Crystal, was real cute. And hadn't she sidled up to him after she'd had a few too many pounders the other night? And didn't she have a sweet little can to die for? Hmm . . . Maybe once he was done down here he could drive straight back and close down the bar a little early and they could toss down a few. After all, his apartment was right above the bar.

***

The county sheriff was waiting for Dave when he got to the house. He stepped out of his patrol car and put on his hat, adjusted his belt, and stood on the side of his car as Dave rolled into the driveway.

"Howdy," said Dave, beaming the biggest smile he could make.

The sheriff didn't say anything, and edged closer to scan the inside of Dave's Ford for a gun, knife, explosive or incendiary device, or any other lethal weapon. Satisfied that he had no malice of intent to inflict severe bodily injury or death upon his about-to-be ex-wife, the sheriff nodded. "You'd be Mr. Jefferson, I guess."

"In the flesh."

The sheriff tugged at his hat. "Sorry 'bout your divorce. Not the divorce maybe so much as the settlement. The whole courthouse is just buzzin' 'bout what she done with those guns – took you for a ride like that."

Dave gunned his engine. "I was about to take a little ride myself."

"You ain'ta gonna hurt her none, are you?"

"Aww . . . hurt a pretty lil' thing like her? Who'd wanna do that."

"Well, I just went through a divorce a couple years ago mysef, similar sort of circumstances. She didn't clean me out nearly as bad as yours did though."

"Yep." Dave looked longingly at the house and thought of all the work he'd put into it. He'd built most of it himself, first clearing the cedars and pulled out all the stumps. Then he'd built the full basement and framed the modified A-frame, a Swiss chalet, no less, with intricate patterns all along the porch. And those flowers there, those beautiful rhododendrons that Gloria had planted with her own two pretty little hands. The vines climbing up the trellis along the porch like that, so pretty, lifting their colorful heads up to catch the last daylight as the sun slipped behind the mountains to bed. Now weren't those rhododendrons just pretty? "Well, if ya'll don't mind, I gotta deed release to deliver to my pretty darlin' lil' wife."

"You can do whatever you want long's you don't harm her, Mr. Jefferson."

Dave beamed. "Really?"

"Sure thing, sir."

"To the house even?"

The sheriff smirked. "I think I gotta call on the radio. I'll go see what it's all about." With that, he tipped his hat and headed for his car.

"Whooee!" Dave mashed the accelerator and the pickup roared straight toward the house. Bing! went the naked Cupid head on the fountain, clipped by the bumper. Bam! went the birdbath, installed by an award-winning designer. Bash! went the garden bench, carved from a single piece of myrtle wood by a famous woodcarver. Gloria stood in horror at the patio door in her bra and panties as he smashed the deck into splinters.

Dave backed up, wheeled around, and went for the

side of the porch now, clipping off the carved wood panels . . . ping, ping, ping, ping, ping, ping, crash went the corner post. Gloria ran out the side door screaming toward the sheriff. In his rearview mirror Dave saw her stand there yelling at the sheriff, jumping, screaming, crying, blubbering tears as the honorable lawman nodded and smiled, admiring a large, luscious breast escaped from her bra like a wild zoo animal from its cage. All the sheriff did was sit there and nod and smile.

Now Dave aimed for the trellis and the rhododendrons – whap, whap, whap, whap, whap, whap. And had he forgotten the roses in the backyard? Aww. He smashed through the swinging bench and headed for the roses – whap, whap, whap, whap, whap, whap. For good measure, he backed up a hundred yards and smashed into the three-season room, shattering panels. Then he backed up again and roared into the breakfast nook, smashing benches, walls, and roof into splinters.

When he was done, Dave figured he'd managed to inflict a minimum of $150,000 damage on the house he'd built with his own hands.

Gloria was screaming and beating on the patrol car roof by then, sweating so hard her bra and panties were totally transparent. The sheriff had a great view sitting right there in his car as she beat on the roof. As Dave pulled up, pickup engine ticking from overheating, the sheriff tipped his hat again.

Dave reached the deed release through his window and handed it to Gloria. "Here you go, honey. It's all yours now." Dave looked at the destroyed house in his rearview mirror. "What's left of it anyway."

Gloria grabbed the paper and leaned over and got in the sheriff's face, too mad to realize her bra had fallen on the ground. "Can't you stop him? Can't you arrest him? Can't you shoot him?" she screamed, breasts jiggling as the sheriff roared.

"Sorry ma'am. Bein's it was his property too 'til that's deed's recorded, I'd say he can do whatever he wants with the house. Insurance claim might be a lil' tricky, but legally speakin', I'd say that's prob'ly your problem now."

"You, you, you bastard!" Gloria screamed at the sheriff, fists pummeling the roof of his car, breasts jiggling in his face.

"Nighty night, sheriff," Dave said with a wink and a wave.

"'Night, Mr. Jefferson. Glad to be of service to ya. Ya might wanna check that tickin' in your engine."

"Just need a li'l oil. Might be warm fer some reason." As Dave pulled away, a huge weight lifted from his shoulders. Now what had Crystal been saying about sexual positions? Now that was a hint he could drive his 350 through.

Windmills

"What's the matter, Dad. Don't you care about our family's legacy?"

Carl Davis looked up from the multipage contract between work-gnarled hands that had seen the ranch through its toughest times. "Legacy? What do you know about legacy. You took off right after high school and went to that fancy college. I don't hear a damn word from you for years. Then you come last year to take over the ranch. What kinda legacy is that?"

"I worked in ag marketing all those years, Dad. I learned how the money side of things works." Gene looked off at the hills rolling past the Belle Fourche River to Bear Butte, and beyond that, the misty-blue Black Hills. "Something you could learn a little more about."

Carl gripped the pen in his right hand until it looked ready to break. "Six windmills at twelve-thousand a year each. Talk about money, you got any idea how much that is?"

"Seventy-two thousand," Gene snarled. "I can do the math."

"Seventy-two thousand," Carl repeated. "And you want to throw away seventh-two thousand?"

Gene's silence was the worst answer he could have given.

"Hi, Grandpa." Carrie came bouncing through the

door, with a smile as wide as the Dakota prairie. Her blond ponytail bounced as she went up to her grandfather and planted a huge, wet kiss on his cheek.

All the fight went out of Carl then, all his resistance to Gene and his demands that "No damned windmills are going up on this ranch." But only for a second. Carl raised the pen above the line to sign.

"I'm telling you, Dad. You're going to ruin everything our family has worked and fought for since the 1870s."

"Got that new combine paid for yet?"

"Course not," Gene scoffed.

Carl signed the contract and folded it and placed it in the pre-stamped envelope and handed it to Carrie. "Wanna take this to the post office when you go to Sturgis, honey?"

"Sure thing, Grandpa." Carrie left the letter on the table and gave him one more kiss before she thundered out the door. She'd go to Sturgis tomorrow. She had better things to do right now.

***

Four generations of Davises had owned the ranch before Carl took it over from his father William in 1970, the same year his sone Gene came into the world, a bawling, demanding mass of life that kept Carl and his wife Amanda up all night. In a way, Gene kept on bawling, kept on demanding, kept on wanting what in his mind was rightfully his – without really working for it. After spending five years to get a four-year business degree, he secured a position at the regional office of a major bank. Even that wasn't good enough for him, so he took a job on the floor at the Chicago Board of Trade and married Lisa and stayed in love with her long enough to have Carrie. Then he started fooling around with cocktail servers and administrative assistants and Lisa took off for L.A., taking Carrie with her. Gene saw Carrie twice a year – Christmas and summer when Gene lured her to his Lake Geneva home with endless spending money. He finally managed to lure her to stay with him and attend the University of Wisconsin. I want to be near Dad, she plaintively told her mother. You've had me all these years. Now give me a chance to know him. Knowing her daughter would just go off anyway if she refused, Lisa relented, and off Carrie went, spending most of the year with her father and the summer between her freshman and sophomore years with her mother. Tension grew between them, though, and Carrie returned to her father that fall and after that she saw her mother as infrequently as she had seen her father in the past.

The land Carl had inherited from William consisted of some of the best bottomland between the Black Hills and the Missouri River. It was dryland, though, and he had to irrigate to make it productive. He ran a herd of Angus-Hereford cross on the higher ground, and in time built it up to four hundred head, sending steers and market heifers to the sale barn and breeding his best heifers to his best bulls.

The farm crisis of the eighties hit western South Dakota ranchers too. As a third of Iowa's farms fell to the auctioneer's hammer, the cattle buyers came around less and less and Carl resorted to growing his own feed grain and fattening his cattle himself. He scrimped and saved and made do with what he had, and except for having to pay for Gene's outrageous college bills, managed to save enough to buy up his neighbors' land as it came up for sale. In 1985, he even managed to buy a section of Meade County dryland on a county tax sale for $5.65 an acre.

By 2018, Carl had amassed 42,000 acres and 600 cattle with no debt. He had improved the bloodlines of his herd, too, his young bulls and breeding heifers commanding top price at livestock exchanges from Sturgis to Fort Pierre. One day Gene called from Chicago and said he missed the ranch and wanted to move back. Would Carl mind?

Carl thought of Gene and Carrie living on the ranch. Through some fluke of genetics, Carrie was the spitting image of Amanda. Carrie had said as much whenever she and her father had visited the ranch and she studied her grandmother's picture on the wall above the stairway. "She was beautiful," Carrie said to her grandfather the first time she had seen her grandmother's picture. "Yes she was," Carl said, switching his gaze between Amanda and Carrie, trying to decide which one of them looked more like the woman he had lost years before.

***

"Have you seen Craig since you've been back?" Gene asked Carrie not long after they moved back to the ranch. They were eating breakfast as the sun slid well past the cottonwoods to the east, a sign that morning was well upon them. Carl had gotten up hours before as was his habit to go check on the cow-calf pairs on the east range with his .270. A neighbor had seen coyotes, and Carl had said the night before he wanted to go check on the calves.

"Craig who?"

Gene set down his fork and rolled his gaze at her. "Larsen. The boy you went
with all during high school. Remember him?"

"Unfortunately, yes." Carrie forked her eggs into her mouth and picked up her last slice of crisp bacon with her left hand and bit it in half just to annoy her father who had always criticized her etiquette.

"He's been asking about you."

"No law against asking." Carrie finished her bacon and washed it down with her orange juice. "Doesn't mean I have to answer, though."

Gene shook his head. "He's finishing his third year of law school and getting ready to take his bar exam."

"Which bar? The No. 10 or The Broken Spoke."

Gene set his jaw at her. "You just don't recognize opportunity when it presents itself, do you."

"I sure recognize disaster when I see it." Carrie took her napkin from her lap and laid it on the table. "I'm going to Sturgis to mail that letter for Grandpa."

"Can't it wait?"

"I need new boots too." She stood just long enough to stare Gene down then grabbed the letter from the table and headed out to her truck.

Her faithful F-150 sat where she had parked it by the front gate the night before. When Grandpa had offered to buy her whatever car she wanted when she was about to graduate and she told him a Nissan Rogue, he scoffed and said he wouldn't be caught dead in a piece of shit like that and insisted on an F-150 at three times the price. Are you sure, Grandpa? she asked. I'm sure I want you to be safe, he answered, and after she told him what color she wanted, it was there in her father's driveway graduation day.

She'd sort of gone cowgirl after that – boots, jeans, chambray shirts – the whole bit. She even started listening to country music, and since it reminded her so much of Grandpa, she turned the volume way up on the radio whenever her dad rode with her, just because she knew it rankled him. At a very early age, she had detected tension between her father and grandfather, and she learned how to milk it to get whatever she wanted. Her grandfather bought her things to win her favor and her dad bought her things to even the score. Not that she was spoiled or anything. It was just her way of getting even with her father for breaking up with her mother.

Sturgis was dead when she entered from East 34. As she turned off the highway and pulled up to the Post Office, another pickup, exactly like hers, pulled alongside. She looked over at the driver and felt her eyes rivetted to the hottest man she had ever seen. He didn't notice her at first. He just sat there, reading a sheet of paper, then looking off. Then he looked down at the paper again and jotted a note on it and stuck it in an envelope and licked it shut.

Carrie waited, deciding, but she didn't wait long. As the other driver's door opened she piled out of her pickup so they reached the Post Office steps at the same time. The man paused and touched his Stetson and let her pass. "'Scuse me, ma'am," he said with a Texas drawl so long she wanted to crawl down it and see what the insides of him looked like. His eyes were the same glimmering blue she had seen in Mirror Lake in the Laramie Range of Wyoming, hair black as coal with narrow sideburns reaching level with earlobes she could have nibbled on all night. He was a good six-four, shoulders as wide as most doorways, his torso narrowing to a slim, hard waist. "I'm sorry, ma'am, do I know you?"

She realized then she'd been standing there a solid minute, looking, no, gawking, at the most perfect example of male flesh she had ever seen. She looked at his left hand and saw no ring then turned and combed her own bare left hand through her ponytail. "Maybe. I'm Carrie Davis," she said, offering him far more information than he had requested and far less than she wanted to give.

"Luke, ma'am," he said, grabbing his hat again and tilting it in his own Texas way. "Luke Shorter."

Carrie laughed.

"Ma'am?"

"Your name should be Luke Taller." She had to look up into his eyes even though she stood one step above him.

Her remark drew a chuckle from Luke. "That's pretty funny, ma'am."

She stepped back down a step so they were on the same level. "Call me Carrie," she insisted.

"Carrie." Luke smiled and looked at the letter in her hand then at Carrie then down the street toward Weimer's. "Would you, uh, like a cup of coffee after we mail these here letters, ma'am? I mean Carrie?"

"I'd love a cup of coffee," she said, as though she hadn't had one in years.

***

Luke told of his two tours in Afghanistan as an Army Ranger then after the service when he was a Ranger again – a Texas Ranger. He loved the work – that is until he and his partner had to apprehend a drug lord crossing the border. His partner was killed and Luke wounded. As he lay in hospital recovering, the windmills in the distance told him of a different future. Two years of college later, he was a wind tech traveling the western US. Now he was site manager for Corona Wind Farm that would start construction in Meade County next April.

"Oh my God. That's the contract I just put in the mail for Grandpa."

"It seems like I remember talking with a Mr. Davis – Carl Davis?"

Yeah, that's Grandpa."

"He's quite a man," said Luke, genuine respect in his voice. "We must have talked a couple hours. He's a very interesting person. Very well read, too."

"I love Grandpa."

As Luke smiled across the table, something unspoken passed between them. "I, uh, was wondering if you might like to have dinner sometime, Carrie."

"How about tonight."

"Uh, sure."

***

Dinner, drinks, and a hike to the top of Bear Butte later, a tall, broad Texan and a feisty, blonde, business school graduate found things in each other they had only dreamt of. They sat and talked and stared at the burning stars atop Bear Butte for hours then made their way back down in the full moon. Carrie tried to quiet Clyde, Carl's black Lab, who started barking as soon as she pulled up to the ranch house at 3 a.m. Clyde finally quieted down as he recognized her and she took off her shoes to make as little noise as possible as she entered.

She crept past the grandfather clock ticking sonorously in the foyer then she passed through the dining room and into the living room.

"I seen you finally made it home," her grandfather said from his chair beside the fireplace.

Carrie jumped and nearly dropped her shoes. "I'm sorry I disturbed you, Grandpa."

"I ain't disturbed." He lifted his old-fashioned glass and sipped his whiskey and smacked his lips.

"Have you been up all night, Grandpa?"

He looked at his watch. "Not yet. Sunlight should break full over the butte to the east in a couple hours. I'll have been up all night then."

"I'm sorry, Grandpa." She stepped quietly toward him. "Were you worried about me?"

"I was. Not now. So, what's his name?"

"What's whose name?"

"The name of the man you was out with half the night."

"Luke Shorter," she said apologetically.

"I was hopin' he'd get his hooks into you – or you into him. That's one damn fine young man."

Carrie couldn't help but give him a broad smile. "'Night, Grandpa."

"'Night, Punkin. Oh, and Carrie?"

"Yes, Grandpa?"

"No need to hurry home early next time on my account – long as it's Luke Shorter you're with."

She chuckled, knowing her secret was safe with him. "Thanks, Grandpa."

"Huh." Carl eyed the whiskey in his glass then finished it. "Guess I can still catch a couple hours shut-eye afore sunup."

***

No one said much to anyone else at the breakfast table the next morning. Carl changed from 80 proof whiskey to black coffee in a matter of hours, trying to decide if he dared drive out to the range and risk arrest. Carrie was wound up tight as a Swiss clock, something festering in her Gene couldn't begin to understand. Gene had thoughts all his own to dwell on – how to pay for a new 32-foot combine his father didn't want plus how to keep those damned windmills from popping up on the same landscape he'd seen as long as he could remember. Windmills his father had agreed to in a legally binding contract his own daughter had mailed. He felt his whole family was turning against him.

Then an idea came to him. Corona Wind Farm wanted all the necessary landowners' agreements in hand before they went before the Meade County Commissioners in a public hearing. He didn't have to oppose this thing after all, did he? He could just get others to do it. And he knew just the person who could speak to all of them.

Craig Olsen didn't fully latch on to the idea at first. Corona Wind Farms was negotiating with his parents and his parents' neighbors, people their families had known for generations. He didn't think the neighbors would take too kindly to sticking his hand in their pockets before the money was even there.

"It's not like you have to oppose them directly," Gene argued, leaning forward in the chair across from Craig's desk to make his point. "Just say you're representing some landowners' concerns."

Craig sighed his frustration at Carl. "I haven't heard any concerns. That's the point."

"No one's said anything about what they'll do to the landscape? Or how about the noise? They're pretty noisy, aren't they? And what about all the birds they kill? How about those?"

Craig steepled his fingers. "Maybe you've lived away from Meade County for too long," said Craig. "Here, people care more about money than views. As for noise, I'm sure most ranchers would find the little sound a wind turbine makes somewhat soothing after spending a day on a tractor or combine. And as for eagles, you'd better talk to the sheep ranchers about those. Lambing season just finished, and I'm sure they might have a thing or two to say about those."

"Well, couldn't you just say at the public hearing that you're representing concerned landowners?"

"What if the commissioners ask them to speak for themselves and no one stands up?"

"I'll pay you."

"I'm not sure I want the job."

"I'll pay you double your usual hourly rate."

"I still don't want the job."

"Carrie's home."

"She is?"

She just graduated from college last week. She's staying at the ranch while she's looking for a job."

Craig looked from Gene to his desk and back to Gene. "Where's this all headed."

"You'd like to get back together with Carrie, wouldn't you?"

Craig's eyes turned hungry. "What do you want me to do."

"Just come out to the ranch and have dinner with Dad and Carrie and me. We'll lay out the main points beforehand. The last thing I want to do is sandbag Dad on this thing. He'll fight like hell if that happens. We'll just sit down and have a nice dinner and I'll bring it up like we're just starting to discuss it. Then you can come in with all the reasons we shouldn't let them put those windmills up on our land. After all, it would be a lot easier if we went into that public hearing with Dad and Carrie on our side – or at least not fighting us."

"So when do you want to do this?"

"The public hearing is two weeks from today, so let's make it a week from Sunday."

***

A week from Sunday later, Luke was just finishing up breakfast in a cafe in Bowman, North Dakota when the call came. A tech had been working on a turbine near Bowman, a sheen of ice on top. Too much slack on his line, he'd slipped and fallen off the edge. His partner tried to help, but he could barely stand up on the ice-slick deck. All he could do was sit there on the edge, calling encouragement, as his partner hung there, blood rushing to his legs and arms. Luke slammed a twenty on the counter and ran out to his truck, spinning gravel like bullets as he sped down the road. An hour and a half. That's how long the guy had hung there. Why in the hell hadn't they called him sooner? Luke skidded sideways on the scoria road as the turbine loomed ahead. He counted the seconds, wondering if the guy was still breathing. Once the blood left the upper body, the heart would slow down and stop. And that was all there was to it. Luke checked the yellow bag with his harness as he finally skidded to a stop, then jumped out of his truck. "Who the hell's site manager here?" Luke demanded. A man several inches shorter paused to hold out his hand. "Paul Evans." Luke ignored Paul's hand. "Who's up there."

"His partner and a couple other guys."

"Does anyone up there know how to suit up and repel down?" Luke was already buckling up his harness and throwing the fall arrest device over his shoulder. No answer, he entered the turbine.

He didn't even pause to catch his breath as he climbed three levels to the top. As he peered out from the top of the tower, frost-peaked buttes stretched for miles on the prairie below. He hooked onto an anchor and made his way across the ice-caked deck to three techs who watched their buddy far below, all shivering from cold but more likely fear.

"Out of the way." Luke hooked up to an anchor at the edge and turned to repel down the tower. The whole thing was a sheet of ice, and his boots kept slipping each time he kicked back.

The tech was unconscious when Luke reached him. Luke hooked onto him and lowered him to the ground, praying he would live long enough to reach the ground and safety. Then he repelled down the rest of the way.

When Luke reached the ground, the site manager was trying to administer CPR, but not very well. Luke took over, and when the tech gasped for breath, Luke finally remembered to take a breath himself. A flash came from the side, and Luke looked up at the photographer and a cameraman beside him. "Get away. Can't you see this man nearly died?"

***

Carrie had waited for Luke all afternoon. They had made plans for Sunday brunch, and he still wasn't here. Six hours, and still no Luke. It was now a little after 5.

"So did your boyfriend forget about you?" asked Gene. He said it with a half-smirk in his voice as though trying to hide his sarcasm but maybe not. Carl and Craig sat on opposite sides of the living room, the four of them squared off with no one yet giving an inch.

Carrie looked out the window where she had hoped Luke would suddenly appear. When her father had told her Craig was coming to dinner and they were going to talk a little business afterward, she sort of fibbed and said she'd already made plans with Luke – and she had, even though it was hours before.

"He's just probably tied up with work," her grandfather reasoned. He went to the sideboard and poured them all a whiskey. Carrie, who normally didn't drink anything stronger than wine, took her shot in a single sip then held her glass out for another.

"A little miffed at Lover Boy?" her father asked.

Craig's chuckle a few feet away drew hate daggers from Carrie.

"Oh well, I guess we can watch the news," said Gene, hitting the TV remote. "Would you like to see how supper's coming, Carrie?"

"I'd love to," she said, preferring that to having to look one more moment at her father and Craig.

The roast was just about done, and she'd just popped the rolls into the oven when the knock came at the front door. Ten to six, the clock said. And Luke was to have been here nearly seven hours before. She threw the potholder on the counter and stalked to the front door.

Luke looked terrible. His face was drawn, almost ashen, and his clothes looked as though he'd been through a war, shirt and pants ripped and grease-streaked.

329

"Where *were* you?" Carrie demanded.

"I'm sorry, Car . . . I was going to call, but it was already hours after I was supposed to be here. Then I had reports to write afterward and the home office to call and . . ."

"You're seven hours late!" she screamed. Her voice lowered as she listened to herself. "Oh well, come in. You might as well eat while you're here." She looked aghast at him. "You look awful!"

"I'm sorry. Late as I was, I didn't want to take time to change."

"You can sit down in the living room while I finish getting dinner ready," she ordered.

They had just entered the living room when the headline, HEROISM IN DAKOTA popped upon the screen, followed by a picture of the turbine where Luke had performed the rescue.

"Hey, that's where I was this morning," said Luke.

The news anchor appeared, voice urgent. "This just in. A daring rescue happened early today when a wind company site manager risked his life and repelled from the sheer, three-hundred-foot face of a wind turbine in southwestern North Dakota to save a technician who had fallen over the side." The next segment clearly showed Luke, repelling toward the victim.

Carrie looked from the television to Luke. "Is this the local news?"

"National," said Carl, hands folded as he pulled up his chair and nearly leaned into the television.

"Luke Shorter attached a rope to the unconscious victim whom he lowered to the ground then came down the rest of the way to administer CPR. Doctors at Bowman Community Hospital said the victim, who would otherwise have died within minutes without Shorter's help, is expected to make a full recovery." The news anchor went on to talk about Luke receiving a Silver Star in Afghanistan and playing a key role in interdicting drug traffic as a Texas Ranger.

Carrie hooked her arm inside Luke's and led him to the leather loveseat where she curled up on his lap and pressed her face against his chest and sobbed. "Please don't ever do anything that stupid again."

Carl stood up and poured a healthy shot of whiskey and carried it over to Luke who downed it and held the glass out for more. "You might just as well be talkin' to a post there, Carrie. Somethin' needs doin', Luke's the man to do it and that's all there is."

Craig rose from his chair and picked up his briefcase and grabbed his coat from the hall tree by the front door.

"Where are you going?" Gene asked.

"Home."

"Why? You haven't had supper yet."

Craig looked at Luke and Carrie together on the couch. "I can't compete with that." He tugged on his coat and picked up his briefcase, then left.

A couple days later, Carl was crossing Main Street toward the bar when a semi honked. Carl flipped the driver off, and whirled his fists in circles like a windmill.

The driver hit his brakes and Carl went up to the driver's window and saw it was Glen Harris, another rancher he'd known for years who was hauling a load of steers to the sale barn. Carl invited him into the bar and after a few drinks crossed to the other side of the street to a law office – not Craig Olsen's.

***

The public hearing went swimmingly. With few objections except for a few typical whackos who said wind turbines caused cancer and epileptic fits and acted as signals to call aliens down from outer space to abduct people for medical experiments – one drunk showed the scars on his stomach as living proof – the Meade County Commissioners approved Corona Wind Farms' permit application and construction started the following spring.

Gene never got his new combine. Carl answered the phone one day and the implement dealer called to say another wheat grower had offered another $5,000 and asked Carl if Gene would like to up the ante. "No he wouldn't," Carl said, answering more for himself than for Gene. "And you can take your combine and shove it up your ass – with the head attached."

Gene was pretty upset about that, asking how he was supposed to harvest 4,000 acres of wheat with a 24-foot-wide head. Carl told him it was simple. "Do a full day's work like the rest of us."

Gene left the next day, vowing never to return, telling his father what a great business mind he'd lost and how he was free now to run his ranch into the dirt if he wanted.

Carl didn't run the ranch into the dirt, though. Carrie took over where her father had left off, and sharpened her pencil as much as Carl's. Soon she was driving combine herself, taking her quarter horse out to cut cattle, and driving the cow-calf pairs onto the home place to the east range. She talked Luke into leaving his job and working the ranch alongside her and Carl. They got married that June and had their first son, Luke Junior, the following May. Two more boys and a girl followed in rapid succession.

***

When Gene got Carrie's call about Carl's passing, it hit him broadside. Sure, things had been strained between him and his dad and to a certain extent, Carrie, ever since he'd left the ranch. He sort of felt like they'd ganged up on him, and he swore he'd never want to have any part of the ranch ever again. He knew he should be there for the reading of the will, though, so he figured he'd might just as well go to the funeral.

The funeral was solemn but lighthearted too. Toward the end of the service, everyone stood at the front of the church and told stories about Carl, his shenanigans, his great love of wild horses, wild women, and whiskey. Above all, they talked about the great love he had for the ranch and his family.

As they drove past the cluster of windmills on the bluffs above the Belle Fourche, Gene grit his teeth and wished he had fought Carl a little harder, maybe found a different lawyer. Then in the reception and the ranch after the funeral, Gene saw what a beautiful place Carrie and Luke and Carl had made it. A huge lawn, new machine shed, a new horse barn with a remuda of great-looking quarter horses. And four, beautiful grandchildren.

The reading of the will came the next day. Gene sat there in the front row, holding his Stetson in his hands, finally feeling a love for his father that he hadn't in years. Now that he was about to take over the ranch, maybe he could patch up things with Carrie and Luke and they could move on with their lives.

" . . . To my son Gene, I leave fifty-thousand dollars and my wishes that he spend it wisely," the lawyer said.

Gene bolted upright. Fifty thousand dollars? Besides the ranch? He started to cry, finally realizing how much his father had loved him.

" . . . And to my beautiful granddaughter Carrie, and her husband Luke, I leave the remainder of my estate, consisting of forty-five thousand acres in Meade County, six hundred head of angus-hereford-cross cattle, and stocks and other investments valued at . . . "

Won't you Write Home, Martha Jane
May 1, 1852
Princeton, Missouri

On the highest hilltop for miles around, Robert Canary was digging. Inside the unpainted wood frame house his wife Charlotte was screaming as Robert set the maple tree, first checking one angle, then another. When her screams turned louder, he set the tree straight, filled the hole with dirt, and stood back to admire his work.

"Mister Canary, you'd best be comin' in to hep," the midwife called. "This here's a breech birth."

Robert stood, shovel in hand, and looked at the rolling hills to the west, south, and north, and seriously studied on heading for one of them. He knew though his wife would finally catch up with him, so he dropped his shovel and headed inside.

The midwife had managed to turn the baby's head but Charlotte was still having a hard time pushing it out. "Ya'll good-fer-nuthin worthless sumnabitch. Wash them hands and help pull this thing outa me."

Robert did as he was told – he always did what his wife told him – and by the time he returned to Charlotte the baby's head had already emerged, drenched in birth fluids and blood. As Robert held out his hands, a baby girl popped out like a colt dropped from a mare, howling like a bobcat. Robert smiled with enormous pride as he held the baby who cocked back her arm and punched him squarely on the nose, her face bearing the same expression as her mother's.

***

When Martha Jane Canary, later known in Western lore as Calamity Jane Burke, came into the world, the nation was on the verge of tearing itself in two, of secessionist factions warring with Union loyalists, of Confederate-sympathizing Missouri State Guards warring with Union-backed Home Guards. Just like other border states such as Maryland, Kentucky, Kansas, and Virginia which would rip itself in half, Missouri was a battleground unto itself. A place where families sent some members North and others South. For some, the wounds would never heal.

Martha Jane took after her mother. When she saw how her father cowered under Charlotte's anger, how he learned to go to the other room or even better yet outside when she had been drinking, Martha Jane learned at an early age that women could have power over men. And when Charlotte took off, sometimes for days, to let herself be squired and used by other men and to squire and use them, Martha Jane learned that marriage was mainly for one reason – to keep the human race going so people could drink and fight and cheat on one another all over again.

She was nine when she heard of the battle over Athens way. The August heat seeped up from the ground to the maple branch where she sat looking over the countryside, wondering what it would be like to be a boy and grown up and able to go to war. She was already a pretty fair shot with her father's squirrel rifle. The maple trees clean shuck of critters were sign enough for that. But she wondered what it would be like if the squirrels should someday decide to shoot back. Now that would be something, wouldn't it?

"Thirty-one casualties," said their neighbor just to the west, Floyd Shannon. Martha liked Floyd, a big man with beard and hair to his shoulders and secessionist loyalties running as long and deep as the Mississippi far off yonder to the east.

"How 'bout them Home Guard bastids," her father asked.

Floyd raised a hooded brow. "Not nearly so bad. Three kilt 'n twenty wounded ah hears."

"Damn shame," said Robert. "Damn dirty shame."

"Sho 'nuff is," said Floyd. So . . . " He eyed Canary squarely. "Y'all gonna take up 'gainst them Home Guards?"

"Caint," said Canary. "Got me a wife 'n three youngins to feed. Leana 'n Lijah, they's spurtin' up like a coupla weeds."

"Hey Pa, watch this." Martha Jane was hanging upside down, legs wrapped around a maple branch, swinging like a monkey.

"Y'all watch yourself, girl. Doc Bates is done gone joined the Union army and they ain't nobody gonna fix your haid y'all falls on top of it."

"I ain't gonna fall, Pa." Martha Jane pulled herself up and sat on the branch, studying him with her chin in her hand. "Kin ah go to war 'gainst them Yankees, Pa?"

"Now girl, y'all knows ya's two young fer that. 'Sides, they don't let girls into the army."

"Ah bet they's some in there anyways. Ah bet they cut they's hair 'n shores up their boobies 'n such so they's kin tote a gun 'n rucksack like the rest of 'em."

Shannon cast a knowing smile. "*How* old you say she is?"

"Not old 'nuff to be talkin' 'bout shorin' boobies." Robert shook his head at his daughter. "Martha Jane, y'all hush your mouth afore ah clean it out with lye soap 'n tans your hide to harness leather. 'N gits out'n that there maple tree afore ya falls out'n it."

"Aw Pa, all right." She dropped eight feet from the tree, landing squarely on her feet like a Pawnee warrior. "Kin ah go over to Tommy's, Pa?"

Canary looked at Shannon. "Ah don't 'spect it'd be no harm. "Long's it's all right with Mistah Shannon here."

"Kin ah go play with Tommy?" Martha Jane asked Shannon, turning on her rare female charm.

"That'd be fine," said Shannon, chuckling.

Canary shook his head as Martha Jane whooped and raced over the field like a jackrabbit, bounding the rail fence in a leap like an antelope. "Ah swears that there girl is gonna kill herself one a these days."

"Or somebody elst," Shannon was quick to add.

***

Martha Jane found Tommy mowing hay with the horse and sickle. For eleven, the boy stood five-eight and his work-knotted arms and back glistened in the August Missouri heat. Martha Jane stood and watched him, first to surprise him, then just to watch him. She had come over to play, but some curious feeling rose up inside her that made her take a different look at Tommy – a look that sort of scared her.

"Hey Tommy," Martha Jane said just as he turned the horse for another pass.

Tommy looked squarely at her, as though not sure he was glad to see her, then deciding he was, he reined the horse to a halt and patted its withers. "Howdy, Martha Jane."

"Y'all wanna play?"

Tommy studied her, eyes flitting down her soiled coveralls, then back again. "Whatcha wanna play."

"Oh, anythin'." Martha Jane held her hands behind her back, leaning foot to foot. "Why ya'll lookin' at me that way, Tommy."

"What way."

"Ya'll know." She looked off shyly. "The way growed-up folks looks at each other."

Tommy chuckled. "Maybe it's 'cause y'all's gettin' growed up."

Martha Jane scuffed her boots in the dirt, something Pa was always on her not to do, given the price of shoe leather. "I spect next thing y'all will wanna kiss me."

Tommy took four big steps toward her before she could even look away. He was a good six inches taller, hair burnt to sand by the sun and blue eyes glimmering back the same color as hers. "So what if I did decide to kiss you right now. What'd you do."

Martha Jane looked side to side. "Ah don't know. Like it, ah 'spect."

Tommy bent over and kissed her on the lips just as square as her Pa taking a pot shot at a turkey in a willow tree. "So whatcha thinka that."

She looked up, not a little bit in awe. "That was right nice, Tommy. Kin we do it agin?"

***

Nearly three years later

"Kin we do it agin?"

It was April 1864 and the war had been raging for three years. Tommy was fourteen and Jane twelve and they held fast to each other like two boll weevils on the same cotton ball.

"Ah 'spects we kin." Tommy leaned over to kiss her, heated, fervent, unrelenting as he kissed her and leaned her back over into the prairie grass so tall a man on a horse could get lost in it.

Martha Jane looked up at him as he finished his kiss and leaned on his elbow to study her. She studied him back. Hard. "Pa wants us to move to Montana. Wherever that is."

"Montana." Tommy's words drifted off toward mountains where the snow never melted. "That's a fur piece for sure."

"Ah don't know as we'll be comin' back – not for a while anyways." Tommy's face blurred as tears traced down her cheek. "Ah'm gonna miss ya, Tommy. Ah'm gonna miss ya sumpin' fierce."

He brushed away her tears and leaned over to kiss her. His hand drifted from her shoulder to her collarbone, then lower.

338

She looked up at him, fevered, tentative, afraid, yet not. "Tommy?

"Yes, Martha Jane?"

"Y'all know how ah always said ah'd kill ya if'n ya tried any of that there stuff?"

"Yes, Martha Jane?"

Her eyes flickered. "Ah wouldn't kill ya if'n ya tried it right now."

***

They were off the next day, Robert driving the team with Charlotte beside him, moody to be leaving but anxious for a new adventure – new places, new people. New men.

Tommy and Floyd Shannon were standing in front of their mud-rutted drive as they passed, Tommy with his straw hat in hand as though a funeral procession were passing. "Ya write home now, all right, Martha Jane?"

She smiled back at him, riding astride her horse like a man, not sidesaddle like a woman, rifle cradled in her hands as she watched for the first jackrabbit to skitter across their path. "Ah'll do that, soon's ah learns writin'." She laughed, then suddenly sobered. "Ah loves ya, Tommy."

Tommy, Floyd Shannon, her folks, the team, and her own horse looked at her as she said it.

"Ah loves ya, Tommy. An' ah always will."

***

She shot not one jackrabbit but three by nightfall, her Pa rolling their carcasses on a spit over the fire as a pot of beans bubbled and biscuits in the Dutch oven browned and puffed up high as toadstools after a soaking spring rain. "Ah swears ya done got us 'nough meat fer a week, Martha Jane. Kin ya lay off'n them poor jackrabbits fer a spell 'fore the prairie's clean shuck of em?"

"Aw Pa, they's more jackrabbits out here 'n fleas on a dog."

"Well, y'all wanna not waste no bullets on 'em?"

"But Pa, I shot them three jackrabbits with three bullets."

339

Robert Canary shook his head and grumbled to himself, unable to argue. Because she had. He still seemed troubled about something. "What's that ah heard 'bout y'all tellin' Tommy ya loved 'em?"

"Aw, it's just a 'spression, Pa."

"'Spression." He stopped turning the spit on the jackrabbits. "Ah loves ya seems a bit more'n a 'spression."

Martha Jane smiled and shrugged.

Robert Canary shook his head as he once more turned the jackrabbits over the fire. "Ah thinks we got ya away from that boy just in time, girl."

Martha Jane turned from him and smiled, this time only to herself.

***

That fall they reached Virginia City, a bustling mining camp of canvas tents and wood-fronted hotels, saloons, and brothels. When a bigger gold strike came up Blackfoot way, they moved up there where in 1866 her mother took sick and up and died. Martha Jane had wanted to write Tommy, but between having to hunt food for the family and driving ore wagon teams, learning to read and write seemed such a waste of time. When there was money to be made running a placer or driving a team, who needed to learn to write, she figured. Long as a person could read a scale good enough to weigh gold dust, that was all that mattered.

After her mother passed on, the family, now Martha Jane with her father and two brothers and three sisters, made their way to Salt Lake where her father died the next year. At fifteen, and with five siblings on her hands, Martha Jane couldn't figure on anything better than heading 120 miles north to Fort Bridger where she found some families willing to take them in before she rode off into immortality.

She came to the Black Hills with the Jenny Expedition in '75, pulled a wounded cavalry Captain Egan onto her own horse to earn the name Calamity Jane, hitched her team up with several men, none of whom would stay around any longer than a tumbleweed before it dried up and blew away. She wore men's clothes and drank, cussed, and fought like a man. And in a smallpox epidemic she nursed a camp full of miners back from the drop edge of yonder.

Her last days were spent in the upstairs of Sheffer and Jays Saloon in Terry, South Dakota. Hand shaking, she scrawled out *Dear Tommy*, but they were the only words she knew. Her dying wish was to be buried next to Wild Bill Hickok, and she was, after a three-mile-long funeral procession carried her to Mount Moriah Cemetery in Deadwood where she still rests today.

ABOUT THE AUTHOR

Michael Tidemann lives between his homes in Iowa, Oregon, and New Mexico

Made in the USA
Columbia, SC
06 September 2024

41896887R00193